A NEW ENGLAND NUN

MARY E. WILKINS

A NEW ENGLAND NUN

AND OTHER STORIES

By Mary E. Freeman (Wilkins)

THE GREGG PRESS / RIDGEWOOD, N. J.

First published in 1891 by Harper & Brothers
Republished in 1967 by
The Gregg Press Incorporated
171 East Ridgewood Avenue
Ridgewood, New Jersey, U.S.A.

Library of Congress Catalog Card Number: 67-29266

Printed in United States of America

AMERICANS
IN
FICTION

INTRODUCTION BY PROFESSOR CLARENCE GOHDES

Editor of *American Literature* Magazine

In the domain of literature the play may once have been the chief abstract and chronicle of the times, but during the nineteenth and twentieth centuries the novel has usurped the chief place in holding the mirror up to the homely face of society. On this account, if for no other, the Gregg Press series of reprints of American fiction merits the attention of all students of Americana and of librarians interested in building up adequate collections dealing with the social and literary history of the United States. Most of the three score and ten novels or volumes of short stories included in the series enjoyed considerable fame in their day but have been so long out of print as to be virtually unobtainable in the original editions.

Included in the list are works by writers not presently fashionable in critical circles — but nevertheless well known to literary historians — among them Joel Chandler Harris, Harriet Beecher Stowe, Thomas Bailey Aldrich, and William Gilmore Simms. A substantial element in the list consists of authors who are known especially for their graphic portrayal of a particular American setting, such as Gertrude Atherton (California), Arlo Bates (Boston), Alice Brown (New England), Edward Eggleston (Indiana), Mary Wilkins Freeman (New England), Henry B. Fuller (Chicago), Richard M. Johnston (Georgia), James Lane Allen (Kentucky), Mary N. Murfree (Tennessee), and Thomas Nelson Page (Virginia). There is even a novel by Frederic Remington, one of the most popular painters of the Western cowboy and Indian — and another, an impressive minor classic on the early mining region of Colorado, from the pen of Mary Hallock Foote. The professional student of American literature will rejoice in the opportunity afforded by the collection to extend his reading of fiction belonging to what is called the "local-color movement" — a major current in the development of the national belles-lettres.

Among the titles in the series are also a number of famous historical novels. Silas Weir Mitchell's *Hugh Wynne* is one of the best fictional treatments of the American Revolution. John Esten Cooke is the foremost Southern writer of his day who dealt with the Civil War. The two books by Thomas Dixon are among the most famous novels on the Reconstruction Era, with sensational disclosures of the original Ku Klux Klan in action. They supplied the grist for the first great movie "spectacular" — "*The Birth of a Nation* (1915).

Paul Leicester Ford's *The Honorable Peter Stirling* is justly ranked among the top American novels which portray American politics in action — a subject illuminated by other novelists in the Gregg list — A. H. Lewis, Frances H. Burnett, and Alice Brown, for example. Economic problems are forcefully put before the reader in works by Aldrich, Mrs. Freeman, and John Hay, whose novels illustrate the ominous concern over the early battles between labor and capital. From the sweatshops of Eastern cities in which newly arrived immigrants toiled for pittances, to the Western mining camps where the laborers packed revolvers, the working class of the times enters into various other stories in the Gregg list. The capitalist class, also, comes in for attention, with an account of a struggle for the ownership of a railroad in Samuel Merwin's *The Short-Line War* and with the devastating documentation of the foibles of the newly rich and their wives in the narratives of David Graham Phillips. It was Phillips whose annoying talent for the exposure of abuses led Theodore Roosevelt to put the term "muck-raker" into currency.

While it is apparent that local-color stories, the historical novel, and the economic novel have all been borne in mind in choosing the titles for this important series of reprints, it is evident that careful consideration has also been given to treatments of various minority elements in the American population. The Negro, especially, but also the Indian, the half-breed, Creoles, Cajuns — and even the West Coast Japanese — appear as characters in various of these novels or volumes of short stories and sketches. Joel Chandler Harris's *Free Joe* will open the eyes of readers who know that author solely as the creator of humorous old Uncle Remus. And there is a revelatory volume of dialect tales, written by a Negro author, *The Conjure Woman* by Charles W. Chesnutt.

In literary conventions and the dominating attitudes toward life, the works in the Gregg series range from the adventurous romance illustrated so well by Mayne Reid or the polite urbanity of Owen Wister to the mordant irony of Kate Chopin and the grimmer realism of Joseph Kirkland's own experiences on bloody Civil War battlefields or the depressing display of New York farm life by Harold Frederic. In short, the series admirably illustrates the general qualities of the fiction produced in the United States during the era covered, just as it generously mirrors the geographical regions, the people, and the problems of the times.

LIST OF STORIES.

A NEW ENGLAND NUN.

It was late in the afternoon, and the light was waning. There was a difference in the look of the tree shadows out in the yard. Somewhere in the distance cows were lowing and a little bell was tinkling; now and then a farm-wagon tilted by, and the dust flew; some blue-shirted laborers with shovels over their shoulders plodded past; little swarms of flies were dancing up and down before the peoples' faces in the soft air. There seemed to be a gentle stir arising over everything for the mere sake of subsidence—a very premonition of rest and hush and night.

This soft diurnal commotion was over Louisa Ellis also. She had been peacefully sewing at her sitting-room window all the afternoon. Now she quilted her needle carefully into her work, which she folded precisely, and laid in a basket with her thimble and thread and scissors. Louisa Ellis could not remember that ever in her life she had mislaid one of these little feminine appurtenances, which had become, from long use and constant association, a very part of her personality.

Louisa tied a green apron round her waist, and got out a flat straw hat with a green ribbon. Then she went into the garden with a little blue crockery bowl, to pick some currants for her tea. After the currants were picked she sat on the back door-step and stemmed them, collecting the stems carefully in her apron, and afterwards throwing them into the hen-coop. She looked sharply at the grass beside the step to see if any had fallen there.

Louisa was slow and still in her movements; it took her a long time to prepare her tea; but when ready it was set forth with as much grace as if she had been a veritable guest to her own self. The little square table stood exactly in the centre of the kitchen, and was covered with a starched linen cloth whose border pattern of flowers glistened. Louisa had a damask napkin on her tea-tray, where were arranged a cut-glass tumbler full of teaspoons, a silver cream-pitcher, a china sugar-bowl, and one pink china cup and saucer. Louisa used china every day — something which none of her neighbors did. They whispered about it among themselves. Their daily tables were laid with common crockery, their sets of best china stayed in the parlor closet, and Louisa Ellis was no richer nor better bred than they. Still she would use the china. She had for her supper a glass dish full of sugared currants, a plate of little cakes, and one of light white biscuits. Also a leaf or two of lettuce, which she cut up daintily. Louisa was very fond of lettuce, which she raised to perfection in her little garden. She ate quite heartily, though in a delicate, pecking way; it seemed almost surprising that any considerable bulk of the food should vanish.

After tea she filled a plate with nicely baked thin corn-cakes, and carried them out into the back-yard.

"Cæsar!" she called. "Cæsar! Cæsar!"

There was a little rush, and the clank of a chain, and a large yellow-and-white dog appeared at the door of his tiny hut, which was half hidden among the tall grasses and flowers.

Louisa patted him and gave him the corn-cakes. Then she returned to the house and washed the tea-things, polishing the china carefully. The twilight had deepened; the chorus of the frogs floated in at the open window wonderfully loud and shrill, and once in a while a long sharp drone from a tree-toad pierced it. Louisa took off her green gingham apron, disclosing a shorter one of pink and white print. She lighted her lamp, and sat down again with her sewing.

In about half an hour Joe Dagget came. She heard his heavy step on the walk, and rose and took off her pink-and-white apron. Under that was still another—white linen with a little cambric edging on the bottom; that was Louisa's company apron. She never wore it without her calico sewing apron over it unless she had a guest. She had barely folded the pink and white one with methodical haste and laid it in a table-drawer when the door opened and Joe Dagget entered.

He seemed to fill up the whole room. A little yellow canary that had been asleep in his green cage at the south window woke up and fluttered wildly, beating his little yellow wings against the wires. He always did so when Joe Dagget came into the room.

"Good-evening," said Louisa. She extended her hand with a kind of solemn cordiality.

"Good-evening, Louisa," returned the man, in a loud voice.

She placed a chair for him, and they sat facing each other, with the table between them. He sat bolt-upright, toeing out his heavy feet squarely, glancing with a good-humored uneasiness around the room. She sat gently erect, folding her slender hands in her white-linen lap.

"Been a pleasant day," remarked Dagget.

"Real pleasant," Louisa assented, softly. "Have you been haying?" she asked, after a little while.

"Yes, I've been haying all day, down in the ten-acre lot. Pretty hot work."

"It must be."

"Yes, it's pretty hot work in the sun."

"Is your mother well to-day?"

"Yes, mother's pretty well."

"I suppose Lily Dyer's with her now?"

Dagget colored. "Yes, she's with her," he answered, slowly.

He was not very young, but there was a boyish look about his large face. Louisa was not quite as old as he, her face was fairer and smoother, but she gave people the impression of being older.

"I suppose she's a good deal of help to your mother," she said, further.

"I guess she is; I don't know how mother'd get along without her," said Dagget, with a sort of embarrassed warmth.

"She looks like a real capable girl. She's pretty-looking too," remarked Louisa.

"Yes, she is pretty fair looking."

Presently Dagget began fingering the books on the table. There was a square red autograph album, and a Young Lady's Gift-Book which had belonged to Louisa's mother. He took them up one after the other and opened them; then laid them down again, the album on the Gift-Book.

Louisa kept eying them with mild uneasiness. Finally she rose and changed the position of the books, putting the album underneath. That was the way they had been arranged in the first place.

Dagget gave an awkward little laugh. "Now what difference did it make which book was on top?" said he.

Louisa looked at him with a deprecating smile. "I always keep them that way," murmured she.

"You do beat everything," said Dagget, trying to laugh again. His large face was flushed.

He remained about an hour longer, then rose to take leave. Going out, he stumbled over a rug, and trying to recover himself, hit Louisa's work-basket on the table, and knocked it on the floor.

He looked at Louisa, then at the rolling spools; he ducked himself awkwardly toward them, but she stopped him. "Never mind," said she; "I'll pick them up after you're gone."

She spoke with a mild stiffness. Either she was a little disturbed, or his nervousness affected her, and made her seem constrained in her effort to reassure him.

When Joe Dagget was outside he drew in the sweet evening air with a sigh, and felt much as an innocent and perfectly well-intentioned bear might after his exit from a china shop.

Louisa, on her part, felt much as the kind-hearted, long-suffering owner of the china shop might have done after the exit of the bear.

She tied on the pink, then the green apron, picked up all the scattered treasures and replaced them in her work-basket, and straightened the rug. Then she set the lamp on the floor, and began sharply examining the carpet. She even rubbed her fingers over it, and looked at them.

"He's tracked in a good deal of dust," she murmured. "I thought he must have."

Louisa got a dust-pan and brush, and swept Joe Dagget's track carefully.

If he could have known it, it would have increased his perplexity and uneasiness, although it would not have disturbed his loyalty in the least. He came twice a week to see Louisa Ellis, and every time, sitting there in her delicately sweet room, he felt as if surrounded by a hedge of lace. He was afraid to stir lest he should put a clumsy foot or hand through the fairy web, and he had always the consciousness that Louisa was watching fearfully lest he should.

Still the lace and Louisa commanded perforce his perfect respect and patience and loyalty. They were to be married in a month, after a singular courtship which had lasted for a matter of fifteen years. For fourteen out of the fifteen years the two had not once seen each other, and they had seldom exchanged letters. Joe had been all those years in Australia, where he had gone to make his fortune, and where he had stayed until he made it. He would have stayed fifty years if it had taken so long, and come home feeble and tottering, or never come home at all, to marry Louisa.

But the fortune had been made in the fourteen years, and he had come home now to marry the woman who had been patiently and unquestioningly waiting for him all that time.

Shortly after they were engaged he had announced to Louisa his determination to strike out into new fields, and secure a competency before they should be married. She had listened and assented with the sweet serenity which never failed her, not even when her lover set forth on that long and uncertain journey. Joe, buoyed up as he was by his sturdy determination, broke down a little at the last, but Louisa kissed him with a mild blush, and said good-by.

"It won't be for long," poor Joe had said, huskily; but it was for fourteen years.

In that length of time much had happened. Louisa's mother and brother had died, and she was all alone in the world. But greatest happening of all—a subtle happening which both were too simple to understand—Louisa's feet had turned into a path, smooth maybe under a calm, serene sky, but so straight and unswerving that it could only meet a check at her grave, and so narrow that there was no room for any one at her side.

Louisa's first emotion when Joe Dagget came home (he had not apprised her of his coming) was consternation, although she would not admit it to herself, and he never dreamed of it. Fifteen years ago she had been in love with him—at least she considered herself to be. Just at that time, gently acquiescing with and falling into the natural drift of girlhood, she had seen marriage ahead as a reasonable feature and a probable desirability of life. She had listened with calm docility to her mother's views upon the subject. Her mother was remarkable for her cool sense and sweet, even temperament. She talked wisely to her daughter when Joe Dagget presented himself, and Louisa accepted him with no hesitation. He was the first lover she had ever had.

She had been faithful to him all these years. She had never dreamed of the possibility of marrying any one else. Her life, especially for the last seven years, had been full of a pleasant peace, she had never felt discontented nor impatient over her lover's absence; still she had always looked forward to his return and their marriage as the inevitable conclusion of things. However, she had fallen into a way of placing it so far in the future that it was almost equal to placing it over the boundaries of another life.

When Joe came she had been expecting him, and expecting to be married for fourteen years, but she was as much surprised and taken aback as if she had never thought of it.

Joe's consternation came later. He eyed Louisa with an instant confirmation of his old admiration. She had changed but little. She still kept her pretty manner and soft grace, and was, he considered, every whit as attractive as ever. As for himself, his stent was done; he had turned his face away from fortune-seeking, and the old winds of romance whistled as loud and sweet as ever through his ears. All the song which he had been wont to hear in them was Louisa; he had for a long time a loyal belief that he heard it still, but finally it seemed to him that although the winds sang always that one song, it had another name. But for Louisa the wind had never more than murmured; now it had gone down, and everything was still. She listened for a little while with half-wistful attention; then she turned quietly away and went to work on her wedding clothes.

Joe had made some extensive and quite magnificent alterations in his house. It was the old homestead; the newly-married couple would live there, for Joe could not desert his mother, who refused to leave her old home. So Louisa must leave hers. Every morning, rising and going about among her neat maidenly possessions, she felt as one looking her last upon the faces of dear friends. It was true that in a measure she could take them with her, but, robbed of their old environments, they would appear in such new guises that they would almost cease to be themselves.

Then there were some peculiar features of her happy solitary life which she would probably be obliged to relinquish altogether. Sterner tasks than these graceful but half-needless ones would probably devolve upon her. There would be a large house to care for; there would be company to entertain; there would be Joe's rigorous and feeble old mother to wait upon; and it would be contrary to all thrifty village traditions for her to keep more than one servant. Louisa had a little still, and she used to occupy herself pleasantly in summer weather with distilling the sweet and aromatic essences from roses and peppermint and spearmint. By-and-by her still must be laid away. Her store of essences was already considerable, and there would be no time for her to distil for the mere pleasure of it. Then Joe's mother would think it foolishness; she had already hinted her opinion in the matter. Louisa dearly loved to sew a linen seam, not always for use, but for the simple, mild pleasure which she took in it. She would have been loath to confess how more than once she had ripped a seam for the mere delight of sewing it together again. Sitting at her window during long sweet afternoons, drawing her needle gently through the dainty fabric, she was peace itself. But there was small chance of such foolish comfort in the future. Joe's mother, domineering, shrewd old matron that she was even in her old age, and very likely even Joe himself, with his honest masculine rudeness, would laugh and frown down all these pretty but senseless old maiden ways.

Louisa had almost the enthusiasm of an artist over the mere order and cleanliness of her solitary home. She had throbs of genuine triumph at the sight of the window-panes which she had polished until they shone like jewels. She gloated gently over her orderly bureau-drawers, with their exquisitely folded contents redolent with lavender and sweet clover and very purity. Could she be sure of the endurance of even this? She had visions, so startling that she half repudiated them as indelicate, of coarse masculine belongings strewn about in endless litter; of dust and disorder arising necessarily from a coarse masculine presence in the midst of all this delicate harmony.

Among her forebodings of disturbance, not the least was with regard to Cæsar. Cæsar was a veritable hermit of a dog. For the greater part of his life he had dwelt in his secluded hut, shut out from the society of his kind and all innocent canine joys. Never had Cæsar since his early youth watched at a woodchuck's hole; never had he known the delights of a stray bone at a neighbor's kitchen door. And it was all on account of a sin committed when hardly out of his puppyhood. No one knew the possible depth of remorse of which this mild-visaged, altogether innocent-looking old dog might be capable; but whether or not he had encountered remorse, he had encountered a full measure of righteous retribution. Old Cæsar seldom lifted up his voice in a growl or a bark; he was fat and sleepy; there were yellow rings which looked like spectacles around his dim old eyes; but there was a neighbor who bore on his hand the imprint of several of Cæsar's sharp white youthful teeth, and for that he had lived at the end of a chain, all alone in a little hut, for fourteen years. The neighbor, who was choleric and smarting with the pain of his wound, had demanded either Cæsar's death or complete ostracism. So Louisa's brother, to whom the dog had belonged, had built him his little kennel and tied him up. It was now fourteen years since, in a flood of youthful spirits, he had inflicted that memorable bite, and with the exception of short excursions, always at the end of the chain, under the strict guardianship of his master or Louisa, the old dog had remained a close prisoner. It is doubtful if, with his limited ambition, he took much pride in the fact, but it is certain that he was possessed of considerable cheap fame. He was regarded by all the children in the village and by many adults as a very monster of ferocity. St. George's dragon could hardly have surpassed in evil repute Louisa Ellis's old yellow dog. Mothers charged their children with solemn emphasis not to go too near to him, and the children listened and believed greedily, with a fascinated appetite for terror, and ran by Louisa's house stealthily, with many sidelong and backward glances at the terrible dog. If perchance he sounded a hoarse bark, there was a panic. Wayfarers chancing into Louisa's yard eyed him with respect, and inquired if the chain were stout. Cæsar at large might have seemed a very ordinary dog, and excited no comment whatever; chained, his reputation overshadowed him, so that he lost his own proper outlines and looked darkly vague and enormous. Joe Dagget, however, with his good-humored sense and shrewdness, saw him as he was. He strode valiantly up to him and patted him on the head, in spite of Louisa's soft clamor of warning, and even attempted to set him loose. Louisa grew so alarmed that he desisted, but kept announcing his opinion in the matter quite forcibly at intervals. "There ain't a better-natured dog in town," he would say, "and it's downright cruel to keep him tied up there. Some day I'm going to take him out."

Louisa had very little hope that he would not, one of these days, when their interests and possessions should be more completely fused in one. She pictured to herself

Cæsar on the rampage through the quiet and unguarded village. She saw innocent children bleeding in his path. She was herself very fond of the old dog, because he had belonged to her dead brother, and he was always very gentle with her; still she had great faith in his ferocity. She always warned people not to go too near him. She fed him on ascetic fare of corn-mush and cakes, and never fired his dangerous temper with heating and sanguinary diet of flesh and bones. Louisa looked at the old dog munching his simple fare, and thought of her approaching marriage and trembled. Still no anticipation of disorder and confusion in lieu of sweet peace and harmony, no forebodings of Cæsar on the rampage, no wild fluttering of her little yellow canary, were sufficient to turn her a hair's-breadth. Joe Dagget had been fond of her and working for her all these years. It was not for her, whatever came to pass, to prove untrue and break his heart. She put the exquisite little stitches into her wedding-garments, and the time went on until it was only a week before her wedding-day. It was a Tuesday evening, and the wedding was to be a week from Wednesday.

There was a full moon that night. About nine o'clock Louisa strolled down the road a little way. There were harvest-fields on either hand, bordered by low stone walls. Luxuriant clumps of bushes grew beside the wall, and trees —wild cherry and old apple-trees—at intervals. Presently Louisa sat down on the wall and looked about her with mildly sorrowful reflectiveness. Tall shrubs of blueberry and meadow-sweet, all woven together and tangled with blackberry vines and horsebriers, shut her in on either side. She had a little clear space between them. Opposite her, on the other side of the road, was a spreading tree;

the moon shone between its boughs, and the leaves twinkled like silver. The road was bespread with a beautiful shifting dapple of silver and shadow; the air was full of a mysterious sweetness. "I wonder if it's wild grapes?" murmured Louisa. She sat there some time. She was just thinking of rising, when she heard footsteps and low voices, and remained quiet. It was a lonely place, and she felt a little timid. She thought she would keep still in the shadow and let the persons, whoever they might be, pass her.

But just before they reached her the voices ceased, and the footsteps. She understood that their owners had also found seats upon the stone wall. She was wondering if she could not steal away unobserved, when the voice broke the stillness. It was Joe Dagget's. She sat still and listened.

The voice was announced by a loud sigh, which was as familiar as itself. "Well," said Dagget, "you've made up your mind, then, I suppose?"

"Yes," returned another voice; "I'm going day after to-morrow."

"That's Lily Dyer," thought Louisa to herself. The voice embodied itself in her mind. She saw a girl tall and full-figured, with a firm, fair face, looking fairer and firmer in the moonlight, her strong yellow hair braided in a close knot. A girl full of a calm rustic strength and bloom, with a masterful way which might have beseemed a princess. Lily Dyer was a favorite with the village folk; she had just the qualities to arouse the admiration. She was good and handsome and smart. Louisa had often heard her praises sounded.

"Well," said Joe Dagget, "I ain't got a word to say."

"I don't know what you could say," returned Lily Dyer.

"Not a word to say," repeated Joe, drawing out the words heavily. Then there was a silence. "I ain't sorry," he began at last, "that that happened yesterday—that we kind of let on how we felt to each other. I guess it's just as well we knew. Of course I can't do anything any different. I'm going right on an' get married next week. I ain't going back on a woman that's waited for me fourteen years, an' break her heart."

"If you should jilt her to-morrow, I wouldn't have you," spoke up the girl, with sudden vehemence.

"Well, I ain't going to give you the chance," said he; "but I don't believe you would, either."

"You'd see I wouldn't. Honor's honor, an' right's right. An' I'd never think anything of any man that went against 'em for me or any other girl; you'd find that out, Joe Dagget."

"Well, you'll find out fast enough that I ain't going against 'em for you or any other girl," returned he. Their voices sounded almost as if they were angry with each other. Louisa was listening eagerly.

"I'm sorry you feel as if you must go away," said Joe, "but I don't know but it's best."

"Of course it's best. I hope you and I have got common-sense."

"Well, I suppose you're right." Suddenly Joe's voice got an undertone of tenderness. "Say, Lily," said he, "I'll get along well enough myself, but I can't bear to think— You don't suppose you're going to fret much over it?"

"I guess you'll find out I sha'n't fret much over a married man."

"Well, I hope you won't—I hope you won't, Lily. God knows I do. And — I hope — one of these days — you'll —come across somebody else—"

"I don't see any reason why I shouldn't." Suddenly her tone changed. She spoke in a sweet, clear voice, so loud that she could have been heard across the street. "No, Joe Dagget," said she, "I'll never marry any other man as long as I live. I've got good sense, an' I ain't going to break my heart nor make a fool of myself; but I'm never going to be married, you can be sure of that. I ain't that sort of a girl to feel this way twice."

Louisa heard an exclamation and a soft commotion behind the bushes; then Lily spoke again—the voice sounded as if she had risen. "This must be put a stop to," said she. "We've stayed here long enough. I'm going home."

Louisa sat there in a daze, listening to their retreating steps. After a while she got up and slunk softly home herself. The next day she did her housework methodically; that was as much a matter of course as breathing; but she did not sew on her wedding-clothes. She sat at her window and meditated. In the evening Joe came. Louisa Ellis had never known that she had any diplomacy in her, but when she came to look for it that night she found it, although meek of its kind, among her little feminine weapons. Even now she could hardly believe that she had heard aright, and that she would not do Joe a terrible injury should she break her troth-plight. She wanted to sound him without betraying too soon her own inclinations in the matter. She did it successfully, and they finally came to an understanding; but it was a difficult thing, for he was as afraid of betraying himself as she.

She never mentioned Lily Dyer. She simply said that while she had no cause of complaint against him, she had lived so long in one way that she shrank from making a change.

"Well, I never shrank, Louisa," said Dagget. "I'm going to be honest enough to say that I think maybe it's better this way; but if you'd wanted to keep on, I'd have stuck to you till my dying day. I hope you know that."

"Yes, I do," said she.

That night she and Joe parted more tenderly than they had done for a long time. Standing in the door, holding each other's hands, a last great wave of regretful memory swept over them.

"Well, this ain't the way we've thought it was all going to end, is it, Louisa?" said Joe.

She shook her head. There was a little quiver on her placid face.

"You let me know if there's ever anything I can do for you," said he. "I ain't ever going to forget you, Louisa." Then he kissed her, and went down the path.

Louisa, all alone by herself that night, wept a little, she hardly knew why; but the next morning, on waking, she felt like a queen who, after fearing lest her domain be wrested away from her, sees it firmly insured in her possession.

Now the tall weeds and grasses might cluster around Cæsar's little hermit hut, the snow might fall on its roof year in and year out, but he never would go on a rampage through the unguarded village. Now the little canary might turn itself into a peaceful yellow ball night after night, and have no need to wake and flutter with wild terror against its bars. Louisa could sew linen seams, and distil roses, and dust and polish and fold away in lavender, as long as she listed. That afternoon she sat with her needle-work at the window, and felt fairly steeped in peace. Lily Dyer, tall and erect and blooming, went past; but she felt no qualm. If Louisa Ellis had sold her birthright she did not know it, the taste of the pottage was so delicious, and had been her sole satisfaction for so long. Serenity and placid narrowness had become to her as the birthright itself. She gazed ahead through a long reach of future days strung together like pearls in a rosary, every one like the others, and all smooth and flawless and innocent, and her heart went up in thankfulness. Outside was the fervid summer afternoon; the air was filled with the sounds of the busy harvest of men and birds and bees; there were halloos, metallic clatterings, sweet calls, and long hummings. Louisa sat, prayerfully numbering her days, like an uncloistered nun.

A VILLAGE SINGER.

THE trees were in full leaf, a heavy south wind was blowing, and there was a loud murmur among the new leaves. The people noticed it, for it was the first time that year that the trees had so murmured in the wind. The spring had come with a rush during the last few days.

The murmur of the trees sounded loud in the village church, where the people sat waiting for the service to begin. The windows were open; it was a very warm Sunday for May.

The church was already filled with this soft sylvan music—the tender harmony of the leaves and the south wind, and the sweet, desultory whistles of birds—when the choir arose and began to sing.

In the centre of the row of women singers stood Alma Way. All the people stared at her, and turned their ears critically. She was the new leading soprano. Candace Whitcomb, the old one, who had sung in the choir for forty years, had lately been given her dismissal. The audience considered that her voice had grown too cracked and uncertain on the upper notes. There had been much complaint, and after long deliberation the church-officers had made known their decision as mildly as possible to the old singer. She had sung for the last time the Sunday before, and Alma Way had been engaged to take her place. With the exception of the organist, the leading soprano was the only paid musician in the large choir. The salary was very modest, still the village people considered it large for a young woman. Alma was from the adjoining village of East Derby; she had quite a local reputation as a singer.

Now she fixed her large solemn blue eyes; her long, delicate face, which had been pretty, turned paler; the blue flowers on her bonnet trembled; her little thin gloved hands, clutching the singing-book, shook perceptibly; but she sang out bravely. That most formidable mountain-height of the world, self-distrust and timidity, arose before her, but her nerves were braced for its ascent. In the midst of the hymn she had a solo; her voice rang out piercingly sweet; the people nodded admiringly at each other; but suddenly there was a stir; all the faces turned toward the windows on the south side of the church. Above the din of the wind and the birds, above Alma Way's sweetly straining tones, arose another female voice, singing another hymn to another tune.

"It's her," the women whispered to each other; they were half aghast, half smiling.

Candace Whitcomb's cottage stood close to the south side of the church. She was playing on her parlor organ, and singing, to drown out the voice of her rival.

Alma caught her breath; she almost stopped; the hymn-book waved like a fan; then she went on. But the long husky drone of the parlor organ and the shrill clamor of the other voice seemed louder than anything else.

When the hymn was finished, Alma sat down. She felt faint; the woman next her slipped a peppermint into her hand. "It ain't worth minding," she whispered, vigorously.

Alma tried to smile; down in the audience a young man was watching her with a kind of fierce pity.

In the last hymn Alma had another solo. Again the parlor organ droned above the carefully delicate accompaniment of the church organ, and again Candace Whitcomb's voice clamored forth in another tune.

After the benediction, the other singers pressed around Alma. She did not say much in return for their expressions of indignation and sympathy. She wiped her eyes furtively once or twice, and tried to smile. William Emmons, the choir leader, elderly, stout, and smooth-faced, stood over her, and raised his voice. He was the old musical dignitary of the village, the leader of the choral club and the singing-schools. "A most outrageous proceeding," he said. People had coupled his name with Candace Whitcomb's. The old bachelor tenor and old maiden soprano had been wont to walk together to her home next door after the Saturday night rehearsals, and they had sung duets to the parlor organ. People had watched sharply her old face, on which the blushes of youth sat pitifully, when William Emmons entered the singing-seats. They wondered if he would ever ask her to marry him.

And now he said further to Alma Way that Candace Whitcomb's voice had failed utterly of late, that she sang shockingly, and ought to have had sense enough to know it.

When Alma went down into the audience-room, in the midst of the chattering singers, who seemed to have descended, like birds, from song flights to chirps, the minister approached her. He had been waiting to speak to her. He was a steady-faced, fleshy old man, who had preached from that one pulpit over forty years. He told Alma, in his slow way, how much he regretted the annoyance to which she had been subjected, and intimated that he would endeavor to prevent a recurrence of it. "Miss Whitcomb—must be—reasoned with," said he ; he had a slight hesitation of speech, not an impediment. It was as if his thoughts did not slide readily into his words, although both were present. He walked down the aisle with Alma, and bade her good-morning when he saw Wilson Ford waiting for her in the doorway. Everybody knew that Wilson Ford and Alma were lovers ; they had been for the last ten years.

Alma colored softly, and made a little imperceptible motion with her head ; her silk dress and the lace on her mantle fluttered, but she did not speak. Neither did Wilson, although they had not met before that day. They did not look at each other's faces—they seemed to see each other without that—and they walked along side by side.

They reached the gate before Candace Whitcomb's little house. Wilson looked past the front yard, full of pink and white spikes on flowering bushes, at the lace-curtained windows ; a thin white profile, stiffly inclined, apparently over a book, was visible at one of them. Wilson gave his head a shake. He was a stout man, with features so strong that they overcame his flesh. "I'm going up home with you, Alma," said he ; "and then—I'm just coming back, to give Aunt Candace one blowing up."

"Oh, don't, Wilson."

"Yes, I shall. If you want to stand this kind of a thing you may ; I sha'n't."

"There's no need of your talking to her. Mr. Pollard's going to."

"Did he say he was?"

"Yes. I think he's going in before the afternoon meeting, from what he said."

"Well, there's one thing about it, if she does that thing again this afternoon, I'll go in there and break that old organ up into kindling-wood." Wilson set his mouth hard, and shook his head again.

Alma gave little side glances up at him, her tone was deprecatory, but her face was full of soft smiles. "I suppose she does feel dreadfully about it," said she. "I can't help feeling kind of guilty, taking her place."

"I don't see how you're to blame. It's outrageous, her acting so."

"The choir gave her a photograph album last week, didn't they?"

"Yes. They went there last Thursday night, and gave her an album and a surprise-party. She ought to behave herself."

"Well, she's sung there so long, I suppose it must be dreadful hard for her to give it up."

Other people going home from church were very near Wilson and Alma. She spoke softly that they might not hear; he did not lower his voice in the least. Presently Alma stopped before a gate.

"What are you stopping here for?" asked Wilson.

"Minnie Lansing wanted me to come and stay with her this noon."

"You're going home with me."

"I'm afraid I'll put your mother out."

"Put mother out! I told her you were coming, this morning. She's got all ready for you. Come along; don't stand here."

He did not tell Alma of the pugnacious spirit with which his mother had received the announcement of her coming, and how she had stayed at home to prepare the dinner, and make a parade of her hard work and her injury.

Wilson's mother was the reason why he did not marry Alma. He would not take his wife home to live with her, and was unable to support separate establishments. Alma was willing enough to be married and put up with Wilson's mother, but she did not complain of his decision. Her delicate blond features grew sharper, and her blue eyes more hollow. She had had a certain fine prettiness, but now she was losing it, and beginning to look old, and there was a prim, angular, old maiden carriage about her narrow shoulders.

Wilson never noticed it, and never thought of Alma as not possessed of eternal youth, or capable of losing or regretting it.

"Come along, Alma," said he; and she followed meekly after him down the street.

Soon after they passed Candace Whitcomb's house, the minister went up the front walk and rang the bell. The pale profile at the window had never stirred as he opened the gate and came up the walk. However, the door was promptly opened, in response to his ring. "Good-morning, Miss Whitcomb," said the minister.

"*Good*-morning." Candace gave a sweeping toss of her head as she spoke. There was a fierce upward curl to her thin nostrils and her lips, as if she scented an adversary. Her black eyes had two tiny cold sparks of fury in them, like an enraged bird's. She did not ask the minister to enter, but he stepped lumberingly into the entry, and she retreated rather than led the way into her little parlor. He settled into the great rocking-chair and wiped his face. Candace sat down again in her old place by the window. She was a tall woman, but very slender and full of pliable motions, like a blade of grass.

"It's a—very pleasant day," said the minister.

Candace made no reply. She sat still, with her head drooping. The wind stirred the looped lace-curtains; a tall rose-tree outside the window waved; soft shadows floated through the room. Candace's parlor organ stood in front of an open window that faced the church; on the corner was a pitcher with a bunch of white lilacs. The whole room was scented with them. Presently the minister looked over at them and sniffed pleasantly.

"You have—some beautiful—lilacs there."

Candace did not speak. Every line of her slender figure looked flexible, but it was a flexibility more resistant than rigor.

The minister looked at her. He filled up the great rocking-chair; his arms in his shiny black coat-sleeves rested squarely and comfortably upon the hair-cloth arms of the chair.

"Well, Miss Whitcomb, I suppose I—may as well come to—the point. There was—a little—matter I wished to speak to you about. I don't suppose you were—at least I can't suppose you were—aware of it, but—this morning, during the singing by the choir, you played and—sung a little too—loud. That is, with—the windows open. It—disturbed us—a little. I hope you won't feel hurt—my dear Miss Candace, but I knew you would rather I would speak of it, for I knew—you would be more disturbed than anybody else at the idea of such a thing."

Candace did not raise her eyes; she looked as if his words might sway her through the window. "I ain't disturbed at it," said she. "I did it on purpose; I meant to."

The minister looked at her.

"You needn't look at me. I know jest what I'm about.

I sung the way I did on purpose, an' I'm goin' to do it again, an' I'd like to see you stop me. I guess I've got a right to set down to my own organ, an' sing a psalm tune on a Sabbath day, 'f I want to; an' there ain't no amount of talkin' an' palaverin' a-goin' to stop me. See there!" Candace swung aside her skirts a little. "Look at that!"

The minister looked. Candace's feet were resting on a large red-plush photograph album.

"Makes a nice footstool, don't it?" said she.

The minister looked at the album, then at her; there was a slowly gathering alarm in his face; he began to think she was losing her reason.

Candace had her eyes full upon him now, and her head up. She laughed, and her laugh was almost a snarl. "Yes; I thought it would make a beautiful footstool," said she. "I've been wantin' one for some time." Her tone was full of vicious irony.

"Why, miss—" began the minister; but she interrupted him:

"I know what you're a-goin' to say, Mr. Pollard, an' now I'm goin' to have my say; I'm a-goin' to speak. I want to know what you think of folks that pretend to be Christians treatin' anybody the way they've treated me? Here I've sung in those singin'-seats forty year. I 'ain't never missed a Sunday, except when I've been sick, an' I've gone an' sung a good many times when I'd better been in bed, an' now I'm turned out without a word of warnin'. My voice is jest as good as ever 'twas; there can't anybody say it ain't. It wa'n't ever quite so high-pitched as that Way girl's, mebbe; but she flats the whole durin' time. My voice is as good an' high to-day as it was twenty year ago; an' if it wa'n't, I'd like to know where the Christianity comes in. I'd like to know if it wouldn't be more to the credit of folks in a church to keep an old singer an' an old minister, if they didn't sing an' hold forth quite so smart as they used to, ruther than turn 'em off an' hurt their feelin's. I guess it would be full as much to the glory of God. S'pose the singin' an' the preachin' wa'n't quite so good, what difference would it make? Salvation don't hang on anybody's hittin' a high note, that I ever heard of. Folks are gettin' as high-steppin' an' fussy in a meetin'-house as they are in a tavern, nowadays. S'pose they should turn you off, Mr. Pollard, come an' give you a photograph album, an' tell you to clear out, how'd you like it? I ain't findin' any fault with your preachin'; it was always good enough to suit me; but it don't stand to reason folks 'll be as took up with your sermons as when you was a young man. You can't expect it. S'pose they should turn you out in your old age, an' call in some young bob squirt, how'd you feel? There's William Emmons, too; he's three years older'n I am, if he does lead the choir an' run all the singin' in town. If my voice has gi'en out, it stan's to reason his has. It ain't, though. William Emmons sings jest as well as he ever did. Why don't they turn him out the way they have me, an' give him a photograph album? I dun know but it would be a good idea to send everybody, as soon as they get a little old an' gone by, an' young folks begin to push, onto some desert island, an' give 'em each a photograph album. Then they can sit down an' look at pictures the rest of their days. Mebbe government 'll take it up.

"There they come here last week Thursday, all the choir, jest about eight o'clock in the evenin', an' pretended they'd come to give me a nice little surprise. Surprise! h'm! Brought cake an' oranges, an' was jest as nice as they could be, an' I was real tickled. I never had a surprise-party before in my life. Jenny Carr she played, an' they wanted me to sing alone, an' I never suspected a thing. I've been mad ever since to think what a fool I was, an' how they must have laughed in their sleeves.

"When they'd gone I found this photograph album on the table, all done up as nice as you please, an' directed to Miss Candace Whitcomb from her many friends, an' I opened it, an' there was the letter inside givin' me notice to quit.

"If they'd gone about it any decent way, told me right out honest that they'd got tired of me, an' wanted Alma Way to sing instead of me, I wouldn't minded so much; I should have been hurt 'nough, for I'd felt as if some that had pretended to be my friends wa'n't; but it wouldn't have been as bad as this. They said in the letter that they'd always set great value on my services, an' it wa'n't from any lack of appreciation that they turned me off, but they thought the duty was gettin' a little too arduous for me. H'm! I hadn't complained. If they'd turned me right out fair an' square, showed me the door, an' said, 'Here, you get out,' but to go an' spill molasses, as it were, all over the threshold, tryin' to make me think it's all nice an' sweet—

"I'd sent that photograph album back quick's I could pack it, but I didn't know who started it, so I've used it for a footstool. It's all it's good for, 'cordin' to my way of thinkin'. An' I ain't been particular to get the dust off my shoes before I used it neither."

Mr. Pollard, the minister, sat staring. He did not look at Candace; his eyes were fastened upon a point straight ahead. He had a look of helpless solidity, like a block of granite. This country minister, with his steady, even temperament, treading with heavy precision his one track for over forty years, having nothing new in his life except the new sameness of the seasons, and desiring nothing new, was incapable of understanding a woman like this, who had lived as quietly as he, and all the time held within herself the elements of revolution. He could not account for such violence, such extremes, except in a loss of reason. He had a conviction that Candace was getting beyond herself. He himself was not a typical New-Englander; the national elements of character were not pronounced in him. He was aghast and bewildered at this outbreak, which was tropical, and more than tropical, for a New England nature has a floodgate, and the power which it releases is an accumulation. Candace Whitcomb had been a quiet woman, so delicately resolute that the quality had been scarcely noticed in her, and her ambition had been unsuspected. Now the resolution and the ambition appeared raging over her whole self.

She began to talk again. "I've made up my mind that I'm goin' to sing Sundays the way I did this mornin', an' I don't care what folks say," said she. "I've made up my mind that I'm goin' to take matters into my own hands. I'm goin' to let folks see that I ain't trod down quite flat, that there's a little rise left in me. I ain't goin' to give up beat yet a while; an' I'd like to see anybody stop me. If I ain't got a right to play a psalm tune on my organ an' sing, I'd like to know. If you don't like it, you can move the meetin'-house."

Candace had had an inborn reverence for clergymen. She had always treated Mr. Pollard with the utmost deference. Indeed, her manner toward all men had been marked by a certain delicate stiffness and dignity. Now she was talking to the old minister with the homely freedom with which she might have addressed a female gossip over the back fence. He could not say much in return. He did not feel competent to make headway against any such tide of passion ; all he could do was to let it beat against him. He made a few expostulations, which increased Candace's vehemence ; he expressed his regret over the whole affair, and suggested that they should kneel and ask the guidance of the Lord in the matter, that she might be led to see it all in a different light.

Candace refused flatly. " I don't see any use prayin' about it," said she. " I don't think the Lord's got much to do with it, anyhow."

It was almost time for the afternoon service when the minister left. He had missed his comfortable noontide rest, through this encounter with his revolutionary parishioner. After the minister had gone, Candace sat by the window and waited. The bell rang, and she watched the people file past. When her nephew Wilson Ford with Alma appeared, she grunted to herself. " She's thin as a rail," said she ; " guess there won't be much left of her by the time Wilson gets her. Little soft-spoken nippin' thing, she wouldn't make him no kind of a wife, anyway. Guess it's jest as well."

When the bell had stopped tolling, and all the people entered the church, Candace went over to her organ and seated herself. She arranged a singing-book before her, and sat still, waiting. Her thin, colorless neck and temples were full of beating pulses ; her black eyes were bright and eager ; she leaned stiffly over toward the music-rack, to hear better. When the church organ sounded out she straightened herself ; her long skinny fingers pressed her own organ-keys with nervous energy. She worked the pedals with all her strength; all her slender body was in motion. When the first notes of Alma's solo began, Candace sang. She had really possessed a fine voice, and it was wonderful how little she had lost it. Straining her throat with jealous fury, her notes were still for the main part true. Her voice filled the whole room; she sang with wonderful fire and expression. That, at least, mild little Alma Way could never emulate. She was full of steadfastness and unquestioning constancy, but there were in her no smouldering fires of ambition and resolution. Music was not to her what it had been to her older rival. To this obscure woman, kept relentlessly by circumstances in a narrow track, singing in the village choir had been as much as Italy was to Napoleon—and now on her island of exile she was still showing fight.

After the church service was done, Candace left the organ and went over to her old chair by the window. Her knees felt weak, and shook under her. She sat down, and leaned back her head. There were red spots on her cheeks. Pretty soon she heard a quick slam of her gate, and an impetuous tread on the gravel-walk. She looked up, and there was her nephew Wilson Ford hurrying up to the door. She cringed a little, then she settled herself more firmly in her chair.

Wilson came into the room with a rush. He left the door open, and the wind slammed it to after him.

"Aunt Candace, where are you?" he called out, in a loud voice.

She made no reply. He looked around fiercely, and his eyes seemed to pounce upon her.

"Look here, Aunt Candace," said he, "are you crazy?" Candace said nothing. "Aunt Candace!" She did not seem to see him. "If you don't answer me," said Wilson, "I'll just go over there and pitch that old organ out of the window!"

"Wilson Ford!" said Candace, in a voice that was almost a scream.

"Well, what say! What have you got to say for yourself, acting the way you have? I tell you what 'tis, Aunt Candace, I won't stand it."

"I'd like to see you help yourself."

"I will help myself. I'll pitch that old organ out of the window, and then I'll board up the window on that side of your house. Then we'll see."

"It ain't your house, and it won't never be."

"Who said it was my house? You're my aunt, and I've got a little lookout for the credit of the family. Aunt Candace, what are you doing this way for?"

"It don't make no odds what I'm doin' so for. I ain't bound to give my reasons to a young fellar like you, if you do act so mighty toppin'. But I'll tell you one thing, Wilson Ford, after the way you've spoke to-day, you sha'n't never have one cent of my money, an' you can't never marry that Way girl if you don't have it. You can't never take her home to live with your mother, an' this house would have been mighty nice an' convenient for you some day. Now you won't get it. I'm goin' to make another will. I'd made one, if you did but know it. Now you won't get a cent of my money, you nor your mother neither. An' I ain't goin' to live a dreadful while longer, neither. Now I wish you'd go home; I want to lay down. I'm 'bout sick."

Wilson could not get another word from his aunt. His indignation had not in the least cooled. Her threat of disinheriting him did not cow him at all; he had too much rough independence, and indeed his aunt Candace's house had always been too much of an air-castle for him to contemplate seriously. Wilson, with his burly frame and his headlong common-sense, could have little to do with air-castles, had he been hard enough to build them over graves. Still, he had not admitted that he never could marry Alma. All his hopes were based upon a rise in his own fortunes, not by some sudden convulsion, but by his own long and steady labor. Some time, he thought, he should have saved enough for the two homes.

He went out of his aunt's house still storming. She arose after the door had shut behind him, and got out into the kitchen. She thought that she would start a fire and make a cup of tea. She had not eaten anything all day. She put some kindling-wood into the stove and touched a match to it; then she went back to the sitting-room, and settled down again into the chair by the window. The fire in the kitchen-stove roared, and the light wood was soon burned out. She thought no more about it. She had not put on the teakettle. Her head ached, and once in a while she shivered. She sat at the window while the afternoon waned and the dusk came on. At seven o'clock the meeting bell rang again, and the people flocked by. This time she did not stir. She had shut her parlor organ. She did not need to out-sing her rival this evening; there was only congregational singing at the Sunday-night prayer-meeting.

She sat still until it was nearly time for meeting to be done; her head ached harder and harder, and she shivered more. Finally she arose. "Guess I'll go to bed," she muttered. She went about the house, bent over and shaking, to lock the doors. She stood a minute in the back door, looking over the fields to the woods. There was a red light over there. "The woods are on fire," said Candace. She watched with a dull interest the flames roll up, withering and destroying the tender green spring foliage. The air was full of smoke, although the fire was half a mile away.

Candace locked the door and went in. The trees with their delicate garlands of new leaves, with the new nests of song birds, might fall, she was in the roar of an intenser fire; the growths of all her springs and the delicate wontedness of her whole life were going down in it. Candace went to bed in her little room off the parlor, but she could not sleep. She lay awake all night. In the morning she crawled to the door and hailed a little boy who was passing. She bade him go for the doctor as quickly as he could, then to Mrs. Ford's, and ask her to come over. She held on to the door while she was talking. The boy stood staring wonderingly at her. The spring wind fanned her face. She had drawn on a dress skirt and put her shawl over her shoulders, and her gray hair was blowing over her red cheeks.

She shut the door and went back to her bed. She never arose from it again. The doctor and Mrs. Ford came and looked after her, and she lived a week. Nobody but herself thought until the very last that she would die; the doctor called her illness merely a light run of fever; she had her senses fully.

But Candace gave up at the first. "It's my last sickness," she said to Mrs. Ford that morning when she first entered; and Mrs. Ford had laughed at the notion; but the sick woman held to it. She did not seem to suffer much physical pain; she only grew weaker and weaker, but she was distressed mentally. She did not talk much, but her eyes followed everybody with an agonized expression.

On Wednesday William Emmons came to inquire for her.

Candace heard him out in the parlor. She tried to raise herself on one elbow that she might listen better to his voice.

"William Emmons come in to ask how you was," Mrs. Ford said, after he was gone.

"I—heard him," replied Candace. Presently she spoke again. "Nancy," said she, "where's that photograph album?"

"On the table," replied her sister, hesitatingly.

"Mebbe—you'd better—brush it up a little."

"Well."

Sunday morning Candace wished that the minister should be asked to come in at the noon intermission. She had refused to see him before. He came and prayed with her, and she asked his forgiveness for the way she had spoken the Sunday before. "I—hadn't ought to—spoke so," said she. "I was—dreadful wrought up."

"Perhaps it was your sickness coming on," said the minister, soothingly.

Candace shook her head. "No—it wa'n't. I hope the Lord will—forgive me."

After the minister had gone, Candace still appeared unhappy. Her pitiful eyes followed her sister everywhere with the mechànical persistency of a portrait.

"What is it you want, Candance?" Mrs. Ford said at last. She had nursed her sister faithfully, but once in a while her impatience showed itself.

"Nancy!"

"What say?"

"I wish—you'd go out when—meetin's done, an'—head off Alma an' Wilson, an'—ask 'em to come in. I feel as if—I'd like to—hear her sing."

Mrs. Ford stared. "Well," said she.

The meeting was now in session. The windows were all open, for it was another warm Sunday. Candace lay listening to the music when it began, and a look of peace came over her face. Her sister had smoothed her hair back, and put on a clean cap. The white curtain in the bedroom window waved in the wind like a white sail. Candace almost felt as if she were better, but the thought of death seemed easy.

Mrs. Ford at the parlor window watched for the meeting to be out. When the people appeared, she ran down the walk and waited for Alma and Wilson. When they came she told them what Candace wanted, and they all went in together.

"Here's Alma an' Wilson, Candace," said Mrs. Ford, leading them to the bedroom door.

Candace smiled. "Come in," she said, feebly. And Alma and Wilson entered and stood beside the bed. Candace continued to look at them, the smile straining her lips.

"Wilson!"

"What is it, Aunt Candace?"

"I ain't altered that—will. You an' Alma can—come here an'—live—when I'm—gone. Your mother won't mind livin' alone. Alma can have—all—my things."

"Don't, Aunt Candace." Tears were running over Wilson's cheeks, and Alma's delicate face was all of a quiver.

"I thought—maybe—Alma 'd be willin' to—sing for me," said Candace.

"What do you want me to sing?" Alma asked, in a trembling voice.

"'Jesus, lover of my soul.'"

Alma, standing there beside Wilson, began to sing. At first she could hardly control her voice, then she sang sweetly and clearly.

Candace lay and listened. Her face had a holy and radiant expression. When Alma stopped singing it did not disappear, but she looked up and spoke, and it was like a secondary glimpse of the old shape of a forest tree through the smoke and flame of the transfiguring fire the instant before it falls. "You flatted a little on—soul," said Candace.

A GALA DRESS.

"I DON'T care anything about goin' to that Fourth of July picnic, 'Liz'beth."

"I wouldn't say anything more about it, if I was you, Em'ly. I'd get ready an' go."

"I don't really feel able to go, 'Liz'beth."

"I'd like to know why you ain't able."

"It seems to me as if the fire-crackers an' the tootin' on those horns would drive me crazy; an' Matilda Jennings says they're goin' to have a cannon down there, an' fire it off every half-hour. I don't feel as if I could stan' it. You know my nerves ain't very strong, 'Liz'beth."

Elizabeth Babcock uplifted her long, delicate nose with its transparent nostrils, and sniffed. Apparently her sister's perverseness had an unacceptable odor to her. "I wouldn't talk so if I was you, Em'ly. Of course you're goin'. It's your turn to, an' you know it. I went to meetin' last Sabbath. You just put on that dress an' go."

Emily eyed her sister. She tried not to look pleased. "I know you went to meetin' last," said she, hesitatingly; "but—a Fourth of July picnic is—a little more of—a rarity." She fairly jumped, her sister confronted her with such sudden vigor.

"Rarity! Well, I hope a Fourth of July picnic ain't

quite such a treat to me that I'd ruther go to it than meetin'! I should think you'd be ashamed of yourself speakin' so, Em'ly Babcock."

Emily, a moment before delicately alert and nervous like her sister, shrank limply in her limp black muslin. "I—didn't think how it sounded, 'Liz'beth."

"Well, I should say you'd better think. It don't sound very becomin' for a woman of your age, an' professin' what you do. Now you'd better go an' get out that dress, an' rip the velvet off, an' sew the lace on. There won't be any too much time. They'll start early in the mornin'. I'll stir up a cake for you to carry, when I get tea."

"Don't you s'pose I could get along without a cake?" Emily ventured, tremulously.

"Well, I shouldn't think you'd want to go, an' be beholden to other folks for your eatin'; I shouldn't."

"I shouldn't want anything to eat."

"I guess if you go, you're goin' like other folks. I ain't goin' to have Matilda Jennings peekin' an' pryin' an' tellin' things, if I know it. You'd better get out that dress."

"Well," said Emily, with a long sigh of remorseful satisfaction. She arose, showing a height that would have approached the majestic had it not been so wavering. The sisters were about the same height, but Elizabeth usually impressed people as being the taller. She carried herself with so much decision that she seemed to keep every inch of her stature firm and taut, old woman although she was.

"Let's see that dress a minute," she said, when Emily returned. She wiped her spectacles, set them firmly, and began examining the hem of the dress, holding it close to her eyes. "You're gettin' of it all tagged out," she declared, presently. "I thought you was. I thought I see some ravellin's hangin' the other day when I had it on. It's jest because you don't stan' up straight. It ain't any longer for you than it is for me, if you didn't go all bent over so. There ain't any need of it."

Emily oscillated wearily over her sister and the dress. "I ain't very strong in my back, an' you know I've got a weakness in my stomach that henders me from standin' up as straight as you do," she rejoined, rallying herself for a feeble defence.

"You can stan' up jest as well as I can, if you're a mind to."

"I'll rip that velvet off now, if you'll let me have the dress, 'Liz'beth."

Elizabeth passed over the dress, handling it gingerly. "Mind you don't cut it rippin' of it off," said she.

Emily sat down, and the dress lay in shiny black billows over her lap. The dress was black silk, and had been in its day very soft and heavy; even now there was considerable wear left in it. The waist and over-skirt were trimmed with black velvet ribbon. Emily ripped off the velvet; then she sewed on some old-fashioned, straight-edged black lace full of little embroidered sprigs. The sisters sat in their parlor at the right of the front door. The room was very warm, for there were two west windows, and a hot afternoon sun was beating upon them. Out in front of the house was a piazza, with a cool uneven brick floor, and a thick lilac growth across the western end. The sisters might have sat there and been comfortable, but they would not.

"Set right out in the face an' eyes of all the neighbors!" they would have exclaimed with dismay had the idea been suggested. There was about these old women and all their belongings a certain gentle and deprecatory reticence. One felt it immediately upon entering their house, or indeed upon coming in sight of it. There were never any heads at the windows; the blinds were usually closed. Once in a while a passer-by might see an old woman, well shielded by shawl and scooping sun-bonnet, start up like a timid spirit in the yard, and softly disappear through a crack in the front door. Out in the front yard Emily had a little bed of flowers—of balsams and nasturtiums and portulacas; she tended them with furtive glances toward the road. Elizabeth came out in the early morning to sweep the brick floor of the piazza, and the front door was left ajar for a hurried flitting should any one appear.

This excessive shyness and secrecy had almost the aspect of guilt, but no more guileless and upright persons could have been imagined than these two old women. They had over their parlor windows full, softly-falling, old muslin curtains, and they looped them back to leave bare the smallest possible space of glass. The parlor chairs retreated close to the walls, the polish of the parlor table lit up a dim corner. There were very few ornaments in sight; the walls were full of closets and little cupboards, and in them all superfluities were tucked away to protect them from dust and prying eyes. Never a door in the house stood open, every bureau drawer was squarely shut. A whole family of skeletons might have been well hidden in these guarded recesses; but skeletons there were none, except, perhaps, a little innocent bone or two of old-womanly pride and sensitiveness.

The Babcock sisters guarded nothing more jealously than the privacy of their meals. The neighbors considered that there was a decided reason for this. "The Babcock girls have so little to eat that they're ashamed to let folks see it," people said. It was certain that the old women regarded intrusion at their meals as an insult, but it was doubtful if they would not have done so had their table been set out with all the luxuries of the season instead of scanty bread and butter and no sauce. No sauce for tea was regarded as very poor living by the village women.

To-night the Babcocks had tea very soon after the lace was sewed on the dress. They always had tea early. They were in the midst of it when the front-door opened, and a voice was heard calling out in the hall.

The sisters cast a dismayed and indignant look at each other; they both arose; but the door flew open, and their little square tea-table, with its green-and-white china pot of weak tea, its plate of bread and little glass dish of butter, its two china cups, and thin silver teaspoons, was displayed to view.

"My!" cried the visitor, with a little backward shuffle. "I do hope you'll scuse me! I didn't know you was eatin' supper. I wouldn't ha' come in for the world if I'd known. I'll go right out; it wa'n't anything pertickler, anyhow." All the time her sharp and comprehensive gaze was on the tea-table. She counted the slices of bread, she measured the butter, as she talked. The sisters stepped forward with dignity.

"Come into the other room," said Elizabeth; and the visitor, still protesting, with her backward eyes upon the tea-table, gave way before her.

But her eyes lighted upon something in the parlor more eagerly than they had upon that frugal and exclusive table. The sisters glanced at each other in dismay. The black silk dress lay over a chair. The caller, who was their neighbor Matilda Jennings, edged toward it as she talked. "I thought I'd jest run over an' see if you wa'n't goin' to the picnic to-morrow," she was saying. Then she clutched the dress and diverged. "Oh, you've been fixin' your dress!" she said to Emily, with innocent insinuation. Insinuation did not sit well upon Matilda Jennings, none of her bodily lines were adapted to it, and the pretence was quite evident. She was short and stout, with a hard, sallow rotundity of cheek, her small black eyes were bright-pointed under fleshy brows.

"Yes, I have," replied Emily, with a scared glance at Elizabeth.

"Yes," said Elizabeth, stepping firmly into the subject, and confronting Matilda with prim and resolute blue eyes. "She has been fixin' of it. The lace was ripped off, an' she had to mend it."

"It's pretty lace, ain't it? I had some of the same kind on a mantilla once when I was a girl. This makes me think of it. The sprigs in mine was set a little closer. Let me see, 'Liz'beth, your black silk dress is trimmed with velvet, ain't it?"

Elizabeth surveyed her calmly. "Yes; I've always worn black velvet on it," said she.

Emily sighed faintly. She had feared that Elizabeth could not answer desirably and be truthful.

"Let me see," continued Matilda, "how was that velvet put on your waist?"

"It was put on peaked."

"In one peak or two?"

"One."

"Now I wonder if it would be too much trouble for you jest to let me see it a minute. I've been thinkin' of fixin' over my old alpaca a little, an' I've got a piece of black velvet ribbon I've steamed over, an' it looks pretty good. I thought mebbe I could put it on like yours."

Matilda Jennings, in her chocolate calico, stood as relentlessly as any executioner before the Babcock sisters. They, slim and delicate and pale in their flabby black muslins, leaned toward each other, then Elizabeth straightened herself. "Some time when it's convenient I'd jest as soon show it as not," said she.

"Well, I'd be much obleeged to you if you would," returned Matilda. Her manner was a trifle overawed, but there was a sharper gleam in her eyes. Pretty soon she went home, and ate her solitary and substantial supper of bread and butter, cold potatoes, and pork and beans. Matilda Jennings was as poor as the Babcocks. She had never, like them, known better days. She had never possessed any fine old muslins nor black silks in her life, but she had always eaten more.

The Babcocks had always delicately and unobtrusively felt themselves above her. There had been in their lives a faint savor of gentility and aristocracy. Their father had been college-educated and a doctor. Matilda's antecedents had been humble, even in this humble community. She had come of wood-sawyers and garden-laborers. In their youth, when they had gone to school and played together, they had always realized their height above Matilda, and even old age and poverty and a certain friendliness could not do away with it.

The Babcocks owned their house and a tiny sum in the bank, upon the interest of which they lived. Nobody knew how much it was, nobody would ever know while they lived. They might have had more if they would have sold or mortgaged their house, but they would have died first. They starved daintily and patiently on their little income. They mended their old muslins and Thibets, and wore one dress between them for best, taking turns in going out.

It seemed inconsistent, but the sisters were very fond of society, and their reserve did not interfere with their pleasure in the simple village outings. They were more at ease abroad than at home, perhaps because there were not present so many doors which could be opened into their secrecy. But they had an arbitrary conviction that their claims to respect and consideration would be forever forfeited should they appear on state occasions in anything but black silk. To their notions of etiquette, black silk was as sacred a necessity as feathers at the English court. They could not go abroad and feel any self-respect in those flimsy muslins and rusty woollens, which were very flimsy and rusty. The old persons in the village could hardly remember when the Babcocks had a new dress. The dainty care with which they had made those tender old fabrics endure so long was wonderful. They held up their skirts primly when they walked; they kept their pointed elbows clear of chairs and tables. The black silk in particular was taken off the minute its wearer entered her own house. It was shaken softly, folded, and laid away in a linen sheet.

Emily was dressed in it on the Fourth of July morning when Matilda Jennings called for her. Matilda came in her voluminous old alpaca, with her tin lunch-pail on her arm. She looked at Emily in the black silk, and her countenance changed. "My! you ain't goin' to wear that black silk trailin' round in the woods, are you?" said she.

"I guess she won't trail around much," spoke up Elizabeth. "She's got to go lookin' decent."

Matilda's poor old alpaca had many a threadbare streak and mended slit in its rusty folds, the elbows were patched, it was hardly respectable. But she gave the skirt a defiant switch, and jerked the patched elbows. "Well, I allers believed in goin' dressed suitable for the occasion," said she, sturdily, and as if that was her especial picnic costume out of a large wardrobe. However, her bravado was not deeply seated, all day long she manœuvred to keep her patches and darns out of sight, she arranged the skirt nervously every time she changed her position, she held her elbows close to her sides, and she made many little flings at Emily's black silk.

The festivities were nearly over, the dinner had been eaten, Matilda had devoured with relish her brown-bread and cheese and cold pork, and Emily had nibbled daintily at her sweet-cake, and glanced with inward loathing at her neighbor's grosser fare. The speeches by the local celebrities were delivered, the cannon had been fired every half-hour, the sun was getting low in the west, and a golden mist was rising among the ferny undergrowth in the grove. "It's gettin' damp; I can see it risin'," said Emily, who was rheumatic; "I guess we'd better walk 'round a little, an' then go home."

"Well," replied Matilda, "I'd jest as soon. You'd better hold up your dress."

The two old women adjusted themselves stiffly upon their feet, and began ranging the grove, stepping warily over the slippery pine-needles. The woods were full of merry calls; the green distances fluttered with light draperies. Every little while came the sharp bang of a fire-cracker, the crash of cannon, or the melancholy hoot of a fish-horn. Now and then blue gunpowder smoke curled up with the golden steam from the dewy ground. Emily was near-sighted; she moved on with innocently peering eyes, her long neck craned forward. Matilda had been taking the lead, but she suddenly stepped aside. Emily walked on unsuspectingly, holding up her precious black silk. There was a quick puff of smoke, a leap of flame, a volley of vicious little reports, and poor Emily Babcock danced as a martyr at her fiery trial might have done; her gentle dignity completely deserted her. "Oh, oh, oh!" she shrieked.

Matilda Jennings pushed forward; by that time Emily was standing, pale and quivering, on a little heap of ashes. "You stepped into a nest of fire-crackers," said Matilda; "a boy jest run; I saw him. What made you stan' there in 'em? Why didn't you get out?"

"I—couldn't," gasped Emily; she could hardly speak.

"Well, I guess it ain't done much harm; them boys ought to be prosecuted. You don't feel as if you was burned anywhere, do you, Em'ly?"

"No—I guess not."

"Seems to me your dress— Jest let me look at your dress, Em'ly. My! ain't that a wicked shame! Jest look at all them holes, right in the flouncin', where it 'll show!"

It was too true. The flounce that garnished the bottom of the black silk was scorched in a number of places. Emily looked at it and felt faint. "I must go right home," she moaned. "Oh, dear!"

"Mebbe you can darn it, if you're real pertickler about it," said Matilda, with an uneasy air.

Emily said nothing; she went home. Her dress switched the dust off the wayside weeds, but she paid no attention to it; she walked so fast that Matilda could hardly keep up with her. When she reached her own gate she swung it swiftly to before Matilda's face, then she fled into the house.

Elizabeth came to the parlor door with a letter in her hand. She cried out, when she saw her sister's face, "What *is* the matter, Em'ly, for pity sakes?"

"You can't never go out again, 'Liz'beth; you can't! you can't!"

"Why can't I go out, I'd like to know? What do you mean, Em'ly Babcock?"

"You can't, you never can again. I stepped into some fire-crackers, an' I've burned some great holes right in the flouncin'. You can't never wear it without folks knowin'. Matilda Jennings will tell. Oh, 'Liz'beth, what will you do?"

"Do?" said Elizabeth. "Well, I hope I ain't so set on goin' out at my time of life as all that comes to. Let's see it. H'm, I can mend that."

"No, you can't. Matilda would see it if you did. Oh, dear! oh, dear!" Emily dropped into a corner and put her slim hands over her face.

"Do stop actin' so," said her sister. "I've jest had a letter, an' Aunt 'Liz'beth is dead."

After a little Emily looked up. "When did she die?" she asked, in a despairing voice.

"Last week."

"Did they ask us to the funeral?"

"Of course they did; it was last Friday, at two o'clock in the afternoon. They knew the letter couldn't get to us till after the funeral; but of course they'd ask us."

"What did they say the matter was?"

"Old age, I guess, as much as anything. Aunt 'Liz'beth was a good deal over eighty."

Emily sat reflectively; she seemed to be listening while her sister related more at length the contents of the letter. Suddenly she interrupted. "'Liz'beth."

"Well?"

"I was thinkin', 'Liz'beth—you know those crape veils we wore when mother died?"

"Well, what of 'em?"

"I—don't see why—you couldn't—make a flounce of those veils, an' put on this dress when you wore it; then she wouldn't know."

"I'd like to know what I'd wear a crape flounce for?"

"Why, mournin' for Aunt 'Liz'beth."

"Em'ly Babcock, what sense would there be in my wearin' mournin' when you didn't?"

"You was named for her, an' it's a very diff'rent thing. You can jest tell folks that you was named for your aunt that jest died, an' you felt as if you ought to wear a little crape on your best dress."

"It 'll be an awful job to put on a different flounce every time we wear it."

"I'll do it; I'm perfectly willin' to do it. Oh, 'Liz'beth, I shall die if you ever go out again an' wear that dress."

"For pity sakes, don't, Em'ly! I'll get out those veils after supper an' look at 'em."

The next Sunday Elizabeth wore the black silk garnished with a crape flounce to church. Matilda Jennings walked home with her, and eyed the new trimming sharply. "Got a new flounce, ain't you?" said she, finally.

"I had word last week that my aunt 'Liz'beth Taylor was dead, an' I thought it wa'n't anything more'n fittin' that I should put on a little crape," replied Elizabeth, with dignity.

"Has Em'ly put on mournin' too?"

"Em'ly ain't any call to. She wa'n't named after her, as I was, an' she never saw her but once, when she was a little girl. It ain't more'n ten year since I saw her. She lived out West. I didn't feel as if Em'ly had any call to wear crape."

Matilda said no more, but there was unquelled suspicion in her eye as they parted at the Babcock gate.

The next week a trunk full of Aunt Elizabeth Taylor's clothes arrived from the West. Her daughter had sent them. There was in the trunk a goodly store of old woman's finery, two black silks among the other gowns. Aunt Elizabeth had been a dressy old lady, although she died in her eighties. It was a great surprise to the sisters. They had never dreamed of such a thing. They palpitated with awe and delight as they took out the treasures. Emily clutched Elizabeth, the thin hand closing around the thin arm.

"'Liz'beth!"

"What is it?"

"We—won't say—anything about this to anybody. We'll jest go together to meetin' next Sabbath, an' wear these black silks, *an' let Matilda Jennings see.*"

Elizabeth looked at Emily. A gleam came into her dim blue eyes; she tightened her thin lips. "*Well, we will,*" said she.

The following Sunday the sisters wore the black silks to church. During the week they appeared together at a sewing meeting, then at church again. The wonder and curiosity were certainly not confined to Matilda Jennings. The eccentricity which the Babcock sisters displayed in not going into society together had long been a favorite topic in the town. There had been a great deal of speculation over it. Now that they had appeared together three consecutive times, there was much talk.

On the Monday following the second Sunday Matilda Jennings went down to the Babcock house. Her cape-bonnet was on one-sided, but it was firmly tied. She opened the door softly, when her old muscles were straining forward to jerk the latch. She sat gently down in the proffered chair, and displayed quite openly a worn place over the knees in her calico gown.

"We had a pleasant Sabbath yesterday, didn't we?" said she.

"Real pleasant," assented the sisters.

"I thought we had a good discourse."

The Babcocks assented again.

"I heerd a good many say they thought it was a good discourse," repeated Matilda, like an emphatic chorus. Then she suddenly leaned forward, and her face, in the depths of her awry bonnet, twisted into a benevolent smile. "I was real glad to see you out together," she whispered, with meaning emphasis.

The sisters smiled stiffly.

Matilda paused for a moment; she drew herself back, as if to gather strength for a thrust; she stopped smiling. "I was glad to see you out together, for I thought it was too bad the way folks was talkin'," she said.

Elizabeth looked at her. "How were they talkin'?"

"Well, I don' know as there's any harm in my tellin' you. I've been thinkin' mebbe I ought to for some time. It's been round consider'ble lately that you an' Em'ly didn't get along well, an' that was the reason you didn't go out more together. I told 'em I hadn't no idea 'twas so, though, of course, I couldn't really tell. I was real glad to see you out together, 'cause there's never any knowin' how folks do get along, an' I was real glad to see you'd settled it if there had been any trouble."

"There ain't been any trouble."

"Well, I'm glad if there ain't been any, an' if there has, I'm glad to see it settled, an' I know other folks will be too."

Elizabeth stood up. "If you want to know the reason why we haven't been out together, I'll tell you," said she. "You've been tryin' to find out things every way you could, an' now I'll tell you. You've drove me to it. We had just one decent dress between us, an' Em'ly an' me took turns wearin' it, an' Em'ly used to wear lace on it, an' I used to rip off the lace an' sew on black velvet when I wore it, so folks shouldn't know it was the same dress. Em'ly an' me never had a word in our lives, an' it's a wicked lie for folks to say we have."

Emily was softly weeping in her handkerchief; there was not a tear in Elizabeth's eyes; there were bright spots on her cheeks, and her slim height overhung Matilda Jennings imposingly.

"My aunt 'Liz'beth, that I was named for, died two or three weeks ago," she continued, "an' they sent us a trunk full of her clothes, an' there was two decent dresses among 'em, an' that's the reason why Em'ly an' me have been out together sence. Now, Matilda Jennings, you have found out the whole story, an' I hope you're satisfied."

Now that the detective instinct and the craving inquisitiveness which were so strong in this old woman were satisfied, she should have been more jubilant than she was. She had suspected what nobody else in town had suspected;

she had verified her suspicion, and discovered what the secrecy and pride of the sisters had concealed from the whole village, still she looked uneasy and subdued. "I sha'n't tell anybody," said she.

"You can tell nobody you're a mind to."

"I sha'n't tell nobody." Matilda Jennings arose; she had passed the parlor door, when she faced about. "I s'pose I kinder begretched you that black silk," said she, "or I shouldn't have cared so much about findin' out. I never had a black silk myself, nor any of my folks that I ever heard of. I ain't got nothin' decent to wear anyway."

There was a moment's silence. "We sha'n't lay up anything," said Elizabeth then, and Emily sobbed responsively. Matilda passed on, and opened the outer door. Elizabeth whispered to her sister, and Emily nodded, eagerly. "You tell her," said she.

"Matilda," called Elizabeth. Matilda looked back. "I was jest goin' to say that, if you wouldn't resent it, it got burned some, but we mended it nice, that you was perfectly welcome to that—black silk. Em'ly an' me don't really need it, and we'd be glad to have you have it."

There were tears in Matilda Jennings's black eyes, but she held them unwinkingly. "Thank ye," she said, in a gruff voice, and stepped along over the piazza, down the steps. She reached Emily's flower garden. The peppery sweetness of the nasturtiums came up in her face; it was quite early in the day, and the portulacas were still out in a splendid field of crimson and yellow. Matilda turned about, her broad foot just cleared a yellow portulaca which had straggled into the path, but she did not notice it. The homely old figure pushed past the flowers and into the house again. She stood before Elizabeth and Emily. "Look here," said she, with a fine light struggling out of her coarse old face, "I want to tell you—*I see them fire-crackers a-sizzlin' before Em'ly stepped in 'em.*"

THE TWELFTH GUEST.

"I DON'T see how it happened, for my part," Mrs. Childs said. "Paulina, you set the table."

"You counted up yesterday how many there'd be, and you said twelve; don't you know you did, mother? So I didn't count to-day. I just put on the plates," said Paulina, smilingly defensive.

Paulina had something of a helpless and gentle look when she smiled. Her mouth was rather large, and the upper jaw full, so the smile seemed hardly under her control. She was quite pretty; her complexion was so delicate and her eyes so pleasant.

"Well, I don't see how I made such a blunder," her mother remarked further, as she went on pouring the tea.

On the opposite side of the table were a plate, a knife and fork, and a little dish of cranberry sauce, with an empty chair before them. There was no guest to fill it.

"It's a sign somebody's comin' that's hungry," Mrs. Childs' brother's wife said, with soft effusiveness which was out of proportion to the words.

The brother was carving the turkey. Caleb Childs, the host, was an old man, and his hands trembled. Moreover, no one, he himself least of all, ever had any confidence in his ability in such directions. Whenever he helped himself to gravy, his wife watched anxiously lest he should spill it, and he always did. He spilled some to-day. There was a great spot on the beautiful clean table-cloth. Caleb set his cup and saucer over it quickly, with a little clatter because of his unsteady hand. Then he looked at his wife. He hoped she had not seen, but she had.

"You'd better have let John give you the gravy," she said, in a stern aside.

John, rigidly solicitous, bent over the turkey. He carved slowly and laboriously, but everybody had faith in him. The shoulders to which a burden is shifted have the credit of being strong. His wife, in her best black dress, sat smilingly, with her head canted a little to one side. It was a way she had when visiting. Ordinarily she did not assume it at her sister-in-law's house, but this was an extra occasion. Her fine manners spread their wings involuntarily. When she spoke about the sign, the young woman next her sniffed.

"I don't take any stock in signs," said she, with a bluntness which seemed to crash through the other's airiness with such force as to almost hurt itself. She was a distant cousin of Mr. Childs. Her husband and three children were with her.

Mrs. Childs' unmarried sister, Maria Stone, made up the eleven at the table. Maria's gaunt face was unhealthily red about the pointed nose and the high cheek-bones; her eyes looked with a steady sharpness through her spectacles.

"Well, it will be time enough to believe the sign when the twelfth one comes," said she, with a summary air. She had a judicial way of speaking. She had taught school ever since she was sixteen, and now she was sixty. She had just given up teaching. It was to celebrate that, and her final home-coming, that her sister was giving a Christmas dinner instead of a Thanksgiving one this year. The school had been in session during Thanksgiving week.

Maria Stone had scarcely spoken when there was a knock on the outer door, which led directly into the room. They all started. They were a plain, unimaginative company, but for some reason a thrill of superstitious and fantastic expectation ran through them. No one arose. They were all silent for a moment, listening and looking at the empty chair in their midst. Then the knock came again.

"Go to the door, Paulina," said her mother.

The young girl looked at her half fearfully, but she rose at once, and went and opened the door. Everybody stretched around to see. A girl stood on the stone step looking into the room. There she stood, and never said a word. Paulina looked around at her mother, with her innocent, half-involuntary smile.

"Ask her what she wants," said Mrs. Childs.

"What do you want?" repeated Paulina, like a sweet echo.

Still the girl said nothing. A gust of north wind swept into the room. John's wife shivered, then looked around to see if any one had noticed it.

"You must speak up quick an' tell what you want, so we can shut the door; it's cold," said Mrs. Childs.

The girl's small sharp face was sheathed in an old worsted hood; her eyes glared out of it like a frightened cat's. Suddenly she turned to go. She was evidently abashed by the company.

"Don't you want somethin' to eat?" Mrs. Childs asked, speaking up louder.

"It ain't—no matter." She just mumbled it.

"What?"

She would not repeat it. She was quite off the step by this time.

"You make her come in, Paulina," said Maria Stone, suddenly. "She wants something to eat, but she's half scared to death. You talk to her."

"Hadn't you better come in, and have something to eat?" said Paulina, shyly persuasive.

"Tell her she can sit right down here by the stove, where it's warm, and have a good plate of dinner," said Maria.

Paulina fluttered softly down to the stone step. The chilly snow-wind came right in her sweet, rosy face. "You can have a chair by the stove, where it's warm, and a good plate of dinner," said she.

The girl looked at her.

"Won't you come in?" said Paulina, of her own accord, and always smiling.

The stranger made a little hesitating movement forward.

"Bring her in, quick! and shut the door," Maria called out then. And Paulina entered with the girl stealing timidly in her wake.

"Take off your hood an' shawl," Mrs. Childs said, "an' sit down here by the stove, an' I'll give you some dinner." She spoke kindly. She was a warm-hearted woman, but she was rigidly built, and did not relax too quickly into action.

But the cousin, who had been observing, with head alertly raised, interrupted. She cast a mischievous glance at John's wife—the empty chair was between them. "For pity's sake!" cried she; "you ain't goin' to shove her off in the corner? Why, here's this chair. She's the twelfth one. Here's where she ought to sit." There was a mixture of heartiness and sport in the young woman's manner. She pulled the chair back from the table. "Come right over here," said she.

There was a slight flutter of consternation among the guests. They were all narrow-lived country people. Their customs had made deeper grooves in their roads; they were more fastidious and jealous of their social rights than many in higher positions. They eyed this forlorn girl, in her faded and dingy woollens which fluttered airily and showed their pitiful thinness.

Mrs. Childs stood staring at the cousin. She did not think she could be in earnest.

But she was. "Come," said she; "put some turkey in this plate, John."

"Why, it's jest as the rest of you say," Mrs. Childs said, finally, with hesitation. She looked embarrassed and doubtful.

"Say! Why, they say just as I do," the cousin went on. "Why shouldn't they? Come right around here." She tapped the chair impatiently.

The girl looked at Mrs. Childs. "You can go an' sit down there where she says," she said, slowly, in a constrained tone.

"Come," called the cousin again. And the girl took the empty chair, with the guests all smiling stiffly.

Mrs. Childs began filling a plate for the new-comer.

Now that her hood was removed, one could see her face more plainly. It was thin, and of that pale brown tint which exposure gives to some blond skins. Still there was a tangible beauty which showed through all that. Her fair hair stood up softly, with a kind of airy roughness which caught the light. She was apparently about sixteen,

"What's your name?" inquired the school-mistress sister, suddenly.

The girl started. "Christine," she said, after a second.

"What?"

"Christine."

A little thrill ran around the table. The company looked at each other. They were none of them conversant with the Christmas legends, but at that moment the universal sentiment of them seemed to seize upon their fancies. The day, the mysterious appearance of the girl, the name, which was strange to their ears—all startled them, and gave them a vague sense of the supernatural. They, however, struggled against it with their matter-of-fact pride, and threw it off directly.

"Christine what?" Maria asked further.

The girl kept her scared eyes on Maria's face, but she made no reply.

"What's your other name? Why don't you speak?"

Suddenly she rose.

"What are you goin' to do?"

"I'd—ruther—go, I guess."

"What are you goin' for? You ain't had your dinner."

"I—can't tell it," whispered the girl.

"Can't tell your name?"

She shook her head.

"Sit down, and eat your dinner," said Maria.

There was a strong sentiment of disapprobation among the company. But when Christine's food was actually before her, and she seemed to settle down upon it, like a bird, they viewed her with more toleration. She was evidently half starved. Their discovery of that fact gave them at once a fellow-feeling toward her on this feast-day, and a complacent sense of their own benevolence.

As the dinner progressed the spirits of the party appeared to rise, and a certain jollity which was almost hilarity prevailed. Beyond providing the strange guest plentifully with food, they seemed to ignore her entirely. Still nothing was more certain than the fact that they did not. Every outburst of merriment was yielded to with the most thorough sense of her presence, which appeared in some subtle way to excite it. It was as if this forlorn twelfth guest were the foreign element needed to produce a state of nervous effervescence in those staid, decorous people who surrounded her. This taste of mystery and unusualness, once fairly admitted, although reluctantly, to their unaccustomed palates, served them as wine with their Christmas dinner.

It was late in the afternoon when they arose from the table. Christine went directly for her hood and shawl, and put them on. The others, talking among themselves, were stealthily observant of her. Christine began opening the door.

"Are you goin' home now?" asked Mrs. Childs.

"No, marm."

"Why not?"

"I ain't got any."

"Where did you come from?"

The girl looked at her. Then she unlatched the door.

"Stop!" Mrs. Childs cried, sharply. "What are you goin' for? Why don't you answer?"

She stood still, but did not speak.

"Well, shut the door up, an' wait a minute," said Mrs. Childs.

She stood close to a window, and she stared out scrutinizingly. There was no house in sight. First came a great yard, then wide stretches of fields; a desolate gray road curved around them on the left. The sky was covered with still, low clouds; the sun had not shone out that day. The ground was all bare and rigid. Out in the yard some gray hens were huddled together in little groups for warmth; their red combs showed out. Two crows flew up, away over on the edge of the field.

"It's goin' to snow," said Mrs. Childs.

"I'm afeard it is," said Caleb, looking at the girl. He gave a sort of silent sob, and brushed some tears out of his old eyes with the back of his hands.

"See here a minute, Maria," said Mrs. Childs.

The two women whispered together; then Maria stepped in front of the girl, and stood, tall and stiff and impressive.

"Now, see here," said she; "we want you to speak up and tell us your other name, and where you came from, and not keep us waiting any longer."

"I—*can't.*" They guessed what she said from the motion of her head. She opened the door entirely then and stepped out.

Suddenly Maria made one stride forward and seized her by her shoulders, which felt like knife-blades through the thin clothes. "Well," said she, "we've been fussing long enough; we've got all these dishes to clear away. It's bitter cold, and it's going to snow, and you ain't going out of this house one step to-night, no matter what you are. You'd ought to tell us who you are, and it ain't many folks that would keep you if you wouldn't; but we ain't goin' to have you found dead in the road, for our own credit. It ain't on your account. Now you just take those things off again, and go and sit down in that chair."

Christine sat in the chair. Her pointed chin dipped down on her neck, whose poor little muscles showed above her dress, which sagged away from it. She never looked up. The women cleared off the table, and cast curious glances at her.

After the dishes were washed and put away, the company were all assembled in the sitting-room for an hour or so; then they went home. The cousin, passing through the kitchen to join her husband, who was waiting with his team at the door, ran hastily up to Christine.

"You stop at my house when you go to-morrow morning," said she. "Mrs. Childs will tell you where 'tis—half a mile below here."

When the company were all gone, Mrs. Childs called Christine into the sitting-room. "You'd better come in here and sit now," said she. "I'm goin' to let the kitchen fire go down; I ain't goin' to get another regular meal; I'm jest goin' to make a cup of tea on the sittin'-room stove by-an'-by."

The sitting-room was warm, and restrainedly comfortable with its ordinary village furnishings—its ingrain carpet, its little peaked clock on a corner of the high black shelf, its red-covered card-table, which had stood in the same spot for forty years. There was a little newspaper-covered stand, with some plants on it, before a window. There was one red geranium in blossom.

Paulina was going out that evening. Soon after the company went she commenced to get ready, and her mother and aunt seemed to be helping her. Christine was alone in the sitting-room for the greater part of an hour.

Finally the three women came in, and Paulina stood before the sitting-room glass for a last look at herself. She had on her best red cashmere, with some white lace around her throat. She had a red geranium flower with some leaves in her hair. Paulina's brown hair, which was rather thin, was very silky. It was apt to part into little soft strands on her forehead. She wore it brushed smoothly back. Her mother would not allow her to curl it.

The two older women stood looking at her. "Don't you think she looks nice, Christine?" Mrs. Childs asked, in a sudden overflow of love and pride, which led her to ask sympathy from even this forlorn source.

"Yes, marm." Christine regarded Paulina, in her red cashmere and geranium flower, with sharp, solemn eyes. When she really looked at any one, her gaze was as unflinching as that of a child.

There was a sudden roll of wheels in the yard.

"Willard's come!" said Mrs. Childs. "Run to the door an' tell him you'll be right out, Paulina, an' I'll get your things ready."

After Paulina had been helped into her coat and hood, and the wheels had bowled out of the yard with a quick dash, the mother turned to Christine.

"My daughter's gone to a Christmas tree over to the church," said she. "That was Willard Morris that came for her. He's a real nice young man that lives about a mile from here."

Mrs. Childs' tone was at once gently patronizing and elated.

When Christine was shown to a little back bedroom that night, nobody dreamed how many times she was to occupy it. Maria and Mrs. Childs, who after the door was closed set a table against it softly and erected a tiltlish pyramid of milkpans, to serve as an alarm signal in case the strange guest should try to leave her room with evil intentions, were fully convinced that she would depart early on the following morning.

"I dun know but I've run an awful risk keeping her," Mrs. Childs said. "I don't like her not tellin' where she come from. Nobody knows but she belongs to a gang of burglars, an' they've kind of sent her on ahead to spy out things an' unlock the doors for 'em."

"I know it," said Maria. "I wouldn't have had her stay for a thousand dollars if it hadn't looked so much like snow. Well, I'll get up an' start her off early in the morning."

But Maria Stone could not carry out this resolution. The next morning she was ill with a sudden and severe attack of erysipelas. Moreover, there was a hard snow-storm, the worst of the season; it would have been barbarous to have turned the girl out-of-doors on such a morning. Moreover, she developed an unexpected capacity for usefulness. She assisted Pauline about the housework with timid alacrity, and Mrs. Childs could devote all her time to her sister.

"She takes right hold as if she was used to it," she told Maria. "I'd rather keep her a while than not, if I only knew a little more about her."

"I don't believe but what I could get it out of her after a while if I tried," said Maria, with her magisterial air, which illness could not subdue.

However, even Maria, with all her well-fostered imperiousness, had no effect on the girl's resolution; she continued as much of a mystery as ever. Still the days went on, then the weeks and months, and she remained in the Childs family.

None of them could tell exactly how it had been brought about. The most definite course seemed to be that her arrival had apparently been the signal for a general decline of health in the family. Maria had hardly recovered when Caleb Childs was laid up with the rheumatism; then Mrs. Childs had a long spell of exhaustion from overwork in nursing. Christine proved exceedingly useful in these emergencies. Their need of her appeared to be the dominant, and only outwardly evident, reason for her stay; still there was a deeper one which they themselves only faintly realized—this poor young girl, who was rendered almost repulsive to these honest downright folk by her persistent cloak of mystery, had somehow, in a very short time, melted herself, as it were, into their own lives. Christine asleep of a night in her little back bedroom, Christine of a day stepping about the house in one of Paulina's old gowns, became a part of their existence, and a part which was not far from the nature of a sweetness to their senses.

She still retained her mild shyness of manner, and rarely spoke unless spoken to. Now that she was warmly sheltered and well fed, her beauty became evident. She grew prettier every day. Her cheeks became softly dimpled; her hair turned golden. Her language was rude and illiterate, but its very uncouthness had about it something of a soft grace.

She was really prettier than Paulina.

The two young girls were much together, but could hardly be said to be intimate. There were few confidences between them, and confidences are essential for the intimacy of young girls.

Willard Morris came regularly twice a week to see Paulina, and everybody spoke of them as engaged to each other.

Along in August Mrs. Childs drove over to town one afternoon and bought a piece of cotton cloth and a little embroidery and lace. Then some fine sewing went on, but with no comment in the household. Mrs. Childs had simply said, "I guess we may as well get a few things made up for you, Paulina, you're getting rather short." And Paulina had sewed all day long, with a gentle industry, when the work was ready.

There was a report that the marriage was to take place on Thanksgiving Day. But about the first of October Willard Morris stopped going to the Childs house. There was no explanation. He simply did not come as usual on Sunday night, nor the following Wednesday, nor the next Sunday. Paulina kindled her little parlor fire, whose sticks she had laid with maiden preciseness; she arrayed herself in her best gown and ribbons. When at nine o'clock Willard had not come, she blew out the parlor lamp, shut up the parlor stove, and went to bed. Nothing was said before her, but there was much talk and surmise between Mrs. Childs and Maria, and a good deal of it went on before Christine.

It was a little while after the affair of Cyrus Morris's note, and they wondered if it could have anything to do with that. Cyrus Morris was Willard's uncle, and the note affair had occasioned much distress in the Childs family for a month back. The note was for twenty-five hundred dollars, and Cyrus Morris had given it to Caleb Childs. The time, which was two years, had expired on the first of September, and then Caleb could not find the note.

He had kept it in his old-fashioned desk, which stood in one corner of the kitchen. He searched there a day and half a night, pulling all the soiled, creasy old papers out of the drawers and pigeon-holes before he would answer his wife's inquiries as to what he had lost.

Finally he broke down and told. "I've lost that note of Morris's," said he. "I dun know what I'm goin' to do."

He stood looking gloomily at the desk with its piles of papers. His rough old chin dropped down on his breast.

The women were all in the kitchen, and they stopped and stared.

"Why, father," said his wife, "where have you put it?"

"I put it here in this top drawer, and it ain't there."

"Let *me* look," said Maria, in a confident tone. But even Maria's energetic and self-assured researches failed. "Well, it ain't here," said she. "I don't know what you've done with it."

"I don't believe you put it in that drawer, father," said his wife.

"It was in there two weeks ago. I see it."

"Then you took it out afterwards."

"I ain't laid hands on't."

"You must have; it couldn't have gone off without hands. You know you're kind of forgetful, father."

"I guess I know when I've took a paper out of a drawer. I know a leetle somethin' yit."

"Well, I don't suppose there'll be any trouble about it, will there?" said Mrs. Childs. "Of course he knows he give the note, an' had the money."

"I dun know as there'll be any trouble, but I'd ruther give a hundred dollar than had it happen."

After dinner Caleb shaved, put on his other coat and hat, and trudged soberly up the road to Cyrus Morris's. Cyrus Morris was an elderly man, who had quite a local reputation for wealth and business shrewdness. Caleb, who was lowly-natured and easily impressed by another's importance, always made a call upon him quite a formal affair, and shaved and dressed up.

He was absent about an hour to-day. When he returned he went into the sitting-room, where the women sat with their sewing. He dropped into a chair, and looked straight ahead, with his forehead knitted.

The women dropped their work and looked at him, and then at each other.

"What did he say, father?" Mrs. Childs asked at length.

"Say! He's a rascal, that's what he is, an' I'll tell him so, too."

"Ain't he goin' to pay it?"

"No, he ain't."

"Why, father, I don't believe it! You didn't get hold of it straight," said his wife.

"You'll see."

"Why, what did he say?"

"He didn't say anything."

"Doesn't he remember he had the money and gave the note, and has been paying interest on it?" queried Maria.

"He jest laughed, an' said 'twa'n't accordin' to law to pay unless I showed the note an' give it up to him. He said he couldn't be sure but I'd want him to pay it over ag'in. *I know where that note is!*"

Caleb's voice had deep meaning in it. The women stared at him.

"Where?"

"*It's in Cyrus Morris's desk—that's where it is.*"

"Why, father, you're crazy!"

"No, I ain't crazy, nuther. I know what I'm talkin' about. I—"

"It's just where you put it," interrupted Maria, taking up her sewing with a switch; "and I wouldn't lay the blame onto anybody else."

"You'd ought to ha' looked out for a paper like that," said his wife. "I guess I should if it had been me. If you've gone an' lost all that money through your carelessness, you've done it, that's all I've got to say. I don't see what we're goin' to do."

Caleb bent forward and fixed his eyes upon the women. He held up his shaking hand impressively. "*If* you'll stop talkin' just a minute," said he, "I'll tell you what I was goin' to. Now I'd like to know just one thing: *Wa'n't Cyrus Morris alone in that kitchen as much as fifteen minutes a week ago to-day? Didn't you leave him there while you went to look arter me? Wa'n't the key in the desk?* Answer me *that!*"

His wife looked at him with cold surprise and severity. "I wouldn't talk in any such way as that if I was you, father," said she. "It don't show a Christian spirit. It's jest layin' the blame of your own carelessness onto somebody else. You're all the one that's to blame. An' when it comes to it, you'd never ought to let Cyrus Morris have the money anyhow. I could have told you better. I knew what kind of a man he was."

"He's a rascal," said Caleb, catching eagerly at the first note of foreign condemnation in his wife's words. "He'd ought to be put in state's-prison. I don't think much of his relations nuther. I don't want nothin' to do with 'em, an' I don't want none of my folks to."

Paulina's soft cheeks flushed. Then she suddenly spoke out as she had never spoken in her life.

"It doesn't make it out because he's a bad man that his

relations are," said she. "You haven't any right to speak so, father. And I guess you won't stop me having anything to do with them, if you want to."

She was all pink and trembling. Suddenly she burst out crying, and ran out of the room.

"You'd ought to be ashamed of yourself, father," exclaimed Mrs. Childs.

"I didn't think of her takin' on it so," muttered Caleb, humbly. "I didn't mean nothin.'"

Caleb did not seem like himself through the following days. His simple old face took on an expression of strained thought, which made it look strange. He was tottering on a height of mental effort and worry which was almost above the breathing capacity of his innocent and placid nature. Many a night he rose, lighted a candle, and tremulously fumbled over his desk until morning, in the vain hope of finding the missing note.

One night, while he was so searching, some one touched him softly on the arm.

He jumped and turned. It was Christine. She had stolen in silently.

"Oh, it's you!" said he.

"Ain't you found it?"

"Found it? No; an' I sha'n't, nuther." He turned away from her and pulled out another drawer. The girl stood watching him wistfully. "It was a big yellow paper," the old man went on—"a big yellow paper, an' I'd wrote on the back on't, 'Cyrus Morris's note.' An' the interest he'd paid was set down on the back on't, too."

"It's too bad you can't find it," said she.

"It ain't no use lookin'; it ain't here, an' that's the hull on't. It's in *his* desk. I ain't got no more doubt on't than nothin' at all."

"Where—does he keep his desk?"

"In his kitchen; it's jest like this one."

"Would this key open it?"

"I dun know but 'twould. But it ain't no use. I s'pose I'll have to lose it." Caleb sobbed silently and wiped his eyes.

A few days later he came, all breathless, into the sitting-room. He could hardly speak; but he held out a folded yellow paper, which fluttered and blew in his unsteady hand like a yellow maple-leaf in an autumn gale.

"Look-a-here!" he gasped—"look-a-here!"

"Why, for goodness' sake, what's the matter?" cried Maria. She and Mrs. Childs and Paulina were there, sewing peacefully.

"Jest look-a-*here!*"

"Why, for mercy's sake, what is it, father? Are you crazy?"

"It's—the *note!*"

"What note? Don't get so excited, father."

"Cyrus Morris's note. That's what note 'tis. Look-a-here!"

The women all arose and pressed around him, to look at it.

"Where *did* you find it, father?" asked his wife, who was quite pale.

"I suppose it was just where you put it," broke in Maria, with sarcastic emphasis.

"No, it wa'n't. No, it wa'n't, nuther. Don't you go to crowin' too quick, Maria. That paper was just where I told you 'twas. What do you think of that, hey?"

"Oh, father, you didn't!"

"It was layin' right there in his desk. That's where 'twas. Jest where I knew—"

"Father, you didn't go over there an' take it!"

The three women stared at him with dilated eyes.

"No, I didn't."

"Who did?"

The old man jerked his head towards the kitchen door. "She."

"Who?"

"Christiny."

"How did she get it?" asked Maria, in her magisterial manner, which no astonishment could agitate.

"She saw Cyrus and Mis' Morris ride past, an' then she run over there, an' she got in through the window an' got it; that's how." Caleb braced himself like a stubborn child, in case any exception were taken to it all.

"It beats everything I ever heard," said Mrs. Childs, faintly.

"Next time you'll believe what I tell you!" said Caleb.

The whole family were in a state of delight over the recovery of the note; still Christine got rather hesitating gratitude. She was sharply questioned, and rather reproved than otherwise.

This theft, which could hardly be called a theft, aroused the old distrust of her.

"It served him just right, and it wasn't stealing, because it didn't belong to him; and I don't know what you would have done if she hadn't taken it," said Maria; "but, for all that, it went all over me."

"So it did over me," said her sister. "I felt just as you did, an' I felt as if it was real ungrateful too, when the poor child did it just for us."

But there were no such misgivings for poor Caleb, with

his money, and his triumph over iniquitous Cyrus Morris. He was wholly and unquestioningly grateful.

"It was a blessed day when we took that little girl in," he told his wife.

"I hope it 'll prove so," said she.

Paulina took her lover's desertion quietly. She had just as many soft smiles for every one ; there was no alteration in her gentle, obliging ways. Still her mother used to listen at her door, and she knew that she cried instead of sleeping many a night. She was not able to eat much, either, although she tried to with pleasant willingness when her mother urged her.

After a while she was plainly grown thin, and her pretty color had faded. Her mother could not keep her eyes from her.

"Sometimes I think I'll go an' ask Willard myself what this kind of work means," she broke out with an abashed abruptness one afternoon. She and Paulina happened to be alone in the sitting-room.

"You'll kill me if you do, mother," said Paulina. Then she began to cry.

"Well, I won't do anything you don't want me to, of course," said her mother. She pretended not to see that Paulina was crying.

Willard had stopped coming about the first of October ; the time wore on until it was the first of December, and he had not once been to the house, and Paulina had not exchanged a word with him in the meantime.

One night she had a fainting-spell. She fell heavily while crossing the sitting-room floor. They got her on to the lounge, and she soon revived ; but her mother had lost all control of herself. She came out into the kitchen and paced the floor.

"Oh, my darlin'!" she wailed. "She's goin' to die. What shall I do? All the child I've got in the world. An' he's killed her! That *scamp!* I wish I could get my hands on him. Oh, Paulina, Paulina, to think it should come to this!"

Christine was in the room, and she listened with eyes dilated and lips parted. She was afraid that shrill wail would reach Paulina in the next room.

"She'll hear you," she said, finally.

Mrs. Childs grew quieter at that, and presently Maria called her into the sitting-room.

Christine stood thinking for a moment. Then she got her hood and shawl, put on her rubbers, and went out. She shut the door softly, so nobody should hear. When she stepped forth she plunged knee-deep into snow. It was snowing hard, as it had been all day. It was a cold storm, too; the wind was bitter. Christine waded out of the yard and down the street. She was so small and light that she staggered when she tried to step firmly in some tracks ahead of her. There was a full moon behind the clouds, and there was a soft white light in spite of the storm. Christine kept on down the street, in the direction of Willard Morris's house. It was a mile distant. Once in a while she stopped and turned herself about, that the terrible wind might smite her back instead of her face. When she reached the house she waded painfully through the yard to the side-door and knocked. Pretty soon it opened, and Willard stood there in the entry, with a lamp in his hand.

"Good-evening," said he, doubtfully, peering out.

"Good-evenin'." The light shone on Christine's face. The snow clung to her soft hair, so it was quite white. Her cheeks had a deep, soft color, like roses; her blue eyes blinked a little in the lamp-light, but seemed rather to flicker like jewels or stars. She panted softly through her parted lips. She stood there, with the snow-flakes driving in light past her, and "She looks like an angel," came swiftly into Willard Morris's head before he spoke.

"Oh, it's you," said he.

Christine nodded.

Then they stood waiting. "Why, won't you come in?" said Willard, finally, with an awkward blush. "I declare I never thought. I ain't very polite."

She shook her head. "No, thank you," said she.

"Did—you want to see mother?"

"No."

The young man stared at her in increasing perplexity. His own fair, handsome young face got more and more flushed. His forehead wrinkled. "Was there anything you wanted?"

"No, I guess not," Christine replied, with a slow softness.

Willard shifted the lamp into his other hand and sighed. "It's a pretty hard storm," he remarked, with an air of forced patience.

"Yes."

"Didn't you find it terrible hard walking?"

"Some."

Willard was silent again. "See here, they're all well down at your house, ain't they?" said he, finally. A look of anxious interest had sprung into his eyes. He had begun to take alarm.

"I guess so."

Suddenly he spoke out impetuously. "Say, Christine, I don't know what you came here for; you can tell me afterwards. I don't know what you'll think of me, but—Well, I want to know something. Say—well, I haven't been 'round for quite a while. You don't—suppose—they've cared much, any of them?"

"I don't know."

"Well, I don't suppose you do, but—you might have noticed. Say, Christine, you don't think she—you know whom I mean—cared anything about my coming, do you?"

"I don't know," she said again, softly, with her eyes fixed warily on his face.

"Well, I guess she didn't; she wouldn't have said what she did if she had."

Christine's eyes gave a sudden gleam. "What did she say?"

"Said she wouldn't have anything more to do with me," said the young man, bitterly. "She was afraid I would be up to just such tricks as my uncle was, trying to cheat her father. That was too much for me. I wasn't going to stand that from any girl." He shook his head angrily.

"She didn't say it."

"Yes, she did; her own father told my uncle so. Mother was in the next room and heard it."

"No, she didn't say it," the girl repeated.

"How do you know?"

"I heard her say something different." Christine told him.

"I'm going right up there," cried he, when he heard that. "Wait a minute, and I'll go along with you."

"I dun know as you'd better—to-night," Christine said,

looking out towards the road, evasively. "She—ain't been very well to-night."

"Who? Paulina? What's the matter?"

"She had a faintin'-spell jest before I came out," answered Christine, with stiff gravity.

"Oh! Is she real sick?"

"She was some better."

"Don't you suppose I could see her just a few minutes? I wouldn't stay to tire her," said the young man, eagerly.

"I dun know."

"I must, anyhow."

Christine fixed her eyes on his with a solemn sharpness. "What makes you want to?"

"What makes me want to? Why, I'd give ten years to see her five minutes."

"Well, mebbe you could come over a few minutes."

"Wait a minute," cried Willard. "I'll get my hat."

"I'd better go first, I guess. The parlor fire 'll be to light."

"Then had I better wait?"

"I guess so."

"Then I'll be along in about an hour. Say, you haven't said what you wanted."

Christine was off the step. "It ain't any matter," murmured she.

"Say—she didn't send you?"

"No, she didn't."

"I didn't mean that. I didn't suppose she did," said Willard, with an abashed air. "What did you want, Christine?"

"There's somethin' I want you to promise," said she, suddenly.

"What's that?"

"Don't you say anything about Mr. Childs."

"Why, how can I help it?"

"He's an old man, an' he was so worked up he didn't know what he was sayin'. They'll all scold him. Don't say anything."

"Well, I won't say anything. I don't know what I'm going to tell her, though."

Christine turned to go.

"You didn't say what 'twas you wanted," called Willard again.

But she made no reply. She was pushing through the deep snow out of the yard.

It was quite early yet, only a few minutes after seven. It was eight when she reached home. She entered the house without any one seeing her. She pulled off her snowy things, and went into the sitting-room.

Paulina was alone there. She was lying on the lounge. She was very pale, but she looked up and smiled when Christine entered.

Christine brought the fresh out-door air with her. Paulina noticed it. "Where have you been?" whispered she.

Then Christine bent over her, and talked fast in a low tone.

Presently Paulina raised herself and sat up. "To-night?" cried she, in an eager whisper. Her cheeks grew red.

"Yes; I'll go make the parlor fire."

"It's all ready to light." Suddenly Paulina threw her arms around Christine and kissed her. Both girls blushed.

"I don't think I said one thing to him that you wouldn't have wanted me to," said Christine.

"You didn't—ask him to come?"

"No, I didn't, honest."

When Mrs. Childs entered, a few minutes later, she found her daughter standing before the glass.

"Why, Paulina!" cried she.

"I feel a good deal better, mother," said Paulina.

"Ain't you goin' to bed?"

"I guess I won't quite yet."

"I've got it all ready for you. I thought you wouldn't feel like sittin' up."

I guess I will; a little while."

Soon the door-bell rang with a sharp peal. Everybody jumped—Paulina rose and went to the door.

Mrs. Childs and Maria, listening, heard Willard's familiar voice, then the opening of the parlor door.

"It's *him!*" gasped Mrs. Childs. She and Maria looked at each other.

It was about two hours before the soft murmur of voices in the parlor ceased, the outer door closed with a thud, and Paulina came into the room. She was blushing and smiling, but she could not look in any one's face at first.

"Well," said her mother, "who was it?"

"Willard. It's all right."

It was not long before the fine sewing was brought out again, and presently two silk dresses were bought for Paulina. It was known about that she was to be married on Christmas Day. Christine assisted in the preparation. All the family called to mind afterwards the obedience so ready as to be loving which she yielded to their biddings during those few hurried weeks. She sewed, she made cake, she ran of errands, she wearied herself joyfully for the happiness of this other young girl.

About a week before the wedding, Christine, saying good-night when about to retire one evening, behaved strangely. They remembered it afterwards. She went up to Paulina and kissed her when saying good-night. It was something which she had never before done. Then she stood in the door, looking at them all. There was a sad, almost a solemn, expression on her fair girlish face.

"Why, what's the matter?" said Maria.

"Nothin'," said Christine. "Good-night."

That was the last time they ever saw her. The next morning Mrs. Childs, going to call her, found her room vacant. There was a great alarm. When they did not find her in the house nor the neighborhood, people were aroused, and there was a search instigated. It was prosecuted eagerly, but to no purpose. Paulina's wedding evening came, and Christine was still missing.

Paulina had been married, and was standing beside her husband, in the midst of the chattering guests, when Caleb stole out of the room. He opened the north door, and stood looking out over the dusky fields. "Christiny!" he called, "Christiny!"

Presently he looked up at the deep sky, full of stars, and called again—"Christiny! Christiny!" But there was no answer save in light. When Christine stood in the sitting-room door and said good-night, her friends had their last sight and sound of her. Their Twelfth Guest had departed from their hospitality forever.

SISTER LIDDY.

THERE were no trees near the almshouse ; it stood in its bare, sandy lot, and there were no leaves or branches to cast shadows on its walls. It seemed like the folks whom it sheltered, out in the full glare of day, without any little kindly shade between itself and the dull, unfeeling stare of curiosity. The almshouse stood upon rising ground, so one could see it for a long distance. It was a new building, Mansard-roofed and well painted. The village took pride in it : no town far or near had such a house for the poor. It was so fine and costly that the village did not feel able to give its insane paupers separate support in a regular asylum ; so they lived in the almshouse with the sane paupers, and there was a padded cell in case they waxed too violent.

Around the almshouse lay the town fields. In summer they were green with corn and potatoes, now they showed ugly plough ridges sloping over the uneven ground, and yellow corn stubble. Beyond the field at the west of the almshouse was a little wood of elms and oaks and wild apple-trees. The yellow leaves had all fallen from the elms and the apple-trees, but most of the brown ones stayed on the oaks.

Polly Moss stood at the west window in the women's

sitting-room and gazed over at the trees. "It's cur'us how them oak leaves hang on arter the others have all fell off," she remarked.

A tall old woman sitting beside the stove looked around suddenly. She had singular bright eyes, and a sardonic smile around her mouth. "It's a way they allers have," she returned, scornfully. "Guess there ain't nothin' very cur'us about it. When the oak leaves fall off an' the others hang on, then you can be lookin' for the end of the world; that's goin' to be one of the signs."

"Allers a-harpin' on the end of the world," growled another old woman, in a deep bass voice. "I've got jest about sick on't. Seems as if I should go crazy myself, hearin' on't the whole time." She was sewing a seam in coarse cloth, and she sat on a stool on the other side of the stove. She was short and stout, and she sat with a heavy settle as if she were stuffed with lead.

The tall old woman took no further notice. She sat rigidly straight, and fixed her bright eyes upon the top of the door, and her sardonic smile deepened.

The stout old woman gave an ugly look at her; then she sewed with more impetus. Now and then she muttered something in her deep voice.

There were, besides herself, three old women in the room —Polly Moss, the tall one, and a pretty one in a white cap and black dress. There was also a young woman; she sat in a rocking-chair and leaned her head back. She was handsome, but she kept her mouth parted miserably, and there were ghastly white streaks around it and her nostrils. She never spoke. Her pretty black hair was rough, and her dress sagged at the neck. She had been living out at a large farm, and had overworked. She had no friends or relatives to take her in; so she had come to the almshouse to rest and try to recover. She had no refuge but the almshouse or the hospital, and she had a terrible horror of a hospital. Dreadful visions arose in her ignorant childish mind whenever she thought of one. She had a lover, but he had not been to see her since she came to the almshouse, six weeks before; she wept most of the time over that and her physical misery.

Polly Moss stood at the window until a little boy trudged into the room, bringing his small feet down with a clapping noise. He went up to Polly and twitched her dress. She looked around at him. "Well, now, Tommy, what do ye want?"

"Come out-doors an' play hide an' coot wis me, Polly."

Tommy was a stout little boy. He wore a calico tier that sagged to his heels in the back, and showed in front his little calico trousers. His round face was pleasant and innocent and charming.

Polly put her arms around the boy and hugged him. "Tommy's a darlin'," she said; "can't he give poor Polly a kiss?"

Tommy put up his lips. "Come out-doors an' play hide an' coot wis me," he said again, breathing the words out with the kiss.

"Now, Tommy, jest look out of the winder. Don't he see that it's rainin', hey?"

The child shook his head stubbornly, although he was looking straight at the window, which revealed plainly enough that long sheets of rain were driving over the fields. "Come out-doors and play hide an' coot wis me, Polly."

"Now, Tommy, jest listen to Polly. Don't he know he can't go out-doors when it's rainin' this way? He'd get all wet, an' Polly too. But I'll tell you what Polly an' Tommy can do. We'll jest go out in the hall an' we'll roll the ball. Tommy go run quick an' get his ball."

Tommy raised a shout, and clapped out of the room; his sweet nature was easily diverted. Polly followed him. She had a twisting limp, and was so bent that she was not much taller than Tommy, her little pale triangular face seemed to look from the middle of her flat chest.

"The wust-lookin' objeck," growled the stout old woman when Polly was out of the room: "looks more like an old cat that's had to airn it's own livin' than a human bein'. It 'bout makes me sick to look at her." Her deep tones travelled far; Polly, out in the corridor waiting for Tommy, heard every word.

"She is a dretful-lookin' cretur," assented the pretty old woman. As she spoke she puckered her little red mouth daintily, and drew herself up with a genteel air.

The stout old woman surveyed her contemptuously. "Well, good looks don't amount to much, nohow," said she, "if folks ain't got common-sense to balance 'em. I'd enough sight ruther know a leetle somethin' than have a dolly-face myself."

"Seems to me she is about the dretfulest-lookin' cretur that I ever did see," repeated the pretty old woman, quite unmoved. Aspersions on her intellect never aroused her in the least.

The stout old woman looked baffled. "Jest turn your head a leetle that way, will you, Mis' Handy?" she said, presently.

The pretty old woman turned her head obediently. "What is it?" she inquired, with a conscious simper.

"Jest turn your head a leetle more. Yes, it's funny I

ain't never noticed it afore. Your nose is a leetle grain crooked—ain't it, Mis' Handy?"

Mrs. Handy's face turned a deep pink—even her little ears and her delicate old neck were suffused; her blue eyes looked like an enraged bird's. "Crooked! H'm! I shouldn't think that folks that's got a nose like some folks had better say much about other folks' noses. There can't nobody tell me nothin' about my nose; I know all about it. Folks that wouldn't wipe their feet on some folks, nor look twice at 'em, has praised it. My nose ain't crooked an' never was, an' if anybody says so it's 'cause they're so spity, 'cause they're so mortal homely themselves. Guess I know." She drew breath, and paused for a return shot, but she got none. The stout old woman sewed and chuckled to herself, the tall one still fixed her eyes upon the top of the door, and the young woman leaned back with her lips parted, and her black eyes rolled.

The pretty old woman began again in defence of her nose; she talked fiercely, and kept feeling of it. Finally she arose and went out of the room with a flirt.

Then the stout old woman laughed. "She's gone to look at her nose in the lookin'-glass, an' make sure it ain't crooked: if it ain't a good joke!" she exclaimed, delightedly.

But she got no response. The young woman never stirred, and the tall old one only lowered her gaze from the door to the stove, which she regarded disapprovingly. "I call it the devil's stove," she remarked, after a while.

The stout old woman gave a grunt and sewed her seam; she was done with talking to such an audience. The shouts of children out in the corridor could be heard. "Pesky young ones!" she muttered.

In the corridor Polly Moss played ball with the children. She never caught the ball, and she threw it with weak, aimless jerks; her back ached, but she was patient, and her face was full of simple childish smiles. There were two children besides Tommy—his sister and a little boy.

The corridor was long; doors in both sides led into the paupers' bedrooms. Suddenly one of the doors flew open, and a little figure shot out. She went down the corridor with a swift trot like a child. She had on nothing but a woollen petticoat and a calico waist; she held her head down, and her narrow shoulders worked as she ran; her mop of soft white hair flew out. The children looked around at her; she was a horrible caricature of themselves.

The stout old woman came pressing out of the sitting-room. She went directly to the room that the running figure had left, and peered in; then she looked around significantly. "I knowed it," she said; "it's tore all to pieces agin. I'd jest been thinkin' to myself that Sally was dretful still, an' I'd bet she was pullin' her bed to pieces. There 'tis, an' made up jest as nice a few minutes ago! I'm goin' to see Mis' Arms."

Mrs. Arms was the matron. The old woman went off with an important air, and presently she returned with her. The matron was a large woman with a calm, benignant, and weary face.

Polly Moss continued to play ball, but several other old women had assembled, and they all talked volubly. They demonstrated that Sally had torn her bed to pieces, that it had been very nicely made, and that she should be punished.

The matron listened; she did not say much. Then she returned to the kitchen, where she was preparing dinner.

Some of the paupers assisted her. An old man, with his baggy trousers hitched high, chopped something in a tray, an old woman peeled potatoes, and a young one washed pans at the sink. The young woman, as she washed, kept looking over her shoulder and rolling her dark eyes at the other people in the room. She was mindful of every motion behind her back.

Mrs. Arms herself worked and directed the others. When dinner was ready the old man clanged a bell in the corridor, and everybody flocked to the dining-room except the young woman at the kitchen sink; she still stood there washing dishes. The dinner was coarse and abundant. The paupers, with the exception of the sick young woman, ate with gusto. The children were all hearty, and although the world had lost all its savor for the hearts and minds of the old ones, it was still somewhat salt to their palates. Now that their thoughts had ceased reaching and grasping, they could still put out their tongues, for that primitive instinct of life with which they had been born still survived and gave them pleasure. In this world it is the child only that is immortal.

The old people and the children ate after the same manner. There was a loud smacking of lips and gurgling noises. The rain drove against the windows of the dining-room, with its bare floor, its board tables and benches, and rows of feeding paupers. The smooth yellow heads of the children seemed to catch all the light in the room. Once in a while they raised imperious clamors. The overseer sat at one end of the table and served the beef. He was stout, and had a handsome, heavy face.

The meal was nearly finished when there was a crash of breaking crockery, a door slammed, and there was a wild shriek out in the corridor. The overseer and one of the old men who was quite able-bodied sprang and rushed out of the room. The matron followed, and the children tagged at her heels. The others continued feeding as if nothing had happened. "That Agnes is wuss agin," remarked the stout old woman. "I've seed it a-comin' on fer a couple of days. They'd orter have put her in the cell yesterday; I told Mis' Arms so, but they're allers puttin' off, an' puttin' off."

"They air a-takin' on her up to the cell now," said the pretty old woman; and she brought around her knifeful of cabbage with a sidewise motion, and stretched her little red mouth to receive it.

Out in the corridor shriek followed shriek; there were loud voices and scuffling. The children were huddled in the doorway, peeping, but the old paupers continued to eat. The sick young woman laid down her knife and fork and wept.

Presently the shrieks and the scuffling grew faint in the distance; the children had followed on. Then, after a little, they all returned and the dinner was finished.

After dinner, when the women paupers had done their share of the clearing away, they were again assembled in their sitting-room. The windows were cloudy with fine mist; the rain continued to drive past them from over the yellow stubbly fields. There was a good fire in the stove, and the room was hot and close. The stout old woman sewed again on her coarse seam, the others were idle. There were now six old women present; one of them was the little creature whom they called Sally. She sat close to the stove, bent over and motionless. Her clothing hardly covered her. The sick young woman was absent; she was lying down on the lounge in the matron's room, and the children too were in there.

Polly Moss sat by the window. The old women began talking among themselves. The pretty old one had taken off her cap and had it in her lap, perking up the lace and straightening it. It was a flimsy rag, like a soiled cobweb. The stout old woman cast a contemptuous glance at it. She raised her nose and her upper lip scornfully. "I don't see how you can wear that nasty thing nohow, Mis' Handy," said she.

Mrs. Handy flushed pink again. She bridled and began to speak, then she looked at the little soft soiled mass in her lap, and paused. She had not the force of character to proclaim black white while she was looking at it. Had the old cap been in the bureau drawer, or even on her head, she might have defended it to the death, but here before her eyes it silenced her.

But after her momentary subsidence she aroused herself; her blue eyes gleamed dimly at the stout old woman. "It was a handsome cap when it was new, anyhow!" said she; "better'n some folks ever had, I'll warrant. Folks that ain't got no caps at all can't afford to be flingin' at them that has, if they ain't quite so nice as they was. You'd orter have seen the cap I had when my daughter was married! All white wrought lace, an' bows of pink ribbon, an' long streamers, an' some artificial roses on't. I don't s'pose you ever see anythin' like it, Mis' Paine."

The stout woman was Mrs. Paine. "Mebbe I ain't," said she, sarcastically.

The tall old woman chimed in suddenly; her thin, nervous voice clanged after the others like a sharply struck bell. "I ain't never had any caps to speak of," she proclaimed; "never thought much of 'em, anyhow; heatin' things; an' I never heard that folks in heaven wore caps. But I have had some good clothes. I've got a piece of silk in my bureau drawer. That silk would stand alone. An' I had a good thibet; there was rows an' rows of velvet ribbon on it. I always had good clothes; my husband, he wanted I should, an' he got 'em fer me. I airned some myself, too. I 'ain't got any now, an' I dunno as I care if I ain't, fer the signs are increasin'."

"Allers a-harpin' on that," muttered the stout old woman.

"I had a handsome blue silk when I was marri'd," vouchsafed Mrs. Handy.

"I've seen the piece of it," returned the tall one; "it ain't near so thick as mine is."

The old woman who had not been present in the morning now spoke. She had been listening with a superior air. She was the only one in the company who had possessed considerable property, and had fallen from a widely differing estate. She was tall and dark and gaunt; she towered up next the pretty old woman like a scraggy old pine beside a faded lily. She was a single woman, and she had lost all her property through an injudicious male relative. "Well," she proclaimed, "everybody knows I've had things if I ain't got 'em now. There I had a whole house, with Brussels carpets on all the rooms except the kitchen, an' stuffed furniture, an' beddin' packed away in chists, an' bureau drawers full of things. An' I ruther think I've had silk dresses an' bunnits an' caps."

"I remember you had a real handsome blue bunnit once, but it warn't so becomin' as some you'd had, you was so dark-complected," remarked the pretty old woman, in a soft, spiteful voice. "I had a white one, drawn silk, an' white feathers on't, when I was married, and they all said it was real becomin'. I was allers real white myself. I had a white muslin dress with a flounce on it, once, too, an' a black silk spencer cape."

"I had a fitch tippet an' muff that cost twenty-five dollars," remarked the stout old woman, emphatically, "*an'* a cashmire shawl."

"I had two cashmire shawls, an' *my* tippet cost fifty dollars," retorted the dark old woman, with dignity.

"My fust baby had an elegant blue cashmire cloak, all worked with silk as deep as that," said Mrs. Handy. She now had the old cap on her head, and looked more assertive.

"Mine had a little wagon with a velvet cushion to ride in; an' I had a tea-set, real chiny, with a green sprig on't," said the stout old woman.

"I had a Brittany teapot," returned Mrs. Handy.

"I had gilt vases as tall as that on my parlor mantel-shelf," said the dark old woman.

"I had a chiny figger, a girl with a basket of flowers on her arm, once," rejoined the tall one; "it used to set side of the clock. An' when I was fust married I used to live in a white house, with a flower-garden to one side. I can smell them pinks an' roses now, an' I s'pose I allers shall, jest as far as I go."

"I had a pump in my kitchen sink, an' things real handy," said the stout old one; "an' I used to look as well as anybody, an' my husband too, when we went to meetin'. I remember one winter I had a new brown alpaca with velvet buttons, an' he had a new great-coat with a velvet collar."

Suddenly the little cowering Sally raised herself and gave

testimony to her own little crumb of past comfort. Her wits were few and scattering, and had been all her days, but the conversation of the other women seemed to set some vibrating into momentary concord. She laughed, and her bleared blue eyes twinkled. "I had a pink caliker gownd once," she quavered out. "Mis' Thompson, she gin it me when I lived there."

"Do hear the poor cretur," said the pretty old woman, with an indulgent air.

Now everybody had spoken but Polly Moss. She sat by the misty window, and her little pale triangular face looked from her sunken chest at the others. This conversation was a usual one. Many and many an afternoon the almshouse old women sat together and bore witness to their past glories. Now they had nothing, but at one time or another they had had something over which to plume themselves and feel that precious pride of possession. Their present was to them a state of simple existence, they regarded their future with a vague resignation; they were none of them thinkers, and there was no case of rapturous piety among them. In their pasts alone they took real comfort, and they kept, as it were, feeling of them to see if they were not still warm with life.

The old women delighted in these inventories and comparing of notes. Polly Moss alone had never spoken. She alone had never had anything in which to take pride. She had been always deformed and poor and friendless. She had worked for scanty pay as long as she was able, and had then drifted and struck on the almshouse, where she had grown old. She had not even a right to the charity of this particular village: this was merely the place where her working powers had failed her; but no one could trace her back to her birthplace, or the town which was responsible for her support. Polly Moss herself did not know—she went humbly where she was told. All her life the world had seemed to her simply standing-ground; she had gotten little more out of it.

Every day, when the others talked, she listened admiringly, and searched her memory for some little past treasure of her own, but she could not remember any. The dim image of a certain delaine dress, with bright flowers scattered over it, which she had once owned, away back in her girlhood, sometimes floated before her eyes when they were talking, and she had a half-mind to mention that, but her heart would fail her. She feared that it was not worthy to be compared with the others' fine departed gowns; it paled before even Sally's pink calico. Polly's poor clothes, covering her pitiful crookedness, had never given her any firm stimulus to gratulation. So she was always silent, and the other old women had come to talk at her. Their conversation acquired a gusto from this listener who could not join in. When a new item of past property was given, there was always a side-glance in Polly's direction.

None of the old women expected to ever hear a word from Polly, but this afternoon, when they had all, down to Sally, testified, she spoke up:

"You'd orter have seen my sister Liddy," said she; her voice was very small, it sounded like the piping of a feeble bird in a bush.

There was a dead silence. The other old women looked at each other. "Didn't know you ever had a sister Liddy," the stout old woman blurted out, finally, with an amazed air.

"My sister Liddy was jest as handsome as a pictur'," Polly returned.

The pretty old woman flushed jealously. "Was she fair-complected?" she inquired.

"She was jest as fair as a lily—a good deal fairer than you ever was, Mis' Handy, an' she had long yaller curls a-hangin' clean down to her waist, an' her cheeks were jest as pink, an' she had the biggest blue eyes I ever see, an' the beautifulest leetle red mouth."

"Lor'!" ejaculated the stout old woman, and the pretty old woman sniffed.

But Polly went on; she was not to be daunted; she had been silent all this time; and now her category poured forth, not piecemeal, but in a flood, upon her astonished hearers.

"Liddy, she could sing the best of anybody anywheres around," she continued; "nobody ever heerd sech singin'. It was so dretful loud an' sweet that you could hear it 'way down the road when the winders was shut. She used to sing in the meetin'-house, she did, an' all the folks used to sit up an' look at her when she begun. She used to wear a black silk dress to meetin', an' a white cashmire shawl, an' a bunnit with a pink wreath around the face, an' she had white kid gloves. Folks used to go to that meetin'-house jest to hear Liddy sing an' see her. They thought 'nough sight more of that than they did of the preachin'.

"Liddy had a feather fan, an' she used to sit an' fan her when she wa'n't singin', an' she allers had scent on her hand-kercher. An' when meetin' was done in the evenin' all the young fellars used to be crowdin' 'round, an' pushin' and bowin' an' scrapin', a-tryin' to get a chance to see her home. But Liddy she wouldn't look at none of them; she married a real rich fellar from Bostown. He was jest as straight as an arrer, an' he had black eyes an' hair, an' he wore a beautiful coat an' a satin vest, an' he spoke jest as perlite.

"When Liddy was married she had a whole chistful of clothes, real fine cotton cloth, all tucks an' laid-work, an' she had a pair of silk stockin's, an' some white shoes. An' her weddin' dress was white satin, with a great long trail to it, an' she had a lace veil, an' she wore great long ear-drops that shone like everythin'. *An'* she come out bride in a blue silk dress, an' a black lace mantilly, an' a white bunnit trimmed with lutestring ribbon."

"Where did your sister Liddy live arter she was married?" inquired the pretty old woman, with a subdued air.

"She lived in Bostown, an' she had a great big house with a parlor an' settin'-room, an' a room to eat in besides the kitchen. An' she had real velvet carpets on all the floors down to the kitchen, an' great pictur's in gilt frames a-hangin' on all the walls. An' her furnitur' was all stuffed, an' kivered with red velvet, an' she had a pianner, an' great big marble images a-settin' on her mantel-shelf. An' she had a coach with lamps on the sides, an' blue satin cushings, to ride in, an' four horses to draw it, an' a man to drive. An' she allers had a hired girl in the kitchen. I never knowed Liddy to be without a hired girl.

"Liddy's husband, he thought everythin' of her; he never used to come home from his work without he brought her somethin', an' she used to run out to meet him. She was allers dretful lovin', an' had a good disposition. Liddy, she had the beautifulest baby you ever see, an' she had a cradle lined with blue silk to rock him in, an' he had a white silk cloak, an' a leetle lace cap—"

"I shouldn't think your beautiful sister Liddy an' her husband would let you come to the poor-house," interrupted the dark old woman.

"Liddy's dead, or she wouldn't."

"Are her husband an' the baby dead, too?"

"They're all dead," responded Polly Moss. She looked out of the window again, her face was a burning red, and there were tears in her eyes.

There was silence among the other old women. They were at once overawed and incredulous. Polly left the room before long, then they began to discuss the matter. "I dun know whether to believe it or not," said the dark old woman.

"Well, I dun know, neither; I never knowed her to tell anythin' that wa'n't so," responded the stout old one, doubtfully.

The old women could not make up their minds whether to believe or disbelieve. The pretty one was the most incredulous of any. She said openly that she did not believe it possible that such a "homely cretur" as Polly Moss could have had such a handsome sister.

But, credulous or not, their interest and curiosity were lively. Every day Polly Moss was questioned and cross-examined concerning her sister Liddy. She rose to the occasion; she did not often contradict herself, and the glories of her sister were increased daily. Old Polly Moss, her little withered face gleaming with reckless enthusiasm, sang the praises of her sister Liddy as wildly and faithfully as any minnesinger his angel mistress, and the old women listened with ever-increasing bewilderment and awe.

It was two weeks before Polly Moss died with pneumonia that she first mentioned her sister Liddy, and there was not one afternoon until the day when she was taken ill that she did not relate the story, with new and startling additions, to the old women.

Polly was not ill long, she settled meekly down under the

disease: her little distorted frame had no resistance in it. She died at three o'clock in the morning. The afternoon before, she seemed better; she was quite rational, and she told the matron that she wanted to see her comrades, the old women. "I've got somethin' to tell 'em, Mis' Arms," Polly whispered, and her eyes were piteous..

So the other old women came into the room. They stood around Polly's little iron bed and looked at her. "I—want to—tell you—somethin'," she began. But there was a soft rush, and the sick young woman entered. She pressed straight to the matron; she disregarded the others. Her wan face seemed a very lamp of life—to throw a light over and above all present darkness, even of the grave. She moved nimbly; she was so full of joy that her sickly body seemed permeated by it, and almost a spiritual one. She did not appear in the least feeble. She caught the matron's arm. "Charley has come, Mis' Arms!" she cried out. "Charley has come! He's got a house ready. He's goin' to marry me, an' take me home, an' take care of me till I get well. I'm goin' right away!"

The old women all turned away from Polly and stared at the radiant girl. The matron sent her away, with a promise to see her in a few minutes. "Polly's dyin'," she whispered, and the girl stole out with a hushed air, but the light in her face was not dimmed. What was death to her, when she had just stepped on a height of life where one can see beyond it?

"Tell them what you wanted to, now, Polly," said the matron.

"I—want to tell you—somethin'," Polly repeated. "I s'pose I've been dretful wicked, but I ain't never had nothin' in my whole life. I—s'pose the Lord orter have been enough, but it's dretful hard sometimes to keep holt of him, an' not look anywheres else, when you see other folks a-clawin' an' gettin' other things, an' actin' as if they was wuth havin'. I ain't never had nothin' as fur as them other things go; I don't want nothin' else now. I've—got past 'em. I see I don't want nothin' but the Lord. But I used to feel dretful bad an' wicked when I heerd you all talkin' 'bout things you'd had, an' I hadn't never had nothin', so—" Polly Moss stopped talking, and coughed. The matron supported her. The old women nudged each other; their awed, sympathetic, yet sharply inquiring eyes never left her face. The children were peeping in at the open door; old Sally trotted past—she had just torn her bed to pieces. As soon as she got breath enough, Polly Moss finished what she had to say. "I—s'pose I—was dretful wicked," she whispered; "but—I never had any sister Liddy."

CALLA-LILIES AND HANNAH.

"MIS' NEWHALL!"

The tall, thin figure on the other side of the street pushed vigorously past. It held it's black-bonneted head back stiffly, and strained its green-and-black woollen shawl tighter across its slim shoulders.

"Mis' *New*hall!"

The figure stopped with a jerk. "Oh, it's you, Marthy. Pleasant afternoon, ain't it?"

"Ain't you comin' in?"

"Well, I don't jest see how I can this afternoon. I was goin' up to Ellen's."

"Can't you jest come over a minute and see my calla-lilies?"

"Well, I don't see how I can. I can see 'em up to the window. Beautiful, ain't they?"

"You can't see nuthin' of 'em out there. Why can't you come in jest a minute? There ain't a soul been in to see 'em this week, and 'tain't often they blow out this way."

"Who's in there?—anybody?"

"No; there ain't a soul but me to home. Hannah's gone over to Wayne. Can't you come in?"

"Well, I dunno but I'll come over jest a minute; but I can't stay. I hadn't ought to stop at all."

Martha Wing waited for her in the door; she was quivering with impatience to show her the lilies. "Come right in," she cried, when the visitor came up the walk.

When she turned to follow her in she limped painfully; one whole side seemed to succumb so nearly that it was barely rescued by a quick spring from the other.

"How's your lameness?" asked Mrs. Newhall.

"Martha's soft withered face flushed. "Here air the lilies," she said, shortly.

"My! ain't they beautiful!"

"'Tain't often you see seven lilies and two buds together."

"Well, 'tain't, that's a fact. Ellen thought hers was pretty handsome, but it can't shake a stick at this. Hers ain't got but three on it. I'd like to know what you do to it, Marthy?"

"I don't do nuthin'. Flowers 'll grow for some folks, and that's all there is about it. I allers had jest sech luck." Martha stood staring at the lilies. A self-gratulation that had something noble about it was in her smiling old face.

"I tell Hannah," she went on, "if I be miser'ble in health, an' poor, flowers 'll blow for me, and that's more than they'll do for some folks, no matter how hard they try. Look at Mis' Walker over there. I can't help thinkin' of it sometimes when I see her go nippin' past with her ruffles and gimcracks. She's young an' good-lookin', but she's had her calla-lily five year, an' she ain't had but one bud, and that blasted."

"Well, flowers is a good deal of company."

"I guess they air. They're most as good as folks. Mis' Newhall, why don't Jennie come in an' see Hannah sometimes?"

All the lines in Mrs. Newhall's face lengthened. She looked harder at the callas. "Well, I dunno, Marthy; Jenny don't go much of anywhere. Those lilies are beautiful. You'd ought to have 'em carried into the meetin'-house next Sunday, an' set in front of the pulpit."

Martha turned white. Her voice quavered up shrilly. 'There's one lily I could mention 's been took out of that meetin'-house, Maria Newhall, an' there ain't no more of mine goin' to be took in, not if I know it."

"Now, Marthy, you know I didn't mean a thing. I no more dreamed of hurtin' your feelin's than the dead."

"No, I don't s'pose you did; an' I don't s'pose your Jenny an' the other girls mean anything by stayin' away an' never comin' near Hannah. They act as if they was afraid of her; but I guess she wouldn't hurt 'em none. She's as good as any of 'em, an' they'll find it out some day."

"Now, Marthy—"

"You needn't talk. I know all about it. I've heerd a good deal of palaver, but I kin see through it. I—"

"Well, I guess I'll have to be goin', Marthy. Good-afternoon."

Martha suddenly recovered her dignity. "Good-afternoon, Mis' Newhall," said she, and relapsed into silence.

After the door had closed behind her guest, she sat down at the window with her knitting. She had an old shawl over her shoulders; the room was very chilly. She pursed up her lips and knitted very fast, a lean, homely figure in the clean, bare room, with its bulging old satin-papered walls. A square of pale sunlight lay on the thin, dull carpet, and the pot of calla-lilies stood in the window.

Before long Hannah came. She entered without a word, and stood silently taking off her wraps.

"Did you git your pay, Hannah?"

"Yes."

When Hannah laid aside her thick, faded shawl, she showed a tall young figure in a clinging old woollen gown of a drab color. She stooped a little, although the stoop did not seem anything but the natural result of her tallness, and was thus graceful rather than awkward. It was as if her whole slender body bent from her feet, lily fashion. She got a brush out of a little chimney cupboard and began smoothing her light hair, which her hood had rumpled a little. She had a full, small face; there was a lovely delicate pink on her cheeks. People said of Hannah, "She is delicate-looking." They said "delicate" in the place of pretty; it suited her better.

"Why don't you say somethin'?" Martha asked, querulously.

"What do you want me to say?"

"Where's your bundle of boots?"

"I haven't got any."

"Ain't got no boots?"

"No."

"Didn't Mr. Allen give you any?"

"No."

"Ain't he going to?"

"No."

"Why not?"

Hannah went on brushing her hair, and made no answer.

"Has—he heard of—that?"

"I suppose so."

"What did he say?"

"Said he couldn't trust me to take any more boots home." One soft flush spread over Hannah's face as she said that, then it receded. She knelt down by the air-tight stove and began poking the fire.

"Course he'd heerd, then. What air you goin' to do, Hannah?"

"I don't know."

"You take it easy 'nough, I hope. Ef you don't hev work, I don't see what's goin' to keep a roof over us."

Hannah, going out into the kitchen, half turned in the doorway. "Don't worry, I'll get some work somewhere, I guess," she said.

But Martha kept on calling out her complaint in a shriller voice, so Hannah could hear as she stepped about in the other room. "I don't see what you're goin' to do; I'm 'bout discouraged. Mis' Newhall, she's been in here, pretended she wanted to see my caller, but she give me no end of digs, the way she allers does. This kind of work is killin' me. Here's this calla-lily's been blowed out the way it has lately, an' not a soul comin' in to see it. Hannah Redman, I don't see what possessed you to do such a thing."

No answering voice came from the kitchen.

"You did do it, didn't you, Hannah? You wouldn't let folks go on in this way if you hadn't."

Hannah said nothing. Martha broke into a fit of loud weeping. She held her hands over her face, and rocked herself back and forth in her chair. "Oh me! Oh me!" she wailed, shrilly.

Hannah paid no attention. She went about getting tea ready. It was a frugal meal, bread and butter and weak tea, but she fried a bit of ham and put it on Martha's plate. The old woman liked something hearty for supper.

"Come," she said at length—"come, Martha, tea's ready."

"I don't want nothin'," wailed the old woman. But she sat sniffing down at the table, and ate heartily.

After tea Hannah got her hood and shawl and went out again. It was a chilly March night; the clouds were flying wildly, there was an uncertain moon, the ground was covered with melting snow. Hannah held up her skirts and stepped along through the slush. The snow-water penetrated her old shoes; she had no rubbers.

Presently she stopped and rang a door-bell. The woman who answered it stood eying her amazedly a minute before she spoke. "Good-evenin', Hannah," she said, stiffly, at length.

"Good-evening, Mrs. Ward. Are your boarders in?"

"Y-e-s."

"Can I see them?"

"Well—I guess so. Mis' Mellen, she's been pretty busy all day. Come in, won't you?"

Hannah followed her into the lighted sitting-room. A young, smooth-faced man and a woman who looked older and stronger were in there. Mrs. Ward introduced them in an embarrassed way to Hannah. "Mis' Mellen, this is Miss Redman," said she, "an' Mr. Mellen."

Hannah opened at once upon the subject of her errand. She had heard that the Mellens wished to begin housekeeping, and were anxious to hire a tenement. She proposed that they should hire her house; she and Martha would reserve only two rooms for themselves. The rent which she suggested was very low. The husband and wife looked at each other.

"We might—go and look at it—to-morrow," he said, hesitatingly, with his eyes on his wife.

"We'll come in some time to-morrow and see how it

suits," said she, in a crisp voice. "Perhaps —" She stopped suddenly. Mrs. Ward had given her a violent nudge. But she looked wonderingly at her and kept on. "We should want—" said she.

"It ain't anything you want, Mis' Mellen," spoke up Mrs. Ward.

"Why, what's the trouble?"

"You don't want it; 'twon't suit you." Mrs. Ward nodded significantly.

Hannah looked at one and the other. The delicate color in her cheeks deepened a little, but she spoke softly. "There are locks and keys on the doors," said she.

Mrs. Ward colored furiously. "I didn't mean—" she began. Then she stopped.

Hannah arose. "If you want to come and look at the rooms, I'll be glad to show them," said she. She stood waiting with a dignity which had something appealing about it.

"Well, I'll see," said Mrs. Mellen.

After Hannah had gone she turned eagerly to Mrs. Ward. "What is the matter?" said she.

"'Tain't safe for you to go there, unless—you want all your things—*stole.*"

"Why, does she—"

"She stole some money from John Arnold up here a year ago. That's a fact."

"You don't mean it!"

"Yes. She was sewin' up there. He left it on the sittin'-room table a minute, an' when he came back it was gone. There hadn't been anybody but her in the room, so of course she took it."

"Did he get the money back?"

"That was the queer part of it. Nobody could ever find out what she did with the money."

"Didn't they take her up?"

"No; they made a good deal of fuss about it at first, but Mr. Arnold didn't prosecute her. I s'pose he thought they couldn't really prove anything, not findin' the money. And then he's a deacon of the church; he'd hate to do such a thing, anyway. But everybody in town thinks she took it, fast enough. Nobody has anything to do with her. She used to go out sewin' for folks, but they say she stole lots of pieces. I heard she took enough black silk here and there to make a dress. Nobody has her now, that I know of. You don't want anybody in your house that you can't trust."

"Of course you don't."

"She was a church member, an' it came up before the church, an' they dismissed her. They asked her if it was so, an' she wouldn't answer one word, yes or no. They couldn't get a thing out of her."

"Well, of course if she hadn't taken it she'd said so."

"It's likely she would."

"I'm real glad you told me. I'd hated awfully to have gone in there with anybody like that."

"I thought you would. I felt as if I ought to tell you, seein' as you was strangers here. I kind of pity her. I s'pose she thought she could raise a littte money that way. I guess she's havin' a pretty hard time. She can't get no work anywhere. She's been sewin' boots for Allen over in Wayne, but I heard the other day he was goin' to shut down on her. She's gettin' some of her punishment in this world. Folks said Arnold's son George had a notion of goin' with her once, but I guess it put a stop to that pretty quick. He's down East somewhere."

Hannah, plodding along out in the windy, moonlit night, knew as well what they were saying as if she had been at their elbows. The wind sung in her ears, the light clouds drove overhead; those nearest the moon had yellow edges. Hannah kept looking up at them.

She had five dollars and fifty cents in her pocket, and no prospect of more. She had herself and a helpless old relative to support. All the village, every friend and acquaintance she had ever had, were crying out against her. That was the case of Hannah Redman when she entered her silent house that night; but she followed her old relative to bed, and went to sleep like a child.

The next morning she got out an old blue cashmere of hers and began ripping it.

"What are you goin' to do?" asked Martha, who had been eying her furtively all the morning.

"I'm going to make over this dress. I haven't got a thing fit to wear."

"I shouldn't think you'd feel much like fixin' over dresses. I don't see what's goin' to become of us. I don't s'pose a soul will be in to see my calla-lily to-day. It's killin' me."

Hannah said nothing, but she worked steadily on the dress all day. She turned it, and it looked like new.

The next day was Sunday. Hannah, going to church in her remodelled dress, heard distinctly some one behind her say, "See, Hannah Redman's got a new dress, I do believe. I shouldn't think she'd feel much like it, should you?"

Hannah sat alone in the pew, where her father and mother had sat before her. They had all been church-going people. Hannah herself had been a member ever since her childhood. Not one Sunday had she missed of stepping modestly up the aisle in her humble Sunday best, and seating herself with gentle gravity. The pew was a conspicuous one beside the pulpit, at right angles with the others. Hannah was in full view of the whole congregation. She sat erect and composed in her pretty dress. The delicate color in her cheeks was the same as ever; her soft eyes were as steady. She found the hymns and sang; she listened to the preaching.

Women looked at her, then at one another. Hannah knew it. Still it had never been as bad since that first Sunday after her dismissal from the church.

There had been a tangible breeze then that had whistled in her ears. Nobody had dreamed that she would come to meeting, but she came.

There was no question but that Hannah's unshaken demeanor brought somewhat harder judgment upon herself. A smile in an object of pity is a grievance. The one claim which Hannah now had upon her friends she did not extort, consequently she got nothing. She showed no need of pity, and was, if anything, more condemned for that than for her actual fault.

"If she wasn't so dreadful bold," they said. "If she acted as if she felt bad about it."

In one of the foremost body-pews sat John Arnold, a large, fair-faced old man, who wore his white hair like a tonsure. He never looked at Hannah. He had a gold-headed cane. He clasped both hands around it, and leaned heavily forward upon it as he listened. It was a habit of his. He settled himself solemnly into this attitude at his entrance. People watched him respectfully. John Arnold was the one wealthy man in this poor country church. Over across the aisle a shattered, threadbare old grandfather leaned impressively upon his poor pine stick in the same way that John Arnold did. He stole frequent, studious glances at him. He was an artist who made himself into a caricature.

There was a communion-service to-day. After the sermon Hannah arose quietly and went down the aisle with the non-communicants. She felt people looking at her, but when she turned, their eyes were somewhere else. No one spoke to her.

"Did anybody speak to you?" old Martha asked when she got home.

"No," said Hannah.

"I don't see how you stand it. I should think it would kill you, an' you don't look as if it wore on you a bit. Hannah, what made you do sech a thing?"

Hannah said nothing.

"I should think, after the way your father an' mother brought you up— Well, it's killin' me. I've been most crazy the whole forenoon thinkin' on't. What air you goin' to do if you can't git no work, Hannah?"

"I guess I can get some, perhaps."

"I don't see where."

The next morning Hannah went over to East Wayne, a town about four miles away. There was a new boot-and-shoe manufactory there, and she thought she might get some employment. The overseer was a pleasant young fellow, who treated her courteously. They had no work just then, but trade was improving. He told her to come again in a month.

"I rather guess I can get some work over at the new shop in East Wayne," she said to Martha when she got home.

"They'll hear on't, an' then you'll lose it, jest the way you've done before," was Martha's reply.

But Hannah lived on the hope of it for a month. She literally lived on little else. They had some potatoes and a few apples in the cellar. Hannah ate them. With her little stock of money she bought food for Martha.

At the end of the month she walked over to East Wayne again. The overseer remembered her. He greeted her very pleasantly, but his honest young face flushed.

"I'm real sorry," he stammered, "but—I'm afraid we can't give you any work."

Hannah turned white. He had heard.

"As far as I am concerned," he went on, "I would; but it don't depend on me, you know." He stood staring irresolutely at Hannah.

"See here, wait a minute," said he, "I'll speak to the boss."

Pretty soon he returned with a troubled look. "It's no use," said he; "he says he hasn't got any work."

"Will he have any by-and-by?" asked Hannah, feebly.

"I'm afraid not," replied the young man, pitifully. He opened the door for her. "Good-by," he said; "don't get down-hearted."

Hannah looked at him, then the tears sprang to her eyes. "Thank you," she said.

When she got past the shop she sat down on a stone beside the road and cried. "I wish he hadn't spoken kind to me," she whispered, sobbingly, to herself—"I wish he hadn't."

The road was bordered with willow bushes; they were just beginning to bud. The new grass was springing, and there was a smell of it in the air. Presently Hannah rose and walked on. She had ten cents in her pocket. She stopped at a store on her way home and bought with it a herring and a couple of fresh biscuit for Martha's supper. She ate nothing herself. She said she was not hungry.

"I knew they'd hear on't," Martha said, when she told her of her disappointment.

The next day Hannah tried to raise some money on her house. It was a large cottage, somewhat out of repair; it was worth some twenty-five hundred dollars.

Hannah could not obtain a loan of a cent upon it. There was no bank in the village, and only one wealthy man, John Arnold. She would not apply to him, and the others, close-fisted, narrow-minded farmers, were afraid of some trap, they knew not what, in the transaction.

"How do I know you'll pay me the interest regular?" asked one man.

"If I don't, you can take the house," said Hannah.

"How do I know I can?" The man looked after her with an air of dull triumph as she went away, drooping more than ever. She was faint from want of food. Still, the look of delicate resolution had not gone from her face. She went home, got out a heavy gold watch-chain which had belonged to her father, took it over to Wayne, and offered it to a jeweller. He looked at her and it curiously. The chain was an old one, but heavy and solid.

"What's your name!" asked the jeweller.

"Hannah Redman."

He pushed it towards her. "No, I guess I can't take it. We have to be pretty careful about these things, you know. If any question should come up—"

Hannah put the chain in her pocket and went home. Old Martha greeted her fretfully.

"I've been dretful lonesome," said she. "There's another lily blowed out, an' there ain't a soul been in to see it."

Hannah sat looking at her moodily. If it were not for this old woman she would lock her house and leave the village this very night. It must be that she would find toleration somewhere in the great world. Some of her kind would be willing to let her live. But here was Martha, whom she would not leave; Martha and her calla-lily, which to a fanciful mind might well seem a very part of her; maybe the grace and beauty which her querulous old age lacked came to her in this form. At all events it recompensed her for them in a measure. Martha plus her calla-lily might equal something almost beautiful—who knew?

Looking at this helpless old creature, something stronger than love took possession of Hannah—a spirit of fierce protection and faithfulness.

"Why don't you take your things off?" Martha groaned.

"I'm going out again."

When Hannah gathered herself up and went out she had a fixed purpose; she was going to get some supper for Martha. There was not a morsel in the house. Martha must have something to eat. There was nothing desperate in her mind, only that fixed intention—the food she would have, she did not know how, but she would have it.

She was so weak from fasting that she could scarcely step herself, but she did not think of that. "It's awful for an old woman to go hungry," she muttered, going down the street.

There was some kindly women in the village; they would give her food if they knew of her terrible need, she was sure of it; she had only to ask. She paused at several gates; once she laid her hand on a latch, then she moved on.

She could not beg with this stigma upon her. Suddenly in her weakness a half delirious fancy took possession of her. She seemed to be thinking other people's thoughts of herself instead of her own. "There's that Hannah Redman," she thought; "the girl that stole. Now she's gone to begging. Who wants to give to a girl like that? What's the sense of her begging? She's down as low as she can be; if she wants anything, why doesn't she steal? It's all over with her. People can't think any worse of her than they do now."

Hannah came to the post-office, and entered mechanically. The post-office merely occupied a corner of the large country store. The postmaster dealt out postage-stamps or cheeses to demand. When Hannah entered there was no one in the great rank room. The proprietor had gone to tea; the two clerks were out in the back yard unloading a team. It was not the hour for customers.

Hannah glanced about. A great heap of fresh loaves was on the counter near the door. She leaned over and smelled of them hungrily, then—she snatched one, hid it under her shawl, and went out.

"Hannah Redman has been stealing again," she thought, with those thoughts of others, as she went down the street.

She made the bread into some toast for Martha, and the old woman ate it complainingly. "I'd ha' relished a leetle bit of bacon," she muttered.

"Hannah Redman might just as well have stolen some bacon while she was about it," she thought. She could not touch the bread herself. She looked badly to-night; her soft eyes glittered, the delicate fineness of her color had deepened. Even Martha noticed it.

"What makes you look so queer, Hannah?" she asked.

" Nothing."

" Don't you feel well? You ain't eatin' a thing. I guess you'd relished a leetle bit of meat."

" I'm all right," said Hannah.

After the supper was cleared away, and old Martha had gone to bed, Hannah sat down by one of the front windows. It was dusk; she could just discern the dark figures passing in the street, but could not identify them. Presently one paused at her gate, unfastened it, and entered. Hannah heard steps on the gravel walk. Then there was a knock on the door.

" They've missed it," Hannah thought. She wondered that she did not care more. " Martha's had her supper, anyhow," she chuckled, fiercely.

She opened the door. " Hannah," said a man's voice.

" Oh!" she gasped. " George Arnold! Go away! go away!"

" Hannah, what's the matter? Oh, you poor girl, have I frightened you to death, after all the rest? Hannah—there; lean against me, dear. You feel better now, don't you? Don't shake so. Come, let's go in and light a lamp, and I'll get you some water."

" Oh, go away!"

" I guess I sha'n't go away till— O Lord! Hannah, I never knew what you'd been through till five minutes ago. I've just heard. Hannah, I'd lie down and die at your feet if it would do any good. Oh, you poor girl!"

The man's voice was all rough and husky. Hannah leaned against the door, gasping faintly, while he struck a match and lit a lamp. She never offered to help him. He went out in the kitchen and brought her a glass of water. She pushed it away.

"No," she motioned with silent lips.

"Do take it, dear; you look dreadfully. You frighten me. Take it just to please me."

She took it then, and drank.

"There, that's a good girl. Now sit down here while I talk to you."

She sat down in the chair he placed for her, and he drew another beside her. He sat for a minute looking at her, then suddenly he reached forward and seized her hands. He held them tightly while he talked. "Hannah, look here; you knew I took that money, didn't you?"

She nodded.

"And you let everybody think you did it; you never said a word to clear yourself. Hannah Redman, there never was a woman like you in the whole world! To think of everybody's being down on you, and—your being turned out of the church! Oh, Lord! Hannah, I can't bear it."

The poor fellow fairly sobbed for a minute. Hannah sat still, looking straight ahead.

"See here," he went on, "I want to tell you the whole story, how I came to do it. It wasn't quite so bad as it looked. It was my money, really; it came from the sale of some woodland that one of my uncles gave me when I was a child, before my mother died. Father sold the land when I was about ten, and put the money in the bank. I knew about it, and I'd ask father a good many times to let me have it, but he never would. You know what father is about money matters. He'd put it in under his name. Well, I wanted a little money dreadfully. There was a good chance—I've made it pay since, too—but father wouldn't give me any. Hannah, father never gave me a dollar to help me in business, and he's a rich man too.

Well, I don't know what possessed him, but the day I was going away he drew that money out of the bank ; he wanted to invest it somewhere. I saw it ; he was counting it over, and he had the bank-book. I asked him for it again, but he wouldn't let me have a dollar of it. Then—I never knew him to be so careless before ; I don't see how it happened—but he laid that money in a roll on the sitting-room table. I saw it when I came in to say good-by to you, and I took it, and crammed it into my pocket. All of a sudden I thought to myself, 'It's my own money, and I'll *have* it.' You were looking right at me when I took it, but I knew you'd think it was mine, I was so cool about it. You did, didn't you?"

"Yes."

"I went down to the depot, expecting every minute I'd hear father behind me, but I got off. I wrote to father after a while and owned up, though I thought he'd know I took it anyway. I never dreamed of his making any fuss about it. I didn't think he'd mention it to a soul ; and as for suspecting you—

"Father wrote me an awful letter, but he didn't say a word about that. He told me I needn't come home again. I ain't stopping there now. He must have known after they accused you, but he never said a word. He knew I liked you, too. Well, I'll clear you, I'll clear you, dear. Every soul in town shall know just what you are, and just what you've done, and then I'm going to take you away from the whole of them, out of the reach of their tongues. I'll do all I can to make it up to you, Hannah."

"Oh, go away, George, please go!"

"Hannah, what do you mean?"

"It's all over."

"Hannah!"

"I wish you'd go away; I can't bear any more."

His face turned pale and rigid as he sat watching her. "Look here," he said, slowly, "I ought to have thought— Of course I'll go right away and never come near you again. I might have known you wouldn't want a fellow that stole. I'll go, Hannah, and I won't say another word."

He rose, and was half-way to the door when he turned. "Good-by," he said.

"Don't, don't! oh, don't! George, you don't know! It's dreadful! I've got to tell you!"

Hannah was beside him, clinging to his arm. All her composure was gone. Her voice rose into a shrill clamor.

"George, George! Oh, what shall I do! what shall I do!"

"Hannah, you'll kill yourself! You mustn't!"

"I can't help it! It isn't you! it isn't you! It was right for you to take it. But it's me! it's me! Oh, what shall I do?"

"Hannah, are you crazy?"

"No; but it's all over. It wasn't true before, but it is now."

"What do you mean?"

"I stole. I did, George, I did!"

"When? You didn't either. You've been dwelling on this till you don't know what you have done."

"Yes, I do. I stole. I did!"

"What did you steal?"

"A loaf of bread."

"Hannah!"

"Martha didn't have anything for supper. Oh, what shall I do?"

"Hannah Redman, you don't mean it's come to this?"

"They wouldn't give me any work; they couldn't trust me, you know, because I'd stole. I never have given up, but now I've got to."

"When—did you have anything to—eat?"

"Yesterday. I didn't eat any of that—bread."

The young man looked at her a moment, then he led her back to her seat.

"See here, Hannah, you sit here a minute till I come back. I won't be gone long."

She sat down weakly. She suddenly felt too exhausted to speak, and leaned her head back and closed her eyes. She hardly knew when George returned.

Presently he came to her with a glass of milk. "Here, drink this, dear," he said.

He held the glass while she drank. In the midst of it she stopped and looked at him piteously.

"What is it, dear?"

"Have you been down to the store?"

"Yes."

"Do they know? Have they found it out yet?"

His tender face grew stern. "No, they hadn't. Don't you think of that again. I've paid them for the bread."

"But they ought to know I—stole it."

"No, you didn't. Hannah, never think of this again. They're paid."

"Did you tell them—I took it?"

"Yes, I told them—all that was necessary. Hannah, dear, don't ever speak of this again, or think of it. Finish your milk now; then I want you to eat some cakes I've got for you. Oh, you poor girl; it seems to me I can't live through this myself. Here I've had plenty to eat, and you—"

A week from the next Sunday Hannah wore a white dress to the meeting. It was an old muslin, but she had washed and ironed it nicely, and sewed some lace in the neck and sleeves. She had trimmed her straw bonnet with white ribbons. Everybody stared when she came up the aisle. George Arnold entered at the same time and seated himself beside her in her pew. The women rustled and whispered. John Arnold was not present to-day. The old grandfather looked across at his empty pew uneasily.

After the service, the minister, an itinerant one—this poor parish had no settled preacher—in a solemn voice requested the congregation to be seated. Then he added—he was an old man, with a certain dull impressiveness of manner—"You are requested to remain a moment. One of your number, a young man whom I this morning joined in the bands of holy wedlock, has something which he wishes to communicate to you."

There was a deathly calm. George Arnold arose. He was a tall, fair man, like his father. His yellow, curled head towered up bravely; the light from the pulpit window settled on it. He was very pale. "I wish to make a statement in the presence of this congregation," he said, in a loud, clear voice. "The lady beside me, who is now my wife, has been accused of theft from my father. The accusation was a false one. I stole the money myself. She has borne what she has had to bear from you all to shield me."

Before he had quite finished Hannah rose; she caught hold of his arm and leaned her cheek against it before them all. They sat down side by side, and waited while the congregation went out. A carriage stood before the church. The bridal couple were to leave town that day. A few stood staring at a distance as George Arnold assisted his bride into the carriage after the crowd had dispersed.

They drove straight to Hannah's house. There was an old figure waiting at the gate. Beside her stood a great pot of calla-lilies.

"You jest lift in them lilies first, afore I git in," said she, "an' be real keerful you don't break 'em. The stalks is tender."

A WAYFARING COUPLE.

A LONG row of little cheap houses stretched on each side of the narrow, dusty street. There was not a tree in the whole length of it except in front of David May's house. A slim young maple, carefully boxed in around the trunk, stood close to his gate.

These poor little houses were all alike; they had been built expressly for the operatives in the Saunders Cotton Mills. There was a little square of ground fenced in before each cottage. Some were miniature vegetable gardens. Araminta May, David's wife, had hers all planted with flowers. They were coarse and gaudy, rather than delicate; her taste ran that way. The flower garden was divided into little fantastic beds edged with cobble-stones, and the narrow footpath leading through the midst of it to the door had on each side a fence of bent willow boughs.

Some morning-glory vines were climbing up on strings towards the two front windows; Araminta's great ambition was to have them thickly screened.

"Folks can't look in an' see us eat then," she said.

They could now. Passers-by might look directly in on the little table set between the windows for tea. The six-o'clock whistle had blown, and the men and girls were coming home from the shops. They straggled along, the men in their calico shirt-sleeves, the girls in their soiled dresses, turning into this yard and that with an air of content.

Araminta had worked in the shop, too, before she was married. Afterwards, David would not let her. "His wife might do his washing and ironing and cooking," he said, "but she should not work for other people as long as he had his two hands."

Every cent that he could spare went to "rig Minty up," as he put it. He could not bear to see her in a poor gown; she dressed as punctiliously as if she had been a fine lady "against Davy comes home."

She had not a fine taste, and admired the cheaply gorgeous. To-night she had on a flimsy blue muslin with a good many flowers, and a deal of wide cotton lace. She was a handsome young woman. She had a long face, with full red lips and an exquisite florid complexion. She flushed pink easily from forehead to throat, but the pink was as fine as a rose's. She had flaxen hair, which she parted and combed straight back.

Araminta's father had been a country minister on a pitiful salary. Her mother had died first, and then her father in his little parish, when she was but a child. Since then she had shifted as best she could. She had lived around in various families, partly dependent, partly working her way, until she was eighteen. Then she came to Saundersville to work in the mills, and there she met David May, and was married to him.

Araminta had not wholly escaped the suspicions liable to attach themselves to a handsome unprotected girl in a humble position. People had said she was a pretty wild kind of a girl, with a meaning look, before she was married.

She had watched for David anxiously to-night. She had a little extra tea—a pie and some hot biscuits.

"I'm awful glad you've come," she said, when the stout, curly-headed young fellow loomed up in the doorway. "The biscuits are all gettin' cold. What made you so late; it ain't pay-night?"

"No," said David, "it's turnin'-off night."

"Now, David May, what do you mean?"

"Just what I say. It's turnin'-off night. I've got turned off."

He dropped down on a chair with that and rested his elbows on his knees and held his head in his two hands—the attitude most indicative of a person's sympathy with his own tired soul.

"Now, Davy, honest an' true, ain't you jokin'?"

"No, I ain't jokin'. Wish to the Lord I was, for your sake!"

"But what have you got turned off fur, Davy? I declare, I'm all upset. They ain't out of work, are they?"

"No; there's work enough. It's some of that Lem Wheelock's doin's. If any feller but him had been foreman, I'd ha' kept my place. He's always had a spite again' me, and I'll be hanged if I know why."

"What did they say was the reason they turned you off?"

"Didn't give me no reason. The boss jest called me into his office, an' told me they wouldn't need my services no more, an' paid me what was owin' me, an' that was jest ten dollars. I tried to talk, but he kep' on writin' in a book an' didn't seem to hear me, an' I quit when I found out I might jest as well be talkin' to a stone wall. I dunno what Wheelock's been tellin' him, and I don't care. Ef he wants me to go, I'll go. I ain't goin' to whine, and tease him fur work. I've got a little feelin', ef I ain't one of the upper crust!"

"That's so, Davy. I'd see him Down East first."

"The worst of it is, Minty, I dunno how we're going to live, or where I'll get work. It's mighty dull times now. It's a mean kind of a box I've got you into."

"Now, don't you go to talkin' like that, David May! I don't want to hear it. Git up an' wash you now, and eat your supper; the biscuits are all gettin' cold."

The poor fellow got up, threw his arms around his wife's waist, and leaned his head on his wife's shoulder. She was as tall as he.

"Oh, Minty, I didn't know but you'd be fur goin' back on me, an' blamin' me, 'cause I'd hed such bad luck. Some women do."

"I ain't some women then; but I will be, if you go to suspectin' me of such a thing again, an' if you don't hurry and wash, an' eat them biscuits before they git cold—"

"Well, mebbe we can weather it. I guess I can find some work pretty soon, an' you'll have enough to eat and wear. I guess we shall git along."

"I'd laugh if we couldn't."

A little later people passing by could look in and see the two at supper just as usual, David's calico shirt-sleeves at one end of the little white-covered table plying vigorously, and Minty's blue-draped arms at the other.

After tea they were standing out in the yard, when Minty caught a glimpse of Lemuel Wheelock, the foreman, coming. She was standing close to her husband, clinging to his arm, when he got up in front of the house; just when he had his eyes fixed full on her she even leaned her head against David's shoulder. She knew why she did, though her husband did not; she knew also why this foreman had turned him off, and this was her method of stabbing him for it.

It was effectual, too. Lemuel Wheelock, who was a handsome young man, with a thin black beard, who threw his shoulders well back when he walked, turned pale, gave a stiff nod, and went by quickly.

"Confound him!" growled David. Minty said nothing for a minute—then she went on with the talk which he had interrupted.

They formed a plan for the future which they set at once to carrying out.

Three days later, early in the morning, before any of the neighbors were up, Minty and David started forth on a hundred-mile tramp.

Coming through her little dewy garden, Minty stopped and picked an enormous bouquet of zinnias and marigolds and balsams. Then she swiftly pulled up the finest of the others by their roots.

"There," she said, "the new folks sha'n't have my flowers! They sha'n't!"

"Why, Minty!" cried David, aghast.

"I don't care. I'd pull up that maple-tree if I could, and you'd carry it."

"I'd look kinder queer startin' out on a hundred-mile tramp with a maple-tree over my shoulder," said David with a chuckle.

Minty could not help laughing. Besides her basket of flowers she carried a basket with some eatables in it. In the pocket of her blue dress were her chief treasures—her little stock of cheap jewelry, and her two keepsakes which she had for remembrances of her father and mother. These last were a Greek Testament and a tiny pincushion made of a bit of her mother's wedding-dress. Of course she could not read a word of the Greek Testament, but she kept it lovingly. She called it "father's book."

David carried the few clothes which they could not do without in a carpet-bag. He had about ten dollars in money. He had tried to persuade Minty to use it to defray her expenses by rail, while he made the journey on foot, alone, but she would not hear to it. White River, the town where they hoped to find work, was a hundred miles distant; if not successful there, they would go fifty miles farther to Waterbury, and they must save their little stock of money for food. She laughed at the idea of the journey's hurting her; it would be fun, she said.

They got out of the village into the woody road before any one was astir. Saundersville was a tiny rural manufacturing town, skirted very closely by forests. It was a cool morning, though it was midsummer; they went along the dark, dewy road gayly enough. They were not half as sad as they had thought they would be. Now they were fairly on the mountain of their affliction, they found out there were flowers on it.

They were young and strong, and walking was a pleasure. It was enough sight better than being cooped up in the shop, David said, looking ahead between the green, dewy boughs. And Minty said she was glad not to be in the house washing dishes such a splendid morning.

She even began to sing as they went along, a Sunday-school tune. The Saundersville folk sang that kind of music principally. Mr. Saunders kept a little church and Sunday-school running vigorously in his domain. David would not sing, but he listened to his wife sympathizingly. She had a strong soprano voice, and was not afraid to let it out.

They walked about twenty miles that day. They ate their dinner and supper from their basket by the roadside, and slept that night in an isolated barn, on a pile of fresh hay.

The next morning they were a little tired and stiff, but they were too young and healthy to mind it much, and they rose and went on.

That day they stopped in a village on their way and spent, cautiously, a portion of their ten dollars for food—bread and crackers. They could pick plenty of blackberries to eat with them along the road.

So they kept on. When they reached White River David could find no work there; the shops were full. There was nothing to do but go farther, to Waterbury. So far their courage had not failed them, but when they reached Waterbury and found no work there, they did not dare to look each other in the face.

They sat down disconsolately to rest on a stone wall on the edge of a pasture, a little out of the village. It was getting late in the afternoon.

"We've got to find some place or other to stay to-night," said David, moodily.

Minty said nothing. She sat staring straight ahead. There were dark hollows under her eyes.

They rose wearily after a little while, and kept on. They hoped to find a barn somewhere which would shelter them for the night. But they walked some miles farther along the country road without finding any kind of a building by the way.

At last, about sunset, they reached a cleared space and a house on the east side of the road. No one lived in it; there was no mistaking that. Its desolateness looked out of its windows as plainly as faces. Where the glass in the front windows was not broken out, it reflected the sunset in blotches of red and gold.

It was a large square building; it had never been painted, and the walls as well as the roof were shingled. The shingles were scaling off now, and a great many of them had a green film of moss on them. The front door stood open with a dreary show of hospitality.

Minty looked in wistfully, when she and David stood on the old door-stone.

"S'pose we had some folks in there waitin' for us, an' supper was ready," said she.

"Be pretty nice, wouldn't it, darlin'?"

"S'pose there were curtains to the windows, an' there was a bed made up white and clean—but there ain't no use talkin' this way. It kinder come over me, that's all."

Minty went in then, laughing. She and David explored the old house, going through all the dingy, echoing rooms. There was not much in them but old rubbish. There was a great barn, which had once sheltered many head of cattle, adjoining the house. Minty and David found a few old rusty tools in there, a heap of hay on one of the dusty scaffolds, and the very phantom of an old sulky. There it stood, tottering on its two half-spokeless wheels, which had borne it over so many of the steep New England hill-roads in its day. Its seat was gone; its covering hung in ribbons; it looked as if it would crumble to dust in a moment, if drawn out of its stall, like an old skeleton if lifted out of its coffin.

"My, what an awful lookin' old carriage," said Minty, peering at it.

"Guess I'd better hitch up, an' we'll go to ride," said David, and they both laughed merrily at the poor joke.

Back of the house had stretched the vegetable garden

and apple orchards. A great sweet apple-tree stood close to the kitchen door ; some of its branches brushed the roof. The tree had deteriorated like the house; some of its limbs were dead, and its apples were not the fair, large things that they had been. They were small and knotty. Still they were eatable, and they were just ripe now. The short grass back of the house was covered with them. The forlorn young couple gathered up some, and carried them into one of the front rooms. They sat down on a heap of hay, which David had brought in from the barn, and supped off sweet apples and crackers.

Before Minty began to eat she pulled her father's book and her mother's pincushion out of her pocket and laid them down beside her. She looked at David and laughed, and flushed pink as she did so.

"What on earth are you doin' that fur, Minty?"

She flushed pinker. "Oh, dear, I don't know; I jest took a notion—I felt kinder lonesome. I declare, Davy, I wish to gracious that I had some folks or you had. They'd be mighty handy jest now."

"That's so," said David slowly. He stopped eating, and his face took on a pitiful expression. "Oh, Minty, I did an awful mean thing marryin' you; an' you a minister's daughter, and so good-lookin'. You'd never been where you are if it hadn't been for me."

"David May, you jest quit."

"I wasn't half good enough for you—"

Minty faced him passionately; she was very white. "Now, David May, you were good enough for me, once fur all, don't you forget. You were good enough fur me! You were good enough, I'm tellin' you the truth, you were! Don't you dare to say you wa'n't again!"

9

"Why, Minty, don't look at me so, darlin', cause I won't if you feel like that; but I can't help thinkin'—"

"Don't you think it! I'll leave you if you think it!"

"Well, I won't think it. Why, Minty!" She fairly frightened him; he did not know what to think of her. But she began to eat, and was talking of something else with her old manner in a minute, and he thought no more about it.

There never was the least danger of David May's knowing anything which other people did not want him to know. There was nothing of the detective element in him. The motives underlying people's actions were to him as the geological strata beneath the surface of the earth. He simply went along through life looking at the snow or the flowers which happened to be in sight, and thinking nothing about the fire or the gold underneath them.

That night they used their heap of hay for a bed; they slept soundly on it, too. The next morning they ate more sweet apples and crackers; then David started for Bassets, a little town three miles distant, in search of work. A man in Waterbury had told him that there was a tub factory in Bassets, and he thought of it now as a forlorn hope.

Minty did not go with him. He came back about noon, bringing some eggs and a pound or so of salt pork, bought with his scanty remaining store of money, but his full, young face looked leaden.

No work in Bassets.

Minty tried to cheer him. She kindled a fire in the wide old fireplace in the kitchen; she scoured an old frying-pan which she had found in the attic, and fried pork and eggs for dinner.

But David could not eat much. His simple heart had taken to desparing more entirely from its very simplicity.

He had very little imagination, and consequently little hope, to which he could resort. He sat with his head in his hands the rest of the day. Minty scolded and vexed, but she could not rouse him.

Discouragement had developed an obstinacy in him of which he had never before seemed capable.

The next morning he was sick—chilly and feverish—and could not get up. His pitiful, helpless look at Minty was hard to be seen.

"Oh, Minty, I'm sick; I can't get up. What will you do?"

"I'll do well enough; just you lay still and not worry. You'll be better by noon."

But he was not. Minty brewed for him a tea of green peppermint leaves which she found near the house; covered him up warm to induce perspiration, and did everything that she could, yet without much effect.

As the day passed he grew no better. He did not seem violently or alarmingly ill, but the fever did not leave him, and he steadily lost strength and flesh. Their pitiable destitution pressed them harder and harder. They would have been reduced to a choice between beggary and starvation if Minty had not found a way out of the difficulty. She took it, right or wrong. She felt at the time very few scruples about the matter; she did later, but she would have done the same thing again, probably, under the same circumstances.

Two or three broad meadows away from the old house there were several cows pastured. They belonged to some farmer. Minty went there every night before the cows went home, and milked them one and another. She used an old earthen jar of a graceful shape, which she had found, for a milking-pail. She strode home with it like a guilty thing, across the fields. She brushed through the sweet fern, knee deep, with the tall jar half-poised on her right hip, carrying her strong, beautiful figure like an Eastern woman.

Minty kept thinking every day that the next day she must call on some one for assistance, have a doctor. But when the next day came David would think that he felt a little better, perhaps, and she would put it off. She had a fierce dislike of asking for charity. She thought it would be equivalent to knocking at an almshouse door, as it probably would have been. She kept all signs of the habitation of the old home resolutely from the few passers-by.

She never looked out of a window without due caution. Her greatest terror was that she should be caught stealing the milk. She used so much art in milking from one cow and another, that she hardly thought the diminution in quantity would betray her, for a while anyway. But she started at every sound on her way to and from the pasture.

She did not tell David how she got the milk. She laughed when he asked her, and said it was all right, it was a secret; when he got well he should know. He was easily enough put off; he did not trouble himself much over that or anything else before long. He grew weaker and weaker. Finally one day he lay most of the time muttering in a half-delirium. He would not move himself much unless Minty left him for a moment. Then he would call after her, "Minty, Minty, Minty," every second until she came back.

Returning from her milking expedition, she could hear him before she reached the house. His greatest fear seemed to be that she would leave him.

"You won't go off and leave me, will you, Minty?" he would say.

"Leave you? Oh, Davy, I guess I won't."

He asked her that question over and over. Her assurances only satisfied him for the moment. The delirious fear kept springing up again in his weak brain.

The next morning Minty watched the pale light coming in at the windows with a new resolution. "Somethin' has got to be done to-day," she whispered to herself. "Somethin' shall be done."

After the sun was up she tried to talk with David, and he seemed to rouse. She sat down on the floor beside him, and took his head in her lap, bending down and leaning her cheek against it.

"Davy, dear, I've got somethin' to tell you, an' I want you to listen jest a minute—"

"Oh, Minty, don't you leave me! Don't you go an' leave me!"

"No; I won't—I ain't goin' to, Davy. Leastways not fur more'n two or three minutes. See here, Davy, darlin', I've got to go and git a doctor to come and see you. I've got to go jest up here to Bassets, you know, and I needn't have to be gone—"

"Oh, Minty! Don't leave me; don't, don't, don't!"

"Oh, jest for two or three minutes; won't you let me, dear? I want to get the doctor, so he can give you some medicine to get you well. Don't you know, Davy?

"Oh, Minty, don't leave me! Oh, Minty, darlin', don't leave me; don't, don't, don't!"

She reasoned with him, and coaxed him for a long time, but it was of no use. All she could get in return was that one despairing cry, "Don't leave me!"

Finally she gave it up, and sat looking straight ahead, her beautiful face held rigid with thought. "There's somethin' got to be done," she muttered.

After a little she rose. He clutched at her dress and set up his pitiful cry again.

"There, there, dear, I ain't goin'. I ain't goin' to Bassets. I'm jest goin' to step out of the room a second. I'll leave the door open."

She ran out of the house to the barn; his cry followed her. There stood the old sulky which she and David had laughed at on the night of their arrival. She took hold of the shafts and pulled it out through the wide doors into the green yard. It was light, and she did it easily enough. She was very strong.

"I can do it," she said, with a nod of her head.

She dragged the sulky along into the road and stopped close to the front door.

Then she ran in, laughing. "Come, Davy, darlin', you're goin' to ride! The carriage is ready."

"Oh, Minty, don't leave me."

"Course I ain't goin' to leave you. I'm goin' with you. Don't you worry a bit, darlin'. Jest let me get your clothes on, an' you'll have a beautiful ride."

She got the poor fellow into his clothes, talking merrily to him all the time. Then she helped him out of the house and into the sulky. She had fixed up a bed of hay in it, and she covered him with her shawl.

He was so exhausted, and near fainting, that at first he hardly noticed anything. When she placed herself between the shafts, and began dragging him slowly out of the yard, however, he set up, from behind, a pitiful, sobbing cry:

"Oh, Minty, you ain't a draggin' me! Let me git out. I won't have it! Oh, Minty, I ain't come to this! Minty, stop—you must stop. Don't you hear me?"

She turned around and looked at him. "David May,

you jest keep still. You don't weigh no more'n a feather; it ain't nothin'. I'm only goin' to take you up to Bassets to see the doctor."

"Minty, stop!"

"Look here, Davy—if you don't lay back an' keep still, I'll—leave you."

He did lie back at that and said no more. Indeed, he was too weak to prolong the struggle. The momentary strength which the sight of Minty in the shafts had given him died away. Minty pressed along. Her pretty face was a deep pink all over; the perspiration rolled down her cheeks; her fair hair clung to her temples. It was a warm day. The flowering bushes which bordered the road were swarming with bees, and the air was full of those rasping and humming sounds which seem to be the very voices of the heat.

It was three miles to Bassets. There was not one house all the way, and the road was not much travelled. Minty did not meet any one.

After a little David seemed asleep, or in a stupor. He lay very still, at any rate, and never spoke. Every little while Minty looked around at him to see if he was safe. When she did so her face was wonderful with the love and strong patience shining through it. Those days of watching over this honest, distressed soul, whose love for her was so unquestioning, had caused all the good elements in her nature to work out a change in it. This was Minty's true flower time. Everything worthy in her was awake and astir and glowing. She, dragging her sick husband over the rough country road, like a beast of burden, was as perfect a woman as she ever would be in this world. She seemed to rise triumphant by this noble abasement from any lower level where she might have been.

She hastened along as fast as she was able. She was not conscious of any great fatigue, though occasionally she stopped to rest a moment.

She reached Bassets about noon. She drew the sulky into the yard of a large white house, the first which she came to, and knocked on the door.

"Can you—tell me—where—the doctor lives?" she asked the man who opened it.

She was leaning against the house, panting; her face was almost purple.

The man stood staring. He was old and large, with a sunburnt face and white hair.

"What in creation," said he at last, "does this mean? Who air ye, anyway? What ails *him?*" pointing at David lying back with deathly face, in the sulky.

Minty told him their pitiful little story in a few panting words. Then she asked again where the doctor lived. She felt almost as if her strength were failing her, now that the struggle was so far over.

"You don't mean to say," said the man, "that you dragged that sulky all the way here? It's a good three miles."

"Yes; it wa'n't much."

"Good Lord! Mother, come here!"

His wife and daughter, who had been peeping, came then to the door with wondering faces.

"Just look here, mother! This young woman's come all the way from the old Shaw house down below here. Dragged her sick husband in that 'ere sulky to see the doctor, she says."

"Won't you please tell me where the doctor lives?" asked poor Minty.

"What's your name?" questioned the old woman.

"May."

"They've come over a hundred mile, lookin' arter work, she says," the man went on, "an' he got sick, and they've been livin' down there, in the old Shaw house; an' she wanted to get the doctor, and he wouldn't let her leave him, so she's dragged him all the way here in the sulky."

"Does the doctor live fur from here?" asked Minty, piteously.

"He's asleep, ain't he?" said the woman.

"I guess so—I want to git to the doctor's."

"An' you dragged him all the way yourself?"

"Yes—"

All of a sudden the woman stepped forward towards Minty, and away, as it were, from her New England suspicion and curiosity.

"You poor thing," said she, with the tears streaming down her sallow cheeks, and her wide, thin mouth working, "I never heerd anythin' like it in my life!"

"You come right in, an' we'll get him in, an' then Cyrus shall go fur the doctor. Mary, you go an' git the bed in the spare room ready."

The daughter went in, wiping her eyes. She was thin and sallow, like her mother, and wore a black calico gown. Her own husband was dead, and she had come here to live with her father and mother. While she was making up the bed in the best bedroom, her tears dropped down on the white sheets.

"I would ha' done as much for *him* if I'd had any need to whilst he was alive," she sobbed to herself.

In a little while poor David May was lying comfortable in that clean, cool bed. Minty was resting; and they had sent for the doctor. He was a skilful man for a country town, and he did his best for David for his wife's sake.

The story of the journey in the sulky spread fast through Bassets. Whatever there was of sweet romance, whatever there was of sweet human pity in those simple, somewhat contracted country folks, was awakened. Poor, pretty, faulty Minty dragging the sulky with her sick husband in it, three miles to Bassets in the heat and dust, was to figure henceforth as the heroine of one of the unwritten folk-lore songs which are handed down from mother to daughter.

Everybody was kind to the poor young couple. When David began to mend, and there was more opportunity for them, there was no end to the kindly services which were proffered.

One day, when they had been there about five weeks, and David was decidedly convalescent, Mrs. Marsh, the woman who had taken them in, was standing at her door, talking to a neighbor, who had just brought over some custard for the sick man.

"Yes," said she, "he's got through the worst on't now, ef he's careful."

"You are goin' to keep 'em a while longer?"

"Keep 'em? I guess I am! I'm goin' to keep 'm till he gits real strong. She's the gratefulest thing you ever see, an' dretful afraid of makin' trouble. She keeps sayin' she guesses he's 'most well enough for 'em to be startin'. But I tell her, no; you're goin' to stay jest where you are till he's able to git out."

"I heard Sampson was goin' to let him have work in the tub factory soon's he gets well."

"Yes; he came over 'bout it. If they wa'n't tickled. They're goin' to live up-stairs in Mis' Eaton's house. They've got some things they left in the place they used to live in, an' they're goin' to send for 'em. He keeps frettin' 'cause she ain't got any more clothes here. He seems to think a sight on her ; wants her to have everythin' and be dressed up. They seem jest as happy as the day is long, now. Hark, there she is, singin'."

Minty's voice rang out from the best bedroom, clear and sweet, in a joyful psalm tune. The women stood, listening.

"I declare," said the neighbor, finally, "she's got a pretty voice, ain't she ? All I kin think of is a bluebird singin', when he first comes back in the spring."

A POETESS.

THE garden-patch at the right of the house was all a gay spangle with sweet-peas and red-flowering beans, and flanked with feathery asparagus. A woman in blue was moving about there. Another woman, in a black bonnet, stood at the front door of the house. She knocked and waited. She could not see from where she stood the blue-clad woman in the garden. The house was very close to the road, from which a tall evergreen hedge separated it, and the view to the side was in a measure cut off.

The front door was open; the woman had to reach to knock on it, as it swung into the entry. She was a small woman and quite young, with a bright alertness about her which had almost the effect of prettiness. It was to her what greenness and crispness are to a plant. She poked her little face forward, and her sharp pretty eyes took in the entry and a room at the left, of which the door stood open. The entry was small and square and unfurnished, except for a well-rubbed old card-table against the back wall. The room was full of green light from the tall hedge, and bristling with grasses and flowers and asparagus stalks.

"Betsey, you there?" called the woman. When she spoke, a yellow canary, whose cage hung beside the front door, began to chirp and twitter.

"Betsey, you there?" the woman called again. The bird's chirps came in a quick volley; then he began to trill and sing.

"She ain't there," said the woman. She turned and went out of the yard through the gap in the hedge; then she looked around. She caught sight of the blue figure in the garden. "There she is," said she.

She went around the house to the garden. She wore a gay cashmere-patterned calico dress with her mourning bonnet, and she held it carefully away from the dewy grass and vines.

The other woman did not notice her until she was close to her and said, "Good-mornin', Betsey." Then she started and turned around.

"Why, Mis' Caxton! That you?" said she.

"Yes. I've been standin' at your door for the last half-hour. I was jest goin' away when I caught sight of you out here."

In spite of her brisk speech her manner was subdued. She drew down the corners of her mouth sadly.

"I declare I'm dreadful sorry you had to stan' there so long!" said the other woman.

She set a pan partly filled with beans on the ground, wiped her hands, which were damp and green from the wet vines, on her apron, then extended her right one with a solemn and sympathetic air.

"It don't make much odds, Betsey," replied Mrs. Caxton. "I ain't got much to take up my time nowadays." She sighed heavily as she shook hands, and the other echoed her.

"We'll go right in now. I'm dreadful sorry you stood there so long," said Betsey.

"You'd better finish pickin' your beans."

"No; I wa'n't goin' to pick any more. I was jest goin' in."

"I declare, Betsey Dole, I shouldn't think you'd got enough for a cat!" said Mrs. Caxton, eying the pan.

"I've got pretty near all there is. I guess I've got more flowerin' beans than eatin' ones, anyway."

"I should think you had," said Mrs. Caxton, surveying the row of bean-poles topped with swarms of delicate red flowers. "I should think they were pretty near all flowerin' ones. Had any peas?"

"I didn't have more'n three or four messes. I guess I planted sweet-peas mostly. I don't know hardly how I happened to."

"Had any summer squash?"

"Two or three. There's some more set, if they ever get ripe. I planted some gourds. I think they look real pretty on the kitchen shelf in the winter."

"I should think you'd got a sage bed big enough for the whole town."

"Well, I have got a pretty good-sized one. I always liked them blue sage-blows. You'd better hold up your dress real careful goin' through here, Mis' Caxton, or you'll get it wet."

The two women picked their way through the dewy grass, around a corner of the hedge, and Betsey ushered her visitor into the house.

"Set right down in the rockin-chair," said she. "I'll jest carry these beans out into the kitchen."

"I should think you'd better get another pan and string 'em, or you won't get 'em done for dinner."

"Well, mebbe I will, if you'll excuse it, Mis' Caxton. The beans had ought to boil quite a while; they're pretty old."

Betsey went into the kitchen and returned with a pan and an old knife. She seated herself opposite Mrs. Caxton, and began to string and cut the beans.

"If I was in your place I shouldn't feel as if I'd got enough to boil a kettle for," said Mrs. Caxton, eying the beans. "I should 'most have thought when you didn't have any more room for a garden than you've got that you'd planted more real beans and peas instead of so many flowerin' ones. I'd rather have a good mess of green peas boiled with a piece of salt pork than all the sweet-peas you could give me. I like flowers well enough, but I never set up for a butterfly, an' I want something else to live on." She looked at Betsey with pensive superiority.

Betsey was near-sighted; she had to bend low over the beans in order to string them. She was fifty years old, but she wore her streaky light hair in curls like a young girl. The curls hung over her faded cheeks and almost concealed them. Once in a while she flung them back with a childish gesture which sat strangely upon her.

"I dare say you're in the right of it," she said, meekly.

"I know I am. You folks that write poetry wouldn't have a single thing to eat growin' if they were left alone. And that brings to mind what I come for. I've been thinkin' about it ever since—our—little Willie—left us." Mrs. Caxton's manner was suddenly full of shamefaced dramatic fervor, her eyes reddened with tears.

Betsey looked up inquiringly, throwing back her curls. Her face took on unconsciously lines of grief so like the other woman's that she looked like her for the minute.

"I thought maybe," Mrs. Caxton went on, tremulously, "you'd be willin' to—write a few lines."

"Of course I will, Mis' Caxton. I'll be glad to, if I can do 'em to suit you," Betsey said, tearfully.

"I thought jest a few—lines. You could mention how —handsome he was, and good, and I never had to punish him but once in his life, and how pleased he was with his little new suit, and what a sufferer he was, and—how we hope he is at rest—in a better land."

"I'll try, Mis' Caxton, I'll try," sobbed Betsey. The two women wept together for a few minutes.

"It seems as if—I couldn't have it so sometimes," Mrs. Caxton said, brokenly. "I keep thinkin' he's in the other —room. Every time I go back home when I've been away it's like—losin' him again. Oh, it don't seem as if I could go home and not find him there—it don't, it don't! Oh, you don't know anything about it, Betsey. You never had any children!"

"I don't s'pose I do, Mis' Caxton; I don't s'pose I do."

Presently Mrs. Caxton wiped her eyes. "I've been thinkin'," said she, keeping her mouth steady with an effort, "that it would be real pretty to have—some lines printed on some sheets of white paper with a neat black border. I'd like to send some to my folks, and one to the Perkinses in Brigham, and there's a good many others I thought would value 'em."

"I'll do jest the best I can, Mis' Caxton, an' be glad to. It's little enough anybody can do at such times."

Mrs. Caxton broke out weeping again. "Oh, it's true, it's true, Betsey!" she sobbed. "Nobody can do anything, and nothin' amounts to anything—poetry or anything else —when he's *gone*. Nothin' can bring him back. Oh, what shall I do, what shall I do?"

Mrs. Caxton dried her tears again, and arose to take

leave. "Well, I must be goin', or Wilson won't have any dinner," she said, with an effort at self-control.

"Well, I'll do jest the best I can with the poetry," said Betsey. "I'll write it this afternoon." She had set down her pan of beans and was standing beside Mrs. Caxton. She reached up and straightened her black bonnet, which had slipped backward.

"I've got to get a pin," said Mrs. Caxton, tearfully. "I can't keep it anywheres. It drags right off my head, the veil is so heavy."

Betsey went to the door with her visitor. "It's dreadful dusty, ain't it?" she remarked, in that sad, contemptuous tone with which one speaks of discomforts in the presence of affliction.

"Terrible," replied Mrs. Caxton. "I wouldn't wear my black dress in it nohow; a black bonnet is bad enough. This dress is 'most too good. It's enough to spoil everything. Well, I'm much obliged to you, Betsey, for bein' willin' to do that."

"I'll do jest the best I can, Mis' Caxton."

After Betsey had watched her visitor out of the yard she returned to the sitting-room and took up the pan of beans. She looked doubtfully at the handful of beans all nicely strung and cut up. "I declare I don't know what to do," said she. "Seems as if I should kind of relish these, but it's goin' to take some time to cook 'em, tendin' the fire an' everything, an' I'd ought to go to work on that poetry. Then, there's another thing, if I have 'em to-day, I can't to-morrow. Mebbe I shall take more comfort thinkin' about 'em. I guess I'll leave 'em over till to-morrow."

Betsey carried the pan of beans out into the kitchen and set them away in the pantry. She stood scrutinizing the shelves like a veritable Mother Hubbard. There was a plate containing three or four potatoes and a slice of cold boiled pork, and a spoonful of red jelly in a tumbler; that was all the food in sight. Betsey stooped and lifted the lid from an earthen jar on the floor. She took out two slices of bread. "There!" said she. "I'll have this bread and that jelly this noon, an' to-night I'll have a kind of dinner-supper with them potatoes warmed up with the pork. An' then I can sit right down an' go to work on that poetry."

It was scarcely eleven o'clock, and not time for dinner. Betsey returned to the sitting-room, got an old black portfolio and pen and ink out of the chimney cupboard, and seated herself to work. She meditated, and wrote one line, then another. Now and then she read aloud what she had written with a solemn intonation. She sat there thinking and writing, and the time went on. The twelve-o'clock bell rang, but she never noticed it; she had quite forgotten the bread and jelly. The long curls drooped over her cheeks; her thin yellow hand, cramped around the pen, moved slowly and fitfully over the paper. The light in the room was dim and green, like the light in an arbor, from the tall hedge before the windows. Great plumy bunches of asparagus waved over the tops of the looking-glass; a framed sampler, a steel engraving of a female head taken from some old magazine, and sheaves of dried grasses hung on or were fastened to the walls; vases and tumblers of flowers stood on the shelf and table. The air was heavy and sweet.

Betsey in this room, bending over her portfolio, looked like the very genius of gentle, old-fashioned, sentimental poetry. It seemed as if one, given the premises of herself and the room, could easily deduce what she would write, and read without seeing those lines wherein flowers rhymed sweetly with vernal bowers, home with beyond the tomb, and heaven with even.

The summer afternoon wore on. It grew warmer and closer; the air was full of the rasping babble of insects, with the cicadas shrilling over them; now and then a team passed, and a dust cloud floated over the top of the hedge; the canary at the door chirped and trilled, and Betsey wrote poor little Willie Caxton's obituary poetry.

Tears stood in her pale blue eyes; occasionally they rolled down her cheeks, and she wiped them away. She kept her handkerchief in her lap with her portfolio. When she looked away from the paper she seemed to see two childish forms in the room—one purely human, a boy clad in his little girl petticoats, with a fair chubby face; the other in a little straight white night-gown, with long, shining wings, and the same face. Betsey had not enough imagination to change the face. Little Willie Caxton's angel was still himself to her, although decked in the paraphernalia of the resurrection.

"I s'pose I can't feel about it nor write about it anything the way I could if I'd had any children of my own an' lost 'em. I s'pose it *would* have come home to me different," Betsey murmured once, sniffing. A soft color flamed up under her curls at the thought. For a second the room seemed all aslant with white wings, and smiling with the faces of children that had never been. Betsey straightened herself as if she were trying to be dignified to her inner consciousness. "That's one trouble I've been clear of, anyhow," said she; "an' I guess I can enter into her feelin's considerable."

She glanced at a great pink shell on the shelf, and remembered how she had often given it to the dead child to play with when he had been in with his mother, and how he had put it to his ear to hear the sea.

"Dear little fellow!" she sobbed, and sat awhile with her handkerchief at her face.

Betsey wrote her poem upon backs of old letters and odd scraps of paper. She found it difficult to procure enough paper for fair copies of her poems when composed; she was forced to be very economical with the first draft. Her portfolio was piled with a loose litter of written papers when she at length arose and stretched her stiff limbs. It was near sunset; men with dinner-pails were tramping past the gate, going home from their work.

Betsey laid the portfolio on the table. "There! I've wrote sixteen verses," said she, "an' I guess I've got everything in. I guess she'll think that's enough. I can copy it off nice to-morrow. I can't see to-night to do it, anyhow."

There were red spots on Betsey's cheeks; her knees were unsteady when she walked. She went into the kitchen and made a fire, and set on the tea-kettle. "I guess I won't warm up them potatoes to-night," said she; "I'll have the bread an' jelly, an' save 'em for breakfast. Somehow I don't seem to feel so much like 'em as I did, an' fried potatoes is apt to lay heavy at night."

When the kettle boiled, Betsey drank her cup of tea and soaked her slice of bread in it; then she put away her cup and saucer and plate, and went out to water her garden. The weather was so dry and hot it had to be watered every night. Betsey had to carry the water from a neighbor's well; her own was dry. Back and forth she went in the deepening twilight, her slender body strained to one side with the heavy water-pail, until the garden-mould looked dark and wet. Then she took in the canary-bird, locked up her house, and soon her light went out. Often on these summer nights Betsey went to bed without lighting a lamp at all. There was no moon, but it was a beautiful starlight night. She lay awake nearly all night, thinking of her poem. She altered several lines in her mind.

She arose early, made herself a cup of tea, and warmed over the potatoes, then sat down to copy the poem. She wrote it out on both sides of note-paper, in a neat, cramped hand. It was the middle of the afternoon before it was finished. She had been obliged to stop work and cook the beans for dinner, although she begrudged the time. When the poem was fairly copied, she rolled it neatly and tied it with a bit of black ribbon; then she made herself ready to carry it to Mrs. Caxton's.

It was a hot afternoon. Betsey went down the street in her thinnest dress—an old delaine, with delicate bunches of faded flowers on a faded green ground. There was a narrow green belt ribbon around her long waist. She wore a green barège bonnet, stiffened with rattans, scooping over her face, with her curls pushed forward over her thin cheeks in two bunches, and she carried a small green parasol with a jointed handle. Her costume was obsolete, even in the little country village where she lived. She had worn it every summer for the last twenty years. She made no more change in her attire than the old perennials in her garden. She had no money with which to buy new clothes, and the old satisfied her. She had come to regard them as being as unalterably a part of herself as her body.

Betsey went on, setting her slim, cloth-gaitered feet daintily in the hot sand of the road. She carried her roll of poetry in a black-mitted hand. She walked rather slowly. She was not very strong; there was a limp feeling in her knees; her face, under the green shade of her bonnet, was pale and moist with the heat.

She was glad to reach Mrs. Caxton's and sit down in her parlor, damp and cool and dark as twilight, for the blinds and curtains had been drawn all day. Not a breath of the fervid out-door air had penetrated it.

"Come right in this way; it's cooler than the sittin'-room," Mrs. Caxton said; and Betsey sank into the hair-cloth rocker and waved a palm-leaf fan.

Mrs. Caxton sat close to the window in the dim light, and read the poem. She took out her handkerchief and wiped her eyes as she read. "It's beautiful, beautiful," she said, tearfully, when she had finished. "It's jest as comfortin' as it can be, and you worked that in about his new suit so nice. I feel real obliged to you, Betsey, and you shall have one of the printed ones when they're done. I'm goin' to see to it right off."

Betsey flushed and smiled. It was to her as if her poem had been approved and accepted by one of the great magazines. She had the pride and self-wonderment of recognized genius. She went home buoyantly, under the wilting sun, after her call was done. When she reached home there was no one to whom she could tell her triumph, but the hot spicy breath of the evergreen hedge and the fervent sweetness of the sweet-peas seemed to greet her like the voices of friends.

She could scarcely wait for the printed poem. Mrs. Caxton brought it, and she inspected it, neatly printed in its black border. She was quite overcome with innocent pride.

"Well, I don't know but it does read pretty well," said she.

"It's beautiful," said Mrs. Caxton, fervently. "Mr. White said he never read anything any more touchin', when I carried it to him to print. I think folks are goin' to think a good deal of havin' it. I've had two dozen printed."

It was to Betsey like a large edition of a book. She had written obituary poems before, but never one had been printed in this sumptuous fashion. "I declare I think it would look pretty framed!" said she.

"Well, I don't know but it would," said Mrs. Caxton. "Anybody might have a neat little black frame, and it would look real appropriate."

"I wonder how much it would cost?" said Betsey.

After Mrs. Caxton had gone, she sat long, staring admiringly at the poem, and speculating as to the cost of a frame. "There ain't no use; I can't have it nohow, not if it don't cost more'n a quarter of a dollar," said she.

Then she put the poem away and got her supper. Nobody knew how frugal Betsey Dole's suppers and breakfasts and dinners were. Nearly all her food in the summer came from the scanty vegetables which flourished between the flowers in her garden. She ate scarcely more than her canary-bird, and sang as assiduously. Her income was almost infinitesimal: the interest at a low per cent. of a tiny sum in the village savings-bank, the remnant of her father's little hoard after his funeral expenses had been paid. Betsey had lived upon it for twenty years, and considered herself well-to-do. She had never received a cent for her poems; she had not thought of such a thing as possible. The appearance of this last in such shape was worth more to her than its words represented in as many dollars.

Betsey kept the poem pinned on the wall under the looking-glass; if any one came in, she tried with delicate hints to call attention to it. It was two weeks after she received it that the downfall of her innocent pride came.

One afternoon Mrs. Caxton called. It was raining hard. Betsey could scarcely believe it was she when she went to the door and found her standing there.

"Why, Mis' Caxton!" said she. "Ain't you wet to your skin?"

"Yes, I guess I be, pretty near. I s'pose I hadn't ought to come 'way down here in such a soak; but I went into Sarah Rogers's a minute after dinner, and something she said made me so mad, I made up my mind I'd come down here and tell you about it if I got drowned." Mrs. Caxton was out of breath; rain-drops trickled from her hair over her face; she stood in the door and shut her umbrella with a vicious shake to scatter the water from it. "I don't know what you're goin' to do with this," said she; "it's drippin'."

"I'll take it out an' put it in the kitchen sink."

"Well, I'll take off my shawl here too, and you can hang it out in the kitchen. I spread this shawl out. I thought it would keep the rain off me some. I know one thing, I'm goin' to have a waterproof if I live."

When the two women were seated in the sitting-room, Mrs. Caxton was quiet for a moment. There was a hesitating look on her face, fresh with the moist wind, with strands of wet hair clinging to the temples.

"I don't know as I had ought to tell you," she said, doubtfully.

"Why hadn't you ought to?"

"Well, I don't care; I'm goin' to, anyhow. I think you'd

ought to know, an' it ain't so bad for you as it is for me. It don't begin to be. I put considerable money into 'em. I think Mr. White was pretty high, myself."

Betsey looked scared. "What is it?" she asked, in a weak voice.

"*Sarah Rogers says that the minister told her Ida that that poetry you wrote was jest as poor as it could be, an' it was in dreadful bad taste to have it printed an' sent round that way.* What do you think of that?"

Betsey did not reply. She sat looking at Mrs. Caxton as a victim whom the first blow had not killed might look at her executioner. Her face was like a pale wedge of ice between her curls.

Mrs. Caxton went on. "Yes, she said that right to my face, word for word. An' there was something else. She said the minister said that you had never wrote anything that could be called poetry, an' it was a dreadful waste of time. I don't s'pose he thought 'twas comin' back to you. You know he goes with Ida Rogers, an' I s'pose he said it to her kind of confidential when she showed him the poetry. There! I gave Sarah Rogers one of them nice printed ones, an' she acted glad enough to have it. Bad taste! H'm! If anybody wants to say anything against that beautiful poetry, printed with that nice black border, they can. I don't care if it's the minister, or who it is. I don't care if he does write poetry himself, an' has had some printed in a magazine. Maybe his ain't quite so fine as he thinks 'tis. Maybe them magazine folks jest took his for lack of something better. I'd like to have you send that poetry there. Bad taste! I jest got right up. 'Sarah Rogers,' says I, 'I hope you won't never do anything yourself in any worse taste.' I trembled so I could hardly speak, and I made up my mind I'd come right straight over here."

Mrs. Caxton went on and on. Betsey sat listening, and saying nothing. She looked ghastly. Just before Mrs. Caxton went home she noticed it. "Why, Betsey Dole," she cried, "you look as white as a sheet. You ain't takin' it to heart as much as all that comes to, I hope. Goodness, I wish I hadn't told you!"

"I'd a good deal ruther you told me," replied Betsey, with a certain dignity. She looked at Mrs. Caxton. Her back was as stiff as if she were bound to a stake.

"Well, I thought you would," said Mrs. Caxton, uneasily; "and you're dreadful silly if you take it to heart, Betsey, that's all I've got to say. Goodness, I guess I don't, and it's full as hard on me as 'tis on you!"

Mrs. Caxton arose to go. Betsey brought her shawl and umbrella from the kitchen, and helped her off. Mrs. Caxton turned on the door-step and looked back at Betsey's white face. "Now don't go to thinkin' about it any more," said she. "I ain't goin' to. It ain't worth mindin'. Everybody knows what Sarah Rogers is. Good-by."

"Good-by, Mis' Caxton," said Betsey. She went back into the sitting-room. It was a cold rain, and the room was gloomy and chilly. She stood looking out of the window, watching the rain pelt on the hedge. The bird-cage hung at the other window. The bird watched her with his head on one side; then he begun to chirp.

Suddenly Betsey faced about and began talking. It was not as if she were talking to herself; it seemed as if she recognized some other presence in the room. "I'd like to know if it's fair," said she. "I'd like to know if you think it's fair. Had I ought to have been born with the wantin' to write poetry if I couldn't write it—had I? Had I ought to have been let to write all my life, an' not know before there wa'n't any use in it? Would it be fair if that canary-bird there, that ain't never done anything but sing, should turn out not to be singin'? Would it, I'd like to know? S'pose them sweet-peas shouldn't be smellin' the right way? I ain't been dealt with as fair as they have, I'd like to know if I have."

The bird trilled and trilled. It was as if the golden down on his throat bubbled. Betsey went across the room to a cupboard beside the chimney. On the shelves were neatly stacked newspapers and little white rolls of writing-paper. Betsey began clearing the shelves. She took out the newspapers first, got the scissors, and cut a poem neatly out of the corner of each. Then she took up the clipped poems and the white rolls in her apron, and carried them into the kitchen. She cleaned out the stove carefully, removing every trace of ashes; then she put in the papers, and set them on fire. She stood watching them as their edges curled and blackened, then leaped into flame. Her face twisted as if the fire were curling over it also. Other women might have burned their lovers' letters in agony of heart. Betsey had never had any lover, but she was burning all the love-letters that had passed between her and life. When the flames died out she got a blue china sugar-bowl from the pantry and dipped the ashes into it with one of her thin silver teaspoons; then she put on the cover and set it away in the sitting-room cupboard.

The bird, who had been silent while she was out, began chirping again. Betsey went back to the pantry and got a lump of sugar, which she stuck between the cage wires. She looked at the clock on the kitchen shelf as she went by. It was after six. "I guess I don't want any supper to-night," she muttered.

She sat down by the window again. The bird pecked at his sugar. Betsey shivered and coughed. She had coughed more or less for years. People said she had the old-fashioned consumption. She sat at the window until it was quite dark; then she went to bed in her little bedroom out of the sitting-room. She shivered so she could not hold herself upright crossing the room. She coughed a great deal in the night.

Betsey was always an early riser. She was up at five the next morning. The sun shone, but it was very cold for the season. The leaves showed white in a north wind, and the flowers looked brighter than usual, though they were bent with the rain of the day before. Betsey went out in the garden to straighten her sweet-peas.

Coming back, a neighbor passing in the street eyed her curiously. "Why, Betsey, you sick?" said she.

"No; I'm kinder chilly, that's all," replied Betsey.

But the woman went home and reported that Betsey Dole looked dreadfully, and she didn't believe she'd ever see another summer.

It was now late August. Before October it was quite generally recognized that Betsey Dole's life was nearly over. She had no relatives, and hired nurses were rare in this little village. Mrs. Caxton came voluntarily and took care of her, only going home to prepare her husband's meals. Betsey's bed was moved into the sitting-room, and the neighbors came every day to see her, and brought little delicacies. Betsey had talked very little all her life; she talked less now, and there was a reticence about her which somewhat intimidated the other women. They would look pityingly and solemnly at her, and whisper in the entry when they went out.

Betsey never complained; but she kept asking if the minister had got home. He had been called away by his mother's illness, and returned only a week before Betsey died.

He came over at once to see her. Mrs. Caxton ushered him in one afternoon.

"Here's Mr. Lang come to see you, Betsey," said she, in the tone she would have used towards a little child. She placed the rocking-chair for the minister, and was about to seat herself, when Betsey spoke:

"Would you mind goin' out in the kitchen jest a few minutes, Mis' Caxton?" said she.

Mrs. Caxton arose, and went out with an embarrassed trot. Then there was silence. The minister was a young man—a country boy who had worked his way through a country college. He was gaunt and awkward, but sturdy in his loose clothes. He had a homely, impetuous face, with a good forehead.

He looked at Betsey's gentle, wasted face, sunken in the pillow, framed by its clusters of curls; finally he began to speak in the stilted fashion, yet with a certain force by reason of his unpolished honesty, about her spiritual welfare. Betsey listened quietly; now and then she assented. She had been a church member for years. It seemed now to the young man that this elderly maiden, drawing near the end of her simple, innocent life, had indeed her lamp, which no strong winds of temptation had ever met, well trimmed and burning.

When he paused, Betsey spoke. "Will you go to the cupboard side of the chimney and bring me the blue sugar-bowl on the top shelf?" said she, feebly.

The young man stared at her a minute; then he went to the cupboard, and brought the sugar-bowl to her. He held it, and Betsey took off the lid with her weak hand. "Do you see what's in there?" said she.

"It looks like ashes."

"It's—the ashes of all—the poetry I—ever wrote."

"Why, what made you burn it, Miss Dole?"

"I found out it wa'n't worth nothin'."

The minister looked at her in a bewildered way. He began to question if she were not wandering in her mind. He did not once suspect his own connection with the matter.

Betsey fastened her eager, sunken eyes upon his face. "What I want to know is—if you'll 'tend to—havin' this—buried with me."

The minister recoiled. He thought to himself that she certainly was wandering.

"No, I ain't out of my head," said Betsey. "I know what I'm sayin'. Maybe it's queer soundin', but it's a notion I've took. If you'll—'tend to it, I shall be—much obliged. I don't know anybody else I can ask."

"Well, I'll attend to it, if you wish me to, Miss Dole," said the minister, in a serious, perplexed manner. She replaced the lid on the sugar-bowl, and left it in his hands.

"Well, I shall be much obliged if you will 'tend to it; an' now there's something else," said she.

"What is it, Miss Dole?"

She hesitated a moment. "You write poetry, don't you?"

The minister colored. "Why, yes; a little sometimes."

"It's good poetry, ain't it? They printed some in a magazine."

The minister laughed confusedly. "Well, Miss Dole, I

don't know how good poetry it may be, but they did print some in a magazine."

Betsey lay looking at him. "I never wrote none that was—good," she whispered, presently; "but I've been thinkin'—if you would jest write a few—lines about me—afterward— I've been thinkin' that—mebbe my—dyin' was goin' to make me—a good subject for—poetry, if I never wrote none. If you would jest write a few lines."

The minister stood holding the sugar-bowl; he was quite pale with bewilderment and sympathy. "I'll—do the best I can, Miss Dole," he stammered.

"I'll be much obliged," said Betsey, as if the sense of grateful obligation was immortal like herself. She smiled, and the sweetness of the smile was as evident through the drawn lines of her mouth as the old red in the leaves of a withered rose. The sun was setting; a red beam flashed softly over the top of the hedge and lay along the opposite wall; then the bird in his cage began to chirp. He chirped faster and faster until he trilled into a triumphant song.

CHRISTMAS JENNY.

The day before there had been a rain and a thaw, then in the night the wind had suddenly blown from the north, and it had grown cold. In the morning it was very clear and cold, and there was the hard glitter of ice over everything. The snow-crust had a thin coat of ice, and all the open fields shone and flashed. The tree boughs and trunks, and all the little twigs, were enamelled with ice. The roads were glare and slippery with it, and so were the door-yards. In old Jonas Carey's yard the path that sloped from the door to the well was like a frozen brook.

Quite early in the morning old Jonas Carey came out with a pail, and went down the path to the well. He went slowly and laboriously, shuffling his feet, so he should not fall. He was tall and gaunt, and one side of his body seemed to slant towards the other, he settled so much more heavily upon one foot. He was somewhat stiff and lame from rheumatism.

He reached the well in safety, hung the pail, and began pumping. He pumped with extreme slowness and steadiness; a certain expression of stolid solemnity, which his face wore, never changed.

When he had filled his pail he took it carefully from the pump spout, and started back to the house, shuffling as before. He was two thirds of the way to the door, when he came to an extremely slippery place. Just there some roots from a little cherry-tree crossed the path, and the ice made a dangerous little pitch over them.

Old Jonas lost his footing, and sat down suddenly; the water was all spilled. The house door flew open, and an old woman appeared.

"Oh, Jonas, air you hurt?" she cried, blinking wildly and terrifiedly in the brilliant light.

The old man never said a word. He sat still and looked straight before him, solemnly.

"Oh, Jonas, you ain't broke any bones, hev you?" The old woman gathered up her skirts and began to edge off the door-step, with trembling knees.

Then the old man raised his voice. "Stay where you be," he said, imperatively. "Go back into the house!"

He began to raise himself, one joint at a time, and the old woman went back into the house, and looked out of the window at him.

When old Jonas finally stood upon his feet it seemed as if he had actually constructed himself, so piecemeal his rising had been. He went back to the pump, hung the pail under the spout, and filled it. Then he started on the return with more caution than before. When he reached the dangerous place his feet flew up again, he sat down, and the water was spilled.

The old woman appeared in the door; her dim blue eyes were quite round, her delicate chin was dropped. "Oh, Jonas!"

"Go back!" cried the old man, with an imperative jerk of his head towards her, and she retreated. This time he arose more quickly, and made quite a lively shuffle back to the pump.

But when his pail was filled and he again started on the return, his caution was redoubled. He seemed to scarcely move at all. When he approached the dangerous spot his progress was hardly more perceptible than a scaly leaf-slug's. Repose almost lapped over motion. The old woman in the window watched breathlessly.

The slippery place was almost passed, the shuffle quickened a little—the old man sat down again, and the tin pail struck the ice with a clatter.

The old woman appeared. "Oh, Jonas!"

Jonas did not look at her; he sat perfectly motionless.

"Jonas, air you hurt? Do speak to me for massy sake!" Jonas did not stir.

Then the old woman let herself carefully off the step. She squatted down upon the icy path, and hitched along to Jonas. She caught hold of his arm—"Jonas, you don't feel as if any of your bones were broke, do you?" Her voice was almost sobbing, her small frame was all of a tremble.

"Go back!" said Jonas. That was all he would say. The old woman's tearful entreaties did not move him in the least. Finally she hitched herself back to the house, and took up her station in the window. Once in a while she rapped on the pane, and beckoned piteously.

But old Jonas Carey sat still. His solemn face was inscrutable. Over his head stretched the icy cherry-branches, full of the flicker and dazzle of diamonds. A woodpecker flew into the tree and began tapping at the trunk, but the ice-enamel was so hard that he could not get any food. Old Jonas sat so still that he did not mind him. A jay flew on the fence within a few feet of him; a sparrow pecked at some weeds piercing the snow-crust beside the door.

Over in the east arose the mountain, covered with frosty foliage full of silver and blue and diamond lights. The air was stinging. Old Jonas paid no attention to anything. He sat there.

The old woman ran to the door again. "Oh, Jonas, you'll freeze, settin' there!" she pleaded. "Can't you git up? Your bones ain't broke, air they?" Jonas was silent.

"Oh, Jonas, there's Christmas Jenny comin' down the road—what do you s'pose she'll think?"

Old Jonas Carey was unmoved, but his old wife eagerly watched the woman coming down the road. The woman looked oddly at a distance: like a broad green moving bush; she was dragging something green after her, too. When she came nearer one could see that she was laden with evergreen wreaths—her arms were strung with them; long sprays of ground-pine were wound around her shoulders, she carried a basket trailing with them, and holding also many little bouquets of bright-colored everlasting flowers. She dragged a sled, with a small hemlock-tree bound upon it. She came along sturdily over the slippery road. When she reached the Carey gate she stopped and looked over at Jonas. "Is he hurt?" she sang out to the old woman.

"I dunno—he's fell down three times."

Jenny came through the gate, and proceeded straight to Jonas. She left her sled in the road. She stooped, brought her basket on a level with Jonas's head, and gave him a little push with it. "What's the matter with ye?" Jonas did not wink. "Your bones ain't broke, are they?"

Jenny stood looking at him for a moment. She wore a black hood, her large face was weather-beaten, deeply tanned, and reddened. Her features were strong, but heavily cut. She made one think of those sylvan faces with features composed of bark-wrinkles and knot-holes, that one can fancy looking out of the trunks of trees. She was not an aged woman, but her hair was iron-gray, and crinkled as closely as gray moss.

Finally she turned towards the house. "I'm comin' in a minute," she said to Jonas's wife, and trod confidently up the icy steps.

"Don't you slip," said the old woman, tremulously.

"I ain't afraid of slippin'." When they were in the house she turned around on Mrs. Carey, "Don't you fuss, he ain't hurt."

"No, I don't s'pose he is. It's jest one of his tantrums. But I dunno what I am goin' to do. Oh, dear me suz, I dunno what I am goin' to do with him sometimes!"

"Leave him alone—let him set there."

"Oh, he's tipped all that water over, an' I'm afeard he'll —freeze down. Oh, dear!"

"Let him freeze! Don't you fuss, Betsey."

"I was jest goin' to git breakfast. Mis' Gill she sent us in two sassage-cakes. I was goin' to fry 'em, an' I jest asked him to go out an' draw a pail of water, so's to fill up the tea-kittle. Oh, dear!"

Jenny sat her basket in a chair, strode peremptorily out of the house, picked up the tin pail which lay on its side near Jonas, filled it at the well, and returned. She wholly ignored the old man. When she entered the door his eyes relaxed their solemn stare at vacancy, and darted a swift glance after her.

"Now fill up the kittle, an' fry the sassages," she said to Mrs. Carey.

"Oh, I'm afeard he won't git up, an' they'll be cold!

Sometimes his tantrums last a consider'ble while. You see he sot down three times, an' he's awful mad."

"I don't see who he thinks he's spitin'."

"I dunno, 'less it's Providence."

"I reckon Providence don't care much where he sets."

"Oh, Jenny, I'm dreadful afeard he'll freeze down."

"No, he won't. Put on the sassages."

Jonas's wife went about getting out the frying-pan, crooning over her complaint all the time. "He's dreadful fond of sassages," she said, when the odor of the frying sausages became apparent in the room.

"He'll smell 'em an' come in," remarked Jenny, dryly. "He knows there ain't but two cakes, an' he'll be afeard you'll give me one of 'em."

She was right. Before long the two women, taking sly peeps from the window, saw old Jonas lumberingly getting up. "Don't say nothin' to him about it when he comes in," whispered Jenny.

When the old man clumped into the kitchen, neither of the women paid any attention to him. His wife turned the sausages, and Jenny was gathering up her wreaths. Jonas let himself down into a chair, and looked at them uneasily. Jenny laid down her wreaths. "Goin' to stay to breakfast?" said the old man.

"Well, I dunno," replied Jenny. "Them sassages do smell temptin'."

All Jonas's solemnity had vanished, he looked foolish and distressed.

"Do take off your hood, Jenny," urged Betsey. "I ain't very fond of sassages myself, an' I'd jest as liv's you'd have my cake as not."

Jenny laughed broadly and good-naturedly, and began

gathering up her wreaths again. "Lor', I don't want your sassage-cake," said she. "I've had my breakfast I'm goin' down to the village to sell my wreaths."

Jonas's face lit up. "Pleasant day, ain't it?" he remarked, affably.

Jenny grew sober. "I don't think it's a very pleasant day; guess you wouldn't if you was a woodpecker or a blue-jay," she replied.

Jonas looked at her with stupid inquiry.

"They can't git no breakfast," said Jenny. "They can't git through the ice on the trees. They'll starve if there ain't a thaw pretty soon. I've got to buy 'em somethin' down to the store. I'm goin' to feed a few of 'em. I ain't goin' to see 'em dyin' in my door-yard if I can help it. I've given 'em all I could spare from my own birds this mornin'."

"It's too bad, ain't it?"

"I think it's too bad. I was goin' to buy me a new caliker dress if this freeze hadn't come, but I can't now. What it would cost will save a good many lives. Well, I've got to hurry along if I'm goin' to git back to-day."

Jenny, surrounded with her trailing masses of green, had to edge herself through the narrow doorway. She went straight to the village and peddled her wares from house to house. She had her regular customers. Every year, the week before Christmas, she came down from the mountain with her evergreens. She was popularly supposed to earn quite a sum of money in that way. In the summer she sold vegetables, but the green Christmas traffic was regarded as her legitimate business—it had given her her name among the villagers. However, the fantastic name may have arisen from the popular conception of Jenny's character. She also was considered somewhat fantastic, although there was no doubt of her sanity. In her early youth she had had an unfortunate love affair, that was supposed to have tinctured her whole life with an alien element. "Love-cracked," people called her.

"Christmas Jenny's kind of love-cracked," they said. She was Christmas Jenny in midsummer, when she came down the mountain laden with green peas and string-beans and summer squashes.

She owned a little house and a few acres of cleared land on the mountain, and in one way or another she picked up a living from it.

It was noon to-day before she had sold all her evergreens and started up the mountain road for home. She had laid in a small stock of provisions, and she carried them in the basket which had held the little bunches of life-everlasting and amaranth flowers and dried grasses.

The road wound along the base of the mountain. She had to follow it about a mile; then she struck into a cart-path which led up to the clearing where her house was.

After she passed Jonas Carey's there were no houses and no people, but she met many living things that she knew. A little field-mouse, scratching warily from cover to cover, lest his enemies should spy him, had appreciative notice from Jenny Wrayne. She turned her head at the call of a jay, and she caught a glimmer of blue through the dazzling white boughs. She saw with sympathetic eyes a woodpecker drumming on the ice-bound trunk of a tree. Now and then she scattered, with regretful sparseness, some seeds and crumbs from her parcels.

At the point where she left the road for the cart-path there was a gap in the woods, and a clear view of the village below. She stopped and looked back at it. It was quite a large village; over it hung a spraying net-work of frosty branches; the smoke arose straight up from the chimneys. Down in the village street a girl and a young man were walking, talking about her, but she did not know that.

The girl was the minister's daughter. She had just become engaged to the young man, and was walking with him in broad daylight with a kind of shamefaced pride. Whenever they met anybody she blushed, and at the same time held up her head proudly, and swung one arm with an airy motion. She chattered glibly and quite loudly, to cover her embarrassment.

"Yes," she said, in a sweet, crisp voice, "Christmas Jenny has just been to the house, and we've bought some wreaths. We're going to hang them in all the front windows. Mother didn't know as we ought to buy them of her, there's so much talk, but I don't believe a word of it, for my part."

"What talk?" asked the young man. He held himself very stiff and straight, and never turned his head when he shot swift, smiling glances at the girl's pink face.

"Why, don't you know? It's town-talk. They say she's got a lot of birds and rabbits and things shut up in cages, and half starves them; and then that little deaf-and-dumb boy, you know—they say she treats him dreadfully. They're going to look into it. Father and Deacon Little are going up there this week."

"Are they?" said the young man. He was listening to the girl's voice with a sort of rapturous attention, but he had little idea as to what she was saying. As they walked, they faced the mountain.

It was only the next day when the minister and Deacon Little made the visit. They started up a flock of sparrows that were feeding by Jenny's door; but the birds did not fly very far—they settled into a tree and watched. Jenny's house was hardly more than a weather-beaten hut, but there was a grape-vine trained over one end, and the front yard was tidy. Just before the house stood a tall pine-tree. At the rear, and on the right, stretched the remains of Jenny's last summer's garden, full of plough-ridges and glistening corn-stubble.

Jenny was not at home. The minister knocked and got no response. Finally he lifted the latch, and the two men walked in. The room seemed gloomy after the brilliant light outside; they could not see anything at first, but they could hear a loud and demonstrative squeaking and chirping and twittering that their entrance appeared to excite.

At length a small pink-and-white face cleared out of the gloom in the chimney-corner. It surveyed the visitors with no fear nor surprise, but seemingly with an innocent amiability.

"That's the little deaf-and-dumb boy," said the minister, in a subdued voice. The minister was an old man, narrow-shouldered, and clad in long-waisted and wrinkly black. Deacon Little reared himself in his sinewy leanness until his head nearly touched the low ceiling. His face was sallow and severely corrugated, but the features were handsome.

Both stood staring remorselessly at the little deaf-and-dumb boy, who looked up in their faces with an expression of delicate wonder and amusement. The little boy was dressed like a girl, in a long blue gingham pinafore. He sat in the midst of a heap of evergreens, which he had been twining into wreaths; his pretty, soft, fair hair was damp, and lay in a very flat and smooth scallop over his full white forehead.

"He looks as if he was well cared for," said Deacon Little. Both men spoke in hushed tones—it was hard for them to realize that the boy could not hear, the more so because every time their lips moved his smile deepened. He was not in the least afraid.

They moved around the room half guiltily, and surveyed everything. It was unlike any apartment that they had ever entered. It had a curious sylvan air; there were heaps of evergreens here and there, and some small green trees leaned in one corner. All around the room—hung on the walls, standing on rude shelves—were little rough cages and hutches, from which the twittering and chirping sounded. They contained forlorn little birds and rabbits and field-mice. The birds had rough feathers and small, dejected heads, one rabbit had an injured leg, one field-mouse seemed nearly dead. The men eyed them sharply. The minister drew a sigh; the deacon's handsome face looked harder. But they did not say what they thought, on account of the little deaf-and-dumb boy, whose pleasant blue eyes never left their faces. When they had made the circuit of the room, and stood again by the fireplace, he suddenly set up a cry. It was wild and inarticulate, still not wholly dissonant, and it seemed to have a meaning of its own. It united with the cries of the little caged wild creatures, and it was all like a soft clamor of eloquent appeal to the two visitors, but they could not understand it.

They stood solemn and perplexed by the fireplace. "Had we better wait till she comes?" asked the minister.

"I don't know," said Deacon Little.

Back of them arose the tall mantel-shelf. On it were a

clock and a candlestick, and regularly laid bunches of brilliant dried flowers, all ready for Jenny to put in her basket and sell.

Suddenly there was a quick scrape on the crusty snow outside, the door flew open, and Jonas Carey's wife came in. She had her shawl over her head, and she was panting for breath.

She stood before the two men, and a sudden crust of shy formality seemed to form over her. "Good-arternoon," she said, in response to their salutations.

She looked at them for a moment, and tightened her shawl-pin; then the restraint left her. "I knowed you was here," she cried, in her weak, vehement voice; "I knowed it. I've heerd the talk. I knowed somebody was goin' to come up here an' spy her out. I was in Mis' Gregg's the other day, an' her husband came home; he'd been down to the store, an' he said they were talkin' 'bout Jenny, an' sayin' she didn't treat Willy and the birds well, an' the town was goin' to look into it. I knowed you was comin' up here when I seed you go by. I told Jonas so. An' I knowed she wa'n't to home, an' there wa'n't nothin' here that could speak, an' I told Jonas I was comin'. I couldn't stan' it nohow. It's dreadful slippery. I had to go on my hands an' knees in some places, an' I've sot down twice, but I don't care. I ain't goin' to have you comin' up here to spy on Jenny, an' nobody to home that's got any tongue to speak for her."

Mrs. Carey stood before them like a ruffled and defiant bird that was frighting herself as well as them with her temerity. She palpitated all over, but there was a fierce look in her dim blue eyes.

The minister began a deprecating murmur, which the

deacon drowned. "You can speak for her all you want to, Mrs. Carey," said he. "We ain't got any objections to hearin' it. An' we didn't know but what she was home. Do you know what she does with these birds and things?"

"Does with 'em? Well, I'll tell you what she does with 'em. She picks 'em up in the woods when they're starvin' an' freezin' an' half dead, an' she brings 'em in here, an' takes care of 'em an' feeds 'em till they git well, an' then she lets 'em go again. That's what she does. You see that rabbit there? Well, he's been in a trap. Somebody wanted to kill the poor little cretur. You see that robin? Somebody fired a gun at him an' broke his wing.

"That's what she does. I dunno but it 'mounts to jest about as much as sendin' money to missionaries. I dunno but what bein' a missionary to robins an' starvin' chippies an' little deaf-an'-dumb children is jest as good as some other kinds, an' that's what she is.

"I ain't afeard to speak; I'm goin' to tell the whole story. I dunno what folks mean by talkin' about her the way they do. There, she took that little dumbie out of the poorhouse. Nobody else wanted him. He don't look as if he was abused very bad, far's I can see. She keeps him jest as nice an' neat as she can, an' he an' the birds has enough to eat, if she don't herself.

"I guess I know 'bout it. Here she is goin' without a new caliker dress, so's to git somethin' for them birds that can't git at the trees, 'cause there's so much ice on 'em.

"You can't tell me nothin'. When Jonas has one of his tantrums she can git him out of it quicker'n anybody I ever see. She ain't goin' to be talked about and spied upon if I can help it. They tell about her bein' love-cracked. H'm. I dunno what they call love-cracked. I know that Anderson fellar went off an' married another girl, when Jenny jest as much expected to have him as could be. He ought to ha' been strung up. But I know one thing—if she did git kind of twisted out of the reg'lar road of lovin', she's in another one, that's full of little dumbies an' starvin' chippies an' lame rabbits, an' she ain't love-cracked no more'n other folks."

Mrs. Carey, carried away by affection and indignation, almost spoke in poetry. Her small face glowed pink, her blue eyes were full of fire, she waved her arms under her shawl. The little meek old woman was a veritable enthusiast.

The two men looked at each other. The deacon's handsome face was as severe and grave as ever, but he waited for the minister to speak. When the minister did speak it was apologetically. He was a gentle old man, and the deacon was his mouthpiece in matters of parish discipline. If he failed him he betrayed how feeble and kindly a pipe was his own. He told Mrs. Carey that he did not doubt everything was as it should be; he apologized for their presence; he praised Christmas Jenny. Then he and the deacon retreated. They were thankful to leave that small, vociferous old woman, who seemed to be pulling herself up by her enthusiasm until she reached the air over their heads, and became so abnormal that she was frightful. Indeed, everything out of the broad, common track was a horror to these men and to many of their village fellows. Strange shadows, that their eyes could not pierce, lay upon such, and they were suspicious. The popular sentiment against Jenny Wrayne was originally the outcome of this characteristic, which was a remnant of the old New England witchcraft superstition. More than anything else, Jenny's eccentricity, her possibly uncanny deviation from the ordinary ways of life, had brought this inquiry upon her. In actual meaning, although not even in self-acknowledgment, it was a witch-hunt that went up the mountain road that December afternoon.

They hardly spoke on the way. Once the minister turned to the deacon. "I rather think there's no occasion for interference," he said, hesitatingly.

"I guess there ain't any need of it," answered the deacon.

The deacon spoke again when they had nearly reached his own house. "I guess I'll send her up a little somethin' Christmas," said he. Deacon Little was a rich man.

"Maybe it would be a good idea," returned the minister. "I'll see what I can do."

Christmas was one week from that day. On Christmas morning old Jonas Carey and his wife, dressed in their best clothes, started up the mountain road to Jenny Wrayne's. Old Jonas wore his great-coat, and had his wife's cashmere scarf wound twice around his neck. Mrs. Carey wore her long shawl and her best bonnet. They walked along quite easily. The ice was all gone now; there had been a light fall of snow the day before, but it was not shoe-deep. The snow was covered with the little tracks of Jenny's friends, the birds and the field-mice and the rabbits, in pretty zigzag lines.

Jonas Carey and his wife walked along comfortably until they reached the cart-path, then the old man's shoestring became loose, and he tripped over it. He stooped and tied it laboriously; then he went on. Pretty soon he stopped again. His wife looked back. "What's the matter?" said she.

"Shoestring untied," replied old Jonas, in a half inarticulate grunt.

"Don't you want me to tie it, Jonas?"

Jonas said nothing more; he tied viciously.

They were in sight of Jenny's house when he stopped again, and sat down on the stone wall beside the path. "Oh, Jonas, what is the matter?"

Jonas made no reply. His wife went up to him, and saw that the shoestring was loose again. "Oh, Jonas, do let me tie it; I'd just as soon as not. Sha'n't I, Jonas?"

Jonas sat there in the midst of the snowy blackberry vines, and looked straight ahead with a stony stare.

His wife began to cry. "Oh, Jonas," she pleaded, "don't you have a tantrum to-day. Sha'n't I tie it? I'll tie it real strong. Oh, Jonas!"

The old woman fluttered around the old man in his great-coat on the wall, like a distressed bird around her mate. Jenny Wrayne opened her door and looked out; then she came down the path. "What's the matter?" she asked.

"Oh, Jenny, I dunno what *to* do. He's got another—tantrum!"

"Has he fell down?"

"No; that ain't it. His shoestring's come untied three times, an' he don't like it, an' he's sot down on the wall. I dunno but he'll set there all day. Oh, dear me suz, when we'd got most to your house, an' I was jest thinkin' we'd come 'long real comfort'ble! I want to tie it for him, but he won't let me, an' I don't darse to when he sets there like that. Oh, Jonas, jest let me tie it, won't you? I'll tie it real nice an' strong, so it won't undo again."

Jenny caught hold of her arm. "Come right into the house," said she, in a hearty voice. She quite turned her back upon the figure on the wall.

"Oh, Jenny, I can't go in an' leave him a-settin' there,

I shouldn't wonder if he sot there all day. You don't know nothin' about it. Sometimes I have to stan' an' argue with him for hours afore he'll stir."

"Come right in. The turkey's most done, an' we'll set right down as soon as 'tis. It's 'bout the fattest turkey I ever see. I dunno where Deacon Little could ha' got it. The plum-puddin's all done, an' the vegetables is 'most ready to take up. Come right in, an' we'll have dinner in less than half an hour."

After the two women had entered the house the figure on the wall cast an uneasy glance at it without turning his head. He sniffed a little.

It was quite true that he could smell the roasting turkey, and the turnip and onions, out there.

In the house, Mrs. Carey laid aside her bonnet and shawl, and put them on the bed in Jenny's little bedroom. A Christmas present, a new calico dress, which Jenny had received the night before, lay on the bed also. Jenny showed it with pride. "It's that chocolate color I've always liked," said she. "I don't see what put it into their heads."

"It's real handsome," said Mrs. Carey. She had not told Jenny about her visitors; but she was not used to keeping a secret, and her possession of one gave a curious expression to her face. However, Jenny did not notice it. She hurried about preparing dinner. The stove was covered with steaming pots; the turkey in the oven could be heard sizzling. The little deaf-and-dumb boy sat in his chimney-corner, and took long sniffs. He watched Jenny, and regarded the stove in a rapture, or he examined some treasures that he held in his lap. There were picture-books and cards, and boxes of candy, and oranges. He held them all tightly gathered into his pinafore. The little caged wild things twittered sweetly and pecked at their food. Jenny laid the table with the best table-cloth and her mother's flowered china. The mountain farmers, of whom Jenny sprang, had had their little decencies and comforts, and there were china and a linen table-cloth for a Christmas dinner, poor as the house was.

Mrs. Carey kept peering uneasily out of the window at her husband on the stone wall.

"If you want him to come in you'll keep away from the window," said Jenny; and the old woman settled into a chair near the stove.

Very soon the door opened, and Jonas came in. Jenny was bending over the potato kettle, and she did not look around. "You can put his great-coat on the bed, if you've a mind to, Mrs. Carey," said she.

Jonas got out of his coat, and sat down with sober dignity; he had tied his shoestring very neatly and firmly. After a while he looked over at the little deaf-and-dumb boy, who was smiling at him, and he smiled back again.

The Careys stayed until evening. Jenny set her candle in the window to light them down the cart-path. Down in the village the minister's daughter and her betrothed were out walking to the church, where there was a Christmas-tree. It was quite dark. She clung closely to his arm, and once in a while her pink cheek brushed his sleeve. The stars were out, many of them, and more were coming. One seemed suddenly to flash out on the dark side of the mountain.

"There's Christmas Jenny's candle," said the girl. And it was Christmas Jenny's candle, but it was also something more. Like all common things, it had, and was, its own poem, and that was—a Christmas star.

A POT OF GOLD.

THE moon came up over the mountain, and suddenly the shadows of the trees grew darker and more distinct. There were four great elm-trees in the Amesbury yard. Over across the road was a cemetery; back of that flowed the river; on the opposite bank of the river arose the mountain. The mountain was wooded to its summit. There were patches of silver on it, where some of the tree-tops waved in the moonlight.

Jonas Amesbury and his mother sat on the door-step; neither of them noticed the beautiful moonlight night much. Once the old woman remarked that the moon made it as bright as day, and Jonas did not even trouble himself to assent.

Jonas looked hardly more than a boy; his curly head had the blond lightness of a baby's; his round face was smooth and delicate. He sat on the lower door-stone, resting his elbows on his knees; his mother, a dark, sallow figure, sat on the upper one. She held herself rigidly, and did not lean against the door-casing. She was very tired, but her will would not let her old bones and muscles relax. Jane Amesbury never "lopped," as she termed it. She was, in her way, a student of human nature and a philosopher. She divided women into two classes: those who "lopped" and those who did not. "I wa'n't never one of the kind that lop," she used to say, with a backward lift of her head so forcible that it seemed as if her neck muscles were made of steel, and one listened for the click, "an' I ain't never thought much of them women that do lop."

One looking at her easily realized the truth of the statement. Old as she was now, it was quite evident that Jane Amesbury had no more leaning necessity than a hardy tree over on the mountain. She required for her growth and support only a rude, stanch soil and a sky.

Her son Jonas seemed different; still, he had something of his mother's character. It was evident in a certain dignity and self-restraint with which he bore himself to-night. He was very unhappy. His mother was looking down upon him with tenderness and a kind of indignation. They had been silent for quite a while; when the moon arose it seemed a signal to them. It was with Jonas as if the shadows in his own soul deepened out, and it seemed as if his mother also saw them, for she began at once: "There ain't no use talkin' 'bout it," said she; "there ain't no sense in a fellar's settin' right down an' givin' up, 'cause he can't git one particular girl. Marryin' ain't everything there is in the world nohow, if folks do act as if 'twas. Folks act like poor fools sometimes. I guess I know."

The old woman gave her head a shake of rage and wisdom. Jonas said nothing. His face, in the moonlight, looked as fair and pretty as a girl's.

Presently his mother began again; she seemed to have a subtle ear for her son's thoughts, and to answer them like spoken arguments.

"I know she's a good-lookin' girl 'nough," said she, "an' she's smart 'nough. I dun know as there *is* anybody 'round here that quite comes up to her; but that don't make no difference. Looks ain't everything, an' smartness ain't everything. There's plenty of girls that's good 'nough, if they can't tear the airth up or set the river on fire. These dretful smart, handsome folks are just the ones that flax out sometimes. They ain't nothin' more'n Fourth of July fireworks; there's more sputter an' fizzle than anything else when you come to find out. I don't think I should give up eatin' an' sleepin', an' go round lookin' as if I'd lost my last friend, on account of one girl, when there's plenty more that would have me. There's Emma Jane Monk—"

Then the young man aroused himself. "I guess," said he, "when you see me going with Emma Jane Monk you'll know it."

"Well, you can turn up your nose at Emma Jane Monk all you want to; she's as good as Rose Tenney any day."

"Mother!"

"What is it?"

"You can talk all you want to, but it ain't going to do any good. I suppose I ain't showing much spunk about it, and I know it ain't any worse for me than for other folks, and I ain't the first one that couldn't get the one he wanted. But I can't bear it, and I ain't going to; that's all there is about it."

"What you goin' to do?" asked his mother, in a stern voice that had in it a frightened inflection.

"I don't know any more than a tree in the wind. I ain't doing anything; I'm being done with."

"Jonas Amesbury, you make me mad talkin' such stuff. I don't see where you got such notions; for my part I know you didn't git 'em from me. Rose Tenney—h'm! S'pose she does curl her hair over her forehead, an' wear her dresses all girt in round her waist, an' act so dreadful soft an' sweet! her folks ain't much, an' everybody knows it; everybody knows what old Joe Tenney is—stole all that land that belonged to his brother; everybody knowed he did it, if they couldn't prove it. I don't think Rose Tenney's got so very much to brag of nohow."

"I'd like to know what good you think it does talking that way, mother?"

"Oh, I don't s'pose it does any good. I s'pose if all Rose Tenney's relations were strung up on the gallows in a row, you'd want her just the same."

"Yes, I would," said Jonas, in a fervent tone, tossing back his head like his mother, with a defiant air. He could fancy himself wedding Rose under the shadow of her swinging relatives, and see nothing ridiculous; he was in such an intense mood that humor was entirely barred out.

"Yes, I s'pose you would; it would be just like you," returned his mother, sarcastically. Then she arose. "Well, I'm goin' in to set the bread a-risin'," said she. "I s'pose the bread might jest as well be riz, if you can't git Rose Tenney."

Jonas did not reply; he got up and went strolling off across the yard. His mother entered the house—the door opened directly into the kitchen. It was dark except for the moonlight. Jane spoke as she stepped over the threshold.

"You there?" said she.

"Yes."

"Where be yer?"

"Over here by the winder."

"Oh, yes, I see yer."

Jane stepped over to the window, where another woman was sitting, and peered out into the yard.

"He's gone out of the yard," said the sitting woman. "You don't s'pose he's goin' down there, do ye?"

"No; he headed up the other way. I see him."

Jane then sat down in a chair near the other woman, who was her unmarried sister. Her name was Elvira Slawson. Elvira was ten years younger than her sister; her blond hair was scarcely gray; she wore it in twisted loops over her ears; she was tall and thin, and her clothes were so loose that all her outlines seemed wavering; one shoulder was a little higher than the other; she had a slow, high-pitched voice.

Jane looked at her; she was in the shadow herself. "I s'pose you heard me talkin' to him, didn't ye?" she remarked.

"I heard a little on't; I couldn't help it. I was settin' right here."

"Well, I dun know what he's goin' to do. I think it's a pretty piece of work, for my part."

"You don't s'pose he'll do anything desprit, do ye?"

"Desprit?—no. If he does, I'll shake him. Desprit! I ain't got no patience with sech kind of work. Ready to pull the house down, 'bout a girl. I s'pose it's what they call—*love!* H'm! it's 'nough to make anybody sick! Love!" Jane's voice as she said "love" had a contemptuous drawl.

Elvira, with her head gently inclined to one side, looked doubtfully at her sister. Being supposed to have no acquaintance with love, she had more respect for him. "Well, I s'pose men do pretty desprit things sometimes on account of love," she said, in a shamefaced way. She was exceedingly timid about alluding to such matters before her sister.

"Desprit things! Well, I s'pose some that's poor fools

do, an' I guess it's good riddance to 'em. Folks that can't see nothin' in this world but the one sugar-plum they ain't able to git had better git out of it. *Love!*"

Jane arose; she went to the shelf and struck a match. "Goin' to mix up bread?" asked her sister.

"Yes, I s'pose so. I thought I'd have some riz biscuit in the mornin', Jonas thinks so much of 'em; but I don't s'pose he'll tech 'em even if I make 'em. He ain't eat enough to-day to feed a fly."

The light flared out; Jane bent her brows over it to see if it were trimmed squarely. Then she went into the pantry for her mixing-bowl and flour. There was now and then a click as her heels struck the floor; the floor was worn into little hillocks, and the nails frequently protruded; one could see here and there one sparkle in the lamp-light. This was an old house; the underpinning sagged in places, and the rooms were full of crooked lines; not a door or window was straight.

Elvira watched her sister mix the bread. Jane did not lose a grain of flour in the process; her knotty fingers were deft and delicate from faithful practice. She left the mixing-bowl polished quite clean when she finally deposited the dough in the pans. There was little treasure in the Amesbury house, but none would be left clinging to the sides of it. Jane had made an appendix to the decalogue to suit her own exigencies; one of the new sins was wastefulness. She did all the housework; she privately believed Elvira to be nothing of a housekeeper. Elvira knitted a great deal of lace edging, and she sold yards of it to people in the village. She also furnished a store with some. She had quite a local reputation for her knitted lace, and was looked upon somewhat in the line of an artist. It was even rumored that she devised new patterns out of her own head. Her sister gave her her board, and all the money she spent was the proceeds of her lace-making. She knitted incessantly, and always had her lace with her in a little bag. Pretty soon she drew her chair up to the table where her sister was making the bread, and drew out her knitting.

"You ain't goin' to knittin' to-night?" remarked Jane, disapprovingly.

"I'm jest goin' to make one scallop."

This lace was considered Elvira's masterpiece, being very broad and intricate. She bent over it, and knitted with a frowning forehead. The light was not very good. She wore spectacles.

"You countin'?" said Jane presently.

"No."

"I'd like to know the hull truth of it 'bout Rose Tenney."

Elvira kept her eyes on her lace. "Do you s'pose she wouldn't have him?" she queried, timidly.

"I dun know; but I do know one thing: it wa'n't her fault if she wouldn't. I know a thing or two. I've had my eyes open. If that girl don't think 'nough of Jonas I'll miss my guess. I've seen her when he was round. A girl don't light up like a rainbow when she sees a fellar comin' if there ain't somethin' in the wind. She thinks 'nough of him. Old Joe Tenney's at the bottom of it. He don't think there's quite 'nough money here. I know him. Since he's got a little money himself, everybody else that ain't got it ain't any more than the dirt under his feet. Joe Tenney always thought more of money than anything else in the world. Cheated his own brother for the sake of it. I shouldn't think he'd want to say much."

Elvira still kept her eyes upon her lace; a red flush mounted on her soft, flabby cheeks. "There didn't nobody really know he cheated him," said she.

"Yes, they did know, too, well's they wanted to. Where did the deeds for that land go to, I'd like to know? They couldn't prove nothin', 'cause they wa'n't registered, but there wa'n't no doubt 'bout it."

"I s'pose he thought that land belonged to him anyhow. You know they said he'd lent Henry consider'ble money. I guess some thought Henry'd agreed to give him them deeds, an' then backed out."

"Elvira Slawson, if you want to stan' up for old Joe Tenney, you can. I should think you was 'bout old 'nough to be off the notion of that by this time."

"I—dun know what you mean, Jane."

"I know what I mean. Well, I s'pose it's—*love.*"

Elvira said no more. She kept her meek suffused face close to her lace. It was quite true that years ago there had been a love affair between herself and Joseph Tenney, and it had come to naught. Her sister had never done twitting her with it: all the prickles in her nature seemed turned against sentiment, perhaps because of its fancied softness, which made her indignant. She had nursed Elvira faithfully through the severe illness which her disappointment had brought upon her, and then had tried a system of mental cauterization to cure the wound. Any symptoms that led her to believe the cure was not complete caused her to apply the iron anew. Now she kept glancing sharply at Elvira over her lace; her lips were compressed, her nose was elevated sarcastically. But soon her anxiety over her son drew her thoughts away from her sister.

"I don't see where he is," she said, standing in the door, after the bread was set away.

"Mebbe he's gone up to Jake Manson's."

"I don't think he has, this time of night. Oh, there he is!"

Neither of the women said anything to Jonas when he entered the kitchen, but they watched him furtively. He went across the room to the mantel-shelf and lighted a candle. "Goin' to bed?" asked his mother then.

Jonas gave an affirmative grunt. He looked as if he had been walking fast, his face was flushed, and his fair hair lay damp and flat on the temples.

Pretty soon the women heard his steps on the stairs. "It's the greatest work I ever see," said Jane. She went about and slammed to the doors and locked them; Elvira put up her lace-work. Then they went to bed in the little bedroom that opened out of the kitchen—they slept together.

A little after midnight Elvira awoke her sister—"Jane, Jane, wake up!" she whispered, fearfully. The dark seemed to loom over her and make her voice echo like a mountain. Jane did not awaken very easily, she had to speak again and shake her a little. When Jane finally aroused it was with a jerk. She sat straight up in bed. "What's the matter?" asked she, in a loud, determined voice.

"Oh, Jane, lay down again; don't be scart. I've jest had the queerest dream."

"Elvira Slawson, you don't mean to say you made all this row an' waked me up out of a sound sleep for a dream!"

"You jest wait till you hear it. You lay down an' I'll tell you what 'twas."

"I don't want to hear it, an' I ain't goin' to. I ain't goin' to listen to any such tomfoolery—wakin' me up out of a sound sleep! I thought the house was afire, or somebody was gittin' in."

"I won't take but jest a minute, Jane."

"I ain't goin' to hear it, an' that's all there is about it." Jane lay down with a thud that made the feather-bed arise in billows.

Elvira begged hard, but she would not let her tell the dream. "If you don't stop carryin' on so I'll go in the spare bedroom an' leave you alone," said she; "I ain't goin' to be broke of my rest this way."

That threat silenced Elvira. All her life she had been afraid of the dark if she were alone in it.

With daylight she began again, but Jane was obdurate. She would not hear the dream at all. She did not believe in dreams. She had always had a contempt for them, and she held the opinion that repeating them caused one to dream more.

So Elvira carried about her dream all day, like a poet his unsung song. She would have told it to Jonas, but he was away all day haying in a distant field. The Amesburys owned this small farm, but their own haying was so meagre that it was done long ago. Now Jonas was hiring out to one of the neighbors. It was a relief to his mother to have him away all day; his miserable face stirred her to keenest agony and wrath. She was utterly distressed and despairing over his misery, and furious with him that he yielded to it.

"I don't see as he looked a mite different when he came home to supper," she told Elvira that night, "and he hadn't eat half what I give him for dinner."

"I wish you'd let me tell you that dream," returned Elvira, eagerly and mysteriously.

"Elvira Slawson, if you don't quit talkin' 'bout that dream I shall go ravin' crazy. I've got enough to stan' up under without that."

The two women were preparing for bed again, and Jane took the hair-pins out of her knot of hair with a conclusive air. Her hair hanging about her face gave her a fierce, haggard look.

"Well, of course I ain't a-goin' to tell it to you if you don't want to hear it," returned Elvira, with some trace of dignity.

"Well, I don't want to hear it, an' I hope you'll remember it."

But again Jane was awakened. This time Elvira clutched her desperately. "Jane," she called, "wake up, for massy sake! *I've dreamed it again.*"

Jane sat up, took hold of her sister, and laid her down peremptorily. Elvira in her excitement had raised herself, and was bending over her. "Now," said she, "you jest listen. I'm a-goin' to lay down again, an' if you speak another word I'm a-goin' into the spare bedroom. As for bein' broke of my rest again to-night, I won't."

Elvira gave a little gasp, but she said nothing more. Soon Jane began to breathe regularly. It was three o'clock in the morning when Elvira aroused her again. This time Elvira had a firm clutch on her arm; her voice was quite loud and decisive.

"Jane!"

"What do you mean actin' so?" Jane asked. feebly. She was now quite alarmed.

"I'm a-goin' to tell you my dream. *I've dreamea it again.*"

"Well, do tell it, for massy sakes. I never see sech work."

"Jane, I've dreamed three times that I found a pot of gold in our field that joins Joe Tenney's oat field. It was under an apple-tree. I dug under it, and I found it."

"H'm!"

"It was an iron pot with a cover, like the one you boil beans in, an' it was chock-full of gold dollars."

"That all?"

"Jane, where you dream about the same thing three times, it comes true. I've always heard it did."

"I s'pose you believe it."

"I dun know as I really believe, but I've heard lots of folks say there was somethin' in it. Don't you remember how mother dreamed three times runnin' how father was goin' on a journey, before he died?"

"Well, if you want to believe sech stuff you can. I wish you'd stop talkin'. I've been broke of my rest 'bout all I want to be. I dun know but I'll go into the spare bedroom anyhow. I s'pose jest as I git fairly to sleep again you'll dream it over again an' grab me."

"Jane, don't you think it means somethin'?"

"It means I'm goin' into the spare bedroom, an' I ain't goin' to lay here talkin' 'bout it."

"Don't, Jane; I won't speak another word."

"You mind you don't, then."

Elvira kept her word. She said no more that night, nor did she the next morning. She never alluded to the dream. She assisted about the dish-washing after breakfast; then she sat down with her lace. After a while Jane went out to feed the hens. When she returned she caught a glimpse of Elvira stealing around the corner of the house. "Where you goin'?" she called.

"I ain't goin' far," answered Elvira, in a trembling voice. Jane strode after her, the hens' dough-dish in her hand. Elvira hustled along, but she soon caught up with her, and saw that she was carrying the shovel.

"Where are you going with that shovel?" asked Jane.

Suddenly Elvira faced her; she held the shovel like a staff. "*I'm—a-goin' to dig.*"

"Elvira Slawson, I never thought you was quite sech a perfect fool."

"I don't care what you say, Jane, I'm goin' to be sure that pot of gold ain't there."

"Well, you ain't goin' to dull up that new shovel diggin', nohow."

"I jest as soon take the old one."

Elvira went back and got the old shovel. Her sister sneered and argued all the way, but she paid no heed. There was on her mild face a kind of rapt expression, like a higher determination. She had gotten her revelation, however petty by comparison, Joan of Arc fashion, and was not to be turned back by banners and spears. Her mission was not to fight, but to dig, and she would dig.

She went forth with her shovel, and left Jane still talking. She did not return until noon; then her face was all flushed with the heat; she tried not to pant. There was a cup of tea and some bread and butter for dinner; they did not have a regular dinner when Jonas was not at home, and Jonas was still haying for the neighbor.

After dinner Elvira put on her sun-bonnet again.

"Then you ain't found the pot of gold yet?" remarked her sister, in a sweet, stinging voice. She had not spoken before except concerning food at the table.

"No," said Elvira, "I ain't found it yet."

"I should think you'd want to finish that lace you was workin' on some time. I should think you'd lose more money than you'll find in the wonderful pot."

"I can finish the lace to-morrow," replied Elvira, going out the door. She had left her shovel in the field. The afternoon passed, and she did not return. Jane got supper ready, and she had not come. Jane did not expect Jonas until late, and there was no one but herself at home for supper. She kept going to the road and looking. Finally she put on her sun-bonnet, and went down the road. It was not far to the field of Elvira's dream. On the farther side a stone wall divided it from Joseph Tenney's land; in the distance she could see the Tenney house —white-painted and piazzaed, a village mansion. The bars at the entrance of the field were let down; she passed through. There were five old apple-trees in the field. Around four of them were heaps of loose earth where Elvira had been digging. The fifth tree stood close to the wall that marked the Tenney land; its branches reached over it. Under this tree crouched Elvira, examining something. Her shovel lay beside her on the ground. Jane approached stealthily. Just as she reached the tree she heard a quick rustle on the other side of the wall; she looked, and saw Joseph Tenney's face through branches of pink dog-bane and over masses of poison-ivy. It was a handsome old face, clean-shaven and blue-eyed, but it was deathly pale. Elvira saw him too. She and Jane looked at him, and he looked at them; then he turned about and went homeward across the wet field, with a step like a slow march. If it was a retreat, it was a dignified one.

The minute Joseph Tenney went away, Elvira sprang up

and grasped the shovel. Jane peered around her. "What you got there?" she asked. Then she repeated the question in an excited tone: "Why, what is it? what have you found?" She had seen a small iron-bound chest, with loam clinging to it; it was open, and overflowing with unfolded papers. She stepped forward, but Elvira was before her in the path. She held the shovel uplifted. "*Don't you go near it!*"

"Course I'm goin' near it. I'd like to know what you mean; I guess I've got jest as good a right to know what 'tis as you have. I should laugh."

"*If you come one step nearer I'll kill you!*" Elvira's eyes were gleaming; there seemed to be sharp lights like steel in them; her face was white and resolute.

Jane started back: she was frightened. "Well, you can keep your old box if you want to," said she. Then she went off across the field. Her sun-bonnet was tilted until it looked of itself aggressive and rampant; she never turned around.

She had not been home long when Elvira returned, leaning upon the shovel. She could scarcely walk, she was so exhausted. When she sat down at the supper-table she turned faint; she laid her head down on the table with a low groan. Jane sprang and brought some water. "It's the greatest piece of work I ever did see," she said, bathing her sister's forehead.

Elvira began to weep. "Oh, Jane, I didn't mean to say such a dreadful thing to you!" she sobbed, weakly. "But I couldn't show it to you, nohow; I couldn't."

"We won't say nothin' more 'bout it," said Jane, shortly. "You'll be sick next. I don't care nothin' 'bout the old box."

After Elvira had had her tea, Jane made her go to bed. She said nothing about the matter to Jonas when he returned. She thought he seemed more depressed than ever.

The next day, in the afternoon, Jane went down to the store for a little shopping. She had a plan to buy some gray flannel and make a nice shirt for Jonas to do haying in. She thought that might perhaps please him and cheer him a little. She was gone an hour. When she returned she found Elvira sitting on the door-step knitting her lace. There was a grape-vine around the door, and some of the light green sprays hung down over Elvira's head. Her face, bent over her lace-work, looked fair and peaceful. Her old muslin dress fell around her in soft folds. She was sixty years old, but she looked maidenly. When Jane stood before her she smiled up at her. Jane sank down on the door-step. "It's a dreadful hot day," she sighed. She eyed Elvira sharply. She felt irascible, and as if she must let go her tongue. Her face was glossy with perspiration, her hands were black from her cotton gloves. She suspected that the flannel was a poor bargain. She eyed Elvira a minute, then she spoke. "There wa'n't no need of your bein' so mighty private 'bout that box. I knowed well 'nough what 'twas all the time."

Elvira dropped the lace and looked at her.

"Mebbe you don't b'lieve it. Well, I'll tell you what 'twas: it was *them deeds.*"

Elvira was trembling violently. "Well, there ain't no harm in it if it was."

"Mebbe there ain't; but that's what was in that box—*them deeds.*"

"His brother's dead now, an' they're his anyway. You can't do nothin'."

"Oh, I ain't goin' to do nothin'. I wouldn't stir a step to tell it to a livin' soul. You needn't worry 'bout that. I ain't afeared but he'll git punishment 'nough some way. I sha'n't do nothin' to bring it on him."

Elvira looked fixedly at her sister; her soft, drawling voice became quite firm. "Jane, he didn't do nothin' wrong 'bout that. He's told me all 'bout it."

"Told you 'bout it? When?"

"Just now—this afternoon."

"Has Joe Tenney been here?"

"Yes."

"Come over 'cause he was scart, I s'pose."

"No, he didn't. He was goin' by, and I called him in. I wanted to tell him where I put it."

"Where did you put it?"

"Under the stone wall, on his side. He told me all 'bout it; jest how it was."

"I'd like to know how he 'counted for hidin' the deeds."

"I can't tell you; I said I wouldn't; but he wa'n't one mite to blame."

"Well, mebbe you believe it."

"Course I believe it."

Jane surveyed her blackened hands. Her right knee ached; she was rheumatic. "P'rhaps he'll have you yet, if you stick up for him so," said she.

Elvira quivered and shrank; her eyes suddenly looked red and weak. "Jane, you know I'm past all that. There ain't no call for you to say sech things as that. Sech a thing ain't never entered into his head. He's been married to a real nice woman, an' he ain't thought of me once a year. 'Twa'n't ever much to him anyway; he wa'n't nothin' but a boy. He don't want me, an' I wouldn't have him if he did. I ain't no fit person for him. He can git somebody that's younger an' smarter if he wants anybody. I ain't nothin' to be married, an' I know it well 'nough."

"You can talk that way all you want to; you'd have him fast enough if you had the chance."

Elvira looked quite solemnly at her sister. "Look a-here, Jane," said she, "mebbe you dun know jest what I mean; but it seems to me as if bein' sure that anybody was all right an' honest was the completest kind of bein' married that anybody could have."

Jane stared at her for a moment; then she looked away; she did not say any more.

Elvira knitted for a few minutes; then she looked up. "I ruther guess," said she, "that it will come out all right 'bout Jonas an' Rose."

"What do you mean?"

"We talked it over some. I guess he thought Jonas hadn't got much, an' there wa'n't much sense in it, in the first place, an' he told Rose she's got to give him up; but I shouldn't wonder if he was kinder thinkin' better of it."

"S'pose he's afraid we'll tell if he don't."

"No, that ain't it. If you knew what I know you wouldn't say so."

"Well, I dun know what you know, but you've got more faith in him than I have."

Elvira's face was lifted; she looked past her sister with an expression as if she were looking at a shrine. "I *know* Joe Tenney is a good man," said she.

The next day Jonas was at home working in the garden. In the afternoon a neighbor drove into the yard and called to him. He had brought a letter to him from the post-office.

Jane was peeping curiously from the window. "What is it?" she called out, after the neighbor had driven away.

Jonas stood out in the yard staring at the letter. "Oh, nothing much," he answered. But smiles were playing all over his face. He went back to the garden, and whistled as he worked.

After tea he went up-stairs, and was gone quite a while. "I believe he's goin' somewhere," Jane said to Elvira. "He washed him real particular, an' he's shaved him. I don't believe but he's goin' down there."

When Jonas came down-stairs he had on his best suit; his curly hair was damp and trained in careful locks over his smooth young forehead; his cheeks were fresh and rosy; he held his neck stiffly in his clean collar and white necktie.

He stood in the kitchen and brushed his hat carefully. His mother and aunt were in the sitting-room, and he stepped softly, hoping they would not come out; but his mother looked out into the kitchen. "Where you goin'?" she inquired.

Jonas blushed beautifully like a girl. Then he laughed. "Oh, I ain't goin' far," he replied, putting on his hat and passing out under the grape-vine.

Jane and Elvira sat up until he returned, although it was quite late. They heard his step out in the yard, and were alert when he came in. He was radiant. He stood in the door looking at them and smiling. "Well," said his mother.

"I guess it's all right," said Jonas. "I shouldn't wonder if one of these days you had a daughter." His face was all pink and glowing, his yellow hair was dry, and the fluffy curls stood out around his forehead and caught the light. Elvira began to cry. His mother laughed and frowned together.

"Well, I hope you'll behave yourself an' eat somethin' now," said she.

After he had gone up-stairs she went out into the kitchen to mix bread. "I guess I'll have some riz biscuit for breakfast," she said to Elvira. "He didn't eat none of them others, but I s'pose he'll eat these fast 'nough. It beats me, but I s'pose it's—*love.*" She tried to say "love" as if it were a clod of mud, but in spite of herself she said it as if it were a jewel.

THE SCENT OF THE ROSES.

CLARISSA MAY's kitchen table was heaped with rose leaves. She was filling a large brown jar with layers of rose leaves and salt. She sprinkled in various spices too, then sniffed at the mixture daintily.

"Needs a little more cinnamon," she murmured.

"I wish you'd let the cinnamon alone," said a quick, sweet voice—"the cinnamon, and the rose leaves, and the salt, and the whole of it. I'd like to fling it into the fire."

"Don't talk so, Anne."

Anne stood in the door. She had just come down from her chamber. She was all ready to go to the picnic. She wore a broad-brimmed white straw hat, trimmed with fine pink flowers. Her ruffled, pink-flowered muslin gown fluttered crisply. She had pinned some pink rose-buds at her throat.

Anne and Clarissa were wonderfully alike, but the comparison would have been less derogatory for Clarissa had they been different. The resemblance brought the regret and humiliation of loss to her. Anne showed what Clarissa had been. She was the rose of this spring, her sister was one of last. If both of them had not been roses, the last year's flower would not have seemed so forlorn.

Clarissa's dull blond hair was brushed smoothly around

her ears; Anne's was crinkled, and there were gold lights in it. Clarissa's skin was tintless and faintly lined; her sister's was warm and rosy and smooth. Clarissa's lips were thin; Anne's, full and red. One's figure showed angles; the other's, curves.

Clarissa, replying with her mild, deprecating voice, gazed admiringly at her sister. "You look real nice," she added.

"Sometimes I don't care whether I look nice or not. You do make me so out of patience!"

"Why, Anne, how you talk!"

"I don't care—you do. The idea of you shutting yourself up here, packing a mess of rose leaves into a jar! There isn't any sense in it."

"You know I'd rather stay at home."

"I don't care if you had. It's real nice for me going alone!"

"Ellen Pierson's going, isn't she?"

"I don't care if she is. Sometimes anybody 'd like their own sister."

"I feel as if I was so much older."

"Older! You're not any older than dozens of girls that go all the time. You're not any older than Addie Leach or Abby Dutton; and I guess they'd be mad enough if anybody was to tell them they were too old to go."

"There's a lock of hair loose. Come round here and let me fix it."

"I don't care if it is," said Anne. But she stepped over to her sister, nevertheless, and Clarissa tucked up the golden lock carefully.

"P'rhaps I'll go next time," said she, appeasingly. "All is, I don't feel much like it, you know. People don't, I suppose, as they grow older."

"If they get up a party to go on West Mountain next week, will you go?"

"I'll see about it."

"I'll crimp your hair, and we'll fix over your blue dress."

"You'll be late, if you don't run along."

"Do I look all right?"

"Yes. I guess your hair'll stay up now."

After Anne had danced out with a crisp swish of muslin skirts, Clarissa went on with her work. She gathered up the soft rose leaves with her little thin veiny hands, and laid them in the jar with the greatest care.

She was soon interrupted again, however. "Oh, here you are!" said another voice. There was a contemptuous inflection in it. A tall, pale woman stood in the door. She held out a package of letters and a little white box stiffly in one hand.

"Oh, is it you, Aunt Joanna?"

"Yes, it's me. Why ain't you gone to the picnic?"

"I didn't feel like it."

"Didn't feel like it! I s'pose you felt more like putterin' over rose leaves. Clarissa May, I b'lieve you're jest about a fool."

"I don't know what you mean." Clarissa glanced at the letters, and her hands trembled.

"Yes, you do know what I mean. I came in the front way, an' went up-stairs. I wanted a piece of brown cambric to line my sleeves, an' I thought I'd see if you hadn't got any. An' I found these things in your bottom bureau drawer, tucked away in the corner out of sight. I'd like to know why you've kept these old letters of Gilman Lane's so dreadful choice for all this time. They were wrote much as ten year ago, some of 'em."

"Aunt Joanna, give me those letters, please."

Clarissa trembled so she could scarcely speak. She felt as if all the light in the world was shining on her heart and showing it forth pitilessly, dispelling all its innocent shadows, which had seemed like guilty ones to her.

"I never see such a mess of nonsense in my life: all 'darling' an' 'dear.' It's enough to make anybody sick."

"Aunt Joanna, you haven't read them?"

"I guess I have read 'em, every line. I rather think I had a right to, as long as you're my sister's daughter. I s'pose he give you this breast-pin too, eh?"

"Aunt Joanna!"

"You needn't look so toppin'. When you've been doin' the way you have late years, never stirrin' out of the house except to meetin', an' actin' as if you'd give up the world, it's about time you was looked out after. Now I jest want to know if Gilman Lane give you the mitten, an' if that's what ails you?"

"Aunt Joanna, if you'll give me those letters—"

"If he has, he's a mean scamp, an' you're an awful fool, that's all I've got to say. Before I'd spend my whole life frettin' over one feller!"

"Aunt Joanna, you haven't any right to come here talking to me so."

"I guess I've got as good a right as anybody. I guess you won't find anybody that thinks much more of you, or is more interested in you, than me. Clarissa May, what I want to know is this—was you engaged to Gilman Lane?"

"No," said Clarissa, shortly. Then she turned her face obstinately away, and went to work on her rose leaves again, and would not speak another word. Her aunt questioned and reproved a while longer; then finding that she could get no further response, threw the letters and box down on the table, and left.

"If I had such soft letters lying around I'd burn 'em. I wouldn't leave 'em where folks could get 'em," said she. She turned around as she went out of the door. "I took that piece of brown cambric you had in your blue box, but I don' know as it's enough."

Clarissa had been intending to use the cambric herself, but she said not a word. After her aunt had gone she carried the letters up-stairs, and put them in their old place; then returned to her work.

She filled the jar quite full, then tidied up her kitchen. When the noon bells were ringing, her Aunt Joanna appeared again. She had a covered plate in her hand. She had brought over some warm dinner. Clarissa thanked her, and took it. Neither of the women alluded to the letters. But the niece looked after her aunt as she went out of the yard, and if she could have smitten her with a total loss of memory, she would have done it in her shame and distress.

Clarissa May knew every line of those old letters by heart. She knew whereabouts the lines stood on the pages, and the words in the lines. The few fond adjectives shone out like jewels among them. Now she thought them all over, she recounted one after another, and she said to herself, "Aunt Joanna has seen this, and this."

She set away the dinner untasted, put on her afternoon dress, and sat down with her sewing at the sitting-room window.

Anne found her there when she returned from the picnic. Anne had lost a little of her crisp daintiness of the morning. Her yellow hair was tumbled, her cheeks were hot, and her muslin dress was crumpled.

She sat down in the first chair with a sigh. "Oh," said she, "I'm glad to get in where it's cool! It's terrible out in the sun."

She looked around the room and at her sister approvingly. There were a certain patience and tranquillity about Clarissa, as she sat there sewing, which were cool and refreshing of themselves.

"You look real cool and comfortable," said Anne.

Clarissa had on an old-fashioned cotton gown of a mixed green-and-white pattern, which suited her soft faded face. This cool old summer-gown had served her mother before her. The daughter wore it with very little alteration in the straight full skirt and long prim body. It came out of its winter seclusion every June and seemed as if it would never be worn out. Clarissa regarded it with gratitude and thankfulness. She wanted Anne to have all the new summer dresses.

The sisters had their small income of one hundred and fifty dollars besides their house. This one hundred and fifty, eked out with a little sewing which Clarissa did, bought their food and clothes. Clarissa was a good manager, she made a little go so far, and she was very careful. There was a good deal of fine darning on the sitting-room carpet, but it took close scrutiny to see it among those faded, whitish-drab scrolls. The room was sweet with roses—living ones, which grew close to the open windows, and dead ones, which lay conserved with salt and spices in Clarissa's jars. She had converted every unused dish in the house into a receptacle for her rose leaves. Old china teapots stood about, and sugar bowls, and earthen jars, all exhaling spicy sweetness. They were in every room in the house. The amusements which life held for Clarissa seemed to be concentrated into this one gentle, erratic one of conserving rose leaves. And the amusement was of such long standing that it was almost like a duty to her. It is doubtful if she did not unconsciously think it wrong to let a rose leaf entirely perish, with all its sweetness, while she could save it.

Years ago Gilman Lane had taught her how to make her first *pot-pourri*. "You ought to save all those roses," he had said one far-off summer day. "My Aunt Celia packs 'em in a jar with salt. I'll show you how."

The two had packed a little blue ginger jar with those old rose leaves. It stood on the shelf in the best parlor now, with the same ones in it.

Something stronger than any rose fragrance floated from it to Clarissa every time she entered the room. It was the fragrance of the old memory, which was better conserved than the rose leaves, and formed the lasting element of that first *pot-pourri*.

"I should think you'd fill up that jar new," Anne said often. She had no sense for that wonderful sweetness which her elder sister got from it.

Anne sat still for quite a while to-day. She did not talk as she usually did on a return from a merrymaking. She leaned her head back in her chair and stared at the opposite wall. There was a thoughtful look in her eyes, but her mouth was half smiling.

"Did you have a good time?" Clarissa asked, finally.

"Real good," Anne said. Then she hesitated. Her conscious smile grew more distinct; the red on her cheeks deepened. "You used to know Gilman Lane, didn't you, Clarissa?" she went on. "Why, what is the matter?"

"Nothing."

"Yes there is, too; you're awful white. Oh, Clarissa, don't you feel well?"

"Just as well as I ever did. Go on. What were you saying? Oh, about Gilman Lane."

"He was there, you know. He's got back from California, where he's been ten years. I didn't remember him. I was nothing but a little girl when he went away, anyhow. You used to know him, didn't you?"

"Yes, some."

"He's real handsome. Ellen introduced him to me; he's a sort of a cousin of hers, you know. She says he's splendid. He's older than I am. Why, didn't he go to school with you, Clarissa?"

"Yes, I believe he did."

"Why, it seems to me I remember his coming here sometimes, now I think of it. Didn't he used to?"

"Yes, he used to run in once in a while, I guess."

"I declare, I do remember it; but I never would have known him. He's splendid-looking."

Anne rose and took off her bonnet slowly. "How soon are you going to have tea, Clarissa?"

"We'll have it now, if you want it."

"Well, I don't know but we'd better, and get it out of the way." Anne stood laughing and fingering her bonnet strings. "To tell you the truth, I shouldn't wonder a bit if he was up here to-night. What is the matter? I know you're sick, Clarissa."

"No, I ain't. I guess I'd better go and get tea right away, then."

"It was a great joke on the other girls, you know. They were all teasing Ellen to introduce them, but he never looked at one of them. P'rhaps he won't come; but I shouldn't be a bit surprised."

Gilman Lane did come. His tall, muscular figure passed

at dusk that night between the descendants of those old roses, up to the front-door porch, which was overgrown with them.

Anne answered his knock. She was aglow with modest delight. She looked up in his face with innocent admiration, which he was foolish not to see. No wonder that this man outshone the gentle village boys in her eyes! Gilman Lane had always been handsome. He was roughened and browned now by his California life, but that only accentuated his beauty to a country girl like Anne, who thought naturally of men as antipodes of flowers and women.

"Good-evening, Mr. Lane," said she, primly, her cheeks pink, her eyes shyly radiant. "Won't you walk in?"

Clarissa, up in her room, heard the knock, the opening door in response, and the firm, manly tread across the entry floor. Then she heard the murmur of voices in the best parlor. She sat on the edge of her little bed, listening. She was rigid; her hands were cold as ice.

In a half-hour or so she heard Anne's step on the stairs, and rose hurriedly. She was lighting a candle when her sister entered.

"Come down-stairs," Anne whispered, "he wants to see you."

"I can't. I was just going over to Aunt Joanna's."

"Come along."

"He doesn't want to see me."

"Yes, he does. He asked if you were at home. He said he used to know you, and he would like to see you. Come along down. If you don't, he'll think you don't want him to come here, or something."

Clarissa, following her imperious young sister down-stairs, went weakly, like an old woman; but Anne, in her joyful impetuosity, never noticed it.

Lane rose as the two entered the parlor, and came across the room. He stumbled over a mat in his progress, and colored. He always managed his great frame a little clumsily.

"Well, how do you do, Clarissa?" said he. His voice was loud and hearty, with a little hesitation in it.

"How do you do, Gilman?" It was that freedom of old days lapsed into formality which is the most chilling of all.

They shook hands; then seated themselves. Clarissa was mute. She felt herself trembling, and wondered if he saw it. He did not; he was thinking to himself how very cool and stiff she was.

He tried to make some conversation. "You're changed some, Clarissa, like all the rest of us," he said, laughing awkwardly. There was a real flush on his brown face.

"I suppose I have," said Clarissa, delicate and pale and outwardly composed. She smiled faintly in his direction.

"I guess you're a little thinner than you used to be, and you haven't got quite so much color. You're well, aren't you?"

There was an odd tone in his voice then that made Anne stare wonderingly at him.

"Very well, thank you," Clarissa said.

"It was a good deal of a joke on me, but I declare when I first saw your sister to-day I thought it was you. She looks just the way you used to, doesn't she?"

"Everybody says she does."

"She does, sure enough. Why didn't you go to the picnic to-day, Clarissa?"

"I don't go out a great deal."

"She'd rather stay in the house and fill old sugar bowls and jars with rose leaves," Anne interrupted, with laughing pettishness. "I've been telling him about it."

"I noticed it the minute I came into the house," said Lane. "I wondered what it was that smelt so sweet."

"Good reason why," laughed Anne; "there are four things full of rose leaves in here, besides that blue ginger-jar on the shelf. They're old in that, and don't smell much. Why don't you fill that one new, Clarissa?"

Lane looked at it gravely. "You ought to," said he; "that's a real pretty jar."

He had forgotten all about it. Whatever consciousness his heart held of those old days did not include that. His man's memory could not keep such small precious things.

"I thought I had about enough," said Clarissa, trying to speak easily. She looked over at the jar. For a moment it seemed more valuable to her than the man who had forgotten it and its storied sweetness. "It's all I've got left of anything," flashed through her mind. She wanted to seize it and cry over it. The forgetting and slighting this poor little jar made it harder for her to control herself. She could scarcely keep the tears back. But no one would have guessed it as she sat there pale and slender and prim.

She excused herself before long. She had to go over to her aunt Joanna's, she said, and pleaded some housewifely errand.

Joanna Emmons was a widow. She kept house with her daughter, also a widow, and two unmarried sons.

The family were all in bed, but the doors were never locked. Clarissa went straight in, and groped her way across the dusky kitchen to her aunt's bedroom door.

"Aunt Joanna!" she called, softly.

"Who is it?" said her aunt, sitting up in bed suddenly. She had not yet fallen asleep.

"It's Clarissa. Say, Aunt Joanna—"

"What are you over here for this time of night? Anne ain't sick, is she?"

"No. I wanted to see you a minute. Aunt Joanna, I wanted to tell you something, and I mean it. It's—about—those letters. If you ever tell Anne or anybody else anything about them, I'll go away somewhere where you'll never see me again, nor any one else either."

"Clarissa May, what do you mean?"

"What I say. You've got to promise me you won't."

"'Tain't very likely I'm goin' all round town tellin' what a fool my sister's daughter made of herself."

"Aunt Joanna, you've got to promise me."

"Clarissa May, let go of my hands! You're crazy. You scare me 'most to death!"

"Promise."

"Well, I'll promise. I won't speak of 'em to a soul. There!"

"Then I'll go home. Don't you forget."

"Clarissa, come back here!" her aunt called after her, as she sped across the kitchen; but she was gone.

Anne was in the sitting-room when she reached home. "He went right after you did," said she, smiling consciously. "I don't think you treated him very well, Clarissa."

"I don't see why," said Clarissa, in a timid way.

"You acted as stiff as a poker. He thought it was awful funny that you didn't go out any more. You've got to go up West Mountain next week, anyhow."

Poor Clarissa went. She dragged herself wearily up those steep inclines, trying all the time to smile with the rest of the merry party. When they reached the summit her face was damp and pale with the heat; her lustreless hair clung close to her forehead. Anne was all rosy and glowing. Gilman Lane was at her side all day. Several times he tried to talk with Clarissa, but she avoided him, keeping close to some of the older young women, her mates.

"Gilman Lane is dead in love with Anne May," she overheard one say, with a furtive glance at her. Some of them remembered that years ago there had been a similar report in connection with the older sister.

"He's perfectly splendid," Anne said that night. "Why don't you say more to him, Clarissa? I'm afraid he'll think you don't want him to come."

So the next time that Gilman called, Clarissa made an effort to be cordial and talkative. She also remained in the room a little longer.

The summer passed, the autumn, and the winter; then the spring came again. Gilman Lane still called nearly every week at the May's.

People said, "Gilman Lane is going with Anne." Still he hardly fulfilled, in their opinions, all the conditions of courtship. He did not come regularly on Sunday evenings, neither did he remain late. Clarissa always saw him during a few minutes of every call. Anne insisted upon it.

"He acts just as if he thought you didn't want him to come and see me, if you don't," said she. "He said once he guessed my sister didn't like to have him calling so often."

Clarissa did not have a doubt as to how it would all end. She was certain that Gilman was fond of Anne. She thought also that her sister liked him, although she had her pretty, smart way about it, as she did about everything else, and laughed rather than sighed.

So Clarissa in her patient certainty overlooked it all. There was one thing which she dreaded: that was any allusion to the past. She had a constant fear lest she should chance to see Gilman when her sister was not there. Several times she did not answer his knock when Anne was away.

Finally the roses were in blossom again. Clarissa's bushes were wonderful this year. The front yard was full of them. The vegetable garden behind the house had a broad walk edged with them, too.

Clarissa went at her old work again. She moved among the rose-trees, a prim, delicate figure, in her old green-and-white gown, and cut every loose rose carefully. She was bent, in her graceful parsimoniousness, on saving all that she could of the sweetness of the world; no matter how poorly she might live herself, her delight in this would not forsake her. She had lost love and youth and beauty, but she still got a little comfort out of her unselfishness and her roses. One is not entirely desolate while one can follow his instincts.

Anne laughed at her. "She's gone to filling jars for the neighbors this year," said Anne. "She filled one for Mrs. Lamson yesterday." She and Gilman were in the parlor that afternoon. Gilman laughed. Then he looked out of the window soberly. Clarissa was in the front yard tending her roses.

"It's real good of her," said he.

"Of course it is. Clarissa never does anything that isn't good, but she is so funny."

The next day Gilman came over with a great bunch of roses from his brother's garden. They were a different variety from any of Clarissa's, and very sweet.

The two sisters were in the garden behind the house. He hunted about until he found them. He held out the roses awkwardly to Clarissa.

"I thought maybe you'd like 'em," said he. "I guess they're different from yours."

"You haven't got any like them, have you, Clarissa?" said Anne, eagerly. "My! I never saw any so sweet."

Clarissa thanked him. "I haven't got any like them," said she. Her voice was a little unsteady.

Presently she carried the roses into the house. Gilman turned to Anne. "Look here," said he, "I want to ask you something."

Anne glanced at him. Then she turned her head so that he could barely see the pink curve of one cheek. She began pulling some roses busily. "I guess I'll pick some to put in the parlor vases," said she. "What is it you wanted to ask?"

"I want to know—I've been coming here pretty near a whole year, and I don't seem to be a bit nearer finding out anything than I was when I started. Now I'm going to ask you point-blank."

"Oh, Gilman!" Anne murmured. She moved a little farther from him, then she came back. She dropped some of her roses.

"I don't see as I can ask anybody but you. I can't see her alone a minute, no matter how hard I try. Oh, Anne, doesn't she ever tell you anything? Don't you know if she cares anything at all about me?"

"Who?"

"Why, Clarissa. Doesn't she ever tell you anything, Anne?"

Anne turned her face farther away. She was very white. Her round young limbs were trembling. "Why don't you go into the house and ask her?" she said, with sweet, shrill incisiveness. "I should say that was the quickest way."

"She'll run if she sees me coming. She doesn't act as if she wanted me to. Oh, Anne, don't you know anything about it?"

"No, I don't know a thing."

"You knew we used to go together some, years ago?"

"No, I didn't."

"We weren't engaged, but it was sort of understood, I'd always thought. It was before I went to California. Father'd lost his money, and mother was sick, and I thought I'd got to stir around and do something before I said much about getting married.

"We wrote to each other quite a while. Then I got kind of discouraged. I wasn't doing very well, and I didn't see as I was ever coming home. I had to send every dollar I could save to father, and I began to think I couldn't get married till I was an old man, and I didn't know but it was sort of silly to say anything about it.

"I dare say my letters showed how I felt. Anyhow, she didn't write quite so often, and then I heard she'd got a beau. That settled me. I should have been home three years ago if I hadn't supposed she was married. I didn't have the courage to ask. I did make up my mind to write and ask mother, though, finally. I thought I could bear it, and might as well know.

"When I found out she wasn't, I came straight here. But she acted so cold and offish the first time I saw her that I thought sure she'd got over thinking anything of me. But once in a while she'd seem a little different, and I couldn't tell. Anne, didn't you ever hear her say anything about me? Sometimes I think I'm a fool to expect she'd remember anything so long ago. I wish I could see her just a minute. I'd like to tell her why I stopped writing, anyhow, though I never supposed she cared much. Her letters had begun to sound rather cool."

"I'll go in and tell Clarissa that you want to speak to her," said Anne. "I don't see any need of so much fuss." Her voice sounded sweet and crisp. She swung her blue muslin skirts between the rose-bushes with an air. Her yellow head was proudly erect.

"She looks just the way Clarissa used to," Gilman thought, as he stared after her.

Presently she reappeared at the entrance of the garden walk. "Go right in," she called out. Then she went around to the front of the house. "They'll see I ain't shut up in my room, crying," she thought to herself.

She sauntered about among the bushes, pulling roses here and there. She heard voices behind the parlor blinds. Her face was still pale, but her mouth began to tremble a little at the corners. Anne had a sweet nature. "It's a great joke on me," she whispered to herself. Then she laughed, with the most unselfish amusement, in the midst of her girlish chagrin and sorrow.

There was a bush of beautiful pink roses down by the gate. Anne stood there picking them when her friend, Ellen Pierson, came down the road, and stopped, leaning her slender elbows on the gate. "What are you picking so many roses for?" asked she.

"I don't know but I shall go to filling up jars with them, like Clarissa," said Anne.

A SOLITARY.

It was snowing hard, as it had been for twenty-four hours. The evergreen-trees hung low with the snow. Nicholas Gunn's little house was almost hidden beneath it. The snow shelved out over the eaves, and clung in damp masses to the walls. Nicholas sat on his door-step, and the snow fell upon him. His old cap had become a tall white crown; there was a ridge of snow upon his bent shoulders. He sat perfectly still; his eyes were fixed upon the weighted evergreens across the road, but he did not seem to see them. He looked as calmly passive beneath the storm as a Buddhist monk.

There were no birds stirring, and there was no wind. All the sound came from the muffled rustle of the snow on the trees, and that was so slight as to seem scarcely more than a thought of sound. The road stretched to the north and south through the forest of pine and cedar and hemlock. Nicholas Gunn's was the only house in sight.

Stephen Forster came up the road from the southward. He bent his head and struggled along; the snow was above his knees, and at every step he lifted his feet painfully, as from a quicksand. He advanced quite noiselessly until he began to cough. The cough was deep and rattling, and he had to stand still in the snow while it was upon him.

Nicholas Gunn never looked up. Stephen bent himself almost double, the cough became a strangle, but Nicholas kept his calm eyes fixed upon the evergreens.

At last Stephen righted himself and kept on. He was very small; his clothes were quite covered with snow, and patches of it clung to his face. He looked like some little winter-starved, white-furred animal, creeping painfully to cover. When he came opposite the house he half halted, but Nicholas never stirred nor looked his way, and he kept on. It was all that he could do to move, the cough had exhausted him; he carried a heavy basket, too.

He had proceeded only a few paces beyond the house when his knees bent under him, he fairly sank down into the snow. He groaned a little, but Nicholas did not turn his head.

After a little, Stephen raised himself, lifted his basket, and went staggering back. "Mr. Gunn," said he.

Nicholas turned his eyes slowly and looked at him, but he did not speak.

"Can't I go into your house an' set down an' rest a few minutes? I'm 'most beat out."

"No, you can't," replied Nicholas Gunn.

"I dun' know as I can git home."

Nicholas made no rejoinder. He turned his eyes away. Stephen stood looking piteously at him. His sharply cut delicate face gleamed white through the white fall of the snow.

"If you'd jest let me set there a few minutes," he said.

Nicholas sat immovable.

Stephen tried to walk on, but suddenly another coughing-fit seized him. He stumbled across the road, and propped himself against a pine-tree, setting the basket down in the snow. He twisted himself about the snowy tree trunk, and the coughs came in a rattling volley.

Nicholas Gunn looked across at him, and waited until Stephen got his breath. Then he spoke. "Look a-here!" said he.

"What say?"

"If you want to set in the house a few minutes, you can. There ain't no fire there."

"Thank ye."

It was some time before Stephen Forster gathered strength enough to return across the road to the house. He leaned against the tree, panting, the tears running down his cheeks. Nicholas did not offer to help him. When at last Stephen got across the road, he arose to let him pass through the door; then he sat down again on the door-step.

Stephen Forster set his basket on the floor, and staggered across the room to a chair. He leaned his head back against the wall and panted. The room was bitterly cold; the snow drifted in through the open door where Nicholas sat. There was no furniture except a cooking-stove, a cot bed, one chair, and a table; but there were ornaments. Upon the walls hung various little worsted and cardboard decorations. There was a lamp-mat on the table, and in one corner was a rude bracket holding a bouquet of wax flowers under a tall glass shade. There was also a shelf full of books beside the window.

Stephen Forster did not notice anything. He sat with his eyes closed. Once or twice he tried feebly to brush the snow off his clothes, that was all. Nicholas never turned his head. He looked like a stone image there in the doorway. In about twenty minutes Stephen arose, took his basket up, and went timidly to the door.

"I'm much obleeged to ye, Mr. Gunn," said he. "I guess I can git along now."

Nicholas got up, and the snow fell from his shoulders in great cakes. He stood aside to let Stephen pass. Stephen, outside the door, paused, and looked up at him.

"I'm much obleeged to ye," he said again. "I guess I can git home now. I had them three coughin'-spells after I left the store, and I got 'most beat out."

Nicholas grunted, and sat down again. Stephen looked at him a minute, then he smiled abashedly and went away, urging his feeble little body through the storm. Nicholas watched him, then he turned his head with a stiff jerk.

"If he wants to go out in such weather, he can. I don't care," he muttered.

It was nearly four o'clock in the afternoon, the snow was gradually ceasing. Presently a yellow light could be seen through the woods in the west. Some birds flew into one of the snowy trees, a wood-sled creaked down the road, the driver stared at Nicholas in the doorway, he turned his head and stared again. It was evident that he was not one of the village people. They had witnessed the peculiarities of Nicholas Gunn for the last six years. They still stared, but not as assiduously.

The driver of the wood-sled, as soon as he went down the slope in the road, and could no longer see Nicholas, began to whistle. The whistle floated back like a wake of merry sound.

Presently Nicholas arose, took off his cap, and beat it against the door-post to rid it of its dome of snow; then he shook himself like a dog, and stamped; then he went into the house, and stood looking irresolutely at the cold stove.

"Should like a fire to heat up my hasty-puddin' mighty well, so—I won't have it," said he.

He took a wooden bucket, and went with it out of doors, around the house, over a snow-covered path, to a spring. The water trickled into its little basin from under a hood of snow. Nicholas plunged in his bucket, withdrew it filled with water, and carried it back to the house. The path led through the woods; all the trees and bushes were white arcs. Some of the low branches bowed over the path, and Nicholas, passing under them, had to stoop.

Nicholas, back in his house, got a bowl out of a rude closet; it was nearly full of cold hasty-pudding. He stood there and swallowed it in great gulps.

The light was waning fast, although it lasted longer than usual on account of the snow, which, now the clouds were gone, was almost like a sheet of white light.

Nicholas, when he had finished his supper, plunged out again into this pale dusk. He tramped, knee-deep, down the road for a long way. He reached the little village centre, left it behind, and went on between white meadow-lands and stretches of woods. Once in a while he met a man plodding down to the store, but there were few people abroad, the road would not be cleared until morning.

Finally Nicholas turned about, and went back until he reached the village store. Its windows and glass door were full of yellow light, in which one could see many heads moving. When Nicholas opened the clanging door and went in, all the heads turned towards him. There was hardly a man there as tall as he. He went across the store with a kind of muscular shamble; his head, with its wild light beard, had a lofty lift to it. The lounging men watched him furtively as he bought some Indian meal and matches at the counter. When he had gone out with his purchases there was a burst of laughter. The store-keeper thrust a small sharp face over the counter.

"If a man is such a darned fool as to live on meal and matches, I ain't got nothin' to say, so long as he pays me the money down," said he. He had a hoarse cold, and his voice was a facetious whisper.

There was another shout of laughter; Nicholas could hear it as he went down the street. The stranger who had driven the wood-sled past Nicholas's house was among the men. He was snow-bound overnight in the village. He was a young fellow, with innocent eyes and a hanging jaw. He nudged the man next him.

"What in creation ails the fellar, anyhow?" said he. "I seed him a-settin' on his door-step this afternoon, and the snow a-drivin' right on him."

"He ain't right in his upper story," replied the man. "Somethin' went again him; his wife run off with another fellar, or somethin', an' he's cracked."

"Why don't they shet him up?"

"He ain't dangerous. Reckon he won't hurt nobody but himself. If he wants to set out in a drivin' snow-storm, and tramp till he's tuckered out, it ain't nothin' to nobody else but himself. There ain't no use bringin' that kind of crazy on the town."

"'Twouldn't cost the town much," chimed in another man. "He's worth property. Shouldn't be surprised if he was worth three thousand dollars. And there he is a-livin' on corn meal and water."

An old man, in a leather-cushioned arm-chair beside the stove, turned his grizzly quizzical face toward the others, and cleared his throat. They all bent forward attentively. He had a reputation for wit.

"Makes me think of old Eph Huntly, and the story Squire Morse used to tell about him," said he. He paused impressively, and they waited. Then he went on. "Seems old Eph got terrible hard up one time. One thing after another went again him. He'd been laid up with the rheumatiz all winter; then his wife she'd been sick, an' they was 'most eat up with medicine an' doctors' bills. Then his hay crop had failed, an' his pertaters had rotted, an' finally, to cap the climax, his best cow died, an' the int'rest money was due on the mortgage, an' he didn't have a cent to pay it with. Well, he couldn't raise the money nohow, an' the day come when he s'posed the farm would have to go. Lawyer Holmes he held the mortgage, an' he expected to see him drive into the yard any time. Well, old Eph he jest goes out in the yard, an' he ketches a nice fat crower, an' he kills him, an' picks him. Then he takes him in to his wife. She was takin' on terrible 'cause she thought the farm had got to go, an' sez he, 'Sukey Ann, I want you to go an' cook this crower jest as good as you know how.' 'Oh, Lor'!' sez she, 'I don't want no crower,' an' she boohooed right out. But old Eph he made her go an' stuff that crower, an' cook him, an' bile onions, turnips, an' squash, an' all the fixin's. He said he never felt so bad in his life, an' he never got to sech a desprit pitch, an' he was goin' to have a good dinner anyhow. Well, it so happened that Lawyer Holmes he driv into the yard jest as old Eph an' his wife were settin' down to dinner, an' he see that nice baked crower an' the fixin's all set out, an' he didn't know what to make on't. It seemed to him Eph couldn't be so dreadful bad off, or he wouldn't have any heart for extra dinners, an' mebbe he had some way of raisin' the money in prospect. Then Lawyer Holmes he was mighty fond of his victuals himself, an' the upshot of it was, he sot down to the table, an' eat a good meal of the crower an' fixin's, an' there wa'n't no mortgage foreclosed that day, an' before long Eph he managed to raise the money somehow. Now if Nicholas Gunn jest had a leetle grain of old Eph's sense, he'd jest git better victuals the wuss he felt, an' let one kinder make up for t'other, instead of livin' on Injun meal an' matches. I ruther guess I wouldn't take to no meal an' matches if my Ann Lizy left me. I'd live jest as high as I could to keep my spirits up."

There was a burst of applause. The old man sat winking and grinning complacently.

"Nicholas Gunn is a darned fool, or else he's cracked," said the storekeeper in his hoarse whisper.

Meanwhile Nicholas Gunn went home. He put his meal away in the closet; he lighted a candle with one of his matches; he read awhile in the Bible; then he went to bed. He did not sleep in the cot bed; that was too luxurious for him. He slept, rolled in a blanket, on the bare floor.

Nicholas Gunn, whether his eccentricities arose from mystical religious fervor or from his own personal sorrows, would have been revered and worshipped as a saintly ascetic among some nations; among New-Englanders he met with the coarse ridicule of the loafers in a country store. Idle meditation and mortification of the flesh, except for gain, were among them irreconcilable with sanity. Nicholas would have had more prestige had he fled to the Himalayas and built himself a cell in some wild pass; however, prestige was not what he sought.

The next morning a wind had arisen; it blew stiff and

cold from the north. The snow was drifted into long waves, and looked like a frozen sea. A flock of sparrows had collected before Nicholas Gunn's door, and he stood watching them. They were searching for crumbs; this deep snow had shortened their resources wofully; all their larders were buried. There were no crumbs before this door; but they searched assiduously, with their feathers ruffled in the wind. Stephen Forster came up the road with his market-basket; it was all he could do to face the wind. His thin coat was buttoned tight across his narrow shoulders; his old tippet blew out. He advanced with a kind of sidewise motion, presenting his body like a wedge to the wind; he could not walk fairly against it.

When he was opposite Nicholas, the sparrows flew up at his feet; he paused, and shifted his basket. "Good-mornin', Mr. Gunn," said he, in a weak voice.

Nicholas nodded. Stephen's face was mottled with purple; his nose and mouth looked shrunken; his shoes were heavy with snow.

"If you want to go in an' set down a few minutes, you can," said Nicholas.

Stephen moved forward eagerly. "Thank ye, Mr. Gunn, I am kinder beat out, an' I'd like to set a few minutes," he said.

He went in and sat down. The wind rushed in great gusts past the open door. Stephen began to cough. Nicholas hesitated, his face was surly, then he shut the door with a bang.

While Stephen rested himself in the house, Nicholas marched up and down before it like a sentinel. He did not seem to see Stephen when he came out, but he stood before him in his track.

"I'm much obleeged, Mr. Gunn," said he.

Nicholas nodded. Stephen hesitated a minute, then he went on up the road. The snow blew up around him in a dazzling cloud, and almost hid him from sight.

"It's the last time I do it," muttered Nicholas.

But it was not. Every morning, storm or shine, Stephen Forster toiled painfully over the road with his market-basket, and every morning Nicholas Gunn invited him into his fireless hermitage to rest. A freezing hospitality, but he offered it, and Stephen accepted it with a fervent gratitude.

It grew apparently more and more necessary. Stephen crept more and more feebly over the road; he had to keep setting his basket down. Nicholas never asked him if he were ill, he never questioned him at all, although he knew nothing about him but his name. Nicholas did not know the names even of many of the village people; he had never offered nor invited confidences. Stephen also did not volunteer any information as to his circumstances during his morning calls upon Nicholas; indeed, he was too exhausted; he merely gave his gentle and timid thanks for the hospitality.

There came a night in January when the cold reached the greatest intensity of the season. The snow creaked underfoot, the air was full of sparkles, there were noises like guns in the woods, for the trees were almost freezing The moon was full, and seemed like a very fire of death, radiating cold instead of heat.

Nicholas Gunn, stern anchorite that he was, could not sleep for the cold. He got up and paced his room. He would not kindle a fire in the stove. He swung his arms and stamped. Suddenly he heard a voice outside. It sounded almost like a child's. "Mr. Gunn!" it cried.

Nicholas stopped and listened. It came again—"Mr. —Gunn!"

"Who's there?" Nicholas sung out, gruffly.

"It's—me."

Then Nicholas knew it was Stephen Forster. He opened the door, and Stephen stood there in the moonlight.

"What are ye out for this time of night?" asked Nicholas.

Stephen chattered so that he could hardly speak. He cowered before Nicholas; the moonlight seemed to strike his little, shivering form like a broadside of icy spears. "I'm 'fraid I'm freezin'," he gasped. "Can't ye take me in?"

"What are ye out for this time of night?" repeated Nicholas, in a rough, loud tone.

"I had to. I'll tell you when I git a leetle warmer. I dun' know but—I'm freezin'."

Stephen's voice, indeed, sounded as if ice were forming over it, muffling it. Nicholas suddenly grasped him by one arm.

"Come in, then, if ye've got to," he growled.

He pulled so suddenly and strongly that Stephen made a run into the house, and his heels flew up weakly. Nicholas whirled him about and seated him on his cot bed.

"Now lay down here," he ordered, "and I'll cover ye up."

Stephen obeyed. Nicholas pulled off his boots, gave his feet a fierce rub, and fixed the coverings over him with rough energy. Then he began pacing the room again.

Presently he went up to the bed. "Warmer?"

"I guess—so." Stephen's shivering seemed to shake the room.

Nicholas hustled a coat off of a peg, and put it over Ste-

15

phen. Then he paced again. Stephen began to cough. Nicholas made an exclamation, and stamped angrily out of the house. There was a little lean-to at the back, and there was some fuel stored in it. Nicholas came back quickly with his arms full of wood. He piled it into the stove, set a match to it, and put on a kettle of water. Then he dragged the cot bed, with Stephen on it, close to the stove, and began to rub him under the bedclothes. His face was knit savagely, but he rubbed with a tender strength.

"Warmer?" said he.

"Yes, I—be," returned Stephen, gratefully.

The fire burned briskly; the sharp air began to soften. Soon the kettle steamed. Nicholas got a measure of meal out of his cupboard, and prepared some porridge in a little stewpan. When it began to boil, he bent over the stove and stirred carefully, lest it should lump. When it was thick enough, he dished it, salted it, and carried it to Stephen.

"There, eat it," said he. "It's the best I've got; it 'll warm ye some. I ain't got no spirits; never keep any in the house."

"I guess I ain't—very hungry, Mr. Gunn," said Stephen, feebly.

"Eat it."

Stephen raised himself, and drained the bowl with convulsive gulps. Tears stood in his eyes, and he gasped when he lay back again. However, the warm porridge revived him. Presently he looked at Nicholas, who was putting more wood on the fire.

"I s'pose you think it's terrible queer that I come here this way," said he; "but there wa'n't no other way. I dun' know whether you know how I've been livin' or not."

"No, I don't."

"Well, I've been livin' with my half-sister, Mis' Morrison. Mebbe you've heard of her?"

"No, I ain't."

"She keeps boarders. We ain't lived in this town more'n three years; we moved here from Jackson. Mis' Morrison's husband's dead, so she keeps boarders. She's consider'ble older'n me. I ain't never been very stout, but I used to tend in a store till I got worse. I coughed so, it used to plague the customers. Then I had to give it up, and when Mis' Morrison's husband died, and she come here, I come with her; she thought there'd be some chores I could do for my board. An' I've worked jest as hard as I could, an' I ain't complained. I've been down to the store to get meat for the boarders' dinner when I couldn't scarcely get along over the ground. But I cough so bad nights that the boarders they complain, an' Mis' Morrison says I must go to—the poor-house. I heard her talkin' with the hired girl about it. She's goin' to get the selectmen to the house to-morrow mornin'. An'—I ain't a-goin' to the poor-house! None of my folks have ever been there, an' I ain't goin'! I'll risk it but what I can get some work to do. I ain't quite so fur gone yet. I waited till the house was still, an' then I cut. I thought if you'd take me in till mornin', I could git down to the depot, an' go to Jackson before the selectmen come. I've got a little money—enough to take me to Jackson—I've been savin' of it up these three years, in case anything happened. It's some I earned tendin' store. I'm willin' to pay you for my night's lodgin'."

Nicholas nodded grimly. He had stood still, listening to the weak, high-pitched voice from the bed.

"It's in my vest pocket, in my pocketbook," said Stephen. "If you'll come here, I'll give it to you, and you can take what you think it's worth. I pinned the pocket up, so's to be sure I didn't lose it."

Stephen began fumbling at his vest. Nicholas lifted a cover from the stove.

"I don't want none of your money," said he. "Keep your money."

"I've got enough to pay you, an' take me to Jackson."

"I tell ye, stop talkin' about your money."

Stephen said no more; he looked terrified. The air grew warmer. Everything was quiet, except for the detonations of the frost in the forest outside, and its sharp cracks in the house walls. Soon Stephen fell asleep, and lay breathing short and hard. Nicholas sat beside him.

It was broad daylight when Stephen aroused himself. He awoke suddenly and completely, and began to get out of bed. "I guess it's time I was goin'," said he. "I'm much obleeged to you, Mr. Gunn."

"You lay still."

Stephen looked at him.

"You lay still," repeated Nicholas.

Stephen sank back irresolutely; his timid, bewildered eyes followed Nicholas, who was smoothing his hair and beard before a little looking-glass near the window. There was a good fire in the cooking-stove, and the room was quite warm, although it was evidently a very cold day. The two windows were thickly coated with frost, and the room was full of dim white light. One of the windows faced towards the east, but the sun was still hidden by the trees across the road.

Nicholas smoothed his hair and his wild beard slowly and punctiliously.

Stephen watched him. "Mr. Gunn," he said, at length.

"What say?"

"I'm afraid—I sha'n't get to the depot before the train goes if I don't start pretty soon."

Nicholas went on smoothing his beard. At length he laid his comb down and turned around. "Look a-here!" said he; "you might jest as well understand it. You ain't a-goin' to any depot to-day, an' you ain't a-goin' to any train, an' you ain't a-goin' to any depot to-morrow nor any train, an' you ain't a-goin' the next day, nor the next, nor the next, nor the next after that."

"What be I a-goin' to do?"

"You are a-goin' to stay jest where you are. I've fought against your comin' as long as I could, an' now you've come, an' I've turned the corner, you are a-goin' to stay. When I've been walkin' in the teeth of my own will on one road, an' havin' all I could do to breast it, I ain't a-goin' to do it on another. I've give up, an' I'm a-goin to stay give up. You lay still."

Stephen's small anxious face on the pillow looked almost childish. His helplessness of illness seemed to produce the same expression as the helplessness of infancy. His hollow, innocent blue eyes were fixed upon Nicholas with blank inquiry. "Won't Mis' Morrison be after me?" he asked, finally.

"No, she won't. Don't you worry. I'm a-goin' over to see her. You lay still." Nicholas shook his coat before he put it on; he beat his cap against the wall, then adjusted it carefully. "Now," said he, "I'm a-goin'. I've left enough wood in the stove, an' I guess it 'll keep warm till I get back. I sha'n't be gone any longer than I can help."

"Mr. Gunn!"

"What say?"

"I ruther guess I'd better be a-goin'."

Nicholas looked sternly at Stephen. "You lay still," he repeated. "Don't you try to get up whilst I'm gone; you ain't fit to. Don't you worry. I'm goin' to fix it all right. I'm goin' to bring you something nice for breakfast. You lay still."

Stephen stared at him, his thin shoulders hitched uneasily under the coverlid.

"You're goin' to lay still, ain't you?" repeated Nicholas.

"Yes; I will, if you say so," replied Stephen. He sighed and smiled feebly.

The truth was that this poor cot in the warm room seemed to him like a couch under the balsam-dropping cedars of Lebanon, and all at once he felt that divine rest which comes from leaning upon the will of another.

"Well, I do say so," returned Nicholas. He looked at the fire again, then he went out. He turned in the doorway, and nodded admonishingly at Stephen. "Mind you don't try to get up," he said again.

Nicholas went out of sight down the road, taking long strides over the creaking snow. He was gone about a half-hour. When he returned, his arms were full of packages. He opened the door, and looked anxiously at the bed. Stephen twisted his face towards him and smiled. Nicholas piled the packages up on the table, and lifted a stove-cover.

"I've seen Mis' Morrison, and it's all right," said he.

"What did she say?" asked Stephen, in an awed voice.

"Well, she didn't say much of anything. She was fryin' griddle-cakes for the boarders' breakfasts. She said she felt real bad about lettin' you go, but she didn't see no other way, an' she'd be glad to have you visit me jest as long as you wanted to. She's goin' to pack up your clothes."

"I ain't got many clothes. There's my old coat an' vest an' my other pants, but they're 'most worn out. I ain't got but one real good shirt besides this one I've got on. That was in the wash, or I'd brought it."

"Clothes enough," said Nicholas.

He crammed the stove with wood, and began undoing the packages. There were coffee, bread, and butter, some little delicate sugar cookies, some slices of ham, and eggs. There were also a pail of milk and a new tin coffee-pot.

Nicholas worked busily. He made coffee, fried the ham and eggs, and toasted slices of bread. When everything was ready, he carried a bowl of water to Stephen for him to wash his hands and face before breakfast. He even got his comb, and smoothed his hair.

Then he set the breakfast out on the table, and brought it up to the bedside. He had placed a chair for himself, and was just sitting down, when he stopped suddenly. "I don't know as it's just fair for me not to tell you a little something about myself before we really begin livin' together," said he. "It won't take but a minute. I don't know but you've heard stories about me that I wa'n't quite right. Well, I am; that is, I s'pose I am. All is, I've had lots of trouble, an' it come mainly through folks I set by; an' I figured out a way to get the better of it. I figured out that if I didn't care anything for anybody, I shouldn't have no trouble from 'em; an' if I didn't care anything for myself, I shouldn't have any from myself. I 'bout made up my mind that all the trouble an' wickedness in this world come from carin' about yourself or somebody else, so I thought I'd quit it. I let folks alone, an' I wouldn't do anything for 'em; an' I let myself alone as near as I could, an' didn't do anything for myself. I kept cold when I wanted to be warm, an' warm when I wanted to be cold. I didn't eat anything I liked, an' I left things around that hurt me to see. My wife she made them wax flowers an' them gimcracks. Then I used to read the Bible, 'cause I used to believe in it an' didn't now, an' it made me feel worse. I did about everything I could to spite myself, an' get all the feelin' out of me, so I could be a little easier in my mind."

Nicholas paused a moment. Stephen was looking at him with bewildered intensity.

"Well, I was all wrong," Nicholas went on. "I've give it all up. I've got to go through with the whole of it like other folks, an' I guess I've got grit enough. I've made up my mind that men's tracks cover the whole world, and there ain't standin'-room outside of 'em. I've got to go with the rest. Now we'll have breakfast."

Nicholas ate heartily; it was long since he had tasted such food; even Stephen had quite an appetite. Nicholas pressed the food upon him; his face was radiant with kindness and delight. Stephen Forster, innocent, honest, and simple-hearted, did not in the least understand him, but that did not matter. There is a higher congeniality than that of mutual understanding; there is that of need and supply.

After breakfast Nicholas cleared away the dishes and washed them. The sun was so high then that it struck the windows, and the frost-work sparkled like diamonds.

Nicholas opened the door; he was going down to the spring

for more water; he saw a flock of sparrows in the bushes across the road, and stopped; then he set his pail down noiselessly and went back for a piece of bread. He broke it and scattered the crumbs before the door, then went off a little way and stood watching. When the sparrows settled down upon the crumbs he laughed softly, and went on towards the spring over the shining crust of snow.

A GENTLE GHOST

OUT in front of the cemetery stood a white horse and a covered wagon. The horse was not tied, but she stood quite still, her four feet widely and ponderously planted, her meek white head hanging. Shadows of leaves danced on her back. There were many trees about the cemetery, and the foliage was unusually luxuriant for May. The four women who had come in the covered wagon remarked it. "I never saw the trees so forward as they are this year, seems to me," said one, gazing up at some magnificent gold-green branches over her head.

"I was sayin' so to Mary this mornin'," rejoined another. "They're uncommon forward, I think."

They loitered along the narrow lanes between the lots: four homely, middle-aged women, with decorous and subdued enjoyment in their worn faces. They read with peaceful curiosity and interest the inscriptions on the stones; they turned aside to look at the tender, newly blossomed spring bushes—the flowering almonds and the bridal wreaths. Once in a while they came to a new stone, which they immediately surrounded with eager criticism. There was a solemn hush when they reached a lot where some relatives of one of the party were buried. She put a bunch of flowers on a grave, then she stood looking at it with red eyes. The others grouped themselves deferentially aloof.

They did not meet any one in the cemetery until just before they left. When they had reached the rear and oldest portion of the yard, and were thinking of retracing their steps, they became suddenly aware of a child sitting in a lot at their right. The lot held seven old, leaning stones, dark and mossy, their inscriptions dimly traceable. The child sat close to one, and she looked up at the staring knot of women with a kind of innocent keenness, like a baby. Her face was small and fair and pinched. The women stood eying her.

"What's your name, little girl?" asked one. She had a bright flower in her bonnet and a smart lift to her chin, and seemed the natural spokeswoman of the party. Her name was Holmes. The child turned her head sideways and murmured something.

"What? We can't hear. Speak up; don't be afraid! What's your name?" The woman nodded the bright flower over her, and spoke with sharp pleasantness.

"Nancy Wren," said the child, with a timid catch of her breath.

"Wren?"

The child nodded. She kept her little pink, curving mouth parted.

"It's nobody I know," remarked the questioner, reflectively. "I guess she comes from—over there." She made a significant motion of her head towards the right. "Where do you live, Nancy?" she asked.

The child also motioned towards the right.

"I thought so," said the woman. "How old are you?"

"Ten."

The women exchanged glances. "Are you sure you're tellin' the truth?"

The child nodded.

"I never saw a girl so small for her age if she is," said one woman to another.

"Yes," said Mrs. Holmes, looking at her critically; "she is dreadful small. She's considerable smaller than my Mary was. Is there any of your folks buried in this lot?" said she, fairly hovering with affability and determined graciousness.

The child's upturned face suddenly kindled. She began speaking with a soft volubility that was an odd contrast to her previous hesitation.

"That's mother," said she, pointing to one of the stones, "an' that's father, an' there's John, an' Marg'ret, an' Mary, an' Susan, an' the baby, and here's—Jane."

The women stared at her in amazement. "Was it your—" began Mrs. Holmes; but another woman stepped forward, stoutly impetuous.

"Land! it's the Blake lot!" said she. "This child can't be any relation to 'em. You hadn't ought to talk so, Nancy."

"It's so," said the child, shyly persistent. She evidently hardly grasped the force of the woman's remark.

They eyed her with increased bewilderment. "It can't be," said the woman to the others. "Every one of them Blakes died years ago."

"I've seen Jane," volunteered the child, with a candid smile in their faces.

Then the stout woman sank down on her knees beside Jane's stone, and peered hard at it.

"She died forty year ago this May," said she, with a gasp.

"I used to know her when I was a child. She was ten years old when she died. You ain't ever seen her. You hadn't ought to tell such stories."

"I ain't seen her for a long time," said the little girl.

"What made you say you'd seen her at all?" said Mrs. Holmes, sharply, thinking this was capitulation.

"I did use to see her a long time ago, an' she used to wear a white dress, an' a wreath on her head. She used to come here an' play with me."

The women looked at each other with pale, shocked faces; one nervous; one shivered. "She ain't quite right," she whispered. "Let's go." The women began filing away. Mrs. Holmes, who came last, stood about for a parting word to the child.

"You can't have seen her," said she, severely, "an' you are a wicked girl to tell such stories. You mustn't do it again, remember."

Nancy stood with her hand on Jane's stone, looking at her. "She did," she repeated, with mild obstinacy.

"There's somethin' wrong about her, I guess," whispered Mrs. Holmes, rustling on after the others.

"I see she looked kind of queer the minute I set eyes on her," said the nervous woman.

When the four reached the front of the cemetery they sat down to rest for a few minutes. It was warm, and they had still quite a walk, nearly the whole width of the yard, to the other front corner where the horse and wagon were.

They sat down in a row on a bank; the stout woman wiped her face; Mrs. Holmes straightened her bonnet. Directly opposite across the street stood two houses, so close to each other that their walls almost touched. One was a large square building, glossily white, with green blinds; the other was low, with a facing of whitewashed stone-work reaching to its lower windows, which somehow gave it a disgraced and menial air; there were, moreover, no blinds.

At the side of the low building stretched a wide ploughed field, where several halting old figures were moving about planting. There was none of the brave hope of the sower about them. Even across the road one could see the feeble stiffness of their attitudes, the half-palsied fling of their arms.

"I declare I shouldn't think them old men over there would ever get that field planted," said Mrs. Holmes, energetically watchful. In the front door of the square white house sat a girl with bright hair. The yard was full of green light from two tall maple-trees, and the girl's hair made a brilliant spot of color in the midst of it.

"That's Flora Dunn over there on the door-step, ain't it?" said the stout woman.

"Yes. I should think you could tell her by her red hair."

"I knew it. I should have thought Mr. Dunn would have hated to have had their house so near the poor-house. I declare I should!"

"Oh, he wouldn't mind," said Mrs. Holmes; "he's as easy as old Tilly. It wouldn't have troubled him any if they'd set it right in his front yard. But I guess *she* minded some. I heard she did. John said there wa'n't any need of it. The town wouldn't have set it so near, if Mr. Dunn had set his foot down he wouldn't have it there. I s'pose they wanted to keep that big field on the side clear; but they would have moved it along a little if he'd made a fuss. I tell you what 'tis, I've 'bout made up my mind—I dun know as it's Scripture, but I can't help it—if folks don't make a fuss they won't get their rights in this world. If you jest lay still an' don't rise up, you're goin' to get stepped on. If people like to be, they can ; I don't."

"I should have thought he'd have hated to have the poor-house quite so close," murmured the stout woman.

Suddenly Mrs. Holmes leaned forward and poked her head among the other three. She sat on the end of the row. "Say," said she, in a mysterious whisper, "I want to know if you've heard the stories 'bout the Dunn house?"

"No; what?" chorussed the other women, eagerly. They bent over towards her till the four faces were in a knot.

"Well," said Mrs. Holmes, cautiously, with a glance at the bright-headed girl across the way—"I heard it pretty straight—they say the house is haunted."

The stout woman sniffed and straightened herself. "Haunted!" repeated she.

"They say that ever since Jenny died there's been queer noises 'round the house that they can't account for. You see that front chamber over there, the one next to the poor-house ; well, that's the room, they say."

The women all turned and looked at the chamber windows, where some ruffled white curtains were fluttering.

"That's the chamber where Jenny used to sleep, you know," Mrs. Holmes went on ; "an' she died there. Well, they said that before Jenny died, Flora had always slept there with her, but she felt kind of bad about goin' back there, so she thought she'd take another room. Well, there was the awfulest moanin' an' takin' on up in Jenny's room, when she did, that Flora went back there to sleep."

"I shouldn't thought she could," whispered the nervous woman, who was quite pale.

"The moanin' stopped jest as soon as she got in there

with a light. You see Jenny was always terrible timid an afraid to sleep alone, an' had a lamp burnin' all night, an it seemed to them jest as if it really was her, I s'pose."

"I don't believe one word of it," said the stout woman, getting up. "It makes me all out of patience to hear people talk such stuff, jest because the Dunns happen to live opposite a graveyard."

"I told it jest as I heard it," said Mrs. Holmes, stiffly.

"Oh, I ain't blamin' you; it's the folks that start such stories that I ain't got any patience with. Think of that dear, pretty little sixteen-year-old girl hauntin' a house!"

"Well, I've told it jest as I heard it," repeated Mrs. Holmes, still in a tone of slight umbrage. "I don't ever take much stock in such things myself."

The four women strolled along to the covered wagon and climbed in. "I declare," said the stout woman, conciliatingly, "I dun know when I've had such an outin'. I feel as if it had done me good. I've been wantin' to come down to the cemetery for a long time, but it's most more'n I want to walk. I feel real obliged to you, Mis' Holmes."

The others climbed in. Mrs. Holmes disclaimed all obligations gracefully, established herself on the front seat, and shook the reins over the white horse. Then the party jogged along the road to the village, past outlying farmhouses and rich green meadows, all freckled gold with dandelions. Dandelions were in their height; the buttercups had not yet come.

Flora Dunn, the girl on the door-step, glanced up when they started down the street; then she turned her eyes on her work; she was sewing with nervous haste.

"Who were those folks, did you see, Flora?" called her mother, out of the sitting-room.

"I didn't notice," replied Flora, absently.

Just then the girl whom the women had met came lingeringly out of the cemetery and crossed the street.

"There's that poor little Wren girl," remarked the voice in the sitting-room.

"Yes," assented Flora. After a while she got up and entered the house. Her mother looked anxiously at her when she came into the room.

"I'm all out of patience with you, Flora," said she. "You're jest as white as a sheet. You'll make yourself sick. You're actin' dreadful foolish."

Flora sank into a chair and sat staring straight ahead with a strained, pitiful gaze. "I can't help it; I can't do any different," said she. "I shouldn't think you'd scold me, mother."

"Scold you; I ain't scoldin' you, child; but there ain't any sense in your doin' so. You'll make yourself sick, an' you're all I've got left. I can't have anything happen to you, Flora." Suddenly Mrs. Dunn burst out in a low wail, hiding her face in her hands.

"I don't see as you're much better yourself, mother," said Flora, heavily.

"I don't know as I am," sobbed her mother; "but I've got you to worry about besides—everything else. Oh, dear! oh, dear, dear!"

"I don't see any need of your worrying about me." Flora did not cry, but her face seemed to darken visibly with a gathering melancholy like a cloud. Her hair was beautiful, and she had a charming delicacy of complexion; but she was not handsome, her features were too sharp, her expression too intense and nervous. Her mother looked like her as to the expression; the features were widely different. It was as if both had passed through one corroding element which had given them the similarity of scars. Certainly a stranger would at once have noticed the strong resemblance between Mrs. Dunn's large, heavy-featured face and her daughter's thin, delicately outlined one—a resemblance which three months ago had not been perceptible.

"I see, if you don't," returned the mother. "I ain't blind."

"I don't see what you are blaming me for."

"I ain't blamin' you, but it seems to me that you might jest as well let me go up there an' sleep as you."

Suddenly the girl also broke out into a wild cry. "I ain't going to leave her. Poor little Jenny! poor little Jenny! You needn't try to make me, mother; I won't!"

"Flora, don't!"

"I won't! I won't! I won't! Poor little Jenny! Oh, dear! oh, dear!"

"What if it is so? What if it is—*her?* Ain't she got me as well as you? Can't her mother go to her?"

"I won't leave her. I won't! I won't!"

Suddenly Mrs. Dunn's calmness seemed to come uppermost, raised in the scale by the weighty impetus of the other's distress. "Flora," said she, with mournful solemnity, "you mustn't do so; it's wrong. You mustn't wear yourself all out over something that maybe you'll find out wasn't so some time or other."

"Mother, don't you think it is—don't you?"

"I don't know what to think, Flora." Just then a door shut somewhere in the back part of the house. "There's father," said Mrs. Dunn, getting up; "an' the fire ain't made."

Flora rose also, and went about helping her mother to get supper. Both suddenly settled into a rigidity of composure; their eyes were red, but their lips were steady. There was a resolute vein in their characters; they managed themselves with wrenches, and could be hard even with their grief. They got tea ready for Mr. Dunn and his two hired men; then cleared it away, and sat down in the front room with their needlework. Mr. Dunn, a kindly, dull old man, was in there too, over his newspaper. Mrs. Dunn and Flora sewed intently, never taking their eyes from their work. Out in the next room stood a tall clock, which ticked loudly; just before it struck the hours it made always a curious grating noise. When it announced in this way the striking of nine, Mrs. Dunn and Flora exchanged glances; the girl was pale, and her eyes looked larger. She began folding up her work. Suddenly a low moaning cry sounded through the house, seemingly from the room overhead. "There it is!" shrieked Flora. She caught up a lamp and ran. Mrs. Dunn was following, when her husband, sitting near the door, caught hold of her dress with a bewildered air; he had been dozing. "What's the matter?" said he, vaguely.

"Don't you hear it? Didn't you hear it, father?"

The old man let go of her dress suddenly. "I didn't hear nothin'," said he.

"Hark!"

But the cry, in fact, had ceased. Flora could be heard moving about in the room overhead, and that was all. In a moment Mrs. Dunn ran up-stairs after her. The old man sat staring. "It's all dum foolishness," he muttered, under his breath. Presently he fell to dozing again, and his vacantly smiling face lopped forward. Mr. Dunn, slow-brained, patient, and unimaginative, had had his evening naps interrupted after this manner for the last three months, and there was as yet no cessation of his bewilderment. He dealt with the simple, broad lights of life; the shadows were beyond his speculation. For his consciousness his daughter Jenny had died and gone to heaven; he was not capable of listening for her ghostly moans in her little chamber overhead, much less of hearing them with any credulity.

When his wife came down-stairs finally she looked at him, sleeping there, with a bitter feeling. She felt as if set about by an icy wind of loneliness. Her daughter, who was after her own kind, was all the one to whom she could look for sympathy and understanding in this subtle perplexity which had come upon her. And she would rather have dispensed with that sympathy, and heard alone those piteous, uncanny cries, for she was wild with anxiety about Flora. The girl had never been very strong. She looked at her distressfully when she came down the next morning.

"Did you sleep any last night?" said she.

"Some," answered Flora.

Soon after breakfast they noticed the little Wren girl stealing across the road to the cemetery again. "She goes over there all the time," remarked Mrs. Dunn. "I b'lieve she runs away. See her look behind her."

"Yes," said Flora, apathetically.

It was nearly noon when they heard a voice from the next house calling, "Nancy! Nancy! Nancy Wren!" The voice was loud and imperious, but slow and evenly modulated. It indicated well its owner. A woman who could regulate her own angry voice could regulate other people. Mrs. Dunn and Flora heard it understandingly.

"That poor little thing will catch it when she gets home," said Mrs. Dunn.

"Nancy! Nancy! Nancy Wren!" called the voice again.

"I pity the child if Mrs. Gregg has to go after her. Mebbe she's fell asleep over there. Flora, why don't you run over there an' get her?"

The voice rang out again. Flora got her hat and stole across the street a little below the house, so the calling woman should not see her. When she got into the cemetery she called in her turn, letting out her thin sweet voice cautiously. Finally she came directly upon the child. She was in the Blake lot, her little slender body, in its dingy cotton dress, curled up on the ground close to one of the graves. No one but Nature tended those old graves now, and she seemed to be lapsing them gently back to her own lines, at her own will. Of the garden shrubs which had been planted about them not one was left but an old low-spraying white rose-bush, which had just gotten its new leaves. The Blake lot was at the very rear of the yard, where it verged upon a light wood, which was silently stealing its way over its own proper boundaries. At the back of the lot stood a thicket of little thin trees, with silvery twinkling leaves. The ground was quite blue with houstonias.

The child raised her little fair head and stared at Flora, as if just awakened from sleep. She held her little pink mouth open, her innocent blue eyes had a surprised look, as if she were suddenly gazing upon a new scene.

"Where's she gone?" asked she, in her sweet, feeble pipe.

"Where's who gone?"

"Jane."

"I don't know what you mean. Come, Nancy, you must go home now."

"Didn't you see her?"

"I didn't see anybody," answered Flora, impatiently. "Come!"

"She was right here."

"What *do* you mean?"

"Jane was standin' right here. An' she had her white dress on, an' her wreath."

Flora shivered, and looked around her fearfully. The fancy of the child was overlapping her own nature. "There wasn't a soul here. You've been dreaming, child. Come!"

"No, I wasn't. I've seen them blue flowers an' the leaves winkin' all the time. Jane stood right there." The child pointed with her tiny finger to a spot at her side. "She hadn't come for a long time before," she added. "She's stayed down there." She pointed at the grave nearest her.

"You mustn't talk so," said Flora, with tremulous severity. "You must get right up and come home. Mrs. Gregg has been calling you and calling you. She won't like it."

Nancy turned quite pale around her little mouth, and sprang to her feet. "Is Mis' Gregg comin'?"

"She will come if you don't hurry."

The child said not another word. She flew along ahead through the narrow paths, and was in the almshouse door before Flora crossed the street.

"She's terrible afraid of Mrs. Gregg," she told her mother when she got home. Nancy had disturbed her own brooding a little, and she spoke more like herself.

"Poor little thing! I pity her," said Mrs. Dunn. Mrs. Dunn did not like Mrs. Gregg.

Flora rarely told a story until she had ruminated awhile over it herself. It was afternoon, and the two were in the front room at their sewing, before she told her mother about "Jane."

"Of course she must have been dreaming," Flora said.

"She must have been," rejoined her mother.

But the two looked at each other, and their eyes said more than their tongues. Here was a new marvel, new evidence of a kind which they had heretofore scented at, these two rigidly walking New England souls; yet walking, after all, upon narrow paths through dark meadows of mysticism. If they never lost their footing, the steaming damp of the meadows might come in their faces.

This fancy, delusion, superstition, whichever one might name it, of theirs had lasted now three months—ever since young Jenny Dunn had died. There was apparently no reason why it should not last much longer, if delusion it were; the temperaments of these two women, naturally nervous and imaginative, overwrought now by long care and sorrow, would perpetuate it.

If it were not delusion, pray what exorcism, what spell of book and bell, could lay the ghost of a little timid child who was afraid alone in the dark?

The days went on, and Flora still hurried up to her chamber at the stroke of nine. If she were a moment late, sometimes if she were not, that pitiful low wail sounded through the house.

The strange story spread gradually through the village. Mrs. Dunn and Flora were silent about it, but Gossip is herself of a ghostly nature, and minds not keys nor bars.

There was quite an excitement over it. People affected with morbid curiosity and sympathy came to the house. One afternoon the minister came and offered a prayer. Mrs. Dunn and Flora received them all with a certain reticence;

they did not concur in their wishes to remain and hear the mysterious noises for themselves. People called them "dreadful close." They got more satisfaction out of Mr. Dunn, who was perfectly ready to impart all the information in his power and his own theories in the matter.

"I never heard a thing but once," said he, "an' then it sounded more like a cat to me than anything. I guess mother and Flora air kinder nervous."

The spring was waxing late when Flora went up-stairs one night with the oil low in her lamp. She had neglected filling it that day. She did not notice it until she was undressed; then she thought to herself that she must blow it out. She always kept a lamp burning all night, as she had in timid little Jenny's day. Flora herself was timid now.

So she blew the light out. She had barely laid her head upon the pillow when the low moaning wail sounded through the room. Flora sat up in bed and listened, her hands clinched. The moan gathered strength and volume; little broken words and sentences, the piteous ejaculations of terror and distress, began to shape themselves out of it.

Flora sprang out of bed, and stumbled towards her west window—the one on the almshouse side. She leaned her head out, listening a moment. Then she called her mother with wild vehemence. But her mother was already at the door with a lamp. When she entered, the moans ceased.

"Mother," shrieked Flora, "it ain't Jenny. It's somebody over there—at the poor-house. Put the lamp out in the entry, and come back here and listen."

Mrs. Dunn set out the lamp and came back, closing the door. It was a few minutes first, but presently the cries recommenced.

"I'm goin' right over there," said Mrs. Dunn. "I'm

goin' to dress myself an' go over there. I'm goin' to have this affair sifted now."

"I'm going too," said Flora.

It was only half-past nine when the two stole into the almshouse yard. The light was not out in the room on the ground-floor, which the overseer's family used for a sitting-room. When they entered, the overseer was there asleep in his chair, his wife sewing at the table, and an old woman in a pink cotton dress, apparently doing nothing. They all started, and stared at the intruders.

"Good-evenin'," said Mrs. Dunn, trying to speak composedly. "We thought we'd come in; we got kind of started. Oh, there 'tis now! What is it, Mis' Gregg?"

In fact, at that moment, the wail, louder and more distinct, was heard.

"Why, it's Nancy," replied Mrs. Gregg, with dignified surprise. She was a large woman, with a masterly placidity about her. "I heard her a few minutes ago," she went on; "an' I was goin' up there to see to her if she hadn't stopped."

Mr. Gregg, a heavy, saturnine old man, with a broad bristling face, sat staring stupidly. The old woman in pink calico surveyed them all with an impersonal grin.

"Nancy!" repeated Mrs. Dunn, looking at Mrs. Gregg. She had not fancied this woman very much, and the two had not fraternized, although they were such near neighbors. Indeed, Mrs. Gregg was not of a sociable nature, and associated very little with anything but her own duties.

"Yes; Nancy Wren," she said, with gathering amazement. "She cries out this way 'most every night. She's ten years old, but she's as afraid of the dark as a baby. She's a queer child. I guess mebbe she's nervous. I don't know but she's got notions into her head, stayin' over in the graveyard so much. She runs away over there every chance she can get, an' she goes over a queer rigmarole about playin' with Jane, and her bein' dressed in white an' a wreath. I found out she meant Jane Blake, that's buried in the Blake lot. I knew there wa'n't any children round here, an' I thought I'd look into it. You know it says 'Our Father,' an' 'Our Mother,' on the old folks' stones. An' there she was, callin' them father an' mother. You'd thought they was right there. I've got 'most out o' patience with the child. I don't know nothin' about such kind of folks." The wail continued. "I'll go right up there," said Mrs. Gregg, determinately, taking a lamp.

Mrs. Dunn and Flora followed. When they entered the chamber to which she led them they saw little Nancy sitting up in bed, her face pale and convulsed, her blue eyes streaming with tears, her little pink mouth quivering.

"Nancy—" began Mrs. Gregg, in a weighty tone. But Mrs. Dunn sprang forward and threw her arms around the child.

"You got frightened, didn't you?" whispered she; and Nancy clung to her as if for life.

A great wave of joyful tenderness rolled up in the heart of the bereaved woman. It was not, after all, the lonely and fearfully wandering little spirit of her dear Jenny; she was peaceful and blessed, beyond all her girlish tumults and terrors; but it was this little living girl. She saw it all plainly now. Afterwards it seemed to her that any one but a woman with her nerves strained, and her imagination unhealthily keen through watching and sorrow, would have seen it before.

She held Nancy tight, and soothed her. She felt almost

as if she held her own Jenny. "I guess I'll take her home with me, if you don't care," she said to Mrs. Gregg.

"Why, I don't know as I've got any objections, if you want to," answered Mrs. Gregg, with cold stateliness. "Nancy Wren has had everything done for her that I was able to do," she added, when Mrs. Dunn had wrapped up the child, and they were all on the stairs. "I ain't coaxed an' cuddled her, because it ain't my way. I never did with my own children."

"Oh, I know you've done all you could," said Mrs. Dunn, with abstracted apology. "I jest thought I'd like to take her home to-night. Don't you think I'm blamin' you, Mis' Gregg." She bent down and kissed the little tearful face on her shoulder: she was carrying Nancy like a baby. Flora had hold of one of her little dangling hands.

"You shall go right up-stairs an' sleep with Flora," Mrs. Dunn whispered in the child's ear, when they were going across the yard; "an' you shall have the lamp burnin' all night, an' I'll give you a piece of cake before you go."

It was the custom of the Dunns to visit the cemetery and carry flowers to Jenny's grave every Sunday afternoon. Next Sunday little Nancy went with them. She followed happily along, and did not seem to think of the Blake lot. That pitiful fancy, if fancy it were, which had peopled her empty childish world with ghostly kindred, which had led into it an angel playmate in white robe and crown, might lie at rest now. There was no more need for it. She had found her place in a nest of living hearts, and she was getting her natural food of human love.

They had dressed Nancy in one of the little white frocks which Jenny had worn in her childhood, and her hat was trimmed with some ribbon and rose-buds which had adorned one of the dead young girl's years before.

It was a beautiful Sunday. After they left the cemetery they strolled a little way down the road. The road lay between deep green meadows and cottage yards. It was not quite time for the roses, and the lilacs were turning gray. The buttercups in the meadows had blossomed out, but the dandelions had lost their yellow crowns, and their filmy skulls appeared. They stood like ghosts among crowds of golden buttercups; but none of the family thought of that; their ghosts were laid in peace.

A DISCOVERED PEARL.

"WONDER what's goin' on in the church?"

Gilman Marlow stopped and stared slowly over at the church. It was a little white building with five pointed windows on each side. The windows were all streaming with light now, and the bright light showed from the door too, for it was open, and people were going in.

Opposite the church, where Marlow stood, the road was lined with thickly set hemlock and pine trees. Behind them was the graveyard: one peering between the branches could see the white stones. The gap for the entrance was a little beyond. There had been a heavy snowfall the day before, and all the trees were loaded with snow now; the boughs bent down heavily; the lowest ones touched the ground.

Marlow stood among the white branches awhile, and looked over at the church with a sort of dull curiosity; then he kept on up the street. He met many little hurrying groups, and he turned out for them readily, plunging into the deep snow at the side of the cleared path.

Some of the people turned and stared after him. "Whc was that?" he heard some one say. "I don't know," said another.

"I guess you don't," muttered Marlow, with a faint chuckle.

When he came in front of a lighted window anywhere, he showed up large and burly, an old rough great-coat shrugged tightly around him, an old fur cap pulled down to his ears. He limped badly.

About a quarter of a mile from the church there was a large white farm-house. The great square front yard was full of smooth snow. Some old rose-bushes under the house walls pricked softly through it, but there was not a foot-track anywhere. All the windows in the house were dark. Marlow stood looking up at the house. A great clod of damp snow struck on his shoulders. It had fallen from a maple-tree which reached out over his head. He shook it off.

"Guess I'll go round to the back door an' see if I can raise anybody," said he, out loud.

"There ain't anybody livin' in that house now," said a voice.

Marlow looked around. A small woman stood beside him; her little upturned face stood out of the dark with its soft paleness, but he could not distinguish the features.

"Is that so?" said he.

"Yes; there ain't anybody been livin' there for some time." The woman caught her breath as she talked.

"Then the old man's dead."

"He died more'n three years ago. The place has been shut up ever since."

"I wonder if I could get in there? I s'pose somebody's got the key. You don't happen to know who, do you? I'm Marlow's son. I don't know who you are, but I don't s'pose it's likely you're anybody that knows me."

"Gilman, is that you?"

"I s'pose it is."

"I knew you the minute you spoke."

"You did? Well, I'm glad of it. I didn't count on anybody in the whole town rememberin' the sound of my voice. But I'll own I can't say as much for myself."

"Don't you know— I live in the next house."

The man hesitated. "It ain't Lucy—well I don't know as it is Lucy Glynn, now." He ended with a little uncertain laugh.

"Yes, it is."

Marlow saw, to his great amazement, that the woman was crying. She was shaken all over with her sobs. She leaned up against the snowy fence. He looked at the house, then at her. He did not know what to do. He had no idea what she was crying about. "I'm real glad to see you, Lucy," said he, finally, in a nervous, apologetic tone. She made no reply. "Is your father livin'?"

"Yes, father's livin'."

Marlow shuffled his feet in the snow. He looked at Lucy, then at the house. "Anything I can do for you?" he said at last, in an embarrassed, solemn way. His face felt hot.

"No." Suddenly the woman straightened herself. "I've got the key to the house," said she, in a tremulous voice, which caught at every word to recover itself.

"Oh, you have!"

"Yes; it's been left at our house ever since he died. If you'll go back with me—"

"All right."

The woman went on ahead, her dark skirts dabbled in the snow. Marlow followed, his eyes on her little narrow shoulders, which had somehow a meek air about them. She gathered her gray shawl up primly on her two arms, and kept it tightly pulled around her. She walked with a little nervous scud. Marlow tramped heavily after her. They had but a little way to go.

"What's goin' on in the church to-night?" said he. "I saw it was all lighted up when I came by."

"They're havin' a Christmas tree there."

"I declare, it is the night before Christmas, ain't it?"

"Didn't you know it?"

"Well, I guess I'd kind of lost my reckonin'. I haven't thought much about Christmas lately. Folks make a great deal more account of it than they used to, anyhow."

"Yes, they do."

The two front windows of the small house in the next lot were golden with light. Some green plants showed in them; the white curtains were drawn only over the upper sashes.

Lucy turned into the gate. As she did so she glanced around at Marlow, and noticed for the first time how he limped. "Why, you're lame," she said.

"Yes. I hurt my knee awhile ago, and then the rheumatism got into it. I've been in the hospital a spell."

The woman gave a little cry. "The hospital!"

"Yes."

"Let me help you up the steps."

"You!"

"I'm real strong."

"Oh, I can get up the steps well enough. It ain't very bad now; I've got kind of used to it. I'd feel lonesome without it, you know. Well, it's better to have an ache stick to you than nothin', I s'pose." Marlow chuckled feebly.

Lucy opened the outer door, then an inner one. The entry was so small that she had to step out of it into the room before her guest could enter at all. There came a rush of warm air, sweet with heliotrope and oleander, and pungent with geraniums.

Marlow snuffed it in, and blinked in the light. "I'll wait here," said he. "You'd better shut your door or you'll cold your house all off."

"Why, you're comin' in?"

"No, thank ye; it wouldn't pay. I'll just stand here till you get the key."

"Ain't you comin' in, just to get warm a minute?"

"No, thank ye; I guess I won't. I'll come some other time. I'll take the key now and go—well, I don't know as I'll say home—over there." He waved his hand towards the dark mass of buildings at the left. Lucy stood looking at him a minute.

"Why don't you shet the door?—you're coldin' the house all off," called a voice out of the light and warmth. "Hey!" called the voice again, "why don't you shet the door? Is that you?"

Then Lucy swung to the inner door and stepped up to Marlow. "You must come in. I don't see what you're thinkin' of. Here's that house all cold and dark. It ain't fit to go into; it's been shut up. You'll catch your death of cold; and you're lame; and there ain't—anybody—there." Her voice sounded weakly sharp; at the end it broke into a sob again.

"Great heavens! she can't want me to come in as bad as that," he said to himself. "I'll get along well enough," he said, ardently, after a minute; "I'm used to 'most everything. 'Twouldn't be worth while for me to come in."

"I was goin' to get you some supper."

"Oh, thank ye; but it don't make any difference to me whether I have any supper or not."

"It ain't any trouble," Lucy said, faintly.

Marlow stood looking irresolutely at her. He could not believe that she was in earnest about wanting him to enter. "I'll track the snow all over your clean house," he said, finally.

That signified that he was coming in. "That ain't any matter," said Lucy, and again threw open the sitting-room door.

Marlow stamped heavily on the door-step, and shook his shoulders; then he went in clumsily. The room was small. Out of his very humility and meekness he saw himself larger than he was; there was a swift multiplication, in his own estimation, of his rough clothes and his rough figure. He held his cap in his hand, and did not dare to stir for a moment. In the corner near him was a great pot with an oleander-tree, its spraying top all pink with blossoms. There was a little yellow stand with pots of geranium and heliotrope on it. Take a step forward, and there was an old man warming his feet at an air-tight stove.

"Here's somebody come to see us, father," said Lucy.

The old man shrank back. He ignored Marlow, who held out his hand, and mumbled something. "I dun know who 'tis," he said, turning to his daughter.

"Why, it's Mr. Marlow, father—Gilman Marlow. He used to live next door—don't you know?"

"'Tain't, nuther; he's dead." The old man set his lips together like a child.

"Yes, father, old Mr. Marlow's dead; he died three years ago. But this ain't him; this is his son Gilman. Don't you remember him?"

"The one that sort of slumped through?"

Lucy started pitifully. Marlow colored; then he grinned.

"Yes, I reckon that just fits my case," said he, with a sort of embarrassed and shamefaced mirthfulness. "I'm the one. I've slumped through ever since I come into the world."

"Father, can't you shake hands with Gilman?"

The old man reached out his hand. His thin mouth curved up at the corners, the wrinkles around his eyes deepened. He would have looked quizzical had he not looked so feeble. Marlow grasped the old hand; then he gave Lucy his cap and coat, and seated himself in the chair which she had proffered him. It was a calico-covered rocker. He sat in it stiffly. It seemed to him that it would be indecorous to relax himself into comfort.

Something brushed his head. He looked up, and it was a soft spray of the oleander blossoms. He moved his chair quickly. Lucy had gone out; he could hear her stepping about in the next room. He wondered vaguely what she was doing. He had no longer any feeling of resistance to her plans. He was nearly exhausted. He was just out of the hospital, and he had walked five miles through the snow that day. His knee began to pain him now. His large, rough-complexioned face was pale.

The old man eyed him intently. He had something which looked like a brown cashmere dress across his knees, and another part of it lay on a chair beside him. "What's she a-doin' on?" he asked Marlow.

"I don't know."

"Lucy!" called her father; "Lucy!"

"What is it, father?" called Lucy back from the other room.

"What air you a-doin' of?"

"Makin' a little tea for Mr. Marlow."

"What air you a-makin' tea for him for?" There was

no reply. "What is she a-makin' tea for you for?" asked the old man of Marlow.

"I don't know."

"She never makes any for me this time o' night. 'Twouldn't do me no harm, nuther, a cup on't warm afore I went to bed." Suddenly the old man caught up the brown cashmere on his lap and threw it over to Marlow. "There," said he, "you kin pick the bastin's out o' that while you're settin'. I've got to pick 'em out of the waist on't."

Marlow looked at the brown cashmere in bewilderment. "What?"

"Pick the bastin's out—them long white stitches in the seams. Lucy dress-makes, an' I hev to pick out all the bastin's. It's ruther more'n I want to do some days. You might jest as well take holt while you air a-settin'."

Marlow began awkwardly pulling at the white thread.

Presently Lucy opened the door. "I've got some tea made," said she, with gentle stiffness. There was a delicate meagreness about the little figure in the best black silk gown. She wore a full white ruche around her slender neck; she held her thin chin erect above it, but her whole head seemed to droop a little. There were bright spots on her cheeks, which were thin, but still softly curved.

Marlow eyed her with admiration, which was the only distinct sentiment which shaped itself out of his bewilderment and fatigue. Lucy had been very pretty, and was now; still she was not as pretty nor as young as she looked to him. He viewed her in the same glass in which he saw himself reflected. Her face beside his own, which thrilled him with humility, got a wonderful beauty of contrast. He eyed his poor clothes, then her nice black silk; the black gloss of it on her shoulders, the cunning loopings, a flutter of black lace on the over-skirt, filled him with respect and awe.

"Wa'n't you goin' out somewhere?" he asked, with feeble politeness. He got up clumsily, and let the brown cashmere slide to the floor.

"No; I was just goin' to look in at the Christmas tree a minute. I wa'n't goin' to stay. Father, what have you done?"

She picked up the dress, and looked at him and Marlow.

"I ain't done nothin' but set him pickin' out a few bastin's," said the old man, defiantly. "He might jest as well be workin' as me."

"Oh, father, you hadn't ought to!"

"I didn't mind," said Marlow, stupidly.

"Father's real feeble and childish," Lucy whispered, when she and her guest were in the other room. "I set him pickin' out bastin's to keep him contented. He frets about doin' it, but he likes it. He's just as uneasy as he can be if he gets out of work."

"It's a great deal better for him, I should think," Marlow assented.

The fragrance of the tea stole into his nostrils. The nicely piled white bread gave out a sweet odor of its own.

Lucy had set out her mother's china cups and saucers—white, with a little green vine on the rims. She offered him her best damson sauce and her fruit cake. Marlow ate without tasting. He was trying to remember something. He remembered it better and better; it was quite clear in his mind by the time he was left to himself in the little sleeping-room up-stairs. It was Lucy's, which she had given up to him. She would sleep on the sitting-room lounge. A little picture hung over the bed. It caught his attention; it had a familiar look: then he recollected. He had given it to Lucy Glynn twenty years ago; they had thought they were in love with each other, though little had been said about it. It was just before he went away. Gradually he recalled some words, a kiss or two. He had almost forgotten. Now the memory came, it was sweet. He felt as if he were thrusting back his head, old and weary and grizzled, out of this wintry misery into some sweet old spring which he had passed. He looked back at it with pitiful regret.

"Why didn't I marry Lucy," he said to himself, "and stay at home, and settle down, and behave myself?"

The next day was Christmas. It snowed again heavily. Marlow got his key and tramped over to his old home through the snow-drifts. So far as he knew, the place was all his. It was quite a little fortune to him, this substantial house, with its environment of sixty acres of meadow and woodland. He could not believe in the reality of it; a whimsical doubt as to the rightfulness of his claim possessed him. He felt as if he were extending his hand for a gift which was begrudged. It was natural enough that he should feel so; he could not remember his father as ever giving him anything willingly. If Gilman Marlow had led a hard life, there had been no parental love and softness to point at as the cause of it. Marlow had a few cents in his pocket. These seemed to him a much more tangible property than this solid estate which he was examining. He walked through the bitter cold rooms with a feeling as if he intruded. His father, dead, became to him a more certain possessor than if living. He saw his father's coat and hat hanging on a peg in the kitchen, and he turned away like a culprit.

After a little he went out in the storm again. He thought he might as well see the man who Lucy had told him had charge of the estate. His name was Nelson ; he was one of the selectmen. Marlow had to pass the church and the graveyard to reach his house. The evergreen branches hung lower than ever ; the new snow-flakes softly bent down the long slim sprays of the graveyard bushes until they lay on the ground ; the mildewed fronts of the slanting old gravestones were hung with irregular, shifting snow-garlands.

Marlow stopped and looked in the solemn white enclosure. The snow settled softly upon him. There was no wind ; everything was very still. Somewhere over there was his father's grave. He brushed away some tears with the back of his hand. "Good Lord," he muttered, "I ain't got much, an' that's a fact." Then he went on. It was a quarter of a mile farther to the selectman's house.

It was noon when he returned along the same road. The snow had gathered a good deal, but he seemed to walk with greater ease—at any rate, he walked faster.

He passed his father's house, and went straight to the Glynns'. He knocked, and the old man shuffled to the door. "Lucy's gone," he said, querulously. "She's been gone all the forenoon, an' I dun know whar she is. It's dinner-time now, an' thar ain't a pertater on, nor nothin', an' I've been a-pickin' out bastin's ever since daylight. I wish you'd find out whar she's gone, an' send her home."

"Well, I'll see," said Marlow. Then he plodded around to the side door of his own house. It opened directly into the kitchen. There was a good fire in the stove, and Lucy stood beside it cooking some eggs. A pot with potatoes was steaming and bubbling over. The table was set out, with a white cloth on it.

"Why, you here?" said Marlow.

Lucy bent over her frying eggs. "I thought I'd get you a little somethin' to eat, seein' you wa'n't willin' to come to our house again. There's a couple of pies in the oven, an'—"

"Lucy," said Marlow, suddenly, "what made you pay up the interest on that mortgage?"

Lucy suddenly turned white. "What do you mean?" she stammered.

"Nelson told me all about it. What made you do it?"

"Mr. Nelson said he wouldn't tell."

"He didn't mean to. I guessed it from somethin' he said, an' then I made him tell me. I think I ought to know it. Lucy, he said you'd put a mortgage on your house to pay up that back interest-money, so it shouldn't be foreclosed. Did you?"

"It ain't worth talkin' about."

"An' then you've paid the interest an' taxes ever since, so I shouldn't lose the place. I don't see how you did it."

"I've had all the dress-makin' I could do." Lucy lifted the frying-pan off the stove. Her hands trembled.

"Stop workin' a minute, an' let's talk," said Marlow.

Lucy set the pan on the hearth, and stood waiting. She cast her eyes down; her face twitched nervously.

"Look here, Lucy, what made you do it?"

"You—was away, an' you didn't know about it."

"How did you know it was worth while—that I'd ever come back?"

"I thought you might."

"You didn't know."

"Mr. Nelson said you would. He got news that you was livin' once; somebody'd seen you; then he lost track of you."

"What made you do it?"

"I thought you hadn't ought to lose the place."

"Well, you shall have the money part of it made up to you." Marlow was silent for a moment. "Lucy," said he, finally, "I never was so beat in my life as I was when Nelson told me that this mornin.' I've been thinkin'— Look here, didn't we go together a little once, years and years ago?"

Lucy turned paler. "There ain't any use in bringin' that up," she said, with a certain dignity.

"I want to know about it. Lucy, did I treat you mean? We wa'n't much more'n children, were we? We didn't talk about gettin' married, did we? We just thought we liked each other, an' kept round together a little while before I went away. That was all, wa'n't it?"

"Yes," whispered Lucy, faintly. Suddenly she put her hands up to her face.

Marlow took a step towards her; then he went back. "Don't cry," said he. "Lucy, see here, I'm goin' to ask you somethin'. Didn't you forget, all this time? Lucy, tell me."

She shook her head.

Marlow shut his mouth tight. He partly turned his head away. Then he spoke again. "Look here, Lucy, I'm goin' to tell you the truth: I hadn't remembered as well as you had."

"I didn't—suppose you had." She turned with a little state, and tried to move towards the door.

"Don't go; I've got somethin' I want to say." He hesitated a moment; then he went on. His face was hot. He had an honest, embarrassed air, like a boy. "I wanted to say that— Well, I thank you more'n I ever thanked any human bein' in my life. I'd lay down an' die, if it could do you any good, to show you that I did. An'—if—I'd come home different, if I'd got rich, or if I'd even come home decent—if I'd behaved myself, and if I looked fit and was fit to be seen beside you—I'd ask you to marry me, an' do all I could to pay you for thinkin' of me all this time; but as 'tis, there ain't any use speakin' of that. All I can say is, I wish the last twenty years was to live over."

Lucy gathered a shawl about her, and turned to go. "I've got to go home and get father's dinner," she said, brokenly. "There ain't any use in bringin' all this up."

"I don't s'pose there is much, but I kind of wanted to speak of it," said Marlow, blushing deeper. "Thank you for gettin' my dinner."

"That's nothin'."

He watched her going with a sinking heart.

"She wouldn't think of havin' me now," he said to himself.

Lucy was half out of the yard, when she turned and came back. Marlow opened the door quickly. There she stood, her knees trembling. She gasped for breath between her words.

"There's—one thing—I didn't mean you to think—I didn't—want—you to think that it would—make any difference to me because—you wa'n't rich or—"

"Lucy, you don't mean to say that you'd have me as I am now?" Marlow took hold of one of her thin arms and pulled her in softly. He led her back to the stove; then he stood looking at her again. "Good Lord, Lucy!" he said, "you can't think anything of me, the way I am now!"

"I don't see why you ain't just as well as you ever was."

"I ain't worth this," said Marlow. He put his arm around Lucy and kissed her forehead.

She stood stiffly; then she released herself, and went over and looked out of a window.

"I'm afraid you don't think enough of me," she said, presently, without looking around.

"I guess you needn't worry about that. I know I ain't been thinkin' about you all these years, as much as you have, accordin' to what you say about me. But—I'll put it this way." He colored and half laughed. These little flights of fancy were natural to him; he took them in his most honest moments; but he was always a little shamefaced about it. "Well, s'pose some day—you know I've been round foreign countries an' on sea-shores a good deal—s'pose some day I'd come across a pearl caught into some sea-weeds, where I hadn't no idea of findin' it. Well, I guess it wouldn't have made much difference to me whether or no I'd been thinkin' about that pearl for twenty years, or whether I'd ever seen it an' forgotten it. There'd been the pearl, an' I'd been the man that had it. I'll think enough of you—you needn't bother about that. I don't know what I'd be made of if I didn't. Good Lord! to think of me havin' *you!*"

After Lucy had been home and attended to her father's wants, she returned and spent all the afternoon making the house comfortable for Marlow.

It was sunset when she went home the last time. It had stopped snowing, and there was a clear, yellow sky in the west. A flock of sparrows flew whistling around one of the maples. A sled loaded with Christmas greens was creaking down the road. One could hear children's voices in the distance. Lucy Glynn sped along. Whether wisely or not, she was full of all Christmas joy. She had given at last her Christmas gift, which she had been treasuring for twenty years.

A VILLAGE LEAR.

"JEST wait a minute, Sary." The old man made a sly backward motion of his hand; his voice was a cautious whisper.

Sarah Arnold stood back and waited. She was a large, fair young woman in a brown calico dress. She held a plate of tapioca pudding that she had brought for the old man's dinner, and she was impatient to give it to him and be off; but she said nothing. The old man stood in the shop door; he had in one hand a stick of red-and-white peppermint candy, and he held it out enticingly towards a little boy in a white frock. The little boy had a sweet, rosy face, and his glossy, fair hair was carefully curled. He stood out in the green yard, and there were dandelions blooming around his feet. It was May, and the air was sweet and warm; over on one side of the yard there was some linen laid out to bleach in the sun.

The little boy looked at the old man and frowned, yet he seemed fascinated.

The old man held out the stick of candy, and coaxed, in his soft, cracked voice. "Jest look a-here, Willy!" said he; "jest look a-here! See what gran'pa's got: a whole stick of candy! He bought it down to the store on purpose for Willy, an' he can have it if he'll jest come here an' give gran'pa a kiss. Does Willy want it, hey?—Willy want it?" The old man took a step forward.

But the child drew back, and shook his head violently, while the frown deepened. "No, no," said he, with baby vehemence.

The old man stepped back and began again. It was as if he were enticing a bird. "Now, Willy," said he, "jest look a-here! Don't Willy like candy?"

The child did not nod, but his blue, solemn eyes were riveted on the candy.

"Well," the grandfather went on, "here's a whole stick of candy come from the store, real nice pep'mint candy, an' Willy shall have it if he'll jest come here an' give gran'-pa a kiss."

The child reached out a desperate hand. "Gimme!" he cried, imperatively.

"Yes, Willy shall have it jest as soon as he gives gran'pa a kiss." The old man waved the stick of candy; his sunken mouth was curved in a sly smile. "Jest look at it! Willy, see it! Red-an'-white candy, real sweet an' nice, with pep'-mint in it. An' it's all twisted! Willy want it?"

The child began to take almost imperceptible steps forward, his eyes still fixed on the candy. His grandfather stood motionless, while his smile deepened. Once he rolled his eyes delightedly around at Sarah. The child advanced with frequent halts.

Suddenly the old man made a spring forward. "Now I've got ye!" he cried. He threw his arms around the boy and hugged him tight.

The child struggled. "Lemme go!—lemme go!" he half sobbed.

"Yes, Willy shall go jest as soon as he gives gran'pa the

kiss," said the old man. "Give gran'pa the kiss, and then he shall have the candy an' go."

The child put up his pretty rosy face and pursed his lips sulkily. The grandfather bent down and gave him an ecstatic kiss.

"There! Now Willy shall have the candy, 'cause he's kissed gran'pa. He's a good boy, an' gran'pa 'll let him have the candy right off. He sha'n't wait no longer."

The child snatched the candy and fled across the yard. The old man laughed, and his laugh was a shrill, rapturous cackle, like the high notes of an old parrot. He turned to the young woman. "I knowed I could toll him in," he said; "I knowed I could. The little fellar likes candy, I tell ye."

Sarah smiled sympathetically and extended the plate of pudding. "I brought you over a little of our pudding," said she. "Mother thought you might relish it."

The old man took it quite eagerly. "Brought a spoon in't, didn't ye?"

"Yes; I thought maybe you'd like to eat it out here."

"Well, I guess I may jest as well eat it out here, an' not carry it into the house. Viny might kinder git the notion that it would clutter up some. I'll jest set down here an' eat this, an' then I won't want no dinner in the house. I guess they're goin' to have beef, an' I don't relish beef much lately. I'd ruther have soft victuals; but Viny she don't cook much soft victuals; the folks in the house don't care much about 'em."

The old man held the plate of pudding, but did not at once begin to eat; his eyes still followed the little boy, who stood aloof under a blooming apple-tree and sucked his candy.

"Jest look at him," he said, admiringly. "I tell ye what 'tis, Sary, that little fellar does like candy. I can allers toll him in with a stick of candy. He's dreadful kind o' bash-ful. I s'pose Ellen she don't jest like to have him round in the shop here much. She dresses him up real nice an' clean in them little white frocks, an' she's afeard he'll get somethin' on 'em; so I guess she tells him he must keep away, an' it makes him kind of afeard. I s'pose she thinks I ain't none too clean nuther to be a-handlin' of him, an' I dun know as I be, but I allers wash my hands real pertick-ler afore I tech him. I've got my tin wash-dish there on the bench, an' I'm real pertickler 'bout it."

The old man waved his hand towards a rusty tin wash-basin on the old shoemaker's bench under the window. There was a smoky curtain over the window; the plastered walls and the ceiling were dark with smoke; the place was full of brown lights. Sarah, in her brown dress, with her fair rosy face, stood waiting until the old man should finish talking.

"Well, I must go now," said she. "I haven't been to dinner myself."

"You jest wait a minute," whispered the old man, with a mysterious air. In the little shop, beside the old shoe-maker's bench, was a table that was brown and dark with age and dirt, and it was heaped with litter. There was a drawer in it, and this the old man opened with an effort; it stuck a little. "Look a-here," he whispered—"look a-here, Sary."

Sarah came close, and peered around his elbow.

The old man took a little parcel from the midst of the leather chips and waxed threads and pegs that half filled the drawer. He unrolled it carefully. "Look a-here," he said again, with a chuckle. He held up a stick of pink candy. "There," he went on, winking an old blue eye at Sarah, "I ain't goin' to give that to him till to-morrer. To-morrer I'll jest toll him in with that, don't ye see? Hey?"

"That's checkerberry, ain't it?"

"Yes, that's checkerberry, an' the tother was pep'mint. I got two sticks of candy down to the store this mornin', one checkerberry an' the tother pep'mint. Ye see, I put a patch on a shoe for the Briggs boy last week, an' he give me ten cents for't. I'd kinder calkilated to lay it out in terbacker—I ain't had none lately—but the more I thought 'bout it the more I thought I'd git a leetle candy. Ye never see sech a chap fer candy as he is; he'll hang off, an' hang off, but he can't stan' it to lose the candy nohow. I dun know but the Old Nick could toll him in with a stick of candy, he's in such a takin' for't; never see sech a fellar fer candy." The old man raised his cackling laugh again, and Sarah laughed too, going out the back door of the shop. "I'm real obleeged to your mother, Sary; you tell her," he called after her.

He replaced the candy in the drawer, still chuckling to himself; then he sat down to his pudding. He sat on his shoemaker's bench, well back from the door, and ate. He smacked his lips loudly; he liked this soft, sweet food.

Barney Swan was a small, frail old man; he stooped weakly, and did not look much larger than a child, sitting there on his bench. His face, too, was like a child's; his sunken mouth had an innocent, infantile expression, and his eyes had that blank, fixed gaze, with an occasional twinkle of shrewdness, that babies' eyes have. His thin white hair hung to his shoulders, and he had no beard. He owned only one decent coat, and that he kept for Sundays: he always went to meeting. On week-days he wore his brown calico shirt sleeves and his old sagging vest. His bagging, brownish black trousers were hauled high around his waist, and his ankles showed like a little boy's.

Old Barney Swan had sat upon that shoemaker's bench the greater part of his time for sixty years. His father before him had been a shoemaker and cobbler; he had learned the trade when a child, and been faithful to it all his life. Now not only his own powers had failed, but hand shoemaking and cobbling were at a discount. There were two thriving boot and shoe factories in the town, and the new boots and shoes were finer to see than the old coarsely cobbled ones. Old Barney was too old to go to work in the shoe factory, but it is doubtful if he would have done so in any case. He had always had a vein of childish obstinacy in spite of his mildness, and it had not decreased with age. "If folks want to wear them manufactured shoes, they can," he would say, with a sudden stiffening of his bent back; "old shackly things! You'd orter seen them shoes the Briggs boy brought in here t'other day; they wa'n't wuth treein' up, an' they never had been."

Although now old Barney's revenue was derived from the Briggs boy and sundry other sturdy, stubbed urchins, whose shoe-leather demanded the cheapest and most thorough repairs to be had, he had accumulated quite a little property through his faithful toil on that leathern seat on the end of that old bench. But it had seemed easier for him to accumulate property than to care for it. His greatest talent was for patient, unremitting labor and economy; his financial conceptions were limited to them. Ten years before, he had made a misadventure and lost a few hundred dollars, and was so humbled and dejected over it that he had made his property over to his daughters on consideration of a life support. They had long been urging him to make such an arrangement. He had two daughters, Malvina and Ellen. His wife had died when they were about twenty. The wife had been a delicate, feeble woman, yet with a certain spirit of her own. In her day the daughters had struggled hard for the mastery of the little household, but with only partial success; after her death they were entirely victorious. Barney had always thought his daughters perfect; they had their own way in everything, with the exception of the money. He clung to that for a while. He was childishly fond of the few dollars he had earned all by himself and stowed away in his house and acres of green meadow-land and the village savings-bank. He was fond of the dollars for themselves; the sense of treasure pleased him. He did not care to spend for himself; there were few things that he wished for except a decent meeting-coat and a little tobacco. The tobacco was one point upon which he displayed his obstinacy; his daughters had never been able entirely to do away with that, although they waged constant war upon it. He would still occasionally have his little comforting pipe, and chew in spite of all berating and disgust. But the tobacco was sadly curtailed since the property had changed hands; he had only his little earnings with which to purchase it. The daughters gave him no money to spend. They argued that "father ain't fit to spend money." So his most urgent necessities were doled out to him.

When the property was divided, Malvina, the elder daughter, had for her share the homestead and a part of the money in the bank; Ellen, the younger, had the larger portion of the bank money and some wooded property.

Malvina stipulated to furnish a home and care for the old man as long as he lived, and Ellen was to pay her sister a certain sum towards his support. Both daughters were married at the time; Malvina had one daughter of her own. Malvina had remained at her old home after her marriage, but Ellen had removed to a town some twenty miles away. Her father had visited there several times, but he never liked to remain long. He would never have gone had not Malvina insisted upon it. She considered that her sister ought to share her burden, and sometimes give her a relief. So Barney would go, although with reluctance; in fact, his little shoe-shop was to him his beloved home, his small solitary nest, where he could fold his old wings in peace. Nobody knew how regretfully he thought of it during his visits at Ellen's. While there he sat mostly in her kitchen, by the cooking-stove, and miserably pored over the almanac or the religious paper. Occasionally he would steal out behind the barn and smoke a pipe, but there was always a hard reckoning with Ellen afterwards, and it was a dearly purchased pleasure. Ellen was a small, fair woman; she was delicate, much as her mother had been, and her weakness and nervousness made her imperious will less evident but more potent. Old Barney stood more in awe of her than of Malvina. He was anxiously respectful towards her husband, who was a stout, silent man, covering his own projects and his own defeats with taciturnity. He was a steady grubber on a farm, and very close with old Barney's money, of which, however, his wife understood that she had full control. She had had out of it a set of red-plush parlor furniture and a new silk dress. Once in a while old Barney, while on a visit, would stand on the parlor threshold and gaze admiringly in at the furniture; but did he venture to step over, his daughter would check him. "Now don't go in there, father," she would cry out; "you'll track in somethin'."

"No, I ain't a-goin' in, Ellen," Barney would reply, and meekly shuffle back.

Old Barney was intensely loyal towards both of his daughters; not even to himself would he admit anything to their disadvantage. He always spoke admiringly of them, and would acknowledge no preference for one above the other. Still he undoubtedly preferred Malvina. She was a large, stout woman, but some people thought that she looked like her father. When the property was divided, Malvina had had every room in the house newly painted and papered; then she stood before them like a vigilant watch-dog. She had been neat before, but with her new paint and paper and a few new carpets her neatness became almost a monomania. She was fairly fierce, and her voice sounded like a bark sometimes when old Barney, with shoes heavy with loam and clothes stained with tobacco juice, shuffled into her spotless house. However, in a certain harsh way she did her duty by her simple old father. She saw to it that his clothes were comfortably warm and mended, and he had enough to eat, although his own individual tastes were never consulted. Still, he was scrupulously bidden to meals, and his plate was well filled. She did not like to have him in the house, and showed that she did not, but she had no compunctions upon that point, for he preferred the shop. She never gave him spending-money, for she did not consider that he was capable of spending money judiciously. She bought all that he had herself. She was a good financier, and made a little go a long way.

Malvina's husband was dead, and her daughter was now

eighteen years old. Her name was Annie. She was a pretty girl, and had a lover. She was to be married soon. They had not told old Barney about it, but he found it out two weeks before the wedding. He stood in his shop door one morning and called cautiously to Sarah Arnold. (The Arnolds lived in the next house, and Sarah was out in the yard picking some roses.) "Sary, come here a minute," he called. And Sarah came, with her roses in her hand. The old man beckoned her mysteriously into the shop. He drew well back from the door, after having peered sharply at the house windows. Then he began: "Ye heard on't, Sary," whispered he—"what's goin' on in there? Hey?" He gave his hand a backward jerk towards the house.

Sarah laughed. "I suppose so," said she.

"How long ye known it? Hey?"

"Well, I've heard 'twas coming off before long."

"The weddin's goin' to be in two weeks. Did ye know that? Hey?"

"I heard so."

"Well, it's the first I've heard on't. I knew that young fellar'd been shinin' round there consider'ble, an' I spos'd 'twas comin' off some time or other, but I didn't have no idee 'twas goin' to be so soon. Look a-here, Sary"—Sarah, placid and fair and pleasant, holding her roses, gazed attentively at him—"*I'm—a-goin' to—give her somethin'!*"

"What are you going to give her?"

"Ye'll see. I've got some money laid up, an' I know a way to raise a leetle more. Ye'll see when the time comes—ye'll see." The old man raised his pleasant cackle, then he hushed it suddenly, with a wary glance towards the house. "You mind you don't say nothin' about it, Sary," said he.

"No, I won't say a word about it," returned Sarah. Then she went home with her roses and her own thoughts. She herself was to be married soon, but there would be no such commotion over her wedding as over Annie's. The Arnolds were very humble folk, according to the social status of the village, and were not on very intimate terms with their neighbors. Old Mr. Arnold took care of people's gardens and sawed wood for a living, and Mrs. Arnold and Sarah sewed, and even went out for extra work when some of the more prosperous village people had company. However, Sarah was going to marry a young man who had saved quite a sum of money. He was building a new house on a cross street at the foot of a meadow that lay behind Barney Swan's shop. Sarah had told Barney all about it, and he often strolled down the meadow and watched the workmen on the new house with a wise and interested air. He was very fond of Sarah. Sarah had her own opinion about Annie and the old man's daughters, but she was calm about expressing it even to her mother. She was a womanly young girl. However, once in a while her indignation grew warm.

"I think it's a shame," she told her mother, when she carried her roses into the house, "that they haven't told Grandpa Swan about Annie's going to be married, and the poor old man's planning to give her a present." The tears stood in Sarah's blue eyes. She crowded the roses into a tumbler.

It was only the next day that old Barney called her into the shop to display the present. He had been so eager about it that he was not able to wait. However, the idea that the gift must not be presented to his granddaughter until her wedding-day was firmly fixed in his mind. He had obtained in some way this notion of etiquette, and he was resolved to abide by it, no matter how impatient he might be. "I've got it here all ready, but I ain't a-goin' to give it to her till the day she's married, ye know," he told Sarah while he was fumbling in the table-drawer (that was his poor little treasure-box). There he kept his surreptitious quids of tobacco and his pipe and his small hoards of pennies. His hands trembled as he drew out a little square parcel. He undid it with slow pains. "Look a-here!" In a little jeweller's box, on a bed of pink cotton, lay a gold-plated brooch with a red stone in the centre. The old man stood holding it, and looking at Sarah with a speechless appeal for admiration.

"Why, ain't it handsome!" said she; "it's just as pretty as it can be!"

Old Barney still did not speak; he stood holding the box, as silent as a statue whose sole purpose is to pose for admiration.

"Where did you get it?" asked Sarah.

The old man ushered in his words with an exultant chuckle. "Down to Bixby's; an' 'twas jest about the pertiest thing he had in his hull store. It cost consider'ble; I ain't a-goin' to tell ye how much, but I didn't pay no ninepence for't, I can tell ye. But I had a leetle somethin' laid up, an' there was some truck I traded off. I was bound I'd git somethin' wuth somethin' whilst I was about it."

As Barney spoke, Sarah noticed that his old silver watch-chain was gone, and a suspicion as to the "truck" seized her, but she did not speak of it. She admired the brooch to Barney's full content, and he stowed it away in the drawer with pride and triumph. He was true to his resolution not to mention the present to his granddaughter, but he could not help throwing out sundry sly hints to the effect that one was forthcoming. However, no one paid any attention to them; they knew too well the state of Barney's exchequer to have any great expectations, and all the family were in the habit of disregarding the old man's chatter. He always talked a great deal, and asked many questions; and they seemed to look upon him much in the light of a venerable cricket, constantly chirping upon their hearth, which for some obscure religious reasons they were bound to harbor.

The question of old Barney's appearance at the marriage was quite a serious one. The wedding was to be a brilliant affair for the village, and the old man was not to be considered in the light of an ornament. Still the idea of not allowing him to be present could not decently be entertained, and Malvina began training him to make the best appearance possible. She instructed him as to his deportment, and had even made a new black silk stock for him to wear at the wedding. He was so delighted that he wanted to take possession at once, and hide it away in his table-drawer, but she would not allow it. She had planned how he should be well shaven and thoroughly brushed, and his pockets searched for tobacco, on the wedding morning. "I should feel like goin' through the floor if your grandfather should come in lookin' the way he does sometimes," she told her daughter Annie.

Annie concerned herself very little about it. She was a young girl of a sweet, docile temperament. She was somewhat delicate physically, and was indolent, partly from that, partly from her nature. Now her mother was making her work so hard over her wedding clothes that she was half ill; her little forefinger was all covered with needle-pricks, and there were hollows under her eyes. Malvina had always been a veritable queen mother to Annie.

Ellen and her little boy visited Malvina for several weeks before the wedding. Ellen assisted about the sewing; she was a fine sewer.

Old Barney did not dare stay much in the house, but he wandered about the yard, and absurdly peeped in at the doors and windows. Back in his second childhood, he had all the delighted excitement of a child over a great occasion. It was perhaps a poor and pitiful happiness, but he was as happy in his own way as Annie was over her coming marriage, and, after all, happiness is only one's own heartful.

But three days before the wedding old Barney was attacked with a severe cold, and all his anticipations came to naught. The cold grew worse, and his daughters promptly decided that he could not be present at the wedding. "There ain't no use talkin' 'bout it, father," said Malvina; "you can't go. You'd jest cough an' sneeze right through it, an' we can't have such work."

The old man pleaded, even with tears, but with no avail; on the wedding day he was almost forcibly exiled to his little shop in the yard. The excitement in the house reached a wild height, and he was not allowed to enter after breakfast; his dinner of bread and butter and tea was brought down to the shop. He sat in the door and watched the house and the hurrying people. He called Sarah Arnold over many times; he was in a panic over his present. "How am I goin' to give her that breastpin, if they don't let me go to the weddin'?" he queried, with sharp anxiety. "There sha'n't nobody else give her that pin nohow."

"I guess you'll have a chance," Sarah said, comfortingly.

When it was time for the people to come to the wedding,

Ellen, in her silk dress, with her hair finely crimped, came rustling out to the shop, and ordered old Barney away from the door.

"Do keep away from the door, father," said she, "for mercy sakes. Such a spectacle as you are, an' the folks beginnin' to come! I should think you'd know better." Ellen's forehead was all corrugated with anxious lines; she was nervous and fretful. She even pushed her father away from the door with one long, veiny hand; then she shut the door with a clash.

Then Barney stood at the window and watched. He held the little jewelry-box tightly clutched in his hand. The window-panes were all clouded and cobwebbed; it was hard for his dim old eyes to see through them, but he held back the stained curtain and peered as sharply as he could.

He saw the neighbors come to the wedding. Several covered wagons were hitched out in the yard. When the minister came into the yard he could scarcely keep himself from rushing to the door.

"There he is!" he said out loud to himself. "There he is! He's come to marry 'em!"

The hubbub of voices in the house reached old Barney's ears. A little after the minister arrived there was a hush. "He's marryin' of 'em!" ejaculated Barney. He danced up and down before the window.

After the hush the voices swelled out louder than before. Barney kept his eyes riveted upon the house. It was some two hours before people began to issue from the doors.

"The weddin's over!" shouted Barney. He looked quite wild; he gave himself a little shake, and opened the shop door and took up his stand there. Everybody could see him in his brown calico shirt-sleeves, and his slouching, untidy vest and trousers. His white locks straggled over his shoulders; his face was not very clean. Suddenly Ellen, standing and smirking in the house door, spied him. Presently she came across the yard, swaying her rattling skirts with a genteel air. She smiled all the way, and old Barney innocently smiled back at her when she reached him. But he jumped, her voice was so fierce.

"You go right in there this minute, father, an' keep that door *shut*," she said between her smiling lips.

She shut the door upon Barney, but she had no sooner reached the house than he opened it again and stood there. He still held the box.

The bridal pair were to set up housekeeping in a village ten miles away. They were to drive over that night. When at last the bridegroom and the bride appeared in the door, old Barney leaned forward, breathless. The bridegroom's glossy buggy and bay horse stood in the yard; the horse was restive, and a young man was holding him by the bridle.

Old Barney did not venture to step outside his shop door. Malvina and Ellen were both in the yard, but it was as if his soul were feeling for ways to approach the young couple. He leaned forward, his eyes were intent and prominent, the hand that held the jewelry-box shook with long, rigid motions.

The bride, at her husband's side, stepped across the green yard to the buggy. This was a simple country wedding, and Annie rode in her wedding dress to her new home. The wedding dress was white muslin, full of delicate frills and loops of ribbons that the wind caught. Annie, coming across the yard, was blown to one side like a white flower. Her slender neck and arms showed pink through the muslin, and she wore her wedding bonnet, which was all white, with bows of ribbon and plumes. Her cheeks were very red.

Old Barney opened his mouth wide. "Good Lord!" said he, with one great gasp of admiration. He laughed in a kind of rapture; he forgot for a minute his wedding present. "Look at 'em!—jest look at 'em!" he repeated. Suddenly he called out, "Annie! Annie! jest look a-here! See what gran'pa's got for ye."

Annie stopped and looked. She hesitated, and seemed about to approach Barney, when the horse started; the young man had hard work to hold him. The bridegroom lifted the bride into the carriage as soon as the horse was quiet enough, sprang in after her, and they flew out of the yard, with everybody shouting merrily after them. Old Barney's piteous cry of "Annie! Annie! jest come here a minute!" was quite lost.

The old man went into the shop and closed the door of his own accord. Then he replaced the little box in the table-drawer. Then he settled down on his old shoe-bench, and dropped his head on his hands. Soon he had a severe coughing-spell. Nobody came near him until it was quite dark; then Malvina came and asked him, in a hard, absent way, if he were not coming into the house to have any supper that night.

Old Barney arose and shuffled after her into the house; he ate the supper that she gave him; then he went to bed. He never took Annie's gold brooch out of the drawer again. He never spoke of it to Sarah Arnold nor any one else. He had the grieved dignity that pertains to the donor of a scorned gift. As the weeks went on, his cold grew no better; he coughed harder and harder. Once Malvina bought some cough medicine for him, but it did no good. The old man grew thinner and weaker, but she did not realize that; the cough arrested her attention; it tired her to hear it so constantly. She told him that there was no need of his coughing so much.

Sarah Arnold was married in August. She and her husband went to live in their new house across the meadow from old Barney's shop.

Sarah had been married a few weeks when one night old Barney came toddling down the meadow to her house. He was so weak that he tottered, but he almost ran. The short growth of golden-rod brushing his ankles seemed enough to throw him over. He waded through it as through a golden sea that would soon throw him from his footing and roll over him, but he never slackened his pace until he reached Sarah's door. She had seen him coming, and ran to meet him.

"Why, what is the matter?" she cried. Old Barney's face was pale and wild. He looked at her and gasped. She caught him by the arm and dragged him into the house, and set him in a chair. "What *is* the matter?" she asked again. She looked white and frightened herself.

Old Barney did not reply for a minute; he seemed to be collecting breath. Then he burst out in a great sobbing cry: "My shop! my shop! She's goin' to have my shop tore down! They're goin' to begin to-morrer. They're movin' my bench. Oh! oh!"

Sarah stood close to him and patted his head. "Who's goin' to have it torn down?"

"Mal—viny."

"When did she say so?"

"Jest—now—come out an' told me. Says the—old—thing looks dreadful bad out—in the yard, an' she wants it—tore down. She's goin' to have me—go to Ellen's an' stay—all winter. Puttin' my bench up—in the garret. I ain't—a-goin' to have the—bench to set on—no longer, I ain't. Oh, hum!"

Sarah's pleasant mouth was set hard. She made old Barney lie down on her sitting-room lounge, and got him a cup of tea. It was evident that the old man was completely exhausted; he could not have walked home had he tried. Sarah sat down beside him and heard his complaint, and tried to comfort him. When her husband came home to tea she told him the story, and he went up across the meadow to the shop before he took off his coat.

"It's so," he growled, when he returned. "They're lugging the things out. It's a blasted shame. Poor old man!"

Sarah's husband had a brown boyish face and a set chin; he took off his coat and began washing his hands at the kitchen sink with such energy that the leather stains might have been the ingratitude of the world.

"Did you say anything about his being down here?" asked Sarah.

"No, I didn't. Let 'em hunt."

About nine o'clock that evening Malvina, holding her skirts up well, came striding over the meadow. She had missed her father, and traced him to Sarah's. Sarah and her husband had put him to bed in their pretty little spare chamber when Malvina came in. It was evident that the old man was very ill; he was wandering a little, and he had terrible paroxysms of coughing; his breath was labored. Malvina stood looking at him; Sarah's husband kept opening his mouth to speak, and his wife kept nudging him to be silent. Finally he spoke—

"He's all upset because his shop's going to be torn down," said he; but his voice was not as bold as his intentions.

"'Tain't that," replied Malvina. "He's dretful careless;

he's been goin' round in his stockin'-feet, an' he's got more cold. I dun know what's goin' to be done. I don't see how I can get him home to-night."

"He can stay here just as well as not," said Sarah, nudging her husband again.

"Well, I'll come over an' git him home in the mornin'," Malvina said.

But she could not get him home when she came over in the morning. Old Barney never went home again. He died the second day after he came to Sarah's. Both of his daughters came to see him, and did what they could, but he did not seem to notice them much. An hour before he died he called Sarah. She ran into the room. Just then there was nobody else in the house. Old Barney sat up in bed, and he was pointing out of the window over the meadow. His pointing forefinger shook, his face was ghastly, but there was a strange, childish delight in it.

"Look a-there, Sary—jest look a-there," said old Barney. "Over in the meader—look. There's Ellen a-comin', an' Viny, an' they look jest as they did when they was young; an' Ellen she's a-bringin' me some tea, an' Viny she's a-bringin' me some custard puddin'. An' there's Willy a-dancin' along. Jest see the leetle fellar a-comin' to see gran'pa all of his own accord. An' there's Annie all in her white dress, jest as pretty as a pictur', a-comin' arter her breastpin. Jest see 'em, Sary." The old man laughed. Out of his ghastly, death-stricken features shone the expression of a happy child. "Jest look at 'em, Sary," he repeated.

Sarah looked, and she saw only the meadow covered with a short waving crop of golden-rod, and over it the September sky.

AMANDA AND LOVE.

AMANDA sewed with a diligence which seemed almost fierce. She jerked out her right elbow at sharp angles, and the stout thread made a rasping sound. She was making a braided rug, which lay stiff and heavy over her knees. Love sat at the other front window. She held some white crotchet-work, but she kept looking away from it out of the window. The cherry-tree and the rose-bushes in the yard were bowing in a light wind. There were no leaves on them, but it was near spring, and the twigs had a red glisten as they moved in the wind.

Now and then Amanda's pale eyes shot a swift, steady glance at Love. "You won't get that tidy done to-night if you keep lookin' out of the window," she remarked presently.

Love started, and colored softly. "I'm goin' to work on it," said she. Then she crocheted steadily, and did not look away from her work for a long time. Love would have been pretty had not her features been too thin and sharply accentuated. She was like a too boldly traced pencil sketch ; the beauty of design could not show through such force of outline. Her hair was too heavy for her delicate little head. It was not very tidy ; when she bent her head over her crochet-work the great slipping knot showed more plainly.

"It does seem as if you might twist up your hair a little tighter; it don't look neat," said Amanda.

"I can't make it stay up anyhow," returned Love, with meek apology.

"I guess I could make it stay up."

Amanda's light hair was parted and brushed so smoothly that there were lines of pale gloss on the sides of her head; the small knot at the back of it was compact and immovable as one on a statue.

After a while Amanda arose. "I'm goin' out to take in the clothes," said she. "I guess they must be dry by this time. I ain't goin' to have 'em beatin' in this wind any longer, anyhow."

"I'll go," said Love.

"No; you stay jest where you are, an' do your tidy. You've got some cold, an' I ain't goin' to have you out in the wind handlin' damp clothes."

When Amanda's tall, slim figure erected itself and moved across the room, it had a kind of stiff majesty about it. Her back and neck were absolutely unbending, there was one unbroken line from her head to her heels, even her dress skirt did not swing, but hung rigidly.

As soon as Amanda had gone, Love let her work fall in her lap, leaned her head back, and looked out of the window again. There was the little front yard, with its green-gray mat of grass and glistening tree and bushes; before it stretched the road; once in a while a team passed, or a woman pushed by with her garments flying back in the wind. Love, looking directly at it all, saw nothing. She had come to a place in her life where the future closed around her so plainly that, whether she would or not, she could see nothing else. Possibilities seemed near enough to sing in her ears, and all her dreams were turned to giants. No one but herself could see them; she was innocently ashamed and terrified to look; but no work and no play could divert her eyes.

When Love heard her sister coming back, she took up her work hurriedly, and began to crochet. Her little thin face looked quite sober and intent; she did not even glance at her sister when she entered. Amanda's face was reddened by the wind, but her hair was not roughened. She held her chilly fingers over the stove, and looked at Love.

"Got the tidy 'most done?" she asked.

"Pretty near."

"Goin' to get it done to-night?"

"I don't know as I can get it quite done. The last rows take longer, you know."

Amanda went suddenly across to Love. "Let me see it," said she.

Love extended the tidy nervously. Amanda scrutinized it.

"Now I want to know jest how much you've worked on this since I went out."

"I don't know as I can tell, Mandy."

"You can tell pretty near. Have you done half a row?"

"I—don't know as I have."

"Have you done quarter of one?"

"I guess not quite."

"Have you done anything at all?"

"Yes, I've done a little."

"I don't believe you've made more'n three shells. Have you?"

Love looked shamefacedly at the tidy, and made no reply.

"You'd ought to be ashamed of yourself," said Amanda.

' It's much as ever you do anything at all lately. I don't see what you think you're comin' to, sittin' all day doin' nothin' at all, starin' out of the window. You act as if you was in a brown study. I'd like to know what ails you."

Love murmured something, and twisted herself away towards the window. Amanda surveyed her imperturbably; her words had been impatient, but her manner of delivery calm. She stood over her sister implacably benignant, like an embodied duty.

" Now, Love, I want to know—an' I think you'd ought to tell me—what are you thinkin' about when you set doin' nothin' so?"

Love quivered. Secret thoughts have more sensitive surfaces than burns, and it seemed to Love that hers were laid bare. " Don't, Mandy. I don't know," she faltered.

" If you are thinkin' about what I think you are," Amanda went on, inexorably, " it's about time you stopped. If you've got any proper pride that a girl ought to have, you won't waste time thinkin' about anybody till you're pretty sure they want you to."

Love turned on her sister with a look as if she were feeling for the claws which nature had denied her. " I never said I was thinkin' about anybody," said she. Then she suddenly put her hands up to her face and began to cry.

" There's nothin' for you to cry about," said Amanda, " nor to get mad about. I'm older than you, an' I know more about the world, an' I'm goin' to look out for you as faithful as I know how, an' that's all there is about it. Now you'd better work on that tidy if you ever want to get it done, while I get supper ready."

Amanda, as she went out of the room, had a look of defiant embarrassment, and her face was flushed. She had not flinched, but she was a New England woman, and she discussed all topics except purely material ones shamefacedly with her sister. She felt as if she had injured her own delicacy as well as her sister's.

Amanda, out in the kitchen, got supper, and Love, in the sitting-room, wiped her eyes and worked on her tidy. It was really necessary it should be finished; she was going to sell it, and she needed the money. The proceeds of Love's little mats and tidies and pincushions all went for her own clothes, while Amanda's heavier and homelier work bought the food, fuel, and her own scanty wardrobe. Love had many a dainty little feature in her attire which Amanda had not, and never fairly knew that she had not. Love's little beribboned gowns and flower-wreathed hats were to Amanda as her own. She never thought of herself as being without them. Love on a Sunday, in her pretty, best attire, was, in a sweet and subtle fashion, Amanda's looking-glass. The elder sister, in her sober shawl and staid bonnet, walking beside her to meeting, saw all the time herself in this younger and fairer guise.

Amanda was old enough to be Love's mother; the two had been left alone in the world when Love was a baby. They had only their little house and an acre or two of land, but Amanda had the head of a financier. She had managed her pennies as firmly and carefully as dollars. She made every inch of their land pay. She sold hay and vegetables. She did heavy tasks in needlework for the neighbors—quilts and braided rugs and rag carpets. She had a little sum at interest in the savings-bank.

While adhering to the letter of her principles in bringing up Love, Amanda had spared her in every possible way. No rough tasks had been imposed upon this little, slender-armed sister. Amanda bought pretty silks and wools and fine threads, and had her taught to do dainty fancy-work, for which she found quite a market among the village women and the storekeepers in a neighboring large town. There were always finished articles on exhibition in the sisters' little front room, which was a studio on an exceedingly small and humble scale. Love's delicately wrought tidies and scarfs decorated the walls on all sides; the table was covered with mats and pin-cushions. Nothing could exceed Amanda's pride in the display. Love had lately finished a silk patchwork bedquilt, which was draped over the mantelshelf like a triumphal banner. Amanda invited people in to see it. She believed it a work of genius.

Love crocheted fast when she kept herself to it. There was quite a piece done on the tidy when Amanda called her out to supper. Amanda had made some milk toast. Love was very fond of it. The two ate their suppers peacefully in the little kitchen. Amanda gave Love the lowermost and best-soaked slices of toast, and Love, whose eyes were still red, ate them meekly.

After supper, when the dishes were cleared away, it was quite dark. Love lighted a lamp, and started to go up-stairs to her chamber.

"Where you goin'?" asked Amanda.

"Up stairs."

"What for?"

"I—thought maybe I'd—better change my dress."

"What are you goin' to change your dress for?"

"I—didn't know but—somebody might come in."

"I'd like to know who's goin' to come that that brown dress you've got on ain't good enough for? Who do you expect?"

"I—don't know as I expect anybody."

"I s'pose you think maybe *he*'ll be in."

"I don't know as anybody'll come. I just thought—I'd change my dress." Love, slight and flat-chested, her shoulder-blades showing through the back of her brown dress, stood before Amanda. She held the lamp unsteadily in both her little bony hands.

"That dress is plenty good enough whoever comes. I don't care if it's the President," said Amanda. "An' I can tell you one thing—if you've got any pride, an' any sense of what's proper, you won't go to dressin' up in that blue dress with all that velvet trimmin' on it, if you think anybody's comin'. If you really want to show anybody you like them before you know whether he likes you or not, you can go an' dress up for them. If anybody's got common-sense, they can read it just like A B C. You'd better go an' set down an' finish that tidy."

Love obeyed. She seated herself at the parlor table with her crochet-work. Once, when her sister was out of the room for a moment, she got up stealthily and looked at herself in the glass behind the table. She smoothed back her hair as well as she could, and adjusted the little brooch at her throat. Then she darted swiftly and noiselessly across the room to the chimney cupboard. A little bottle of cologne stood on the middle shelf. Love sprinkled some on her handkerchief; then she flew back to her chair. She hardly gained it before Amanda entered, and almost at the same moment there was a knock on the front door. Love gave a great start, and half arose. Amanda looked at her.

"I'll go," said she, sternly. Love sat down.

Amanda had reached the sitting-room door, when she

turned around and sniffed sharply. "What's that I smell?" said she.

Love said nothing.

"Have you been puttin' some of that cologne on your handkerchief?"

"A little."

"You're a silly girl."

Love crocheted with her heart beating loudly, while her sister opened the front door and let in the visitor. She could hear Amanda's voice and a subdued masculine one. Amanda was asking the visitor to lay aside his hat and coat in very much the same way that she might have asked an enemy to lay down his arms.

Amanda preceded a young man into the sitting-room. She set the lamp on the shelf and blew it out. Love half arose. She and the young man looked at each other; they extended their hands, then drew them back. Love sank into her chair with a soft, bashful titter, and the young man sat gravely and stiffly down on the sofa. Amanda seated herself at the table with her braided rug. She got it in place, and began sewing.

"How's your mother?" she asked the young man, in a dry, constrained voice.

"She's pretty well, thank you," he replied.

He was young and very tall. His feet, in their well-blacked shoes, sprawled far out from the sofa. His handsome face was red with embarrassment, but his blue eyes looked at Amanda quite sturdily and steadily.

"Has she begun on her cleanin' yet?" said Amanda.

"No, ma'am; I guess not."

"I s'pose you can help her some about the carpets."

"Yes, ma'am."

Amanda sewed, and Love crocheted on her tidy. The young man drew his feet farther in.

"It's a pleasant evening out," he remarked, after a while. Amanda nodded, with cold acquiescence.

"Yes, I s'pose 'tis," said she. Love smiled softly, without looking up.

There was a long silence. The sisters worked steadily. The visitor sat on the sofa, with his unoccupied masculine hands on his knees. Now and then he glanced at Love's bowed head. There was a calla-lily in a big pot behind her, and the broad leaves threw shadows over her. Love herself looked like a flower which for some reason was not giving out its natural fragrance. It seemed as if she needed to be stirred and shaken.

The time went on. Once in a while Amanda vouchsafed an abrupt question, and the young man replied. Love never spoke until he arose to take leave. Then she started and looked up.

"It ain't late," said she, and the blushes flamed over her cheeks.

"I guess I must be goin'," said he. There was something pitiful about the young fellow, in his Sunday suit and light necktie, with his shiny shoes and curly hair dampened and brushed as smoothly as possible. All these little humble masculine furbishings had gone for naught, and he was going home disappointed and hurt after a painfully dull evening. However, he held up his head like a man, and there was a stiffness in his way of taking leave which betokened resentment as well as dejection.

Amanda went to the door with him, and watched him put on his coat and hat. "Remember me to your mother," said she, when he went out.

When Amanda returned to the sitting-room, Love had her head bent very low over her work.

"You hadn't ought to have said it wa'n't late when he got up to go," said Amanda. "It looked dreadful forward, as if you wanted him to stay whether or no. I was surprised at you."

Love put her hands over her face, and her shoulders twitched.

"What is the matter?" asked Amanda.

"I don't believe he'll—ever—come again as long as he lives."

"I'd like to know why he won't come?"

Love made no reply. She sobbed convulsively.

"Come, you'd better go to bed," said Amanda. "You're actin' dreadful silly. Ain't you got any pride at all? I guess before I'd sit and cry because I was afraid a fellow wouldn't come to see me— An' he'll come again fast enough. I'll go an' heat a flat-iron to put to your feet. It'll be kind of chilly up-stairs to-night."

Amanda got Love into bed with the hot flat-iron at her feet, and herself lay half the night listening to hear if she were awake crying. The sisters slept in the two cottage chambers; Love had the large sunny front one. There were muslin curtains at Love's windows; she had a clean, faded woollen carpet, a large looking-glass over her bureau, and the best feather-bed. Amanda's little room was as bare and poor as could well be, her tiny looking-glass was blurred, and her bed was hard and lumpy.

If Love lay awake weeping, she wept so softly that her sister did not hear her. This was a Wednesday night. Love's admirer had been calling upon her occasionally on Wednesday evenings for some time. The next Wednesday evening he did not come, nor the next, nor the next. The sisters said nothing to each other about it. Love did not attempt to change her dress and make herself smart for him again. Her fancy-work dragged more than ever, but she always tried to be industrious when Amanda was in the room. One afternoon a neighbor called and asked Amanda out in the entry, when she was taking leave, if her sister was well.

"She always did look dreadful delicate," said she, "but now she looks to me as if you could see the light through her if you held her the right way. I should think you'd better get her something strength'nin' to take, Amanda. You know her mother died of the consumption."

"I guess she's well enough," returned Amanda, shortly. "She's always thin as a rail."

But when she went back into the sitting-room she saw Love with the neighbor's eyes; before, she had seen her with her own, to which her desires had been like soft-hued spectacles. That night she tried to get something for supper that Love would relish, but the girl scarcely tasted it. She only pecked at it like a little thin bird. Amanda made up her mind to get some medicine for her, as the neighbor had advised, and the next day she did, and Love took it, with no perceptible effect.

Five weeks from the Wednesday on which the young man had called, Amanda heard that he had procured some work in another village, and left town. She hesitated whether or not to tell Love. Finally she decided to. Love had just lighted her lamp to go to bed one night when she told her.

"They say he's left town an' gone to Sharon," said she, in a harsh, constrained voice.

Love did not make a sound, but her face moved as if she screamed. She went weakly up-stairs with her lamp, and Amanda sat down in the parlor and thought. It was midnight before she went up-stairs.

She listened a minute at Love's door, then she tiptoed in and bent over her. Love was asleep; her little face had a peaceful look, but her skin was dank and pale with perspiration; great beads stood on her forehead.

"That's the way mother used to look when she was asleep," Amanda said to herself.

Suddenly Love opened her eyes. She did not seem startled, but she turned away from Amanda and the light.

"Now, Love, I want to know what all this means," said Amanda. "Are you frettin' yourself sick because that fellow don't come?"

Love did not reply; her face was hidden, but her slender shoulders heaved convulsively.

"Well," said Amanda, slowly, "it beats all. I've heard of such things, but I never knew they were true." She smoothed out the bedclothes over Love and straightened her pillow. "Now you'd better stop cryin', an' go to sleep," said she. "He'll come again fast enough, don't you worry."

Amanda went out with the light. She did not sleep at all that night. She lay in her little chamber and wrestled for another with a problem of nature which she had never had to face for herself.

The next day was Saturday. In the afternoon Amanda dressed herself to go out. "I'm goin' out a little ways, it's so pleasant," she told Love, when she went into the sitting-room with her bonnet and shawl on.

Love smiled listlessly. She was at the window with her fancy-work as usual. Amanda glanced back as she went down the path to the front gate, but Love did not look after her; her head was bent over her work.

Amanda went down the road until she reached a large white cottage set in a deep yard. There were four front windows. Amanda saw a head at one of them, but it disappeared when she turned in at the gate. She drew her old cashmere shawl tightly over her shoulders, and went, slim and stately, up the front walk. There was a strong sweet odor of pine-apple in the air; it came from an odd brown flowering bush near the gate. It might have been gunpowder, and Amanda might have been marching up to hostile guns, from her feelings. She felt a pair of inimical female eyes upon her behind a closed blind, but she set her face steadily ahead, went up to the door, and knocked.

She waited a long time, but no one came. She knocked again and again. Finally she compressed her lips and tried the door. It was not locked. She went into the entry, and knocked on the sitting-room door. No one came. She opened the door and walked in. Directly the opposite door closed with a bang. Amanda walked across to that door and opened it. There stood an elderly woman in a little entry between the sitting-room and kitchen. She looked at Amanda with a kind of defiant embarrassment. Her handsome fleshy face was quite red.

"Good-afternoon, Mis' Dale," said Amanda.

"Good-afternoon."

There was a pause. "I want to speak to you a minute," said Amanda.

"Well, come into the sitting-room."

Amanda began at once when she and Mrs. Dale were seated opposite each other. "I wanted to ask you," said she, "how your son was."

"He's well as common."

"I heard he'd left town."

"Yes, he has."

"Does he ever come home?"

"Sometimes."

"Well, some time when he does come, I should be happy to have him call at our house."

Mrs. Dale's face grew redder, her round eyes gave out a blue glare. "Well, I'll tell you one thing right to your face, Amandy Perry, an' I ain't afraid to neither. My son ain't comin' over to your house again to be snubbed, not if I can help it. I guess he's full as good as your sister—full as good."

"It wa'n't that, Mis' Dale."

"I'd like to know what it was, then."

"I rather guess I talked to Love, an' said some things that made her act kind of bashful. I ain't never had a thing against your son. I've always thought he was one of the likeliest young men in town."

"I ruther guess my son is full as good as anybody that little meachin' thing is likely to get—full as good. I don't know what you think you are, nor where you come from: folks that have had to live from hand to mouth the way you have, an' never have had any parlor. My folks have always had parlors an' sittin'-rooms, an' I guess some of 'em would have thought my son was stoopin' if they'd known."

The channel in which Mrs. Dale's ideas ran was so narrow that it had to be well cleared of one set before others could enter. She was a kindly enough woman, but just now she was possessed of maternal resentment to the exclusion of everything else. Mrs. Dale was like an enraged mother bird with one note, she screamed it over and over in

Amanda's ears in spite of all she could say. Finally Amanda arose to go, and Mrs. Dale followed her to the door, still talking. Amanda noticed a hat on the entry table. "He's come home to spend Sunday," she thought, but she said nothing.

Mrs. Dale closed the door after her with a bang, and Amanda went slowly down the path, looking on either hand. Over in the field south of the house there was a low red fire leaping in the dry grass, and a man's figure moving about, knee-deep in curling smoke. Amanda went straight across to the field and up to the man. She held her skirts close around her, and stepped unflinchingly over the blackened ground.

"Good-afternoon, Willis," said she.

"Good-afternoon," the young man returned, stiffly.

"Come to spend Sunday?"

"Yes, ma'am."

"Why don't you come over and see us? You ain't been for a long time."

Willis stood straight and tall before Amanda; his eyes looked like his mother's. "Because I ain't goin' anywhere where I'm shown so plain I ain't wanted," said he.

"You're wanted enough. We should be real glad to see you any time. I s'pose I'm kind of stiff sometimes, but I don't mean to be; an' Love is a little quiet an' bashful, but you mustn't think we mean to act offish. If you ain't goin' anywheres to-morrow night, we'd be glad to see you. Love, she ain't very well."

Willis moved around and beat a little at the burning grass.

"Love, she ain't very well, an' I guess she's kind of frettin' because she thinks you're put out," said Amanda, in a pitiful voice.

"Well, maybe I'll come if you'd like to have me," said Willis, hesitatingly.

"We'll be happy to have you." Amanda started off; then she turned. "What—are you going to do to-night?" she asked, timidly.

"To-night?"

"Yes."

"Nothing particular that I know off."

"Can't you come to-night?"

"I—don't know but I can," Willis said, in a bewildered way.

Amanda went home in the early spring afternoon. Her limbs trembled; her face had a shocked, desperate expression. She was full of a solemn shame and terror at what she had done. People when they overstep their bounds of conduct are apt to step high and wide; poor Amanda had cleared hers well. The frogs were singing in a stretch of low meadow-land that she passed. They would have seemed to her like the chorus of a Greek tragedy had she ever heard of one.

When she got home she sat down with Love and sewed until supper-time. She said nothing about Willis Dale. She got supper early, and cleared it away. Then she got a brush and comb and basin of water, and called Love out into the kitchen. "Come here a minute, Love," said she.

Love crept out obediently.

"I'm goin' to see if I can't make your hair look neat for once," said Amanda, in a resolute tone.

She dampened Love's pretty wild hair, brushed it energetically, and twisted it tight and hard on the top of her head. Love's thin childish face looked strange and severe with her hair in flat dark curves around her temples. Amanda surveyed her approvingly.

"There," said she. "Now you'd better go an' put on your other dress; I want to fix that place that's ripped in this one."

"I thought I'd go to bed pretty soon," said Love.

"No, you ain't goin' to bed, neither. Now go an' put on your dress. You look nice an' neat for once in your life."

Willis came at eight o'clock. Amanda let him in, and left him with Love in the sitting-room. She herself sat down at the kitchen window in the deepening dusk, and stared out over the shadowy fields. She could hear the voices of her sister and her lover, now fairly started upon that path of love which was as strange to this rigid-lived single woman as that of death, and whither she was far less able to follow. Amanda sat there, and wept patiently, leaning her head against the window-casing.

UP PRIMROSE HILL.

"WE can, Mis' Rowe; this winder ain't fastened. I can slide it up easy 'nough."

"Where does it go to?"

"Into the kitchen. I declare, there's the tea-kittle on the stove; an' I should think the door was open into the butt'ry. Yes, 'tis. Mis' Rowe, the dishes are settin' on the shelves jest the way they were left."

"Can you see 'em?"

"Yes, I can. I don't b'lieve there's one speck of harm in our gettin' in an' lookin' round a little."

"Oh, Mis' Daggett, do you think we'd ought to?"

"I'd like to know what harm 'twould do."

"S'pose they should find it out?"

"I don't see who *they* is. There ain't one of the Primroses left but Maria, an' it ain't likely she'll be round here to find it out very soon."

"It's awful 'bout her, ain't it?"

"I dun know as I think it's very awful; it ain't any more than she deserves for treatin' Abel Rice the way she did."

"I've heard her husband had spent 'most all her money."

"Guess it's true 'nough. They said once she was goin' to leave him."

"I never really believed he struck her the way they said he did; did you?"

"Guess it's true 'nough. I tell you what it is, Mis' Rowe, I b'lieve folks get their desarts in this world sometimes.—We can get in here jest as easy as not, if we are a mind to."

"Oh, Mis' Daggett, I dun know 'bout it."

"There ain't a bit of harm in't," said Mrs. Daggett, who was long and vigorous and sinewy. Then with no more ado she pushed up the grating old window.

Mrs. Rowe, who was a delicate little body, stood timorously aloof in a bed of mint that had grown up around the kitchen door of the old Primrose house. There was a small wilderness of mint and sweetbrier and low pink-flowering mallow around the door. All the old foot-tracks were concealed by them.

The window was not very high; Mrs. Daggett put one knee on the sill and climbed in easily enough. Mrs. Rowe watched her with dilated eyes; occasionally she peered behind her; she had a sideway poise like a deer. It was perfectly evident that if she were to see any one approaching she would fly and leave her companion to her fate.

"Come, you get in now," said Mrs. Daggett. Her harsh, yellow old face peered out of the window; back of it was a dark green gloom. All the windows but that were closed and blinded.

"Oh, Mis' Daggett, I dun know as I darse to!"

"Come along!"

"I don't b'lieve I can get in."

"Yes, you can; it ain't high."

Mrs. Rowe approached slowly; she lifted one feeble knee. "It's no use, I can't noway," said she.

Mrs. Daggett caught hold of her arms and pulled. "Now you climb while I pull!" she cried.

"Oh, I can't noway, Mis' Daggett! You'll pull my arms out by the roots. I guess you'd better stop."

"I'll get out an' boost you in," Mrs. Daggett said, briskly, and strode over the window-sill.

But the "boosting" was not successful; finally little Mrs. Rowe recoiled in terror. "I'm afraid you'll make me go in there head-first," said she. "I guess you'd better stop, Mis' Daggett. You go in an' look round, an' I'll wait here for you."

"I'll tell you what we can do: I'll set out a chair; you can climb in jest as easy as not, then."

Mrs. Daggett again climbed in, set out one of the dusty kitchen chairs, and Mrs. Rowe with many quavers made her entry. For a moment the two women stood close together, looking about them; Mrs. Rowe was quite pale, Mrs. Daggett shrewdly observant. "I'm goin' to open them other blinds an' have a little more light," she declared at length.

"Oh, do you s'pose you'd better?"

"I'd like to know what harm it can do." Mrs. Daggett forced up the old windows, and defiantly threw open the blinds.

The kitchen was a large one, with an old billowy floor and the usual furnishings. Mrs. Daggett lifted the teakettle and examined it. "It's all one bed of rust," said she; "set up with water in't, most likely; that Mis' Loomis that was here when old Mr. Primrose died wa'n't no kind of a housekeeper. I'm a-goin' into the butt'ry."

"Oh, do you think we'd better?"

"I'd like to know what harm it can do."

Mrs. Daggett advanced with virtuous steadfastness, and the other woman, casting fearful backward glances, followed hesitatingly in her wake. They entered the pantry, which was as large as a small room, and stood with their chins tipped, scanning the shelves. "There's a whole set of white ware," said Mrs. Daggett, "an' there's some blue packed away on the top shelf. I s'pose there's a chiny closet in the parlor, where the chiny is: they must have had some chiny dishes. Ain't that a nice platter? That's jest what I want, a platter that size. What's in here?"

"Oh, don't, Mis' Daggett; seems to me I wouldn't!"

"What's the harm, I'd like to know?"

Mrs. Daggett lifted the cover from a small jar. "It's quince sauce, sure's you live," said she, sniffing cautiously. "It don't look to me as if it was hurt one mite. I'm goin' to taste of it."

"Oh, Mis' Daggett!"

"I am." Mrs. Daggett found a knife, and plunged it defiantly into the quince sauce. "It's jest as good as ever 'twas; it ain't worked one mite. You taste of it, Mis' Rowe."

"Oh, I don't b'lieve I'd better, Mis' Daggett." Mrs. Rowe looked with tremulous longing at the sauce which her friend held towards her on the tip of the knife.

"Land sakes! take it! What harm can it do?" Mrs. Daggett gave the knife a shove nearer, and Mrs. Rowe opened her mouth.

"It is good, ain't it?" she said, after tasting reflectively.

"I don't see why it ain't. Have some more."

"I guess I hadn't better."

"I'm goin' to. Might just as well; it's only spoilin' here." Mrs. Daggett helped herself to some generous dips of the sauce, and Mrs. Rowe also took sundry tastes between her remonstrances. They found nothing else that was edible, except some spices. Mrs. Daggett took a pinch of the cinnamon. "Ain't lost its strength one mite," she remarked; "thought I'd like to see if it had."

The Primrose house was a large, old-fashioned edifice. It had been the mansion-house of this tiny village, and its owners had been the grandees. The town was named for them; they had been almost like feudal lords of the little settlement. Now they all were dead with the exception of one daughter, and she had not been near her old home for twenty years. The house had been shut up since her father's death, five years ago. The great square rooms were damp and musty, and even the furniture seemed to have acquired an air of distance and reserve.

When the two curious women penetrated the statelier and more withdrawn recesses of the house, Mrs. Rowe eyed every chair as if it were alive and drawing up itself haughtily before interlopers. But Mrs. Daggett had no such feelings. She investigated everything unsparingly. She began opening a bureau drawer in one of the front chambers. Mrs. Rowe, watching her, fairly danced with weak and fascinated terror. "Oh, don't, Mis' Daggett—don't you open them drawers! You scare me dreadfully!" she cried.

"I'd like to know what harm it can do." Mrs. Daggett pulled out the drawer with a jerk. "Oh, my!" she exclaimed; "ain't this elegant!"

Mrs. Rowe tremblingly slid towards her and peeped around her shoulder, and just then came a loud peal of the door-bell. Mrs. Rowe clutched Mrs. Daggett: "Oh, Mis' Daggett, come—come quick, for mercy sake! That's the door-bell! Oh, Mis' Daggett, they'll ketch us here—they will! they will!"

"Keep still!" returned Mrs. Daggett. "No, they won't ketch us, neither. I dun know as we're doin' any harm if they did." She gave the bureau drawer a shove to, and led the retreat. "Come on down the back stairs," she said. "Don't break your neck; there's time 'nough."

When they were half-way down the stairs the bell rang again. "Oh!" gasped Mrs. Rowe—"oh, Mis' Daggett, they'll ketch us!"

"No, they won't, neither; come along." Mrs. Daggett climbed first out of the kitchen window. She thought that she could assist her friend better in that way. "I'll stand outside here and lift you down," she said. "Don't hurry so; you'll fall an' break your bones."

Mrs. Rowe mounted a chair with frantic haste, and got into the window. Mrs. Daggett extended both arms, and she jumped. "Mercy sakes! I'm ketched onto somethin'!" she screamed. "Oh, Mis' Daggett!" In fact, Mrs. Rowe's skirt had caught on something inside, and she pitched helplessly against her friend. "I hear 'em a-comin'," she groaned. "Oh, what shall I do! what shall I do!"

"Can't you hang here a minute, till I reach in an' unhitch it?"

"Oh, I can't!—I can't! Don't you let go of me, Mis' Daggett—don't you! I shall fall and break my bones if you do. Oh, I hear 'em a-comin'! Oh, Mis' Daggett, you pull as hard as you can! It's my alpacky dress. I ain't had it but three years, but I don't care nothin' 'bout that. Oh, Mis' Daggett!"

Mrs. Rowe struggled wildly, and Mrs. Daggett pulled; finally the alpaca skirt gave way. Mrs. Rowe as she turned and fled cast one despairing glance at it. "It's spoilt!" she groaned; "a great three-cornered piece gouged out of it. Oh, Mis' Daggett, do hurry!"

Mrs. Daggett paused to shut the window; then she overtook her friend with long, vigorous strides. "I wa'n't goin' to leave that window up," she remarked, "not if I knew it."

The women skirted the house well to the right, and passed into the road.

"Now I'm goin' to walk by an' see who 'tis," said Mrs. Daggett.

"Oh, don't, Mis' Daggett; let's go right home."

"I'm jest goin' to walk up by the path where I can see in. Come along; they won't know we've been in the house."

Mrs. Daggett fairly pushed her timid friend in the direction that she wished.

The Primrose house was thickly surrounded by trees, and stood far back from the road; one could only get an uninterrupted view of the front door by looking directly up the walk.

Mrs. Daggett took a cautious glance as she passed the gate; then she stopped short. "Good land!" she exclaimed, "it ain't anybody but Abel Rice. If we ain't a passel of fools!" She could see between the trees a tall man with a yellow beard leaning against the front door of the Primrose house.

"Are you sure it's him?" quavered Mrs. Rowe.

"Course I'm sure. Don't you s'pose I know Abel Rice? If it ain't the greatest piece of work! There, I knew all about his goin' there an' ringin' the bell."

"I never knew as he did really."

"Well, I knew he did. Mrs. Adoniram White said she'd seen him time an' time again. To think of our runnin' away for a luny like Abel Rice!"

"It's awful 'bout his goin' there, ain't it?"

"Yes, 'tis awful. They say they've talked an' talked to

him, but they can't make him b'lieve Maria Primrose don't live there; an' every once in a while, no matter what he's doin', hoein' potatoes or what, he'll steal off an' go up there an' ring the door-bell. I wish Maria could see him sometimes, an' realize what she did when she jilted him for that rich feller she married."

"It would serve her jest right; don't you think 'twould?"

"Yes, I do think it would serve her jest right."

The two were now walking along the sidewalk, leaving the Primrose house out of sight. Presently they came to the house where Mrs. Rowe lived, and she turned in at the gate. "Good-afternoon, Mis' Daggett," said she.

"Good-afternoon. Say, Mis' Rowe, look here a minute."

Mrs. Rowe stepped back obediently. Mrs. Daggett approached her lips to her ear and dropped her voice to a whisper: "If—I was you, I wouldn't say nothin' about our goin' in there to Marthy."

"I ain't goin' to," rejoined Mrs. Rowe, with a wise air; "you needn't be afraid of that, Mis' Daggett."

"I ain't done nothin' I'm ashamed of, but it's jest as well not to tell everything you know. I'm dreadful sorry you tore your dress so, Mis' Rowe."

The rent in Mrs. Rowe's black alpaca dress attracted immediate attention when she entered the house; she turned herself cautiously, but her sister, Mrs. Joy, noticed it at once. "Why, Hannah, how did you tear your dress so?" said she.

"I ketched it," replied Mrs. Rowe, with a meek sigh, turning her head to look at the three-cornered rent.

"Why, I should think you did! I guess you'll have one job mendin' it. What did you ketch it onto?"

"On a nail. I see Abel Rice a-standin' ringin' the front-door bell at the Primrose house when I come by." Mrs. Rowe had very little diplomacy in her nature, but she could fly as skittishly as any other woman from a distasteful subject.

"I want to know!" said Mrs. Joy, with ready interest. "I never really knew whether to b'lieve them stories about his ringin' that bell or not."

"I see him with my own eyes." Mrs. Rowe was laying aside her bonnet and shawl, uncovering her small gray head and her narrow alpaca shoulders, which had a deprecating slope to them. One could judge more correctly of her character from her shoulders than from her face, which was shifty, reflecting lights and shadows from others; her shoulders were the immovable sign of herself.

Mrs. Joy did not resemble her in the least; she was larger and stouter, with a rosy face whose lines were all drawn with decision. When she was talking she surveyed one steadily with her full bright eyes that seldom winked. People called her a handsome woman. Her daughter Annie, who sat at the window with her crochet-work, resembled her, only she was young and girlishly slim, her bright, clear eyes were blue instead of black, and her hair was light. There was a brilliant color on her rather thin cheeks. She crocheted some scarlet worsted very rapidly. making her slender fingers fly. Her mother had a significant side tone for her in her voice when she spoke again.

"Well, there's no use talkin', Abel Rice couldn't have had any brains to speak of, or he wouldn't have lost 'em so easy," said she. "This goin' crazy for love is something I don't put much stock in, for my part. Folks must have a weak spot somewhere, or it would take something more than love to tip 'em over. I guess none of the Rices are any too smart, when it comes right down to it. It ain't a family I should want to get into."

Annie never said a word; she crocheted faster.

Mrs. Rowe had dropped her shawl-pin, and had been hunting for it. Just then she found it, and rose up. "I should be kind of afraid if Frank Rice had any—such kind of trouble, it might affect him the same way. Shouldn't you?" said she.

She fairly jumped when her sister replied: "Afraid of it? No, I guess I shouldn't be afraid of it. I guess there don't many folks get crazy for—love." Mrs. Joy pronounced "love" with an affectedly sweet drawl.

Mrs. Rowe colored shamefacedly. "I s'pose Abel did; don't you?"

"No, I don't, neither. Most likely he'd got crazy anyway; it was in him."

"Well, I dun know." Mrs. Rowe always departed from an argument with a mild profession of ignorance. She stood in awe of her sister.

When she left the room to put away her bonnet, Mrs. Joy turned to Annie: "Ain't you goin' to see him to-night?" she asked.

"I—haven't made up my mind."

"I should think it was about time you did. There's the picnic comin' off to-morrow."

"No, it isn't, either."

"When is it, I'd like to know?"

"The day after to-morrow."

"Well, you ain't got any too much time; you'd ought to let him know a little beforehand, so he can get somebody else. I should think you'd better see him when he goes home to-night; it will do jest as well as any way."

Annie kept her eyes upon her crocheting; her cheeks grew redder. "I've—about made up my mind that I shall go with him, anyway," she muttered.

"What?"

"I've about made up my mind to go with Frank the way I said I would."

Mrs. Joy's eyes snapped. "Well, if you do, you'll have to give up all thoughts of Henry Simpson, that's all," said she. "If he sees you at that picnic with Frank Rice, he'll think it's all decided, an' he'll let you alone."

"Sometimes I think I'd rather wish he would."

"I'd like to know what you mean."

"I've made up my mind that I don't want him, anyway."

"H'm! I'd like to know why."

Annie crocheted silently for a minute. "Well, I suppose that I like Frank the best," she murmured, with a shamefaced air.

"Oh! Well, I s'pose that's all that's necessary, then. I s'pose if you—*love* him, there ain't anything more to be said."

The manner with which her mother's voice lingered upon *love* made it seem at once shameful and ridiculous to the girl; but she raised a plea in her own defence.

"I don't care," said she; "I don't think it's right to get married unless you do love the one you marry."

"I guess you'll find out that there's something besides *love* if you do get married to Frank Rice, or I'll miss my guess. When you get settled down there in that little cooped-up house with his father and mother and crazy uncle, an' don't have enough money to buy you a calico dress, you'll find out it ain't all—*love.*"

"He'd build a piece on to the house."

"An' run in debt for it; you know he ain't got a cent. Well, Annie Joy, I've said all I'm goin' to. You know how things are jest as well as I can tell you. You know how I've dug an' scrimped all my life, an' you know how we're situated now; it's jest all we can do to get along, an' your father's an old man. If you marry Frank Rice you'll have to live jest as I've done, only you won't be so well off, if anything; your father had a good house, all paid for, when we started. You'll have to work an' slave, an' never go anywhere nor have anything; you'll have to make up your mind to it. An' if you have Henry Simpson, you'll live over in Lennox, an' have everything nice, an' people will look up to you. You'll have to take your choice, that's all I've got to say."

Mrs. Joy got up and went out of the room with a heavy flourish. On the threshold she turned: "Ain't it most time for him to go by?"

Annie nodded. Soon after her mother left the room she saw at a swift glance the young man of whom they had been speaking coming down the sidewalk. She looked quickly away, and never raised her eyes from her crocheting when he went by.

"Has he been past?" asked her mother when she came in.

"Yes."

Mrs. Joy compressed her lips. "Well, you can do jest as you are a mind to," said she.

Yet she continued to talk and advance arguments. If Annie did not go to the picnic with Frank, she had little doubt that matters would be brought to a favorable climax with regard to the other young man, who had lately paid her much attention. She was making a new dress for

Annie to wear, and she sewed and reasoned with her all that evening and during the next day.

In the afternoon a young girl, an acquaintance of Annie's, came in. She had just returned from Lennox, where she had been shopping. Lennox was a large village—the city for this little hamlet of Primrose Hill.

"I saw somebody there," said the girl, with a significant smile at Annie, "and he looked real handsome. He was driving a beautiful horse, and he's got one of those new-style carriages. If I was some folks I should feel pretty fine."

"Alice would give all her old shoes to get a chance like you," remarked Mrs. Joy after the visitor had gone.

"I don't believe she'd treat another fellow mean to get it," said Annie. She had looked doubtfully pleased at the girl's joking.

"I don't see as your treatin' him mean if you let him know beforehand. I guess you ain't the only girl that changes her mind. Mebbe he'll take up with Alice. I should think she'd make him a real good wife."

"He won't: I can tell you that much. He can't bear her."

"Well, he'll find somebody. It's 'most time for him to go by, ain't it?"

"I suppose so," replied Annie, coldly.

It was late in the afternoon. An hour ago Mrs. Daggett had called for Mrs. Rowe, and the two old women had sauntered up the street together. "I didn't tell you what I see in that bureau drawer," Mrs. Daggett had whispered when they started forth; "it was the handsomest black satin I ever laid my eyes on. I—*mean to see it again.*"

"Oh, Mis' Daggett!"

"I'd like to know what harm it can do."

The two, in their homely black gowns, had moved on towards the Primrose house. Frank Rice would have to pass it on his way home from his work: he lived a half-mile beyond.

Mrs. Joy, as she talked to Annie, kept her face turned towards the road, watching for him. "There he is," she said, presently. Annie bent over her work. "Do you hear?" her mother repeated, sharply.

"Yes, I hear." Suddenly Annie sat up straight and looked in her mother's eyes. "I can't do it," said she.

"I'd like to know why not. Hurry, or he'll be gone by."

Annie sat quite still for a minute; her eyes were staring and her mouth set hard. Then she arose and went out of the front door and down the walk. The man reached the gate just as she did. She started, and turned a white face back towards the window; it was Frank Rice's uncle Abel, who, people said, had lost his wits because Maria Primrose had jilted him. He passed, and Annie clung to the gate. An awful voice of prophetic denunciation seemed to cry through all her weakness and ignoble ambition. Her mother appeared in the door, and drew back hastily; she had seen Frank Rice coming, following in the track of his uncle. She remarked for the first time a strong resemblance between the two men, and it thrilled her with a strange horror. She went back into the sitting-room, and peered around a corner of a window. When Frank reached the gate, she saw Annie step forward. She saw them stand and talk for a few minutes; then they walked slowly up the street together.

"What's she doin' that for?" muttered her mother with a bewildered air; she felt singularly shocked and subdued.

Annie and Frank went out of sight in the direction of the Primrose house.

It might have been an hour later when a woman came slowly up the hill which gave its name to the little settlement. She had walked from Lennox; she had not money enough to pay her fare in the coach which ran between the two villages. It rattled past her on the road; the passengers thrust out their heads and stared at her. "I declare, I believe that's Maria Primrose," said one woman to another. Maria Primrose, to call her as her old neighbors did by her maiden name, toiled slowly up Primrose Hill. She was a middle-aged woman, with a slender figure like a girl's; but her face, which had been handsome, had not kept its youth so well; one on passing her saw it with a certain disappointment. Her black clothes had an elegant and almost foreign air; some of the rich silk pleatings were frayed, but that did not hurt the general effect.

When she had come within half a mile of the Primrose house she saw a man at work in a potato field on the left of the road. She stopped and looked at him. Everything was very dusty, and the wind blew; great clouds of dust rolled up from the road, and passed like smoke over the fields; now the setting sun shone through it and gave it a gold color. Maria saw the man through a cloud of golden dust.

He threw down his hoe and came towards her, and she stood waiting. When he was near enough, on the other side of the stone wall, she looked in his face. His large blue eyes looked straight at her with a gentle and indifferent stare, his yellow-bearded mouth smiled pleasantly and vacantly.

Maria went on. Presently she heard a quick shuffle behind her, and Abel Rice passed, never turning his head; he was soon out of sight. When Maria Primrose went up the path to her old home, he stood straight and gaunt before the door; he had pulled the bell, and he was listening. When he saw Maria he shuffled off the end of the piazza, and disappeared among the trees. She looked after him for a second, then she unlocked the door.

There was a scream and a patter of feet up in the second story, then a scramble over the back stairs; Mrs. Daggett and Mrs. Rowe were making their escape from the house. Annie Joy and Frank Rice were also fleeing from the precincts of the Primrose house. Its front piazza had looked quiet and isolated, and they had strolled up there and seated themselves. They arose and went away when Abel Rice came and rang the bell to summon his lost sweetheart; they held each other's hands, and sped along between the trees. They saw Maria, and quickened their pace; but before they had passed out into the road, Frank cast a hasty glance around, and the two kissed each other.

Maria Primrose entered her old home to pass the remainder of her life in lonely and unavailing regret and a dulness which was not peace; the two curious old women hustled guiltily out of the kitchen window; Abel Rice went his solemn and miserable way; and the young lovers passed happily forth, starting up before her like doves. There had been a wreck, and the sight of it had prevented another.

A STOLEN CHRISTMAS.

"I DON'T s'pose you air goin' to do much Christmas over to your house."

Mrs. Luther Ely stood looking over her gate. There was a sweet, hypocritical smile on her little thin red mouth. Her old china-blue eyes stared as innocently as a baby's, although there was a certain hardness in them. Her soft wrinkled cheeks were pink and white with the true blond tints of her youth, which she had never lost. She was now an old woman, but people still looked at her with admiring eyes, and probably would until she died. All her life long her morsel of the world had had in it a sweet savor of admiration, and she had smacked her little feminine lips over it greedily. She expected every one to contribute towards it, even this squat, shabby, defiant old body standing squarely out in the middle of the road. Marg'ret Poole had stopped unwillingly to exchange courtesies with Mrs. Luther Ely. She looked aggressive. She eyed with a sidewise glance the other woman's pink, smirking face.

"'Tain't likely we be," she said, in a voice which age had made gruff instead of piping. Then she took a step forward.

"Well, we ain't goin' to do much," continued Mrs. Ely, with an air of subdued loftiness. "We air jest goin' to hev a little Christmas tree for the children. Flora's goin' to git a few things. She says there's a very nice 'sortment up to White's."

Marg'ret gave a kind of affirmative grunt; then she tried to move on, but Mrs. Ely would not let her.

"I dun know as you have noticed our new curtains," said she.

Had she not! Poor Marg'ret Poole, who had only green paper shades in her own windows, had peeped slyly around the corner of one, and watched mournfully, though not enviously, her opposite neighbor tacking up those elegant Nottingham-lace draperies, and finally tying them back with bows of red ribbon.

Marg'ret would have given much to have scouted scornfully the idea, but she was an honest old woman, if not a sweet one.

"Yes, I see 'em," said she, shortly.

"Don't you think they're pretty?"

"Well 'nough," replied Marg'ret, with another honest rigor.

"They cost consider'ble. I told Flora I thought she was kind of extravagant; but then Sam's airnin' pretty good wages. I dun know but they may jest as well have things. Them white cotton curtains looked dreadful kind of gone by."

Marg'ret thought of her green paper ones. She did not hate this other old woman; she at once admired and despised her; and this admiration of one whom she despised made her angry with herself and ashamed. She was never at her ease with Mrs. Luther Ely.

Mrs. Ely had run out of her house on purpose to intercept her and impress her with her latest grandeur—the curtains and the Christmas tree. She was sure of it. Still she looked with fine appreciation at the other's delicate pinky face, her lace cap adorned with purple ribbons, her black gown with a flounce around the bottom. The gown was rusty, but Marg'ret did not notice that; her own was only a chocolate calico. Black wool of an afternoon was sumptuous to her. She thought how genteel she looked in it. Mrs. Ely still retained her slim, long-waisted effect. Marg'ret had lost every sign of youthful grace; she was solidly square and stout.

Mrs. Ely had run out, in her haste, without a shawl; indeed, the weather was almost warm enough to go without one. It was only a week before Christmas, but there was no snow, and the grass was quite bright in places. There were green lights over in the field, and also in the house yards. There was a soft dampness in the air, which brought spring to mind. It almost seemed as if one, by listening intently, might hear frogs or bluebirds.

Now Marg'ret stepped resolutely across the street to her little house, which was shingled, but not painted, except on the front. Some one had painted that red many years before.

Mrs. Ely, standing before her glossy white cottage, which had even a neat little hood over its front door, cried, patronizingly, after her once again:

"I'm comin' over to see you as soon as I can," said she, "arter Christmas. We air dretful busy now."

"Well, come when ye can," Marg'ret responded, shortly. Then she entered between the dry lilac bushes, and shut the door with a bang.

Even out in the yard she had heard a shrill clamor of children's voices from the house; when she stood in the little entry it was deafening.

"Them children is raisin' Cain," muttered she. Then she threw open the door of the room where they where. There were three of them in a little group near the window. Their round yellow heads bobbed, their fat little legs and arms swung wildly. "Granny! granny!" shouted they.

"For the land sake, don't make such a racket! Mis' Ely can hear you over to her house," said Marg'ret.

"Untie us. Ain't ye goin' to untie us now? Say, Granny."

"I'll untie ye jest as soon as I can get my things off. Stop hollerin'."

In the ceiling were fixed three stout hooks. A strong rope was tied around each child's waist, and the two ends fastened securely around a hook. The ropes were long enough to allow the children free range of the room, but they kept them just short of one dangerous point—the stove. The stove was the fiery dragon which haunted Marg'ret's life. Many a night did she dream that one of those little cotton petticoats had whisked too near it, and the flames were roaring up around a little yellow head. Many a day, when away from home, the same dreadful pictures had loomed out before her eyes; her lively fancy had untied these stout knots, and she had hurried home in a panic.

Marg'ret took off her hood and shawl, hung them carefully in the entry, and dragged a wooden chair under a hook. She was a short woman, and she had to stretch up on her tiptoes to untie those hard knots. Her face turned a purplish red.

This method of restriction was the result of long thought and study on her part. She had tried many others, which had proved ineffectual. Willy, the eldest, could master knots like a sailor. Many a time the grandmother had returned to find the house empty. Willy had unfastened his own knot and liberated his little sisters, and then all three had made the most of their freedom. But even Willy, with his sharp five-year-old brain and his nimble little fingers, could not untie a knot whose two ends brushed the ceiling. Now Marg'ret was sure to find them all where she left them.

After the children were set at liberty she got their supper, arranging it neatly on the table between the windows. There was a nice white table cover, and the six silver teaspoons shone. The teaspoons were the mark of a flood-tide of Marg'ret's aspirations, and she had had aspirations all her life. She had given them to her daughter, the children's mother, on her marriage. She herself had never owned a bit of silver, but she determined to present her daughter with some.

"I'm goin' to have you have things like other folks," she had said.

Now the daughter was dead, and she had the spoons. She regarded the daily use of them as an almost sinful luxury, but she brought them out in their heavy glass tumbler every meal.

"I'm goin' to have them children learn to eat off silver spoons," she said, defiantly, to their father; "they'll think more of themselves."

The father, Joseph Snow, was trying to earn a living in the city, a hundred miles distant. He was himself very young, and had not hitherto displayed much business capacity, although he was good and willing. They had been very poor before his wife died; ever since he had not been able to do much more than feed and clothe himself. He had sent a few dollars to Marg'ret from time to time—dollars which he had saved and scrimped pitifully to accumulate—but the burden of their support had come upon her.

She had sewed carpets and assisted in spring cleanings—everything to which she could turn a hand. Marg'ret was a tailoress, but she could now get no employment at her trade. The boys all wore "store clothes" in these days. She could only pick up a few cents at a time; still she managed to keep the children in comfort, with a roof over their heads and something to eat. Their cheeks were fat and pink; they were noisy and happy, and also pretty.

After the children were in bed that night she stood in her kitchen window and gazed across at Mrs. Luther Ely's house. She had left the candle in the children's room—the little things were afraid without it—and she had not yet lighted one for herself; so she could see out quite plainly, although the night was dark. There was a light in the parlor of the opposite house; the Nottingham-lace curtains showed finely their pattern of leaves and flowers. Marg'ret eyed them. "'Tain't no use my tryin' to git up a notch," she muttered. "'Tain't no use for some folks. They ain't worked no harder than I have; Louisa Ely ain't never begun to work so hard; but they can have lace curtains an' Christmas trees."

The words sounded envious. Still she was hardly that; subsequent events proved it. Her "tryin' to git up a notch" explained everything. Mrs. Luther Ely, the lace-curtains, and the Christmas tree were as three stars set on that higher "notch" which she wished to gain. If the other woman had dressed in silk instead of rusty wool, if the lace draperies had been real, Marg'ret would hardly have wasted one wistful glance on them. But Mrs. Luther Ely had been all her life the one notch higher, which had seemed almost attainable. In that opposite house there was only one carpet; Marg'ret might have hoped for one carpet. Mrs. Ely's son-in-law earned only a comfortable living for his family; Marg'ret's might have done that. Worst of all, each woman had one daughter, and Marg'ret's had died.

Marg'ret had been ambitious all her life. She had made struggle after struggle. The tailoress trade was one of them. She made up her mind that she would have things like other people. Then she married, and her husband spent her money. One failure came after another. She slipped back again and again on the step to that higher notch. And here she was to-night, old and poor, with these three helpless children dependent upon her.

But she felt something besides disappointed ambition as she stood gazing out to-night.

"There's the children," she went on; "can't have nuthin' for Christmas. I ain't got a cent I can spare. If I git 'em enough to eat, I'm lucky."

Presently she turned away and lighted a lamp. She had some sewing to do for the children, and was just sitting down with it, when she paused suddenly and stood reflecting.

"I've got a good mind to go down to White's an' see what he's got in for Christmas," said she. "Mebbe Joseph 'll send some money 'long next week, an' if he does, mebbe I can git 'em some little thing. It would be a good plan for me to kind of price 'em."

Marg'ret laid her work down, got her hood and shawl, and went out, fastening the house securely, and also the door of the room where the stove was.

To her eyes the village store which she presently entered

was a very emporium of beauty and richness. She stared at the festoons of evergreens, the dangling trumpets and drums, the counters heaped with cheap toys, with awe and longing. She asked respectfully the price of this and that, some things less pretentious than the others. But it was all beyond her. She might as well have priced diamonds and bronzes. As she stood looking, sniffing in the odor of evergreen and new varnish, which was to her a very perfume of Christmas, arising from its fulness of peace and merriment, Flora Trask, Mrs. Ely's daughter, entered. Marg'ret went out quickly. "She'll see I ain't buyin' anything," she thought to herself.

But Marg'ret Poole came again the next day, and the next, and the next—morning, afternoon, and evening. "I dun know but I may want to buy some things by-an'-by," she told the proprietor, apologetically, "an' I thought I'd kind of like to price 'em."

She stood about, eying, questioning, and fingering tenderly. No money-letter came from Joseph. She inquired anxiously at the post-office many times a day. She tried to get work to raise a little extra money, but she could get none at this time of the year. She visited Mrs. White, the storekeeper's wife, and asked with forlorn hope if she had no tailor-work for her. There were four boys in that family. But Mrs. White shook her head. She was a good woman. "I'm sorry," said she, "but I haven't got a mite. The boys wouldn't wear home-made clothes."

She looked pitifully at Marg'ret's set, disappointed face when she went out.

Finally those animals of sugar and wood, those pink-faced, straight-bodied dolls, those tin trumpets and express wagons, were to Marg'ret as the fair apples hanging over the garden wall were to Christiana's sons in the *Pilgrim's Progress.* She gazed and gazed, until at last the sight and the smell of them were too much for her.

The evening before Christmas she went up to the post-office. The last mail was in, and there was no letter for her. Then she kept on to the store. It was rather early, and there were not as yet many customers. Marg'ret began looking about as usual. She might have been in the store ten minutes when she suddenly noticed a parcel on the corner of a counter. It was nicely tied. It belonged evidently to one of the persons who were then trading in the store or was to be delivered outside later. Mr. White was not in; two of his sons and a boy clerk were waiting upon the customers.

Marg'ret, once attracted by this parcel, could not take her eyes from it long. She pored over the other wares with many sidelong glances at it. Her thoughts centred upon it, and her imagination. What could be in it? To whom could it belong?

Marg'ret Poole had always been an honest woman. She had never taken a thing which did not belong to her in her whole life. She suddenly experienced a complete moral revulsion. It was as if her principles, whose weights were made shifty by her long watching and longing, had suddenly gyrated in a wild somersault. While they were reversed, Marg'ret, warily glancing around, slipped that parcel under her arm, opened the door, and sped home.

It was better Christmas weather than it had been a week ago. There was now a fine level of snow, and the air was clear and cold. Marg'ret panted as she walked. The snow creaked under her feet. She met many people hurrying along in chattering groups. She wondered if they could see the parcel under her shawl. It was quite a large one.

When she got into her own house she hastened to strike a light. Then she untied the parcel. There were in it some pink sugar cats and birds, two tin horses and a little wagon, a cheap doll, and some bright picture-books, besides a paper of candy.

"My land!" said Marg'ret, "won't they be tickled!"

There was a violent nervous shivering all over her stout frame. "Why can't I keep still?" said she.

She got out three of the children's stockings, filled them, and hung them up beside the chimney. Then she drew a chair before the stove, and went over to the bureau to get her Bible: she always read a chapter before she went to bed. Marg'ret was not a church member, she never said anything about it, but she had a persistent, reticent sort of religion. She took up the Bible; then laid it down; then she took it up again with a clutch.

"I don't care," said she, "I ain't done nothin' so terrible out of the way. What can't be airned, when anybody's willin' to work, ought to be took. I'm goin' to wait till arter Christmas; then I'm jest goin' up to Mis' White's some arternoon, an' I'm goin' to say, 'Mis' White,' says I, 'the day before Christmas I went into your husband's store, an' I see a bundle a-layin' on the counter, an' I took it, an' said nothin' to nobody. I shouldn't ha' done such a thing if you'd give me work, the way I asked you to, instead of goin' outside an' buyin' things for your boys, an' robbin' honest folks of the chance to airn. Now, Mis' White, I'll tell you jest what I'm willin' to do: you give me somethin' to do, an' I'll work out twice the price of them things I took, an' we'll call it even. If you don't, all is, your husband will have to lose it.' I wonder what she'll say to that."

Marg'ret said all this with her head thrown back, in a tone of indescribable defiance. Then she sat down with her Bible and read a chapter.

The next day she watched the children's delight over their presents with a sort of grim pleasure.

She charged them to say nothing about them, although there was little need of it. Marg'ret had few visitors, and the children were never allowed to run into the neighbors'.

Two days after Christmas the postmaster stopped at Marg'ret's house: his own was just beyond.

He handed a letter to her. "This came Christmas morning," said he. "I thought I'd bring it along on my way home. I knew you hadn't been in for two or three days, and I thought you were expecting a letter."

"Thank ye," said Marg'ret. She pulled the letter open, and saw there was some money in it. She turned very white.

"Hope you ain't got any bad news," said the postmaster.

"No, I ain't." After he had gone she sat down and read her letter with her knees shaking.

Joseph Snow had at last got a good situation. He was earning fifty dollars a month. There were twenty dollars in the letter. He promised to send her that sum every month.

"Five dollars a week!" gasped Marg'ret. "My land! An' I've—*stole!*"

She sat there looking at the money in her lap. It was quite late; the children had been in bed a long time. Finally she put away the money, and went herself. She did not read in her Bible that night.

She could not go to sleep. It was bitterly cold. The old timbers of the house cracked. Now and then there was a sharp report like a pistol. There was a pond near by, and great crashes came from that. Marg'ret might have been, from the noise, in the midst of a cannonade, to which her own guilt had exposed her.

"'Tain't nothin' but the frost," she kept saying to herself.

About three o'clock she saw a red glow on the wall opposite the window.

"I'm 'maginin' it," muttered she. She would not turn over to look at the window. Finally she did. Then she sprang, and rushed towards it. The house where Mrs. Luther Ely lived was on fire.

Marg'ret threw a quilt over her head, unbolted her front door, and flew. "Fire! fire!" she yelled. "Fire! fire! Oh, Mis' Ely, where be you? Fire! fire! Sam — Sam Trask, you're all burnin' up! Flora! Oh! fire! fire!"

By the time she got out in the road she saw black groups moving in the distance. Hoarse shouts followed her cries. Then the church bell clanged out.

Flora was standing in the road, holding on to her children. They were all crying. "Oh, Mis' Poole!" sobbed she, "ain't it dreadful? ain't it awful?"

"Have you got the children all out?" asked Marg'ret.

"Yes; Sam told me to stand here with 'em."

"Where's your mother?"

"I don't know. She's safe. She waked up first." The young woman rolled her wild eyes towards the burning house. "There she is!" cried she.

Mrs. Ely was running out of the front door with a box in her hand. Her son-in-law staggered after her with a table on his shoulder.

"Don't you go in again, mother," said he.

There were other men helping to carry out the goods, and they chimed in. "No," cried they; "'tain't safe. Don't you go in again, Mis' Ely!"

Marg'ret ran up to her. "Them curtains," gasped she, "an' the parlor carpet, have they got them out?"

"Oh, I dun know—I dun know! I'm afraid they ain't. Oh, they ain't got nothin' out! Everything all burnin' up! Oh, dear me! oh, dear! Where *be* you goin'?"

Marg'ret had rushed past her into the house. She was going into the parlor, when a man caught hold of her. "Where are you going?" he shouted. "Clear out of this."

"I'm a-goin' to git out them lace curtains an' the carpet."

"It ain't any use. We stayed in there just as long as we could, trying to get the carpet up; but we couldn't stand it any longer; it's chock full of smoke." The man shouted it out, and pulled her along with him at the same time. "There!" said he, when they were out in the road; "look at that." There was a flicker of golden fire in one of the parlor windows. Then those lace curtains blazed. "There!" said the man again: "I told you it wasn't any use."

Marg'ret turned on him. There were many other men within hearing. "Well, I wouldn't tell of it," said she, in a loud voice. "If I was a pack of stout, able-bodied men, and couldn't ha' got out them curtains an' that carpet afore they burnt up, I wouldn't tell of it."

Flora and the children had been taken into one of the neighboring houses. Mrs. Ely still stood out in the freezing air, clutching her box and wailing. Her son-in-law was trying hard to persuade her to go into the house where her daughter was.

Marg'ret joined them. "I would go if I was you, Mis' Ely," said she.

"No, I ain't goin'. I don't care where I be. I'll stay right here in the road. Oh, dear me!"

"Don't take on so."

"I ain't got a thing left but jest my best cap here. I did git that out. Oh, dear! oh, dear! everything's burnt up but jest this cap. It's all I've got left. I'll jest put it on an' set right down here in the road an' freeze to death. Nobody 'll care. Oh, dear! dear! dear!"

"Oh, don't, Mis' Ely." Marg'ret, almost rigid herself with the cold, put her hand on the other woman's arm. Just then the roof of the burning house fell in. There was a shrill wail from the spectators.

"Do come, mother," Sam begged when they stood staring for a moment.

"Yes, do go, Mis' Ely," said Marg'ret. "You mustn't feel so."

"It's easy 'nough to talk," said Mrs. Ely. "'Tain't your house; an' if 'twas, you wouldn't had much to lose—nothin' but a passel of old wooden cheers an' tables."

"I know it," said Marg'ret.

Finally Mrs. Ely was started, and Marg'ret hurried home. She thought suddenly of the children and the money. But the children had not waked in all the tumult, and the money was where she had left it. She did not go to bed again, but sat over the kitchen stove thinking, with her elbows on her knees, until morning. When morning came she had laid out one plan of action.

That afternoon she took some of her money, went up to Mr. White's store, and bought some Nottingham-lace curtains like the ones her neighbors had lost. They were off the same piece.

That evening she went to call on Mrs. Ely, and presented them. She had tried to think that she might send the parcel anonymously—leave it on the door-step; but she could not.

"'Twon't mortify me so much as 'twill the other way," said she, "an' I'd ought to be mortified."

So she carried the curtains, and met with a semblance of gratitude and a reality of amazement and incredulity which shamed her beyond measure.

After she got home that night she took up the Bible, then laid it down. "Here I've been talkin' and worryin' about gettin' up a higher notch," said she, "an' kind of despisin' Mis' Ely when I see her on one. Mis' Ely wouldn't have stole. I ain't nothin' 'side of her now, an' I never can be."

The scheme which Marg'ret had laid to confront Mrs. White was never carried out. Her defiant spirit had failed her.

One day she was there and begged for work again. "I'm willin' to do 'most anything," said she. "I'll come an' do your washin', or anything, an' I don't want no pay."

Mrs. White was going away the next day, and she had no work to give the old woman; but she offered her some fuel and some money.

Marg'ret looked at her scornfully. "I've got money enough, thank ye," said she. "My son sends me five dollars a week."

The other woman stared at her with amazement. She told her husband that night that she believed Marg'ret Poole was getting a little unsettled. She did not know what to make of her.

Not long after that Marg'ret went into Mr. White's store, and slyly laid some money on the counter. She knew it to be enough to cover the cost of the articles she had stolen. Then she went away and left it there.

That night she went after her Bible. "I declare I *will* read it to-night," muttered she. "I've paid for 'em." She stood eying it. Suddenly she began to cry. "Oh, dear!" she groaned; "I can't. There don't anything do any good—the lace curtains, nor payin' for 'em, nor nothin'. I dun know what I shall do."

She looked at the clock. It was about nine. "He won't be gone yet," said she. She stood motionless, thinking. "If I'm goin' to-night, I've got to," she muttered. Still she did not start for a while longer. When she did, there was no more hesitation. No argument could have stopped Marg'ret Poole, in her old hood and shawl, pushing up the road, fairly started on her line of duty. When she got to the store she went in directly. The heavy door slammed to, and the glass panels clattered. Mr. White was alone in the store. He was packing up some goods preparatory to closing. Marg'ret went straight up to him, and laid a package before him on the counter.

"I brought these things back," said she; "they belong to you."

"Why, what is it?" said Mr. White, wonderingly.

"Some things I stole last Christmas for the children."

"What!"

"I stole 'em."

She untied the parcel, and began taking out the things one by one. "They're all here but the candy," said she; "the children ate that up; an' Aggie bit the head off this pink cat the other day. Then they've jammed this little horse consider'ble. But I brought 'em all back."

Mr. White was an elderly, kind-faced man. He seemed

slowly paling with amazement as he stared at her and the articles she was displaying.

"You say you stole them?" said he.

"Yes; I stole 'em."

"When?"

"The night afore Christmas."

"Didn't Henry give 'em to you?"

"No."

"Why, I told him to," said Mr. White, slowly. "I did the things up for you myself that afternoon. I'd seen you looking kind of wishful, you know, and I thought I'd make you a present of them. I left the bundle on the counter when I went to supper, and told Henry to tell you to take it, and I supposed he did."

Marg'ret stood staring. Her mouth was open, her hands were clinched. "I dun know—what you mean," she gasped out at length.

"I mean you ain't been stealing as much as you thought you had," said Mr. White. "You just took your own bundle."

LIFE-EVERLASTIN'.

"AIN'T that your sister goin' 'long the other side of the street, Mis' Ansel?"

Mrs. Ansel peered, scowling—the sun was in her face. "Yes, that's her."

"She's got a basket. I guess she's been somewheres."

"She's been somewheres after life-everlastin' blossoms. They keep forever, you know. She's goin' to make a pillow for old Oliver Weed's asthma; he's real bad off."

"So I've heard. I declare it makes me all out of patience, folks that have got as much money as them Weeds have, not havin' a doctor an' havin' something done. I don't believe his wife amounts to much in sickness either."

"I guess she don't either. I could tell a few things if it wa'n't for talkin' against my neighbors. I tell Luella if she's mind to be such a fool as to slave for folks that's got plenty to do for themselves with, she can. I want to know, now, Mis' Slate, if you think this bonnet is big enough for me. Does it set fur enough onto my head?"

"It sets jest as fur on as the fashion, Mis' Ansel, an' a good deal further on than some. I wish you could see some of 'em."

"Well, I s'pose this ain't a circumstance to some, but it looks dreadful odd to me."

"Of course it looks a little odd at first, you've wore your bonnets so much further forward. You might twist up your hair a little higher if you was a mind to; that would tip it forward a little; but it ain't a mite too fur back for the fashion."

"Land! I can't do my hair any different from what I always do it, bonnet or no bonnet."

"You might friz your hair a little more in front; the hair ought to be real fluffy an' careless with this kind of a bonnet. Let me fix it a little."

Mrs. Ansel stood still before the glass while Mrs. Slate fixed her hair. She smiled a faint, foolish smile, and her homely face had the same expression as a pretty one on seeing itself in a new bonnet. Mrs. Ansel had never known that her face was homely. She was always pleased and satisfied with anything that was her own, and possession was to her the law of beauty.

Mrs. Slate, the milliner, was shorter than she. She stretched up, cocked her head, and twisted her mouth to one side with a superior air while she arranged her customer's thin front locks. Finally they lay tossed loosely over her flat, shiny forehead. "There," said the milliner; "that looks a good deal better. You see what you think."

Mrs. Ansel surveyed herself in the glass; her smile deepened. "Yes, it does look better, I guess."

"It's what I call a real stylish bonnet. You wouldn't be ashamed to wear it to meetin' anywhere, I don't care if it was in Boston or New York. I tell you what 'tis, Mis' Ansel, your sister would look nice in this kind of a bonnet." The milliner's prominent nose sloped her profile out sharply in the centre, like the beak of a bird; her little hands were skinny as claws, and restless; she always smiled, and her voice was subdued.

Mrs. Ansel still looked fondly at herself, but her tone changed; she sighed. "Yes, Luella would look good in it," said she. "I don't know as it would be quite so becomin' to her as it is to me; she never looked so well with anything that set back; but I guess she'd look pretty good in it. But I don't know when Luella's had a new bonnet, Mis' Slate. Of course she don't need any, not goin' to meetin' or anything."

"She don't ever go to meetin', does she?"

"No; she ain't been for twenty-five years. I feel bad 'nough about it. It seems to me sometimes if Luella would jest have a pretty new bonnet, an' go to meetin' Sabbath-days like other folks, I wouldn't ask for anything else."

"It must be a dreadful trial to you, Mis' Ansel."

"You don't know anything about it, Mis' Slate. You think there's bows enough on it, don't you?"

"Oh, plenty. I was speakin' to Jennie the other day about your sister—"

"An' the strings ain't too long?"

"Not a mite. You ain't never had a bonnet that become you any better than this does, Mis' Ansel. To tell the truth, I think you look a little better in it than you did in your summer one."

Mrs. Ansel began taking off the new bonnet, untying the crisp ribbon strings tenderly. "Well, I don't know but it's all right," said she.

"I'll get some paper an' do it up," said the milliner. "I ain't 'fraid but what you'll like it when you get used to it. You've always got to get used to anything new."

When Mrs. Ansel had gone down the street, delicately holding the new bonnet in its soft tissue wrapper, the milliner went into her little back room. There was one window in the room, and a grape-vine hung over it. A girl with fair hair and a delicately severe profile sat sewing by the window, with the grape-vine for a background.

"Well, I'm thankful that woman has gone," said the milliner. "I never saw such a fuss."

The girl said nothing. She nodded a little coldly, that was all.

"Are you puttin' in that linin' full enough?"

"It's all she brought."

"Oh, well, you can't do any better, then, of course. P'rhaps I hadn't ought to speak so about Mis' Ansel; she's a real nice woman; all is, she's kind of tryin' sometimes when anybody feels nervous. It's as hard work to get a bonnet onto her head that suits her as it would be if she was a queen; but after she once gets it she's settled on it, that's one comfort. She's a real nice woman, and I shouldn't want you to repeat what I said, Clara."

"I sha'n't say anything." There was a kind of mild *hauteur* about the girl that made the milliner color and twitch embarrassingly. She took a bonnet off the table and fell to work; but soon some one entered the shop, and she arose again.

Presently she was whispering over the counter to the customer that she had Clara Vinton working for her now; that she was a nice girl, but she'd acted dreadful kind of stiff somehow ever since the minister had been going with her, and she wasn't much company for her; but she didn't want her to say anything about it, for she was a real nice girl.

"I see Mis' Ansel goin' home with her new bonnet," remarked the customer.

"Yes; she jest went out with it."

When she reached home she found her sister, Luella Norcross, sitting on the door-step.

Luella followed her sister into the house. It was quite a smart house. Mrs. Ansel loved to furbish it, and she had a little income of her own. There were no dull colors anywhere; the walls gleamed with gold paper, and the carpets were brilliant.

Luella sat in the sitting-room and waited, while her sister went for a sheet which she had promised her. The mantel-shelf was marble, and there were some tall gilded glass vases on it. The stove shone like a mirror; there was a bright rug before it, and over on the table stood a lamp, whose shade was decorated with roses.

Luella plunged her hand down into the mass of everlasting flowers in her basket; the soft, healing fragrance came up in her face. "They're packed pretty solid," she muttered. "I guess there's enough."

When Mrs. Ansel returned with the sheet she was frowning. "There," said she, "I can't hunt no more to-night. I've had every identical thing out of that red chist, an' that's all I can seem to see. I don't know whether there's any more or not; if there is, you'll have to wait till I ain't jest home from down street, and can hunt better'n I can to-night."

Luella unfolded the sheet and examined it. "Oh, well, this is pretty good; it 'll make three, I guess. I'll wait, and maybe you'll come across the others some time."

"You'll have to wait if you have 'em. Did you see the new lamp?"

"Well, no, I didn't notice it, as I know of. That it?"

"You ain't been sittin' right here an' never seen that new lamp?"

"I guess I must have been lookin' at somethin' else."

"I never see such a woman! Anything like that sittin' right there before your face an' eyes, an' you never pay any attention to it! I s'pose if I had Bunker Hill Monument posted up here in the middle of the sittin'-room, you'd set right down under it an' think, an' never notice there was anything uncommon."

"It's a pretty lamp—ain't it?"

"It's real handsome." Luella arose and gathered her shawl about her; she had laid the folded sheet over the top of her basket.

"Wait a minute," said Mrs. Ansel; "you ain't seen my new bonnet."

Luella rested her basket on the chair, and stood patiently while her sister took the bonnet out of the wrapper and adjusted it before the looking-glass.

"There!" said she, turning around, "what do you think of it?"

"I should think it was real pretty."

"You don't think it sets too far back, do you?"

"I shouldn't think it did."

"Shouldn't you rather have this changeable ribbon than plain?"

"Seems to me I should." Luella's voice had unmistakably an abstracted drawl.

Her sister turned on her. "You don't act no more as if you cared anything about my new bonnet than you would if I was the pump with a new tin dipper on the top of it," said she. "If I was you I'd act a little more like other folks, or I'd give up. It's bad enough for you to go 'round lookin' like a scarecrow yourself; you might take a little interest in what your own sister has to wear."

Luella said nothing; she gathered up her basket of everlasting blossoms again.

Her sister paused and eyed her fiercely for a second; then she continued: "For my part, I'm ashamed," said she—"mortified to death. It was only this afternoon that I heard somebody speakin' about it. Here you've been wearin' that old black bonnet, that you had when father died, all these years, an' never goin' to meetin'. If you'd only have a decent new bonnet—I don't know as you'd want one that sets quite so far back as this one—an' go to meetin' like other folks, there'd be some sense in it."

Luella, her basket on her arm, started for the door. Although her shoulders were round, she carried her handsome head in a stately fashion. "We've talked this over times enough," said she.

"Here you are roamin' the woods an' pastures Sabbath-days in that old bonnet, an' jest as likely as not to meet all the folks goin' to meetin'. What do you s'pose I care about havin' a new bonnet if I meet you gettin' along in that old thing—my own sister?"

Luella marched out of the house. When she was nearly out of the yard her sister ran to the door and called after her. "Luella," said she.

The stately figure paused, but did not turn around. "What is it?"

"Look here a minute," said Mrs. Ansel, mysteriously; "I want to tell you something."

Luella stepped back, her sister bent forward—she still

had on the new bonnet—"I went into Mis' Plum's on my way down street," said she, "an' she said the minister wanted to marry the Vinton girl, but she won't have him, 'cause there ain't no parsonage, an' she don't think there's 'nough to live on. Mis' Plum says she thinks she shows her sense; he don't have but four hundred a year, an' there'd be a lot of children, the way there always is in poor ministers' families, an' nothin' to keep 'em on. Mis' Plum says she heard he applied to the church to see if they wouldn't give him a parsonage; he didn't know but they'd hire that house of yours that's next to the meetin'-house; but they wouldn't; they say they can't afford it."

"I shouldn't think four hundred dollars was much if preachin' was worth anything," remarked Luella.

"Oh, well, it does very well for you to talk when you don't give anything for preachin'."

Luella again went out of the yard. She was in the street when her sister called her again.

"Look 'round here a minute."

Luella looked.

"Do you think it sets too far back?"

"No, I don't think it does," Luella answered, loudly, then she kept on down the road. She had not far to go. The house where she lived stood at the turn of the road, on a gentle rise of ground; next to it was the large unoccupied cottage which she owned; next to that was the church. Luella lived in the old Norcross homestead; her grandfather had built it. It was one of those old buildings which aped the New England mansion-houses without once approaching their solid state. It settled unevenly down into its place. Its sparse front yard was full of evergreens, lilac bushes, and phlox; its windows, gleaming with green lights, were awry, and all its white clapboards were out of plumb.

Luella went around to the side door: the front one was never used—indeed, it was swollen and would not open—and the front walk was green. The side door opened into a little square entry. On one side was the sitting-room, on the other the kitchen. Luella went into the kitchen, and an old woman rose up from a chair by the stove. She was small as a child, but her muscles were large, her flaxen hair was braided lightly, her round blue eyes were filmy, and she grinned constantly without speaking.

"Got the cleanin' done, 'Liza?" asked Luella. The old woman nodded, and her grin widened. She was called foolish; her humble capabilities could not diffuse themselves, but were strong in only one direction: she could wash and scrub, and in that she took delight. Luella harbored her, fed and clothed her, and let her practise her one little note of work.

After Luella had taken off her bonnet and shawl, she went to work preparing supper. The old woman was not smart enough to do that. She sat watching her. When Luella set the tea-pot on the stove and cut the bread, she fairly crowed like a baby.

"Maria offered me a piece of her new apple-pie an' a piece of sage-cheese," remarked Luella, "but I wouldn't take it. If I'm a mind to stint myself and pay up Joe Perry's rent it's nobody's business, but I ain t goin' to be mean enough to live on other folks to do it."

The old woman grinned as she ate. Luella had fallen into the habit of talking quite confidentially to her, unreciprocative as she was.

After supper Luella put away the tea-things—that was

too fine work for the old woman—then she lighted her sitting-room lamp, and sat down there to make the case for the life-everlasting pillow. The old woman crept in after her, and sat by the stove in a little chair, holding her sodden hands in her lap.

"I hope to goodness this pillow will help him some," said Luella. "They're real good for asthma. Mother used to use 'em." She sewed with strong jerks. The old man for whom she was making the pillow was rich in the village sense, and miserly. Ill as he sometimes was, he and his wife would not call in a doctor on account of the expense; they scarcely kept warm and fed themselves. Public opinion was strong against them; very little pity was given to the feeble old man; but Luella viewed it all with a broad charity which was quite past the daily horizon of the village people. "I don't care if they are rich an' able to buy things themselves, we hadn't ought to let 'em suffer," she argued. "Mebbe they can't help bein' close any more'n we can help somethin' we've got. It's a failin', and folks ought to help folks with failin's, I don't care what they are." So Luella Norcross made broth and gruel, and carried them in to old Oliver Weed, and even gave him some of her dry cedar-wood; and people said she was as foolish as old Eliza. All the burly whining tramps, and beseeching pedlars of unsalable wares, who came to the village, flocked to her door, sure of a welcome.

On a summer's day the tramps sat on her door-step, and ate their free lunches, in winter they ate them comfortably by the kitchen fire. Many a time her barn and warm haymow harbored them over a cold stormy night.

"Might jest as well stick out a sign, 'Tramps' Tavern,' on the barn, an' done with it," Mrs. Ansel said. "If you don't get set on fire some night by them miserable sneakin' tramps, I miss my guess."

But she never did, and the tramp slouched peaceably out of her yard, late in the frosty morning, after she had given him a good breakfast in the warm kitchen.

There was an old pedlar of essences who came regularly, and she always bought of him, although his essences were poor, and her cake scantily flavored in consequence. Him she often lodged in her nice spare chamber, although she distrusted his cleanliness, and she and old Eliza had much scrubbing to do thereafter.

Luella even traded faithfully with a sly-eyed Italian woman, who went about, bent to one side by a great basket of vases and plaster images. "You'd ought to be ashamed of yourself encouragin' such folks," Mrs. Ansel remonstrated, "she's jest as miserable an' low as she can be."

"I don't care how low she is," said Luella. "She's keepin' one commandment sellin' plaster images to get her livin', an' I'm a-goin' to help her."

And Luella crowded the little plaster flower girls and fruit boys together on the sitting-room shelf, to make room for the new little shepherdess.

This very day she had been visited by an old broken-down minister, who often stood at her door, tall and tremulous in his shiny black broadcloth, with a heavy bag of undesirable books. There were some hanging shelves in Luella's sitting-room which were filled with these books, but to-day she had bought another.

"There ain't room on the shelves for another one, but I s'pose I can stow it away somewhere," she told Eliza, after he had gone. "I've give away all I can seem to. The book ain't very interestin'."

Luella usually lodged the book agent over night, when he came to the village, although he also had his failings. Many a night she was awakened by the creaking of the cellar-stairs, when the old minister crept down stealthily, a lamp balanced unsteadily in his shaking hand, to the cider-barrel. She would listen anxiously until she heard him return to his room, then get up and look about and sniff for fire.

There was not a woman in the village who had so many blessings, worth whatever they might be, offered to her. If she was not in full orthodox flavor among the respectable part of the town, her fame was bright among the poor and maybe lawless element, whom she befriended. They showed it by their shuffling footprints thick in her yard, and the frequency of their petitions at her door. It was the only way in which they could show it. The poor can show their love and gratitude only by the continual out-reaching of their hands.

This evening, while Luella sewed on her life-everlasting pillow, and the old woman sat grinning in the corner, there was a step in the yard. Luella laid down her work, and looked at Eliza, and listened. The step came steadily up the drive; the shoes squeaked. Luella took up her work again.

"I know who 'tis," said she. "It's the book man; his shoes squeak just that way, an' I told him he'd better come back here to-night an' stay over. It saves him payin' for lodgin'."

There came a sharp knock on the side door.

"You go let him in, 'Liza," said Luella.

The old woman patted out of the room. Presently she looked in again, and her grin was a broad laugh. "It's the minister," she chuckled.

Luella arose and went herself. There in the entry stood a young man, short and square-shouldered, with a pleasant boyish face. He looked bravely at Luella, and tried to speak with suave fluency, but his big hands twitched at the ends of his short coat sleeves.

"Good-evening, Miss Norcross, good-evening," said he.

"Oh, it's you, Mr. Sands!" said Luella. "Good-evenin'. Walk in an' be seated."

Luella herself was a little stiff. She pushed forward the big black-covered rocking-chair for the minister, then she sat down herself, and took up her sewing.

"It is a charming evening," remarked the minister.

"I thought it seemed real pleasant when I looked out after supper," said Luella.

She and the minister spoke about the conditions of several of the parish invalids, they spoke about a fire and a funeral which had taken place that week, and all the time there was a constraint in their manners. Finally there was a pause; then the minister burst out. A blush flamed out to the roots of his curly hair. He tried to make his voice casual, but it slipped into his benediction cadences.

"I don't see you at church very often, Miss Norcross," said he.

"You don't see me at all," returned Luella.

The minister tried to smile. "Well, maybe that is a little nearer the truth, Miss Norcross."

Luella sewed a few stitches on her life-everlasting pillow; then she laid it down in her lap, straightened herself, and looked at the minister. Her deep-set blue eyes seemed to see every atom of him; her noble forehead even, from which the gray hair was pulled well back, and which was scarcely lined, seemed to front him with a kind of visual power of its own.

"I may just as well tell you the truth, Mr. Sands," said she, "an' we may just as well come to the point at once. I know what you've come for; my sister told me you was comin' to see about my not going to meetin'. Well, I'll tell you once for all, I'm just as much obliged to you, but it won't do any good. I've made up my mind I ain't goin' to meetin', an' I've got good reasons."

"Would you mind giving them, Miss Norcross?"

"I ain't going to argue."

"But just giving me a few of your reasons wouldn't be arguing." The young man had now acquired the tone which he wished. He smiled on Luella with an innocent patronage, and crossed his legs. Luella thought he looked very young.

"The fact is," said she, "I'm not a believer, an' I won't be a hypocrite. That's all there is about it."

The minister looked at her. It was the first time he had encountered an outspoken doubter, and it was for a minute to him as if he faced one of the veritable mediæval dragons of the church. This simple and untutored village agnostic filled him with amazement and terror. When he spoke it was not to take up the argument for the doctrine, but to turn its gold side, as it were, towards his opponent, in order to persuade belief. "Your soul's salvation—do you never think of that?" he queried, solemnly. "You know heaven and your soul's salvation depend upon it."

"I ain't never worried much about my soul's salvation," said Luella. "I've had too many other souls to think about. An' it seems to me I'd be dreadful piggish to make goin' to heaven any reason for believin' a thing that ain't reasonable."

The minister made a rally; he remembered one of the things he had planned to say. "But you've read the New Testament, Miss Norcross," said he, "and you must admit that 'never man spake like this man.' When you read the words of Christ you must see that there was never any man like him."

"I know there wa'n't," said Luella, "that's jest the reason why the whole story don't seem sensible."

The minister gave a kind of a gasp. "But you believe in God, don't you, Miss Norcross?" said he.

"I ain't a fool," replied Luella. She arose with a decided air. "Do you like apples, Mr. Sands?" said she.

The minister gasped again, and assented.

"I've got some real nice sweet ones and some Porters," said Luella, in a cheerful tone, "an' I'm goin' to get you a plate of 'em, Mr. Sands."

Luella went out and got the plate of apples, and the minister began eating them. He felt uneasily that it was his duty to reopen the argument. "If you believe in God—" he began.

But Luella shook her head at him as if she were his mother. "I'd rather not argue any more," said she. "Try that big Porter; I guess it's meller." And the minister ate his apples with enjoyment. Luella filled his pockets with some when he went home. "He seems like a real good young man," she said to old Eliza after the minister had gone; "an' that Vinton girl would make him jest the kind of a wife he'd ought to have. She's real up an' comin', an' she'd prop him up firm on his feet. I s'pose if I let him have that house he'd be tickled 'most to death. I'd kind of 'lotted on the rent of it, but I s'pose I could get along."

The old woman grinned feebly. She had been asleep in

her corner, and her blue eyes looked dimmer than ever. She comprehended not a word; but that did not matter to Luella, who had fallen into the habit of utilizing her as a sort of spiritual lay-figure upon which to drape her own ideas.

The next morning, about nine o'clock, she carried the pillow, which she had finished and stuffed with the life-everlasting blossoms, to old Oliver Weed's. The house stood in a wide field, and there were no other houses very near. The grass was wet with dew, and all the field was sweet in the morning freshness. Luella, carrying her life-everlasting pillow before her, went over the fragrant path to the back door. She noticed as she went that the great barn doors were closed.

"Queer the barn ain't open," she thought to herself. "I wonder what John Gleason's about, late as this in the mornin'?"

John Gleason was old Oliver Weed's hired man. He had been a tramp. Luella herself had fed him, and let him sleep off a drunken debauch in her barn once. People had wondered at Oliver Weed's hiring him, but he had to pay him much less than the regular price for farm hands.

Luella heard the cows low in the barn as she opened the kitchen door. "Where—did all that—blood come from?" said she.

She began to breathe in quick gasps; she stood clutching her pillow, and looking. Then she called: "Mr. Weed! Mr. Weed! Where be you? Mis' Weed! Is anything the matter? Mis' Weed!" The silence seemed to beat against her ears. She went across the kitchen to the bedroom. Here and there she held back her dress. She reached the bedroom door, and looked in.

Luella pressed back across the kitchen into the yard. She went out into the road, and turned towards the village. She still carried the life-everlasting pillow, but she carried it as if her arms and that were all stone. She met a woman whom she knew, and the woman spoke; but Luella did not notice her; she kept on. The woman stopped and looked after her.

Luella went to the house where the sheriff lived, and knocked. The sheriff himself opened the door. He was a large, pleasant man. He began saying something facetious about her being out calling early, but Luella stopped him.

"You'd—better go up to the—Weed house," said she, in a dry voice. "There's some—trouble."

The sheriff started. "Why, what do you mean, Luella?"

"The old man an' his wife are—both killed. I went in there to carry this, an'—I saw them."

"My God!" said the sheriff. He caught up his hat, and started on a run to the barn for his horse.

The sheriff's wife and daughter pressed forward and plied Luella with horrified questions; they urged her to come in and rest, she looked so pale; but she said little, and turned towards home. Flying teams passed her on the road; men rushed up behind her and questioned her. When she reached the Weed house the field seemed black with people. When she got to her own house she went into the sitting-room and sat down. She felt faint. She did not think of lying down; she never did in the daytime. She leaned her head back in her chair and turned her face towards the yard. Everything out there, the trees, the grass, the crowding ranks of daisies, the next house, looked strange, as if another light than that of the sun was on them. But she somehow noticed even then how a blind on the second floor of the house was shut that had been open. "I wonder how that come shut?" she muttered, feebly.

Pretty soon her sister, Mrs. Ansel, came hurrying in. She was wringing her hands. "Oh, ain't it awful? ain't it awful?" she cried. "Good land, Luella, how you look! You'll faint away. I'm goin' to mix you up some peppermint before I do another thing."

Mrs. Ansel made a cup of hot peppermint tea for her, and she drank it.

"Now tell me all about it," said Mrs. Ansel. "What did you see first? What was you goin' in there for?"

"To carry the pillow," said Luella, pointing to it. "I can't talk about it, Maria."

Mrs. Ansel went over to the lounge and took up the pillow. "Mercy sakes! what's that on it?" she cried, in horror.

"I—s'pose I—hit it against the wall somehow," replied Luella. "I can't talk about it, Maria."

Mrs. Ansel could not learn much from her sister. Presently she left, and lingered slowly past the Weed house, to which her curiosity attracted her, but which her terror and horror would not let her approach closely.

The peppermint revived Luella a little. After a while she got up and put on the potatoes for dinner. Old Eliza was scrubbing the floor. When dinner was ready she ate all the potatoes, and Luella sat back and looked at her.

All the afternoon people kept coming to the house and questioning her, and exclaiming with horror. It seemed to Luella that her own horror was beyond exclamations. There was no doubt in the public mind that the murderer was the hired man, John Gleason. He was nowhere to be found; the constables and detectives were searching fiercely for him.

That night when Luella went to bed she stood at her chamber window a minute, looking out. It was bright moonlight. Her window faced the unoccupied house, and she noticed again how the blind was shut.

"It's queer," she thought, "for that blind wouldn't stay shut; the fastenin' wa'n't good." As she looked, the blind swung slowly open. "The wind is jest swingin' it back and forth," she thought. Then she saw distinctly the chamber window open, a dark arm thrust out, and the blind closed again.

"*He's in there*," said Luella. She had put out her lamp. She went down-stairs in the dark, and made sure that all the doors and windows were securely fastened. She even put chairs and tables against them. Then she went back to her chamber, dressed herself, and watched the next house. She did not stir until morning. The next day there was a cold rain. The search for John Gleason continued, the whole village was out, and strange officials were driving through the streets. Everybody thought that the murderer had escaped to Canada, taking with him the money which he had stolen from the poor old man's strong-box under his bed.

All the day long Luella watched the next house through the gray drive of the rain. About sunset she packed a basket with food, stole across to the house, and set it in the corner of the door. She got back before a soul passed on the road. She had set Eliza at a task away from the windows.

The moon rose early. After supper Luella sat again in her chamber without any lamp and watched. About nine o'clock she saw the door of the next house swing open a little, and the basket was drawn in.

"*He's in there*," said Luella. She went down and fastened

up the house as she had done the night before. Old Eliza went peacefully to bed, and she watched again. She put a coverlid over her shoulders, and sat, all huddled up, peering out. The rain had stopped ; the wall of the next house shone like silver in the moonlight. She watched until the moon went down and until daylight came ; then she went to bed, and slept an hour.

After breakfast that morning she set old Eliza at a task, and went up to her chamber again. She sank down on her knees beside the bed. "O God," said she, "have I got to give him up—have I? Have I got to give him up to be hung? What's goin' to become of him then? Where'll he go to when he's been so awful wicked? Oh, what shall I do? Here he is a-takin' my vittles, an' comin' to my house, an' a-trustin' me!" Luella lifted her arms ; her face was all distorted. She seemed to see the whole crew of her pitiful dependents crowding around her, and pleading for the poor man who had thrown himself upon her mercy. She saw the old drunken essence man, the miserable china women, all the wretched and vicious tramps and drunkards whom she had befriended, pressing up to her, and pleading her to keep faith with their poor brother.

The thought that John Gleason had trusted her, had taken that food when he knew that she might in consequence betray him to the gallows, filled her with a pity that was almost tenderness, and appealed strongly to her loyalty and honor.

On the other hand, she remembered what she had seen in the Weed house. The poor old man and woman seemed calling to her for help. She reflected upon what she had heard the day before: that the detectives were after John Gleason for another murder; this was not the first. She called to mind the danger that other helpless people would be in if this murderer were at large. Would not their blood be upon her hands? She called to mind the horrible details of what she had seen, the useless cruelty, and the horror of it.

Once she arose with a jerk, and got her bonnet out of the closet. Then she put it back, and threw herself down by the bed again. "Oh!" she groaned, "I don't know what to do!"

Luella shut herself in her own room nearly all day. She went down and got the meals, then returned. The sodden old woman did not notice anything unusual. At dusk she watched her chance, and carried over more food, and she watched and saw it taken in again.

This night she did not lock the house. All she fastened was old Eliza's bedroom door; that she locked securely, and hid the key. All the other doors and windows were unfastened, and when she went up-stairs she set the side door partly open. She set her lamp on the bureau, and looked at her face in the glass. It was white and drawn, and there was a desperate look in her deep-set eyes. "Mebbe it's the last time I shall ever see my face," said she. "I don't know but I'm awful wicked to give him the chance to do another murder, but I can't give him up. If he comes in an' kills me, I sha'n't have to, an' maybe he'll jest take the money an' go, an' then I sha'n't have to."

Luella had two or three hundred dollars in an old wallet between her feather-bed and the mattress. She took it out and opened it, spreading the bills. Then she laid it on the bureau. She took a gold ring off her finger, and unfastened her ear-rings and laid them beside it, and a silver watch that had belonged to her father. Down-stairs she had arranged the teaspoons and a little silver cream-jug in full sight on the kitchen table.

After the preparations were all made she blew out her lamp, folded back the bed-spread, lay down in her clothes, and pulled it over her smoothly. She folded her hands and lay there. There was not a bolt or a bar between her and the murderer next door. She closed her eyes and lay still. Every now and then she thought she heard him down-stairs; but the night wore on, and he did not come. At daylight Luella arose. She was so numb and weak that she could scarcely stand. She put away the money and the jewelry, then she went down-stairs and kindled the kitchen fire and got breakfast. The silver was on the table just as she had left it, the door half open, and the cold morning wind coming in. Luella gave one great sob when she shut the door. "He must have seen it," she said, "but he wouldn't do nothin' to hurt me, an' I've got to give him up."

She said no more after that; she was quite calm getting breakfast. After the meal was finished and the dishes cleared away she told old Eliza to put on her other dress and her bonnet and shawl. She had made up her mind to take the old creature with her; she was afraid to leave her alone in the house, with the murderer next door to spy out her own departure.

When the two women were ready they went out of the yard, and Luella felt the eyes of John Gleason upon her. They went down the road to the village, old Eliza keeping a little behind her mistress. Luella aimed straight for the sheriff's house. He drove into the yard as she entered; he had been out all night on a false scent. He stopped when he saw Luella, and she came up to him. "John Gleason is in that vacant house of mine," said she. He caught at the reins, but she stopped him. "You've got to wait long enough to give me time to get home, so I sha'n't be right in the midst of it, if you've got any mercy," said she, in a loud, strained voice. Then she turned and ran. She stopped only long enough to tell old Eliza to follow her straight home and go at once into the house. She ran through the village street like a girl. People came to the windows and stared after her. Every minute she fancied she heard wheels behind her; but the sheriff did not come until after she had been in the house fifteen minutes, and old Eliza also was at home.

Luella was crouching at her chamber window, peering around the curtain, when the sheriff and six men came into the yard and surrounded the next house. She had a wild hope that John Gleason might not be there, that he might have escaped during the night. She watched. The men entered, there was the sound of a scuffle and loud voices, and then she saw John Gleason dragged out.

Presently Luella went down-stairs; she had to keep hold of the banister. Old Eliza was gaping at the kitchen window. "Come away from that window, 'Liza," said Luella, "and wash up the floor right away." Then Luella began cleaning potatoes and beets for dinner.

The next Sunday Luella went to church for the first time in twenty-five years. Old Eliza also went shuffling smilingly up the aisle behind her mistress. Everybody stared. Luella paused at her sister's pew, and her brother-in-law sat a little while looking at her before he arose to let her in.

Mrs. Ansel was quite flushed. She pulled her new bonnet farther on her head; she glanced with agitated hauteur across her sister at old Eliza; then her eyes rolled towards her sister's bonnet.

Presently she touched Luella. "What possessed you to bring her, an' come out lookin' so?" she whispered. "Why didn't you get a new bonnet before you came to meetin'?"

Luella looked at her in a bewildered fashion for a minute, then she set her face towards the pulpit. She listened to the sermon; it had in it some innocent youthful conceits, and also considerable honest belief and ardent feeling. The minister saw Luella, and thought with a flush of pride that his arguments had convinced her. The night before, he had received a note from her tendering him the use of her vacant house. After the service he pressed forward to speak to her. He thanked her for her note, said that he was glad to see her out to meeting, and shook her hand vehemently. Then he joined Clara Vinton quite openly, and the two walked on together. There was quite a little procession passing up the street. The way led between pleasant cottages with the front yards full of autumn flowers —asters and pansies and prince's-feathers. Presently they passed a wide stretch of pasture-land where life-everlasting flowers grew. Luella walked with an old woman with a long, saintly face; old Eliza followed after.

Luella's face looked haggard and composed under her flimsy black crape frillings. She kept her eyes, with a satisfied expression, upon the young minister and the tall girl who walked beside him with a grave, stately air.

"I hear they're goin' to be married," whispered the old woman.

"I guess they are," replied Luella.

Just then Clara turned her face, and her fine, stern profile showed.

"She'll make him a good wife, I guess," said the old woman. She turned to Luella, and her voice had an indescribably shy and caressing tone. "I was real glad to see you to meetin' to-day," she whispered. "I knew you'd feel like comin' some time; I always said you would." She flushed all over her soft old face as she spoke.

Luella also flushed a little, but her voice was resolute. "I ain't got much to say about it, Mis' Alden," said she, "but I'm goin' to say this much—it ain't no more'n right I should, though I don't believe in a lot of palaver about things like this—I've made up my mind that I'm goin' to believe in Jesus Christ. I ain't never, but I'm goin' to now, for"—Luella's voice turned shrill with passion—"*I don't see any other way out of it for John Gleason!*"

AN INNOCENT GAMESTER.

"DON'T stan' there lookin' at me that way, Charlotte."

"Why, Aunt Lucinda!"

Lucinda Moss put her slender red fingers over her face. "I—didn't think it was—anything out of the—way," she sniffed, weakly.

Charlotte stood before her as relentless and handsome as an accusing angel. Her full, strong young figure seemed to tower over her aunt; her firm, rosy face and clear blue eyes seemed to spy out her inmost weaknesses like sunlight. "I must say I am surprised," said Charlotte. Her voice was loud and even and sweet. Charlotte, no matter how indignant she might be, never altered her voice.

"I didn't think it was anything so much out of the way, Charlotte."

"Well, I must say, Aunt Lucinda, I never thought, from all I've known of you, that you'd do such a thing as to sit down and play cards."

Lucinda's eyes, all pink and watery, rested appealingly on Charlotte, then on the table before her. Charlotte had on a light cambric gown that displayed a rigor of starch and cleanliness. She had worn her white apron in school all day, but it still flared as stiffly as when she had put it on in the morning. Her brown hair was brushed until it shone;

there was not a stray lock anywhere. All this perfect order and nicety made her seem more pitiless to her aunt. Lucinda shrank weakly down in her chair. She was lean and delicate, in flimsy old black muslin and a shiny old black silk apron. She wore a tumbled muslin kerchief around her neck, and had lax, faded curls behind her ears. She looked from Charlotte to the table. There was a printed red cloth on it, and a row of books piled up against the wall under the gilt-framed glass. There was an old-fashioned work-box with a gilt ball on each corner, and a little china vase with some violets in it. But Lucinda eyed ruefully the objects directly before her on the corner of the table. There lay a pack of little old-fashioned cards and a large green-covered Bible. The cards were scattered about, and some of them were tucked under the Bible.

"And for you to try to hide the cards under the Bible!" continued Charlotte. "I shouldn't have thought you could have done that, Aunt Lucinda."

"It was layin' right there. I'd jest been readin' some in it." Lucinda's voice took on a sharper tone. There is a wall of limitation for all human patience, and she was being crowded against hers. She stood against it, and displayed what small defensive powers she had, although her defence was principally appeal and excuse. "I didn't have anything to do," she proceeded — "not anything. I'd been knittin' till I got cramps, an' I read a chapter, an' then I thought I'd jest get out the cards. It's dreadful dull sometimes, Charlotte."

"I should think you could find some amusement in your own mind," replied Charlotte, with no abatement of severity.

Lucinda eyed her in a bewildered way, as if called upon

to consider an argument based upon some unknown equation.

"I know perfectly well," continued Charlotte, "that it isn't my place to dictate to you, for you are my aunt, and a good deal older than I am. But I must say it surprised me a good deal to come in and find you playing cards, for I wasn't brought up to see them in the house."

Lucinda sat bolt-upright; there were hot red spots on her cheeks; one near enough could have seen pulses beating here and there through the delicate skin on her neck and forehead. "I wa'n't playin' cards," said she.

"Why, what were you doing, then? I don't know what you mean, Aunt Lucinda."

"Well, I was— I s'pose you'll think I'm dreadful silly, Charlotte, but I ain't had much to 'muse me, an' I've kinder got in the way of it."

"For pity's sake, Aunt Lucinda, what are you coming at?" Charlotte stared at her, and wrinkled her fair high forehead in a way she had when perplexed.

"I didn't mean to do anything out of the way, but I s'pose you'll think it was dreadful silly, Charlotte. I was jest tellin' my fortune."

"What?"

The tears stood in the old woman's eyes. She shook visibly. In her simple life her little foolishnesses had come to take the place of sins, and she was shamefaced over them as such. "I was jest—tellin' my fortune."

"I don't believe I know what you mean, Aunt Lucinda." Charlotte's blue eyes were raised, her round rosy face was all furrowed with those lines of perplexity.

"Why, don't you know, Charlotte? You can tell your fortune with cards. There's a way of doin' it. I learnt it when I was a girl. Didn't you know it?" asked Lucinda, with tremulous eagerness.

"I've heard of it."

"I s'pose it is kind of silly; but it's kind of 'musin' sometimes, when I'm feelin' dull, you know." Lucinda trembled, and still kept her eyes fastened upon her niece's face, which expressed a calm contempt.

Presently Lucinda began again, with more stress of appeal: "I was jest tellin' my fortune, Charlotte; I didn't s'pose there was any harm in it. Once in a while I take a notion to tell it, jest for the fun of it, you know."

"I shouldn't think it would be much fun."

"Well, I dun know as 'tis, Charlotte; but it's kind of 'musin' sometimes."

Charlotte still gazed at her aunt with that look of contemptuous perplexity, and the old woman could not take her eyes from her face.

"It's jest because it's kind of 'musin'," she pleaded again. "An' when anybody ain't had any more change than I've had 'most all their life, it's kind of comfortin' to spread out the cards an' try to calculate if there ain't somethin' different comin'. It don't never come, an' I don't s'pose it's ever goin' to; course I don't put any faith in it, but it's kind of 'musin'."

Charlotte turned away, and put her face down to the little bunch of violets on the table: one of her scholars had brought them to her. "Well, I can't stop to talk any more about it," said she. "I must go out and get supper."

Charlotte righted herself and went out of the room with a firm step, and proceeded to get supper ready. She had her own ideas about supper, and indeed about all the other meals. Lucinda Moss's household plan had been revolutionized since her niece had come to live with her. She had no longer any voice in anything, and she had come almost to forget what her own original note had been. She was growing deprecatory and shamefaced about herself, and she no longer openly confessed in many cases her preferences. It took some new emergency, like this of the cards, to arouse her at all.

Lucinda had always liked a bit of cold pork, some left-over dinner vegetables, some little savory relish, for supper, but now she ate a slice of bread-and-butter and a spoonful of sauce, and drank a glass of milk. Charlotte had decreed that that was better for her. Lucinda had not even her cup of tea since Charlotte reigned.

Lucinda had been fond of a rich cup-cake, which she had also enjoyed stirring up once a week for herself. She had taken an innocent pride in its excellence, and she had treated her few callers to it. She had liked a slice of it between meals. But that was now all done away with; there was no cake baked in the house. "That rich cake is not fit for you to eat, Aunt Lucinda," Charlotte had said. "I think we had better not have any more of it." And poor Lucinda came gently down to her niece's views on diet, and put cup-cake and cold pork and vegetables away from her like devices of Satan. She concealed from herself her longing for them; and she felt the most sincere love and gratitude to Charlotte for her interest in her welfare. Indeed, Charlotte did everything from the purest motives. She had meant to do her very best by her old aunt Lucinda when she had come to live with her, after her father's death, from a sense of duty. She had given up her school in her native village, and taken another, that she did not like nearly as well, here in Foster. She had found Lucinda old and feeble, and at once set to work about taking care of her and relieving her from all her household labors.

Charlotte had not much time out of school, but she kept the house, and would have only a modicum of assistance from her aunt. Lucinda soon did not venture to prepare a meal nor set away a dish, she met with such kind and determined remonstrances from her niece. Charlotte was so determined, when she set about being good and doing her whole duty, that she was quite capable of tyrannizing over goodness itself. And then it was undeniably better that an old and feeble woman like her aunt Lucinda should not eat rich cup-cake between meals, nor wear herself out at house-work, although Lucinda had never worn herself out at house-work. There was considerable scandal of a modest kind about her in the village. There was a rumor that Lucinda Moss had not taken up her sitting-room carpet for ten years, nor her parlor carpet within the memory of man, and that she deliberately shut up one or two chambers, and let them stay so, with no application of broom or duster, year after year. But Charlotte had every carpet in the house taken up spring and fall. She hung all the feather-beds out of the windows, and dusted in all the dark corners. Poor old Lucinda sometimes felt as if there was so much cleanliness that she was almost chilly. But she never remonstrated about anything, unless it was for a moment, when she happened to be taken by surprise, as in the matter of the cards. She seemed quite to fall in with Charlotte's views that her own tastes were not to be considered when they interfered with her own good, and that most of them did so interfere.

When she came out to supper that night she looked meekly and unquestioningly at the cold milk, the bread-and-butter, and sauce. Her very soul thirsted for a cup of tea, and she felt as guilty as any wine-bibber that it should be so. Charlotte had said that it was as bad to drink tea as to drink strong liquor, and that it was very unhealthy for her.

It did not take long for them to eat supper; they never dallied over their meals. Charlotte did not dally over anything; indeed, she could not, with so much on her hands. She sent Lucinda into the sitting-room while she put away the supper dishes. When that was done she went into the sitting-room herself, and sat down with some needle-work at the window opposite her aunt. There was still an hour of daylight left.

There was a cunning look in Lucinda's face; she was smiling and quite talkative. She spoke about the weather, and the neighbors, and Charlotte's school; then she gave a sudden sharp glance at her niece. "Charlotte?"

"What say, Aunt Lucinda?"

"Charlotte." The old woman was smiling hard, and her voice was soft and tremulously sweet. "Did you ever have your fortune told?"

"No, I never did."

"Well, now, Charlotte, don't you want me to tell it?" Lucinda twisted her face up towards her niece, and her smile was as bland and cunning as a witch's.

"No, thank you, Aunt Lucinda," Charlotte replied, stiffly.

"It's real remarkable how they do turn out sometimes, Charlotte. I might tell you somethin' 'bout—who you was goin' to marry, you know."

"I haven't any wish to try it, and I am never going to marry anybody." Charlotte blushed, but she looked with dignified scorn at her aunt's delicate old face, that still smirked up at her. "To say just what I think, Aunt Lucinda," she continued, "it seems to me very silly, and I should think the cards would be better in the fire than anywhere else."

"I'd kind of hate to burn 'em, Charlotte. I've had 'em ever since I was a girl."

Charlotte made no reply. Lucinda watched her pitifully. The cunning smile had faded entirely from her face. She seemed to sit lower in her chair.

"Well, mebbe I had ought to burn 'em," she remarked, finally, with a hard breath. Pretty soon she arose. "I guess I'll go to bed," said she.

"Why, it isn't dark yet," responded Charlotte.

"I know it ain't, but I'm kind of tired somehow." Lucinda went across the room with a weak shuffle. Charlotte looked after her, and thought to herself that she aged rapidly. She did not think any more about the cards and the fortune-telling. She could not treat any subject lightly, and had to bring her mind down with a heavy step upon all matters, however trivial, that it stopped to consider. She knew quite well that her gentle, weak old aunt's whim for fortune-telling was not a subject for very serious controversy. She expressed her opinion strongly, as was her wont; then let the matter slip away entirely from her thoughts.

The days went on, and nothing more was said about the cards. Charlotte did not know whether they were burned, as she had advised, or not. She thought no more about them. She noticed that her aunt ate even less than usual, and seemed more spiritless. She thought also that she grew thin.

"What's the matter, Aunt Lucinda; don't you feel well?" she asked one night when the old woman announced her intention of going to bed immediately after supper,

Lucinda paused in her onward shuffle. "Well, I dun know," said she; "I guess I'm well 'nough, but I feel kind of poorly. I've been thinkin' if I had some of that root-beer I used to make, it might kind of set me up."

"Milk is a good deal better for you," said Charlotte, promptly. "You don't drink enough milk."

"Well, I dun know; I drink consider'ble, Charlotte."

"How much did you drink to-night?"

"Well, I dun know; 'most a cupful, I guess."

Charlotte went to the table and poured out a cup quite full of milk. "Now, Aunt Lucinda, you just drink this down before you go to bed," said she.

"Oh, Charlotte, I dun know as I can."

"Yes, you can, too; it's good for you."

Lucinda put out her hand for the milk; then she drew it back. "Oh, Charlotte, I can't, noways in the world."

Charlotte held the milk quite under her nose, and her face contracted with disgust when she looked down at it. "Drink it right down," said Charlotte.

The old woman took the cup, and drank down the milk with desperate gulps. When she had finished she gave the cup to Charlotte and clapped her hand over her mouth.

"That's right," said Charlotte, in a commendatory tone. "It'll do you good. You don't drink half enough milk."

Lucinda gave her head an unmeaning shake. She was quite speechless. She kept her hand pressed tightly to her mouth all the way out of the room.

The next morning Charlotte made her drink two cups of milk for breakfast, and she did so more easily. Lucinda looked quite alert that morning, and Charlotte thought to herself that she was improving.

"You feel better, don't you, Aunt Lucinda?" she said.

"Well, I dun know; I ruther guess I do feel a little rested," answered Lucinda.

She had an odd expression that morning. Charlotte kept regarding her; she could not think what made her look so strange. Finally she decided that it was because her aunt had her hair pushed back a little farther than usual from her temples. It took away from her expression of gentle weakness, and gave her something of a wild air. Charlotte was not nervous; after she had decided as to the cause of it, her aunt's strange look no longer dwelt in her mind. She taught school placidly all the forenoon. But when she came home at noon, and could find Lucinda nowhere in the house, that odd look of hers started up afresh in her memory. After she had hunted through the house and garden, and inquired at the neighbors', she stood in the middle of the sitting-room, and that strange face swam before her eyes. "It meant something," she said to herself; "she meant to do something."

Some of the neighbors came running in. There were three men (two old ones and one young one), two middle-aged women, and two girls. They had just risen from their dinner-tables; the women were in calico gowns and aprons, and the men in their shirt sleeves—all except the young man; he had stopped to put on his coat.

"Oh, have you found her?" two or three of the women gasped out as they entered; the others stared in breathless inquiry. Charlotte shook her head. The neighbors circled around her and asked questions. Nobody knew what to do first. "The trouble is, there don't seem to be anywhere that there's any sense in to look for her," said one of the women, with a sage air. And it was quite true. There was no reasonable place outside of her own house in which to look for her. Lucinda might almost have been regarded as a gentle and timid crustacean, and that house in which she had been born and lived her whole life as her shell. She never stirred out of it, except into her little garden, from one week's end to the other. She never went into a neighbor's. It had seemed a mere farce to inquire of one. It was almost impossible to imagine Lucinda outside of her own house; the very windows seemed full of her to people on the street, and the neighbors were bewildered, standing there in the sitting-room and trying to think of her as away.

The young man in the company surveyed Charlotte with anxious, honest eyes. He was tall, and his fair curly head overtopped all the others. He was the brother of one of the girls. Charlotte never looked at him. The talk and speculation went on; then finally the young man made a start. "I'll go and put my horse in the buggy," he said, in a determined tone, "and I'll go a piece on all the roads, and see if anybody has seen anything of her."

"I'll go an' help you harness," returned one of the old men, promptly.

Then Charlotte and the others searched the house again from garret to cellar. Charlotte was not easily timorous nor imaginative, but fearful imaginations could come to her, as to all human beings, and when they did come they had weighty presences. Charlotte probably would never see a ghost, but if she ever did it would come with a mighty march upon her. After the second fruitless search through the house was finished, she turned upon the people with her. "Something dreadful has happened," said she, in a quick, strained tone.

"Oh, mebbe there ain't," one of the women said, soothingly; but her eyes were wild and scared.

"Yes, there has."

They all stood in the side entry, where they had come from the second story. Charlotte looked from one to the other; then she set her mouth hard, and went out into the yard. In the middle of the yard there was a well with an old-fashioned sweep. Charlotte went with rigid strides straight to the well, and the people followed her, the young girls hanging back a little. Charlotte stretched herself up, leaned over the curb, and looked down; the others crowded close to her, and did the same. They could see nothing but their own faces in the far-away dark water. They gazed down at the young rosy faces and the old ones, with the flecks of sunlight around them, but they could see nothing beyond. It was that reflection of life which is all that one sees upon the farthest point of investigation.

"We can't see nothin' but ourselves," said one of the women. "Father, you'd better get a pole somewhere, an' poke down there."

"Where can I git a pole?" asked the old man, who was the woman's husband. He had an important, solemn voice; his wife, no matter how great her awe, was always sharply vociferous.

One of the young girls clutched the other by the arm when the pole was mentioned. Charlotte and the old man went into the garden, where there was a pile of last year's bean-poles, and he spliced some together with clumsy pains. They all stood back when he stepped up and began probing the well. He had bent a nail in the end of the pole, and he poked about warily. Finally he turned about on his spectators. He had a large face, and he carried himself pompously.

"There ain't nothin' there," said he. There was a slight

savor of disappointment in his tone. He had a natural scent for glory, but he was like an animal reared at a distance from his native prey, and had little opportunity to exercise it. He wished no harm to have befallen poor Lucinda; but if there had, he would have liked that distinction which belonged to the discoverer of it.

"Are you sure?" asked his wife.

"Course I'm sure. There ain't no use standin' pokin' any longer." The old man stepped down and stood in a stately attitude, with a pole at his side like a spear. "There ain't any other well, is there?" he inquired of Charlotte.

"No."

"No cistern nor nothin'? There wa'n't nothin' covered up that she could have stepped into?"

"No, there wasn't," said Charlotte. She struck out of the yard as she spoke.

"Where you goin'?" one of the women asked.

"Down to the salt-meadow."

Charlotte kept on down the street, and they all straggled after her. Others joined them, with eager questions, as they progressed. It was quite a crowd that reached the marsh that the Foster people called the salt-meadow. High tides flooded it. The rest of the time it lay a bare level, burned by the sun and swept by the salt wind. Here and there were pools of sea-water quite deep. Charlotte had thought of them.

Away over to the eastward there was a blue line between the marsh and a white cloudy sky; that was the sea. The people ran about here and there over the marsh; they looked taller than they were. There were now many boys in the company, and when they got into the distance, and showed up against the sky, they looked like men on the level meadow. They whooped and hallooed. Charlotte never spoke a word. She went from pool to pool, and the old man with the pole went with her. Here and there lay great mats of long and sunburnt marsh-grass. They looked like fleeces of wild animals. Charlotte eyed one with a desire to lift it up and see if her aunt were not lying hidden beneath it. Charlotte, neither knowing why, nor fully understanding that she was, began to be tortured by remorse. Lucinda had never spoken to blame her, but there was no need, for silence and absence will grind with accusing voices. Charlotte's ears were full of the voices, although she could not yet understand what they said.

She did not until that evening. When she returned from her fruitless search on the marsh she found the house and yard quite full of people. Some of the kindly women had been getting supper. They had brought in of their own stores. The hygienic food in the house looked rather poor to them. They agreed that Lucinda must have been pretty well pinched. The table was loaded with hot biscuits, cake, and cold meats, and there was a pot of strong tea. Charlotte would not eat anything, although the women urged her. Finally they sat down and drank the tea themselves. After supper, the house cleared gradually. Two of the women volunteered to stay with Charlotte all night, and the young girl, sister of the fair-haired young man, was to sleep with her. The two older women went home for a little while to mix some bread and fold clothes, and the young girl and Charlotte were alone in the sitting-room.

Now and then they could hear voices out in the street. Charlotte kept going to the door to listen. Once, as she returned, she hit Lucinda's little old work-box that stood on the corner of the table, and knocked it to the floor. All the things fell out; Charlotte groaned. It seemed as if she hurt her lost aunt. The girl came to her aid, and they began picking up the things and replacing them. Suddenly Charlotte gave a cry, and took something to the light and examined it closely. Then she sank into a chair, and rocked herself to and fro, and cried.

"Oh, dear! oh, dear! poor Aunt Lucinda! poor Aunt Lucinda! What shall I do? what shall I do?" she wailed.

The girl arose, and stood regarding her in a frightened way. She had a sweet, homely face, and was very small, much smaller than Charlotte. She had always been rather afraid of Charlotte, she was so large and handsome and peremptory. Finally she went up to her timidly. "Why, what *is* it?" she asked; "what *is* the matter, Charlotte?"

Charlotte held out something. "Look at that," she said, convulsively.

The girl took it and looked at it curiously. It was a playing-card, the jack of hearts, and one corner was scorched and shrivelled by fire. "Why, it's a card," said she, vaguely; "and it's been burnt."

Charlotte uncovered her face, and showed it wet and swollen and distorted. "Yes," said she, "it's a card. And I'll tell you what I did. I'll tell you all about it. I've been wicked; I've been dreadful wicked and cruel. I found her trying to tell her fortune with those cards one day, and I scolded her for it, and I told her she ought to burn them up. She was telling her fortune, and trying to get a little bit of comfort and amusement out of it, and she's never had much in her life. She was cooped up here in this house all the best part of her life with her mother, that was nervous and half crazy, and had to be taken care of like a baby. She never went anywhere nor had anything, and she got a little bit of comfort out of the cards telling her fortune, and I told her to burn them. And she tried to. Oh, she tried to!—she tried to! Poor Aunt Lucinda! I can see it, just how it was. She put them into the fire, and she felt dreadfully to see them burn. She'd had them ever since she was a girl, and she'd taken so much comfort with them! It was just like burning up all the little hope she had left. And she just pulled out this card, when it was all afire, and saved it. I remember she had burned her fingers, and she wouldn't tell me how. That was how she did it. Oh, poor Aunt Lucinda! poor Aunt Lucinda!"

The other girl looked from her to the card with a puzzled and distressed air. "Don't feel so bad," she ventured, hesitatingly.

"Oh, I've got to feel bad! I've got to! I've got to all my life! The cards ain't all. Oh, I can tell you things—things that I never knew before. They all come up now. I haven't let her have tea when she wanted it, nor cake, nor cold pork and potatoes for supper, nor anything between meals. And she wanted some root-beer last night, and I said she couldn't have it. I've been setting myself up, because I thought I knew more; and I knew the things weren't good for her perhaps, but they were all her little comforts, all she had, and nobody ought to have taken them away but God. Oh, I've been doing a dreadful thing! I've been stealing from her. And I've done more than that. Oh, I have! I have! I've been stealing *her*. I've been taking the self out of her. Oh, poor Aunt Lucinda! poor Aunt Lucinda! What shall I do? what shall I do?"

The girl was quite pale; she held her lips parted. She did not comprehend it at all, nor know what to say. Suddenly there was a touch on her shoulder, and she looked around. It was her brother; he had been standing in the room a minute or two, but they had not noticed him.

"What's the matter with her?" he asked his sister in a whisper.

Charlotte went on wailing. Both of them had an odd feeling that she was not fairly there, and that they could speak of her.

"She feels awfully. She thinks she hasn't treated her well."

"What stuff!" The young man hesitated a moment; his face flushed; he looked at his sister. Finally he went up to Charlotte, knelt down on the floor beside her, and slid his arm around her waist. "Don't take on so—don't; you mustn't," he whispered. "I'll find her. I'm going now to give my horse his supper, and then I'm going to get a fresh one at Joe Grayson's, and I'm going to start out again. I'll find her before morning, and bring her back safe and sound. Don't take on so."

But Charlotte never hushed her wail. She did not seem to notice that his arm was around her.

The young man arose; he did not meet his sister's eye when he spoke to her. "I'm going home, and will send mother over right away," said he.

"She's coming as soon as she's folded the clothes," replied the sister.

"She's got to come now."

His steps sounded heavy and quick on the front walk. In spite of his pity he had an odd feeling of elation. He also had been rather afraid of Charlotte; she had seemed like a goddess in armor. He had now a feeling that he had caught her outside of her panoply.

He lived only three houses away, and his mother came

running over in a few minutes. She was a woman with as weighty a will as Charlotte's, although her softness and slowness of manner disguised it. Her will to Charlotte's was as feathers to steel, but the weight was there. She made Charlotte drink a bowl of sage tea and go to bed. She and the other woman sat up all night in the sitting-room, and listened and watched. They felt as if dreadful tidings might arrive at any moment, but none did. When Charlotte came down-stairs in the morning nothing more was known about her aunt than when she had gone to bed. Charlotte had not slept any, but she was quite calm. All her old repose of manner had returned, but there was no longer any strength in it. She did not stand as erect, with her shoulders back, as formerly. She looked ten years younger. Charlotte was quite a young girl, but everybody had considered her older.

The search for Lucinda continued: the roads were scoured for miles around, every well and pool was dragged, a close watch was kept upon the sea-shore; but nothing was seen of her until five o'clock in the afternoon. Then she came walking into the house. She entered at the side door, and went straight into the sitting-room. There were some women there with Charlotte. They all sat about the room like mourners. When they saw Lucinda they screamed with shrill voices, and more women came in from the kitchen. Charlotte did not speak nor scream. She went over to her aunt and clutched her arm hard.

Lucinda looked about with a bewildered air. Her cheeks were quite pink, her eyes shone, her curls were all untwisted and lay on her shoulders. Her bonnet, which was flat and old-fashioned, had slipped far back, her cashmere shawl with a green centre was pinned on one side, and the point trailed. But with all her disorder and bewilderment she was full of gentle but triumphant assertion.

"What are they all in here for this way?" she asked Charlotte, quite openly.

"Oh, Aunt Lucinda, where have you been?"

Lucinda looked about on them all with a sort of mild dignity. She stood quite straight. "I've been a-visitin'."

"What?"

"I've been a-visitin'."

"Oh, Aunt Lucinda, where?"

"I've been to Denham."

"Denham?"

"Yes; it's forty mile away, an' I've been on the cars. I've been a-visitin' my cousin on my mother's side that lives there—Mary Ellen Taylor. She's livin' with her oldest son, an' she's situated real pleasant. I hadn't seen her for twenty-five year."

"Oh! how did you get there?"

"I went on the steam-cars," replied Lucinda, with a lofty air.

"But how? Nobody saw you. How did you get started, Aunt Lucinda?"

Lucinda surveyed her niece with a look of pleasant cunning. "I jest went down 'cross-lots an' got on. I didn't see nobody," said she.

It was quite true, and had been quite feasible, as everybody saw. There was no regular depot at Foster, nothing but a little rude shed with a bench, where passengers, if there were any, waited. That day there had been none, and the road was lonely. Lucinda had been quite unseen and unmolested in her journey across-lots and her waiting at the station. Now that she had appeared, it seemed strange that no one had thought of such a solution of her disappearance. But people would have dreamed as soon of a marsh-flower taking to the railroad as of Lucinda Moss. She had been so long in one place that it seemed that it must be with her as with the flower, and that nothing but the wind of death could take her away.

The women had stood about, astonished and panic-stricken. Finally one spoke up. "Well," said she, "I know one thing: if I was to say what I thought, it would be somethin' pretty plain. All this go-round—"

Charlotte interposed. She stepped before her aunt, who had begun to shrink. "Don't you say a word to blame her, I won't have it," said she.

"Well, if you want to excuse it, after all the trouble and worry we've had and you've had—"

"I won't hear a word," repeated Charlotte.

After a while the neighbors had one by one departed, and Charlotte and Lucinda were alone together. Charlotte went directly about getting supper. When she called out Lucinda there was a fine array on the table: plenty of cake and pie, and some cold meat and vegetables. The room was full of the fragrance of tea. Charlotte poured out a cup, and passed it to Lucinda. "I thought we'd have tea to-night," said she. "And I've been thinking—this cake is some the neighbors brought in, but I don't think it is nearly as good as that cup-cake you used to make, and I wish you'd make some to-morrow, Aunt Lucinda, if you feel like it."

"I'd jest as lief as not." Lucinda's face was all trembling with smiles.

The next night, when Charlotte came home from school, she had a little parcel that she handed to Lucinda. "Here's something I bought for you, Aunt Lucinda," said she. Lucinda opened the parcel. It was a pack of cards. "I don't know but I'll let you tell my fortune, after all, if you'd like to," observed Charlotte, after a while.

After supper that evening Lucinda moved the things on the table back, and spread out the cards. She bent over them, and her face took on a wise and important expression. "Well," said she, finally, in a meditative voice, "there's a light-complected man right close to you, Charlotte, an' a weddin'-ring, for the first thing—"

LOUISA.

"I DON'T see what kind of ideas you've got in your head, for my part." Mrs. Britton looked sharply at her daughter Louisa, but she got no response.

Louisa sat in one of the kitchen chairs close to the door. She had dropped into it when she first entered. Her hands were all brown and grimy with garden-mould; it clung to the bottom of her old dress and her coarse shoes.

Mrs. Britton, sitting opposite by the window, waited, looking at her. Suddenly Louisa's silence seemed to strike her mother's will with an electric shock; she recoiled, with an angry jerk of her head. "You don't know nothin' about it. You'd like him well enough after you was married to him," said she, as if in answer to an argument.

Louisa's face looked fairly dull; her obstinacy seemed to cast a film over it. Her eyelids were cast down; she leaned her head back against the wall.

"Sit there like a stick if you want to!" cried her mother.

Louisa got up. As she stirred, a faint earthy odor diffused itself through the room. It was like a breath from a ploughed field.

Mrs. Britton's little sallow face contracted more forcibly. "I s'pose now you're goin' back to your potater patch."

said she. "Plantin' potaters out there jest like a man, for all the neighbors to see. Pretty sight, I call it."

"If they don't like it, they needn't look," returned Louisa. She spoke quite evenly. Her young back was stiff with bending over the potatoes, but she straightened it rigorously. She pulled her old hat farther over her eyes.

There was a shuffling sound outside the door and a fumble at the latch. It opened, and an old man came in, scraping his feet heavily over the threshold. He carried an old basket.

"What you got in that basket, father?" asked Mrs. Britton.

The old man looked at her. His old face had the round outlines and naïve grin of a child.

"Father, what you got in that basket?"

Louisa peered apprehensively into the basket. "Where did you get those potatoes, grandfather?" said she.

"Digged 'em." The old man's grin deepened. He chuckled hoarsely.

"Well, I'll give up if he ain't been an' dug up all them potaters you've been plantin'!" said Mrs. Britton.

"Yes, he has," said Louisa. "Oh, grandfather, didn't you know I'd jest planted those potatoes?"

The old man fastened his bleared blue eyes on her face, and still grinned.

"Didn't you know better, grandfather?" she asked again.

But the old man only chuckled. He was so old that he had come back into the mystery of childhood. His motives were hidden and inscrutable; his amalgamation with the human race was so much weaker.

"Land sakes! don't waste no more time talkin' to him," said Mrs. Britton. "You can't make out whether he knows what he's doin' or not. I've give it up. Father, you jest set them pertaters down, an' you come over here an' set down in the rockin'-chair ; you've done about 'nough work to-day."

The old man shook his head with slow mutiny.

"Come right over here."

Louisa pulled at the basket of potatoes. "Let me have 'em, grandfather," said she. "I've got to have 'em."

The old man resisted. His grin disappeared, and he set his mouth. Mrs. Britton got up, with a determined air, and went over to him. She was a sickly, frail-looking woman, but the voice came firm, with deep bass tones, from her little lean throat.

"Now, father," said she, "you jest give her that basket, an' you walk across the room, and you set down in that rockin'-chair."

The old man looked down into her little, pale, wedge-shaped face. His grasp on the basket weakened. Louisa pulled it away, and pushed past out of the door, and the old man followed his daughter sullenly across the room to the rocking-chair.

The Brittons did not have a large potato field ; they had only an acre of land in all. Louisa had planted two thirds of her potatoes ; now she had to plant them all over again. She had gone to the house for a drink of water ; her mother had detained her, and in the meantime the old man had undone her work. She began putting the cut potatoes back in the ground. She was careful and laborious about it. A strong wind, full of moisture, was blowing from the east. The smell of the sea was in it, although this was some miles inland. Louisa's brown calico skirt blew out in it like a sail. It beat her in the face when she raised her head.

"I've got to get these in to-day somehow," she muttered. "It 'll rain to-morrow."

She worked as fast as she could, and the afternoon wore on. About five o'clock she happened to glance at the road—the potato field lay beside it—and she saw Jonathan Nye driving past with his gray horse and buggy. She turned her back to the road quickly, and listened until the rattle of the wheels died away. At six o'clock her mother looked out of the kitchen window and called her to supper.

"I'm comin' in a minute," Louisa shouted back. Then she worked faster than ever. At half-past six she went into the house, and the potatoes were all in the ground.

"Why didn't you come when I called you?" asked her mother.

"I had to get the potatoes in."

"I guess you wa'n't bound to get 'em all in to-night. It's kind of discouragin' when you work, an' get supper all ready, to have it stan' an hour, I call it. An' you've worked 'bout long enough for one day out in this damp wind, I should say."

Louisa washed her hands and face at the kitchen sink, and smoothed her hair at the little glass over it. She had wet her hair too, and made it look darker: it was quite a light brown. She brushed it in smooth straight lines back from her temples. Her whole face had a clear bright look from being exposed to the moist wind. She noticed it herself, and gave her head a little conscious turn.

When she sat down to the table her mother looked at her with admiration, which she veiled with disapproval.

"Jest look at your face," said she; "red as a beet. You'll be a pretty-lookin' sight before the summer's out, at this rate."

Louisa thought to herself that the light was not very strong, and the glass must have flattered her. She could not look as well as she had imagined. She spread some butter on her bread very sparsely. There was nothing for supper but some bread and butter and weak tea, though the old man had his dish of Indian-meal porridge. He could not eat much solid food. The porridge was covered with milk and molasses. He bent low over it, and ate large spoonfuls with loud noises. His daughter had tied a towel around his neck as she would have tied a pinafore on a child. She had also spread a towel over the table-cloth in front of him, and she watched him sharply lest he should spill his food.

"I wish I could have somethin' to eat that I could relish the way he does that porridge and molasses," said she. She had scarcely tasted anything. She sipped her weak tea laboriously.

Louisa looked across at her mother's meagre little figure in its neat old dress, at her poor small head bending over the tea-cup, showing the wide parting in the thin hair.

"Why don't you toast your bread, mother?" said she. "I'll toast it for you."

"No, I don't want it. I'd jest as soon have it this way as any. I don't want no bread, nohow. I want somethin' to relish—a herrin', or a little mite of cold meat, or somethin'. I s'pose I could eat as well as anybody if I had as much as some folks have. Mis' Mitchell was sayin' the other day that she didn't believe but what they had butcher's meat up to Mis' Nye's every day in the week. She said Jonathan he went to Wolfsborough and brought home great pieces in a market-basket every week. I guess they have everything."

Louisa was not eating much herself, but now she took another slice of bread with a resolute air. "I guess some folks would be thankful to get this," said she.

"Yes, I s'pose we'd ought to be thankful for enough to keep us alive, anybody takes so much comfort livin'," returned her mother, with a tragic bitterness that sat oddly upon her, as she was so small and feeble. Her face worked and strained under the stress of emotion; her eyes were full of tears; she sipped her tea fiercely.

"There's some sugar," said Louisa. "We might have had a little cake."

The old man caught the word. "Cake?" he mumbled, with pleased inquiry, looking up, and extending his grasping old hand.

"I guess we ain't got no sugar to waste in cake," returned Mrs. Britton. "Eat your porridge, father, an' stop teasin'. There ain't no cake."

After supper Louisa cleared away the dishes; then she put on her shawl and hat.

"Where you goin'?" asked her mother.

"Down to the store."

"What for?"

"The oil's out. There wasn't enough to fill the lamps this mornin'. I ain't had a chance to get it before."

It was nearly dark. The mist was so heavy it was almost rain. Louisa went swiftly down the road with the oil-can. It was a half-mile to the store where the few staples were kept that sufficed the simple folk in this little settlement. She was gone a half-hour. When she returned, she had besides the oil-can a package under her arm. She went into the kitchen and set them down. The old man was asleep in the rocking-chair. She heard voices in the adjoining room. She frowned, and stood still, listening.

"Louisa!" called her mother. Her voice was sweet, and higher pitched than usual. She sounded the *i* in Louisa long.

"What say?"

"Come in here after you've taken your things off."

Louisa knew that Jonathan Nye was in the sitting-room. She flung off her hat and shawl. Her old dress was damp, and had still some earth stains on it; her hair was roughened by the wind, but she would not look again in the glass; she went into the sitting-room just as she was.

"It's Mr. Nye, Louisa," said her mother, with effusion.

"Good-evenin', Mr. Nye," said Louisa.

Jonathan Nye half arose and extended his hand, but she did not notice it. She sat down peremptorily in a chair at the other side of the room. Jonathan had the one rocking-chair; Mrs. Britton's frail little body was poised anxiously on the hard rounded top of the carpet-covered lounge. She looked at Louisa's dress and hair, and her eyes were stony with disapproval, but her lips still smirked, and she kept her voice sweet. She pointed to a glass dish on the table.

"See what Mr. Nye has brought us over, Louisa," said she.

Louisa looked indifferently at the dish.

"It's honey," said her mother; "some of his own bees made it. Don't you want to get a dish an' taste of it? One of them little glass sauce dishes."

"No, I guess not," replied Louisa. "I never cared much about honey. Grandfather 'll like it."

The smile vanished momentarily from Mrs. Britton's lips, but she recovered herself. She arose and went across the room to the china closet. Her set of china dishes was on the top shelves, the lower were filled with books and papers. "I've got somethin' to show you, Mr. Nye," said she.

This was scarcely more than a hamlet, but it was incorporated, and had its town books. She brought forth a pile of them, and laid them on the table beside Jonathan Nye. "There," said she, "I thought mebbe you'd like to look at these." She opened one and pointed to the school report. This mother could not display her daughter's accomplishments to attract a suitor, for she had none. Louisa did not own a piano or organ; she could not paint; but she had taught school acceptably for eight years—ever since she was sixteen—and in every one of the town books was testimonial to that effect, intermixed with glowing eulogy. Jonathan Nye looked soberly through the books; he was a slow reader. He was a few years older than Louisa, tall and clumsy, long-featured and long-necked. His face was a deep red with embarrassment, and it contrasted oddly with his stiff dignity of demeanor.

Mrs. Britton drew a chair close to him while he read. "You see, Louisa taught that school for eight year," said she; "an' she'd be teachin' it now if Mr. Mosely's daughter hadn't grown up an' wanted somethin' to do, an' he put her in. He was committee, you know. I dun' know as I'd ought to say so, an' I wouldn't want you to repeat it, but they do say Ida Mosely don't give very good satisfaction, an' I guess she won't have no reports like these in the town books unless her father writes 'em. See this one."

Jonathan Nye pondered over the fulsome testimony to Louisa's capability, general worth, and amiability, while she sat in sulky silence at the farther corner of the room. Once in a while her mother, after a furtive glance at Jonathan, engrossed in a town book, would look at her and gesticulate fiercely for her to come over, but she did not stir. Her eyes were dull and quiet, her mouth closely shut; she looked homely. Louisa was very pretty when pleased and animated, at other times she had a look like a closed flower. One could see no prettiness in her.

Jonathan Nye read all the school reports; then he arose heavily. "They're real good," said he. He glanced at Louisa and tried to smile; his blushes deepened.

"Now don't be in a hurry," said Mrs. Britton.

"I guess I'd better be goin'; mother's alone."

"She won't be afraid; it's jest on the edge of the evenin'."

"I don't know as she will. But I guess I'd better be goin'." He looked hesitatingly at Louisa.

She arose and stood with an indifferent air.

"You'd better set down again," said Mrs. Britton.

"No; I guess I'd better be goin'." Jonathan turned towards Louisa. "Good-evenin'," said he.

"Good-evenin'."

Mrs. Britton followed him to the door. She looked back and beckoned imperiously to Louisa, but she stood still. "Now come again, do," Mrs. Britton said to the departing caller. "Run in any time; we're real lonesome evenin's. Father he sets an' sleeps in his chair, an' Louisa an' me often wish somebody 'd drop in; folks round here ain't none too neighborly. Come in any time you happen to feel like it, an' we'll both of us be glad to see you. Tell your mother I'll send home that dish to-morrer, an' we shall have a real feast off that beautiful honey."

When Mrs. Britton had fairly shut the outer door upon Jonathan Nye, she came back into the sitting-room as if her anger had a propelling power like steam upon her body.

"Now, Louisa Britton," said she, "you'd ought to be ashamed of yourself—ashamed of yourself! You've treated him like a—hog!"

"I couldn't help it."

"Couldn't help it! I guess you could treat anybody decent if you tried. I never saw such actions! I guess you needn't be afraid of him. I guess he ain't so set on you that he means to ketch you up an' run off. There's other girls in town full as good as you an' better-lookin'. Why didn't you go an' put on your other dress? Comin' into the room with that old thing on, an' your hair all in a frowse! I guess he won't want to come again."

"I hope he won't," said Louisa, under her breath. She was trembling all over.

"What say?"

"Nothin'."

"I shouldn't think you'd want to say anything, treatin' him that way, when he came over and brought all that beautiful honey! He was all dressed up, too. He had on a real nice coat—cloth jest as fine as it could be, an' it was kinder damp when he come in. Then he dressed all up to come over here this rainy night an' bring this honey." Mrs. Britton snatched the dish of honey and scudded into the kitchen with it. "Sayin' you didn't like honey after he took all that pains to bring it over!" said she. "I'd said I liked it if I'd lied up hill and down." She set the dish in the pantry. "What in creation smells so kinder strong an' smoky in here?" said she, sharply.

"I guess it's the herrin'. I got two or three down to the store."

"I'd like to know what you got herrin' for?"

"I thought maybe you'd relish 'em."

"I don't want no herrin's, now we've got this honey. But I don't know that you've got money to throw away." She shook the old man by the stove into partial wakefulness, and steered him into his little bedroom off the kitchen. She herself slept in one off the sitting-rooms; Louisa's room was up-stairs.

Louisa lighted her candle and went to bed, her mother's scolding voice pursuing her like a wrathful spirit. She cried when she was in bed in the dark, but she soon went to sleep. She was too healthfully tired with her out-door work not to. All her young bones ached with the strain of manual labor as they had ached many a time this last year since she had lost her school.

The Brittons had been and were in sore straits. All they had in the world was this little house with the acre of land. Louisa's meagre school money had bought their food and clothing since her father died. Now it was almost starvation for them. Louisa was struggling to wrest a little sustenance from their stony acre of land, toiling like a European peasant woman, sacrificing her New England dignity. Lately she had herself split up a cord of wood which she had bought of a neighbor, paying for it in instalments with work for his wife.

"Think of a school-teacher goin' into Mis' Mitchell's house to help clean!" said her mother.

She, although she had been of poor, hard-working people all her life, with the humblest surroundings, was a born aristocrat, with that fiercest and most bigoted aristocracy which sometimes arises from independent poverty. She had the feeling of a queen for a princess of the blood about her school-teacher daughter; her working in a neighbor's kitchen was as galling and terrible to her. The projected marriage with Jonathan Nye was like a royal alliance for the good of the state. Jonathan Nye was the only eligible young man in the place; he was the largest land-owner; he had the best house. There were only himself and his mother; after her death the property would all be his. Mrs. Nye was an older woman than Mrs. Britton, who forgot her own frailty in calculating their chances of life.

"Mis' Nye is considerable over seventy," she said often to herself; "an' then Jonathan will have it all."

She saw herself installed in that large white house as reigning dowager. All the obstacle was Louisa's obstinacy, which her mother could not understand. She could see no fault in Jonathan Nye. So far as absolute approval went, she herself was in love with him. There was no more sense, to her mind, in Louisa's refusing him than there would have been in a princess refusing the fairy prince and spoiling the story.

"I'd like to know what you've got against him," she said often to Louisa.

"I ain't got anything against him."

"Why don't you treat him different, then, I want to know?"

"I don't like him." Louisa said "like" shamefacedly, for she meant love, and dared not say it.

"*Like!* Well, I don't know nothin' about such likin's as some pretend to, an' I don't want to. If I see anybody is good an' worthy, I like 'em, an' that's all there is about it."

"I don't—believe that's the way you felt about—father," said Louisa, softly, her young face flushed red.

"Yes, it was. I had some common-sense about it."

And Mrs. Britton believed it. Many hard middle-aged years lay between her and her own love-time, and nothing is so changed by distance as the realities of youth. She believed herself to have been actuated by the same calm reason in marrying young John Britton, who had had fair prospects, which she thought should actuate her daughter in marrying Jonathan Nye.

Louisa got no sympathy from her, but she persisted in her refusal. She worked harder and harder. She did not spare herself in doors or out. As the summer wore on her face grew as sunburnt as a boy's, her hands were hard and brown. When she put on her white dress to go to meeting on a Sunday there was a white ring around her neck where the sun had not touched it. Above it her face and neck showed browner. Her sleeves were rather short, and there were also white rings above her brown wrists.

"You look as if you were turnin' Injun by inches," said her mother.

Louisa, when she sat in the meeting-house, tried slyly to pull her sleeves down to the brown on her wrists; she gave a little twitch to the ruffle around her neck. Then she glanced across, and Jonathan Nye was looking at her. She thrust her hands, in their short-wristed, loose cotton gloves, as far out of the sleeves as she could; her brown wrists showed conspicuously on her white lap. She had never heard of the princess who destroyed her beauty that she might not be forced to wed the man whom she did not love, but she had something of the same feeling, although she did not have it for the sake of any tangible lover. Louisa had never seen anybody whom she would have preferred to Jonathan Nye. There was no other marriageable young man in the place. She had only her dreams, which she had in common with other girls.

That Sunday evening before she went to meeting her

mother took some old wide lace out of her bureau drawer. "There," said she, "I'm goin' to sew this in your neck an' sleeves before you put your dress on. It 'll cover up a little; it's wider than the ruffle."

"I don't want it in," said Louisa.

"I'd like to know why not? You look like a fright. I was ashamed of you this mornin'."

Louisa thrust her arms into the white dress sleeves peremptorily. Her mother did not speak to her all the way to meeting. After meeting, Jonathan Nye walked home with them, and Louisa kept on the other side of her mother. He went into the house and stayed an hour. Mrs. Britton entertained him, while Louisa sat silent. When he had gone, she looked at her daughter as if she could have used bodily force, but she said nothing. She shot the bolt of the kitchen door noisily. Louisa lighted her candle. The old man's loud breathing sounded from his room; he had been put to bed for safety before they went to meeting; through the open windows sounded the loud murmur of the summer night, as if that, too, slept heavily.

"Good-night, mother," said Louisa, as she went up-stairs; but her mother did not answer.

The next day was very warm. This was an exceptionally hot summer. Louisa went out early; her mother would not ask her where she was going. She did not come home until noon. Her face was burning; her wet dress clung to her arms and shoulders.

"Where have you been?" asked her mother.

"Oh, I've been out in the field."

"What field?"

"Mr. Mitchell's."

"What have you been doin' out there?"

"Rakin' hay."

"Rakin' hay with the men?"

"There wasn't anybody but Mr. Mitchell and Johnny. Don't, mother!"

Mrs. Britton had turned white. She sank into a chair. "I can't stan' it nohow," she moaned. "All the daughter I've got."

"Don't, mother! I ain't done any harm. What harm is it? Why can't I rake hay as well as a man? Lots of women do such things, if nobody round here does. He's goin' to pay me right off, and we need the money. Don't, mother!" Louisa got a tumbler of water. "Here, mother, drink this."

Mrs. Britton pushed it away. Louisa stood looking anxiously at her. Lately her mother had grown thinner than ever; she looked scarcely bigger than a child. Presently she got up and went to the stove.

"Don't try to do anything, mother; let me finish getting dinner," pleaded Louisa. She tried to take the pan of biscuits out of her mother's hands, but she jerked it away.

The old man was sitting on the door-step, huddled up loosely in the sun, like an old dog.

"Come, father," Mrs. Britton called, in a dry voice, "dinner's ready—what there is of it!"

The old man shuffled in, smiling.

There was nothing for dinner but the hot biscuits and tea. The fare was daily becoming more meagre. All Louisa's little hoard of school money was gone, and her earnings were very uncertain and slender. Their chief dependence for food through the summer was their garden, but that had failed them in some respects.

One day the old man had come in radiant, with his shaking hands full of potato blossoms; his old eyes twinkled over them like a mischievous child's. Reproaches were useless; the little potato crop was sadly damaged. Lately, in spite of close watching, he had picked the squash blossoms, piling them in a yellow mass beside the kitchen door. Still, it was nearly time for the pease and beans and beets; they would keep them from starvation while they lasted.

But when they came, and Louisa could pick plenty of green food every morning, there was still a difficulty: Mrs. Britton's appetite and digestion were poor; she could not live upon a green-vegetable diet; and the old man missed his porridge, for the meal was all gone.

One morning in August he cried at the breakfast-table like a baby, because he wanted his porridge, and Mrs. Britton pushed away her own plate with a despairing gesture.

"There ain't no use," said she. "I can't eat no more garden-sauce nohow. I don't blame poor father a mite. You ain't got no feelin' at all."

"I don't know what I can do; I've worked as hard as I can," said Louisa, miserably.

"I know what you can do, and so do you."

"No, I don't, mother," returned Louisa, with alacrity. "He ain't been here for two weeks now, and I saw him with my own eyes yesterday carryin' a dish into the Moselys', and I knew 'twas honey. I think he's after Ida."

"Carryin' honey into the Moselys'? I don't believe it."

"He was; I saw him."

"Well, I don't care if he was. If you're a mind to act decent now, you can bring him round again. He was dead set on you, an' I don't believe he's changed round to that Mosely girl as quick as this."

"You don't want me to ask him to come back here, do you?"

"I want you to act decent. You can go to meetin' to-night, if you're a mind to—I sha'n't go; I ain't got strength 'nough—an' 'twouldn't hurt you none to hang back a little after meetin', and kind of edge round his way. 'Twouldn't take more'n a look."

"Mother!"

"Well, I don't care. 'Twouldn't hurt you none. It's the way more'n one girl does, whether you believe it or not. Men don't do all the courtin'—not by a long shot. 'Twon't hurt you none. You needn't look so scart."

Mrs. Britton's own face was a burning red. She looked angrily away from her daughter's honest, indignant eyes.

"I wouldn't do such a thing as that for a man I liked," said Louisa; "and I certainly sha'n't for a man I don't like."

"Then me an' your grandfather 'll starve," said her mother; "that's all there is about it. We can't neither of us stan' it much longer."

"We could—"

"Could what?"

"Put a—little mortgage on the house."

Mrs. Britton faced her daughter. She trembled in every inch of her weak frame. "Put a mortgage on this house, an' by-an'-by not have a roof to cover us! Are you crazy? I tell you what 'tis, Louisa Britton, we may starve, your grandfather an' me, an' you can follow us to the graveyard over there, but there's only one way I'll ever put a mortgage on this house. If you have Jonathan Nye, I'll ask him to take a little one to tide us along an' get your weddin' things."

"Mother, I'll tell you what I'm goin' to do."

"What?"

"I am goin' to ask Uncle Solomon."

"I guess when Solomon Mears does anythin' for us you'll know it. He never forgave your father about that wood lot, an' he's hated the whole of us ever since. When I went to his wife's funeral he never answered when I spoke to him. I guess if you go to him you'll take it out in goin'."

Louisa said nothing more. She began clearing away the breakfast dishes and setting the house to rights. Her mother was actually so weak that she could scarcely stand, and she recognized it. She had settled into the rocking-chair, and leaned her head back. Her face looked pale and sharp against the dark calico cover.

When the house was in order, Louisa stole up-stairs to her own chamber. She put on her clean old blue muslin and her hat, then she went slyly down and out the front way.

It was seven miles to her uncle Solomon Mears's, and she had made up her mind to walk them. She walked quite swiftly until the house windows were out of sight, then she slackened her pace a little. It was one of the fiercest dog-days. A damp heat settled heavily down upon the earth; the sun scalded.

At the foot of the hill Louisa passed a house where one of her girl acquaintances lived. She was going in the gate with a pan of early apples. "Hullo, Louisa," she called.

"Hullo, Vinnie."

"Where you goin'?"

"Oh, I'm goin' a little way."

"Ain't it awful hot? Say, Louisa, do you know Ida Mosely's cuttin' you out?"

"She's welcome."

The other girl, who was larger and stouter than Louisa, with a sallow, unhealthy face, looked at her curiously. "I don't see why you wouldn't have him," said she. "I should have thought you'd jumped at the chance."

"Should you if you didn't like him, I'd like to know?"

"I'd like him if he had such a nice house and as much money as Jonathan Nye," returned the other girl.

She offered Louisa some apples, and she went along the road eating them. She herself had scarcely tasted food that day.

It was about nine o'clock; she had risen early. She calculated how many hours it would take her to walk the seven miles. She walked as fast as she could to hold out. The heat seemed to increase as the sun stood higher. She had walked about three miles when she heard wheels behind her. Presently a team stopped at her side.

"Good-mornin'," said an embarrassed voice.

She looked around. It was Jonathan Nye, with his gray horse and light wagon.

"Good-mornin'," said she.

"Goin' far?"

"A little ways."

"Won't you—ride?"

"No, thank you. I guess I'd rather walk."

Jonathan Nye nodded, made an inarticulate noise in his throat, and drove on. Louisa watched the wagon bowling lightly along. The dust flew back. She took out her handkerchief and wiped her dripping face.

It was about noon when she came in sight of her uncle Solomon Mears's house in Wolfsborough. It stood far back from the road, behind a green expanse of untrodden yard. The blinds on the great square front were all closed; it looked as if everybody were away. Louisa went around to the side door. It stood wide open. There was a thin blue cloud of tobacco smoke issuing from it. Solomon Mears sat there in the large old kitchen smoking his pipe. On the table near him was an empty bowl; he had just eaten his dinner of bread and milk. He got his own dinner, for he had lived alone since his wife died. He looked at Louisa. Evidently he did not recognize her.

"How do you do, Uncle Solomon?" said Louisa.

"Oh, it's John Britton's daughter! How d'ye do?"

He took his pipe out of his mouth long enough to speak, then replaced it. His eyes, sharp under their shaggy brows, were fixed on Louisa; his broad bristling face had a look of stolid rebuff like an ox; his stout figure, in his soiled farmer dress, surged over his chair. He sat full in the doorway. Louisa standing before him, the perspiration trickling over her burning face, set forth her case with a certain dignity. This old man was her mother's nearest relative. He had property and to spare. Should she survive him, it would be hers, unless willed away. She, with her unsophisticated sense of justice, had a feeling that he ought to help her.

The old man listened. When she stopped speaking he took the pipe out of his mouth slowly, and stared gloomily past her at his hay field, where the grass was now a green stubble.

"I ain't got no money I can spare jest now," said he. "I s'pose you know your father cheated me out of consider'ble once?"

"We don't care so much about money, if you have got something you could spare to—eat. We ain't got anything but garden-stuff."

Solomon Mears still frowned past her at the hay field. Presently he arose slowly and went across the kitchen. Louisa sat down on the door-step and waited. Her uncle was gone quite a while. She, too, stared over at the field, which seemed to undulate like a lake in the hot light.

" Here's some things you can take, if you want 'em," said her uncle, at her back.

She got up quickly. He pointed grimly to the kitchen table. He was a deacon, an orthodox believer; he recognized the claims of the poor, but he gave alms as a soldier might yield up his sword. Benevolence was the result of warfare with his own conscience.

On the table lay a ham, a bag of meal, one of flour, and a basket of eggs.

" I'm afraid I can't carry 'em all," said Louisa.

" Leave what you can't then." Solomon caught up his hat and went out. He muttered something about not spending any more time as he went.

Louisa stood looking at the packages. It was utterly impossible for her to carry them all at once. She heard her uncle shout to some oxen he was turning out of the barn. She took up the bag of meal and the basket of eggs and carried them out to the gate; then she returned, got the flour and ham, and went with them to a point beyond. Then she returned for the meal and eggs, and carried them past the others. In that way she traversed the seven miles home. The heat increased. She had eaten nothing since morning but the apples that her friend had given her. Her head was swimming, but she kept on. Her resolution was as immovable under the power of the sun as a rock. Once in a while she rested for a moment under a tree, but she soon arose and went on. It was like a pilgrimage, and the Mecca at the end of the burning, desert-like road was her own maiden independence.

It was after eight o'clock when she reached home. Her mother stood in the doorway watching for her, straining her eyes in the dusk.

"For goodness sake, Louisa Britton! where have you been?" she began; but Louisa laid the meal and eggs down on the step.

"I've got to go back a little ways," she panted.

When she returned with the flour and ham, she could hardly get into the house. She laid them on the kitchen table, where her mother had put the other parcels, and sank into a chair.

"Is this the way you've brought all these things home?" asked her mother.

Louisa nodded.

"All the way from Uncle Solomon's?"

"Yes."

Her mother went to her and took her hat off. "It's a mercy if you ain't got a sunstroke," said she, with a sharp tenderness. "I've got somethin' to tell you. What do you s'pose has happened? Mr. Mosely has been here, an' he wants you to take the school again when it opens next week. He says Ida ain't very well, but I guess that ain't it. They think she's goin' to get somebody. Mis' Mitchell says so. She's been in. She says he's carryin' things over there the whole time, but she don't b'lieve there's anything settled yet. She says they feel so sure of it they're goin' to have Ida give the school up. I told her I thought Ida would make him a good wife, an' she was easier suited than some girls. What do you s'pose Mis' Mitchell says? She says old Mis' Nye told her that there was one thing about it: if

Jonathan had you, he wa'n't goin' to have me an' father hitched on to him; he'd look out for that. I told Mis' Mitchell that I guess there wa'n't none of us willin' to hitch, you nor anybody else. I hope she'll tell Mis' Nye. Now I'm a-goin' to turn you out a tumbler of milk—Mis' Mitchell she brought over a whole pitcherful; says she's got more'n they can use—they ain't got no pig now—an' then you go an' lay down on the sittin'-room lounge, an' cool off; an' I'll stir up some porridge for supper, an' boil some eggs. Father 'll be tickled to death. Go right in there. I'm dreadful afraid you'll be sick. I never heard of anybody doin' such a thing as you have."

Louisa drank the milk and crept into the sitting-room. It was warm and close there, so she opened the front door and sat down on the step. The twilight was deep, but there was a clear yellow glow in the west. One great star had come out in the midst of it. A dewy coolness was spreading over everything. The air was full of bird calls and children's voices. Now and then there was a shout of laughter. Louisa leaned her head against the door-post.

The house was quite near the road. Some one passed — a man carrying a basket. Louisa glanced at him, and recognized Jonathan Nye by his gait. He kept on down the road toward the Moselys', and Louisa turned again from him to her sweet, mysterious, girlish dreams.

A CHURCH MOUSE.

"I NEVER heard of a woman's bein' saxton."

"I dun' know what difference that makes; I don't see why they shouldn't have women saxtons as well as men saxtons, for my part, nor nobody else neither. They'd keep dusted 'nough sight cleaner. I've seen the dust layin' on my pew thick enough to write my name in a good many times, an' ain't said nothin' about it. An' I ain't goin' to say nothin' now again Joe Sowen, now he's dead an' gone. He did jest as well as most men do. Men git in a good many places where they don't belong, an' where they set as awkward as a cow on a hen-roost, jest because they push in ahead of women. I ain't blamin' 'em; I s'pose if I could push in I should, jest the same way. But there ain't no reason that I can see, nor nobody else neither, why a woman shouldn't be saxton."

Hetty Fifield stood in the rowen hay-field before Caleb Gale. He was a deacon, the chairman of the selectmen, and the rich and influential man of the village. One looking at him would not have guessed it. There was nothing imposing about his lumbering figure in his calico shirt and baggy trousers. However, his large face, red and moist with perspiration, scanned the distant horizon with a stiff and reserved air; he did not look at Hetty.

"How'd you go to work to ring the bell?" said he. "It would have to be tolled, too, if anybody died."

"I'd jest as lief ring that little meetin'-house bell as to stan' out here an' jingle a cow-bell," said Hetty; "an' as for tollin', I'd jest as soon toll the bell for Methusaleh, if he was livin' here! I'd laugh if I ain't got strength 'nough for that."

"It takes a kind of a knack."

"If I ain't got as much knack as old Joe Sowen ever had, I'll give up the ship."

"You couldn't tend the fires."

"Couldn't tend the fires—when I've cut an' carried in all the wood I've burned for forty year! Couldn't keep the fires a-goin' in them two little wood-stoves!"

"It's consider'ble work to sweep the meetin'-house."

"I guess I've done 'bout as much work as to sweep that little meetin'-house, I ruther guess I have."

"There's one thing you ain't thought of."

"What's that?"

"Where'd you live? All old Sowen got for bein' saxton was twenty dollar a year, an' we couldn't pay a woman so much as that. You wouldn't have enough to pay for your livin' anywheres."

"Where am I goin' to live whether I'm saxton or not?"

Caleb Gale was silent.

There was a wind blowing, the rowen hay drifted round Hetty like a brown-green sea touched with ripples of blue and gold by the asters and golden-rod. She stood in the midst of it like a May-weed that had gathered a slender toughness through the long summer; her brown cotton gown clung about her like a wilting leaf, outlining her harsh little form. She was as sallow as a squaw, and she had pretty black eyes; they were bright, although she was old. She kept them fixed upon Caleb. Suddenly she raised herself upon her toes; the wind caught her dress and made it blow out; her eyes flashed. "I'll tell you where I'm goin' to live," said she. "*I'm goin' to live in the meetin'-house.*"

Caleb looked at her. "*Goin' to live in the meetin'-house!*"

"Yes, I be."

"Live in the meetin'-house!"

"I'd like to know why not."

"Why—you couldn't—live in the meetin'-house. You're crazy."

Caleb flung out the rake which he was holding, and drew it in full of rowen. Hetty moved around in front of him, he raked imperturbably; she moved again right in the path of the rake, then he stopped. "There ain't no sense in such talk."

"All I want is jest the east corner of the back gall'ry, where the chimbly goes up. I'll set up my cookin'-stove there, an' my bed, an' I'll curtain it off with my sunflower quilt, to keep off the wind."

"A cookin'-stove an' a bed in the meetin'-house!"

"Mis' Grout she give me that cookin'-stove, an' that bed I've allers slept on, before she died. She give 'em to me before Mary Anne Thomas, an' I moved 'em out. They air settin' out in the yard now, an' if it rains that stove an' that bed will be spoilt. It looks some like rain now. I guess you'd better give me the meetin'-house key right off."

"You don't think you can move that cookin'-stove an' that bed into the meetin'-house — I ain't goin' to stop to hear such talk."

"My worsted-work, all my mottoes I've done, an' my wool flowers, air out there in the yard."

Caleb raked. Hetty kept standing herself about until he was forced to stop, or gather her in with the rowen hay. He looked straight at her, and scowled ; the perspiration trickled down his cheeks. "If I go up to the house can Mis' Gale git me the key to the meetin'-house?" said Hetty.

"No, she can't."

"Be you goin' up before long?"

"No, I ain't." Suddenly Caleb's voice changed : it had been full of stubborn vexation, now it was blandly argumentative. "Don't you see it ain't no use talkin' such nonsense, Hetty? You'd better go right along, an' make up your mind it ain't to be thought of."

"Where be I goin' to-night, then?"

"To-night?"

"Yes ; where be I a-goin'?"

"Ain't you got any place to go to?"

"Where do you s'pose I've got any place? Them folks air movin' into Mis' Grout's house, an' they as good as told me to clear out. I ain't got no folks to take me in. I dun' know where I'm goin' ; mebbe I can go to your house?"

Caleb gave a start. "We've got company to home," said he, hastily. "I'm 'fraid Mis' Gale wouldn't think it was convenient."

Hetty laughed. "Most everybody in the town has got company," said she.

Caleb dug his rake into the ground as if it were a hoe, then he leaned on it, and stared at the horizon. There was a fringe of yellow birches on the edge of the hay-field ; beyond them was a low range of misty blue hills. "You ain't got no place to go to, then?"

"I dun' know of any. There ain't no poor-house here, an' I ain't got no folks."

Caleb stood like a statue. Some crows flew cawing over the field. Hetty waited. "I s'pose that key is where Mis' Gale can find it?" she said, finally.

Caleb turned and threw out his rake with a jerk. "She knows where 'tis; it's hangin' up behind the settin'-room door. I s'pose you can stay there to-night, as long as you ain't got no other place. We shall have to see what can be done."

Hetty scuttled off across the field. "You mustn't take no stove nor bed into the meetin'-house," Caleb called after her; "we can't have that, nohow."

Hetty went on as if she did not hear.

The golden-rod at the sides of the road was turning brown; the asters were in their prime, blue and white ones; here and there were rows of thistles with white tops. The dust was thick; Hetty, when she emerged from Caleb's house, trotted along in a cloud of it. She did not look to the right or left, she kept her small eager face fixed straight ahead, and moved forward like some little animal with the purpose to which it was born strong within it.

Presently she came to a large cottage-house on the right of the road; there she stopped. The front yard was full of furniture, tables and chairs standing among the dahlias and clumps of marigolds. Hetty leaned over the fence at one corner of the yard, and inspected a little knot of household goods set aside from the others. There were a small cooking-stove, a hair trunk, a yellow bedstead stacked up against the fence, and a pile of bedding. Some children in the yard stood in a group and eyed Hetty. A woman appeared in the door—she was small, there was a black smutch on her face, which was haggard with fatigue, and she scowled in the sun as she looked over at Hetty. "Well, got a place to stay in?" said she, in an unexpectedly deep voice.

"Yes, I guess so," replied Hetty.

"I dun' know how in the world I can have you. All the beds will be full — I expect his mother some to-night, an' I'm dreadful stirred up anyhow."

"Everybody's havin' company; I never see anything like it." Hetty's voice was inscrutable. The other woman looked sharply at her.

"You've got a place, ain't you?" she asked, doubtfully.

"Yes, I have."

At the left of this house, quite back from the road, was a little unpainted cottage, hardly more than a hut. There was smoke coming out of the chimney, and a tall youth lounged in the door. Hetty, with the woman and children staring after her, struck out across the field in the little foot-path towards the cottage. "I wonder if she's goin' to stay there?" the woman muttered, meditating.

The youth did not see Hetty until she was quite near him, then he aroused suddenly as if from sleep, and tried to slink off around the cottage. But Hetty called after him. "Sammy," she cried, "Sammy, come back here, I want you!"

"What d'ye want?"

"Come back here!"

The youth lounged back sulkily, and a tall woman came to the door. She bent out of it anxiously to hear Hetty.

"I want you to come an' help me move my stove an' things," said Hetty.

"Where to?"

"Into the meetin'-house."

"The meetin'-house?"

"Yes, the meetin'-house."

The woman in the door had sodden hands; behind her arose the steam of a wash-tub. She and the youth stared at Hetty, but surprise was too strong an emotion for them to grasp firmly.

"I want Sammy to come right over an' help me," said Hetty.

"He ain't strong enough to move a stove," said the woman.

"Ain't strong enough!"

"He's apt to git lame."

"Most folks are. Guess I've got lame. Come right along, Sammy!"

"He ain't able to lift much."

"I s'pose he's able to be lifted, ain't he?"

"I dun' know what you mean."

"The stove don't weigh nothin'," said Hetty; "I could carry it myself if I could git hold of it. Come, Sammy!"

Hetty turned down the path, and the youth moved a little way after her, as if perforce. Then he stopped, and cast an appealing glance back at his mother. Her face was distressed. "Oh, Sammy, I'm afraid you'll git sick," said she.

"No, he ain't goin' to git sick," said Hetty. "Come, Sammy." And Sammy followed her down the path.

It was four o'clock then. At dusk Hetty had her gay sunflower quilt curtaining off the chimney-corner of the church gallery; her stove and little bedstead were set up, and she had entered upon a life which endured successfully for three months. All that time a storm brewed; then it broke; but Hetty sailed in her own course for the three months.

It was on a Saturday that she took up her habitation in the meeting-house. The next morning, when the boy who had been supplying the dead sexton's place came and shook the door, Hetty was prompt on the other side. "Deacon Gale said for you to let me in so I could ring the bell," called the boy.

"Go away," responded Hetty. "I'm goin' to ring the bell; I'm saxton."

Hetty rang the bell with vigor, but she made a wild, irregular jangle at first; at the last it was better. The village people said to each other that a new hand was ringing. Only a few knew that Hetty was in the meeting-house. When the congregation had assembled, and saw that gaudy tent pitched in the house of the Lord, and the resolute little pilgrim at the door of it, there was a commotion. The farmers and their wives were stirred out of their Sabbath decorum. After the service was over, Hetty, sitting in a pew corner of the gallery, her little face dark and watchful against the flaming background of her quilt, saw the people below gathering in groups, whispering, and looking at her.

Presently the minister, Caleb Gale, and the other deacon came up the gallery stairs. Hetty sat stiffly erect. Caleb Gale went up to the sunflower quilt, slipped it aside, and looked in. He turned to Hetty with a frown. To-day his dignity was supported by important witnesses. "Did you bring that stove an' bedstead here?"

Hetty nodded.

"What made you do such a thing?"

"What was I goin' to do if I didn't? How's a woman as old as me goin' to sleep in a pew, an' go without a cup of tea?"

The men looked at each other. They withdrew to another corner of the gallery and conferred in low tones;

then they went down-stairs and out of the church. Hetty smiled when she heard the door shut. When one is hard pressed, one, however simple, gets wisdom as to vantage-points. Hetty comprehended hers perfectly. She was the propounder of a problem; as long as it was unguessed, she was sure of her foothold as propounder. This little village in which she had lived all her life had removed the shelter from her head; she being penniless, it was beholden to provide her another; she asked it what. When the old woman with whom she had lived died, the town promptly seized the estate for taxes—none had been paid for years. Hetty had not laid up a cent; indeed, for the most of the time she had received no wages. There had been no money in the house; all she had gotten for her labor for a sickly, impecunious old woman was a frugal board. When the old woman died, Hetty gathered in the few household articles for which she had stipulated, and made no complaint. She walked out of the house when the new tenants came in; all she asked was, "What are you going to do with me?" This little settlement of narrow-minded, prosperous farmers, however hard a task charity might be to them, could not turn an old woman out into the fields and highways to seek for food as they would a Jersey cow. They had their Puritan consciences, and her note of distress would sound louder in their ears than the Jersey's bell echoing down the valley in the stillest night. But the question as to Hetty Fifield's disposal was a hard one to answer. There was no almshouse in the village, and no private family was willing to take her in. Hetty was strong and capable; although she was old, she could well have paid for her food and shelter by her labor; but this could not secure her an entrance even among this hard-working and thrifty people, who would ordinarily grasp quickly enough at service without wage in dollars and cents. Hetty had somehow gotten for herself an unfortunate name in the village. She was held in the light of a long-thorned brier among the beanpoles, or a fierce little animal with claws and teeth bared. People were afraid to take her into their families; she had the reputation of always taking her own way, and never heeding the voice of authority. "I'd take her in an' have her give me a lift with the work," said one sickly farmer's wife; "but, near's I can find out, I couldn't never be sure that I'd get molasses in the beans, nor saleratus in my sour-milk cakes, if she took a notion not to put it in. I don't dare to risk it."

Stories were about concerning Hetty's authority over the old woman with whom she had lived. "Old Mis' Grout never dared to say her soul was her own," people said. Then Hetty's sharp, sarcastic sayings were repeated; the justice of them made them sting. People did not want a tongue like that in their homes.

Hetty as a church sexton was directly opposed to all their ideas of church decorum and propriety in general; her pitching her tent in the Lord's house was almost sacrilege; but what could they do? Hetty jangled the Sabbath bells for the three months; once she tolled the bell for an old man, and it seemed by the sound of the bell as if his long, calm years had swung by in a weak delirium; but people bore it. She swept and dusted the little meeting-house, and she garnished the walls with her treasures of worsted-work. The neatness and the garniture went far to quiet the dissatisfaction of the people. They had a crude taste. Hetty's skill in fancy-work was quite celebrated. Her wool flowers were much talked of, and young girls tried to copy them. So these wreaths and clusters of red and blue and yellow wool roses and lilies hung as acceptably between the meeting-house windows as pictures of saints in a cathedral.

Hetty hung a worsted motto over the pulpit; on it she set her chiefest treasure of art, a white wax cross with an ivy vine trailing over it, all covered with silver frost-work. Hetty always surveyed this cross with a species of awe; she felt the irresponsibility and amazement of a genius at his own work.

When she set it on the pulpit, no queen casting her rich robes and her jewels upon a shrine could have surpassed her in generous enthusiasm. "I guess when they see that they won't say no more," she said.

But the people, although they shared Hetty's admiration for the cross, were doubtful. They, looking at it, had a double vision of a little wax Virgin upon an altar. They wondered if it savored of popery. But the cross remained, and the minister was mindful not to jostle it in his gestures.

It was three months from the time Hetty took up her abode in the church, and a week before Christmas, when the problem was solved. Hetty herself precipitated the solution. She prepared a boiled dish in the meeting-house, upon a Saturday, and the next day the odors of turnip and cabbage were strong in the senses of the worshippers. They sniffed and looked at one another. This superseding the legitimate savor of the sanctuary, the fragrance of peppermint lozenges and wintergreen, the breath of Sunday clothes, by the homely week-day odors of kitchen vegetables, was too much for the sensibilities of the people. They looked indignantly around at Hetty, sitting before her sunflower hanging, comfortable from her good dinner of the day before, radiant with the consciousness of a great plateful of cold vegetables in her tent for her Sabbath dinner.

Poor Hetty had not many comfortable dinners. The selectmen doled out a small weekly sum to her, which she took with dignity as being her hire; then she had a mild forage in the neighbors' cellars and kitchens, of poor apples and stale bread and pie, paying for it in teaching her art of worsted-work to the daughters. Her Saturday's dinner had been a banquet to her: she had actually bought a piece of pork to boil with the vegetables; somebody had given her a nice little cabbage and some turnips, without a thought of the limitations of her housekeeping. Hetty herself had not a thought. She made the fires as usual that Sunday morning; the meeting-house was very clean, there was not a speck of dust anywhere, the wax cross on the pulpit glistened in a sunbeam slanting through the house. Hetty, sitting in the gallery, thought innocently how nice it looked.

After the meeting, Caleb Gale approached the other deacon. "Somethin's got to be done," said he. And the other deacon nodded. He had not smelt the cabbage until his wife nudged him and mentioned it; neither had Caleb Gale.

In the afternoon of the next Thursday, Caleb and the other two selectmen waited upon Hetty in her tabernacle. They stumped up the gallery stairs, and Hetty emerged from behind the quilt and stood looking at them scared and defiant. The three men nodded stiffly; there was a pause; Caleb Gale motioned meaningly to one of the others, who shook his head; finally he himself had to speak. "I'm 'fraid you find it pretty cold here, don't you, Hetty?" said he.

"No, thank ye; it's very comfortable," replied Hetty, polite and wary.

"It ain't very convenient for you to do your cookin' here, I guess."

"It's jest as convenient as I want. I don't find no fault."

"I guess it's rayther lonesome here nights, ain't it?"

"I'd 'nough sight ruther be alone than have comp'ny, any day."

"It ain't fit for an old woman like you to be livin' alone here this way."

"Well, I dun' know of anything that's any fitter; mebbe you do."

Caleb looked appealingly at his companions; they stood stiff and irresponsive. Hetty's eyes were sharp and watchful upon them all.

"Well, Hetty," said Caleb, "we've found a nice, comfortable place for you, an' I guess you'd better pack up your things, an' I'll carry you right over there." Caleb stepped back a little closer to the other men. Hetty, small and trembling and helpless before them, looked vicious. She was like a little animal driven from its cover, for whom there is nothing left but desperate warfare and death.

"Where to?" asked Hetty. Her voice shrilled up into a squeak.

Caleb hesitated. He looked again at the other selectmen. There was a solemn, far-away expression upon their faces. "Well," said he, "Mis' Radway wants to git somebody, an'—"

"You ain't goin' to take me to that woman's!"

"You'd be real comfortable—"

"I ain't goin'."

"Now, why not, I'd like to know?"

"I don't like Susan Radway, hain't never liked her, an' I ain't goin' to live with her."

"Mis' Radway's a good Christian woman. You hadn't ought to speak that way about her."

"You know what Susan Radway is, jest as well's I do; an' everybody else does too. I ain't goin' a step, an' you might jest as well make up your mind to it."

Then Hetty seated herself in the corner of the pew nearest her tent, and folded her hands in her lap. She looked over at the pulpit as if she were listening to preaching. She panted, and her eyes glittered, but she had an immovable air.

"Now, Hetty, you've got sense enough to know you can't stay here," said Caleb. "You'd better put on your bonnet, an' come right along before dark. You'll have a nice ride."

Hetty made no response.

The three men stood looking at her. "Come, Hetty," said Caleb, feebly; and another selectman spoke. "Yes, you'd better come," he said, in a mild voice.

Hetty continued to stare at the pulpit.

The three men withdrew a little and conferred. They did not know how to act. This was a new emergency in their simple, even lives. They were not constables; these three steady, sober old men did not want to drag an old woman by main force out of the meeting-house, and thrust her into Caleb Gale's buggy as if it were a police wagon.

Finally Caleb brightened. "I'll go over an' git mother," said he. He started with a brisk air, and went down the gallery stairs; the others followed. They took up their stand in the meeting-house yard, and Caleb got into his buggy and gathered up the reins. The wind blew cold over the hill. "Hadn't you better go inside and wait out of the wind?" said Caleb.

"I guess we'll wait out here," replied one; and the other nodded.

"Well, I sha'n't be gone long," said Caleb. "Mother'll know how to manage her." He drove carefully down the hill; his buggy wings rattled in the wind. The other men pulled up their coat collars, and met the blast stubbornly.

"Pretty ticklish piece of business to tackle," said one, in a low grunt.

"That's so," assented the other. Then they were silent, and waited for Caleb. Once in a while they stamped their feet and slapped their mittened hands. They did not hear Hetty slip the bolt and turn the key of the meeting-house door, nor see her peeping at them from a gallery window.

Caleb returned in twenty minutes; he had not far to go. His wife, stout and handsome and full of vigor, sat beside him in the buggy. Her face was red with the cold wind; her thick cashmere shawl was pinned tightly over her broad bosom. "Has she come down yet?" she called out, in an imperious way.

The two selectmen shook their heads. Caleb kept the horse quiet while his wife got heavily and briskly out of the buggy. She went up the meeting-house steps, and reached out confidently to open the door. Then she drew back and looked around. "Why," said she, "the door's locked; she's locked the door. I call this pretty work!"

She turned again quite fiercely, and began beating on the door. "Hetty!" she called; "Hetty, Hetty Fifield! Let me in! What have you locked this door for?"

She stopped and turned to her husband.

"Don't you s'pose the barn key would unlock it?" she asked.

"I don't b'lieve 'twould."

"Well, you'd better go home and fetch it."

Caleb again drove down the hill, and the other men searched their pockets for keys. One had the key of his corn-house, and produced it hopefully; but it would not unlock the meeting-house door.

A crowd seldom gathered in the little village for anything short of a fire; but to-day in a short time quite a number of people stood on the meeting-house hill, and more kept coming. When Caleb Gale returned with the barn key his daughter, a tall, pretty young girl, sat beside him, her little face alert and smiling in her red hood. The other selectmen's wives toiled eagerly up the hill, with a young daughter of one of them speeding on ahead. Then the two young girls stood close to each other and watched the proceedings. Key after key was tried; men brought all the large keys they could find, running importantly up the hill, but none would unlock the meeting-house door. After Caleb had tried the last available key, stooping and screwing it anxiously, he turned around. "There ain't no use in it, any way," said he; "most likely the door's bolted."

"You don't mean there's a bolt on that door?" cried his wife.

"Yes, there is."

"Then you might jest as well have tore 'round for hen's feathers as keys. Of course she's bolted it if she's got any wit, an' I guess she's got most as much as some of you men that have been bringin' keys. Try the windows."

But the windows were fast. Hetty had made her sacred castle impregnable except to violence. Either the door would have to be forced or a window broken to gain an entrance.

The people conferred with one another. Some were for

retreating, and leaving Hetty in peaceful possession until time drove her to capitulate. "She'll open it to-morrow," they said. Others were for extreme measures, and their impetuosity gave them the lead. The project of forcing the door was urged; one man started for a crow-bar.

"They are a parcel of fools to do such a thing," said Caleb Gale's wife to another woman. "Spoil that good door! They'd better leave the poor thing alone till to-morrow. I dun' know what's goin' to be done with her when they git in. I ain't goin' to have father draggin' her over to Mis' Radway's by the hair of her head."

"That's jest what I say," returned the other woman.

Mrs. Gale went up to Caleb and nudged him. "Don't you let them break that door down, father," said she.

"Well, well, we'll see," Caleb replied. He moved away a little; his wife's voice had been drowned out lately by a masculine clamor, and he took advantage of it.

All the people talked at once; the wind was keen, and all their garments fluttered; the two young girls had their arms around each other under their shawls; the man with the crow-bar came stalking up the hill.

"Don't you let them break down that door, father," said Mrs. Gale.

"Well, well," grunted Caleb.

Regardless of remonstrances, the man set the crow-bar against the door; suddenly there was a cry, "There she is!" Everybody looked up. There was Hetty looking out of a gallery window.

Everybody was still. Hetty began to speak. Her dark old face, peering out of the window, looked ghastly; the wind blew her poor gray locks over it. She extended her little wrinkled hands. "Jest let me say one word," said she; "jest one word." Her voice shook. All her coolness was gone. The magnitude of her last act of defiance had caused it to react upon herself like an overloaded gun.

"Say all you want to, Hetty, an' don't be afraid," Mrs. Gale called out.

"I jest want to say a word," repeated Hetty. "Can't I stay here, nohow? It don't seem as if I could go to Mis' Radway's. I ain't nothin' again' her. I s'pose she's a good woman, but she's used to havin' her own way, and I've been livin' all my life with them that was, an' I've had to fight to keep a footin' on the earth, an' now I'm gittin' too old for't. If I can jest stay here in the meetin'-house, I won't ask for nothin' any better. I sha'n't need much to keep me, I wa'n't never a hefty eater; an' I'll keep the meetin'-house jest as clean as I know how. An' I'll make some more of them wool flowers. I'll make a wreath to go the whole length of the gallery, if I can git wool 'nough. Won't you let me stay? I ain't complainin', but I've always had a dretful hard time; seems as if now I might take a little comfort the last of it, if I could stay here. I can't go to Mis' Radway's nohow." Hetty covered her face with her hands; her words ended in a weak wail.

Mrs. Gale's voice rang out clear and strong and irrepressible. "Of course you can stay in the meetin'-house," said she; "I should laugh if you couldn't. Don't you worry another mite about it. You sha'n't go one step to Mis' Radway's; you couldn't live a day with her. You can stay jest where you are; you've kept the meetin'-house enough sight cleaner than I've ever seen it. Don't you worry another mite, Hetty."

Mrs. Gale stood majestically, and looked defiantly around; tears were in her eyes. Another woman edged up to her.

"Why couldn't she have that little room side of the pulpit, where the minister hangs his hat?" she whispered. "He could hang it somewhere else."

"Course she could," responded Mrs. Gale, with alacrity, "jest as well as not. The minister can have a hook in the entry for his hat. She can have her stove an' her bed in there, an' be jest as comfortable as can be. I should laugh if she couldn't. Don't you worry, Hetty."

The crowd gradually dispersed, sending out stragglers down the hill until it was all gone. Mrs. Gale waited until the last, sitting in the buggy in state. When her husband gathered up the reins, she called back to Hetty: "Don't you worry one mite more about it, Hetty. I'm comin' up to see you in the mornin'!"

It was almost dusk when Caleb drove down the hill; he was the last of the besiegers, and the feeble garrison was left triumphant.

The next day but one was Christmas, the next night Christmas Eve. On Christmas Eve Hetty had reached what to her was the flood-tide of peace and prosperity. Established in that small, lofty room, with her bed and her stove, with gifts of a rocking-chair and table, and a goodly store of food, with no one to molest or disturb her, she had nothing to wish for on earth. All her small desires were satisfied. No happy girl could have a merrier Christmas than this old woman with her little measure full of gifts. That Christmas Eve Hetty lay down under her sunflower quilt, and all her old hardships looked dim in the distance, like far-away hills, while her new joys came out like stars.

She was a light sleeper; the next morning she was up early. She opened the meeting-house door and stood looking out. The smoke from the village chimneys had not yet begun to rise blue and rosy in the clear frosty air. There was no snow, but over all the hill there was a silver rime of frost; the bare branches of the trees glistened. Hetty stood looking. "Why, it's Christmas mornin'," she said, suddenly. Christmas had never been a gala-day to this old woman. Christmas had not been kept at all in this New England village when she was young. She was led to think of it now only in connection with the dinner Mrs. Gale had promised to bring her to-day.

Mrs. Gale had told her she should have some of her Christmas dinner, some turkey and plum-pudding. She called it to mind now with a thrill of delight. Her face grew momentarily more radiant. There was a certain beauty in it. A finer morning light than that which lit up the wintry earth seemed to shine over the furrows of her old face. "I'm goin' to have turkey an' plum-puddin' to-day," said she; "it's Christmas." Suddenly she started, and went into the meeting-house, straight up the gallery stairs. There in a clear space hung the bell-rope. Hetty grasped it. Never before had a Christmas bell been rung in this village; Hetty had probably never heard of Christmas bells. She was prompted by pure artless enthusiasm and grateful happiness. Her old arms pulled on the rope with a will, the bell sounded peal on peal. Down in the village, curtains rolled up, letting in the morning light, happy faces looked out of the windows. Hetty had awakened the whole village to Christmas Day.

A KITCHEN COLONEL.

BACK of the kitchen proper in the Lee house there was another shed-kitchen, unplastered and unpainted, that was used for rough work like soap-boiling and washing. Each kitchen had its own door opening directly into the green yard on the north side of the house.

Abel Lee sat in the door of the back kitchen cleaning dandelion greens. His long limbs in stiff blue cotton overalls sprawled down over the low wooden step into the grass. His white head showed out against the dark unpainted interior at his back. He had a tin pan full of dandelions between his knees, and he was scraping them assiduously with an old shoe-knife, and throwing them into another pan on the step beside him.

That morning the narrow green yard that stretched along the north side of the house had been all thickly set with yellow dandelion disks; now there were very few left, for Abel had dug them up for dinner.

It was early in May, and the air was full of sudden sweet calls of birds and delicate rustles of flowering boughs. In Ephraim Cole's next-door yard, on the other side of the gray picket-fence, stood three blossoming peach-trees. They were young and symmetrical trees, they stood in a line, and were in full pink bloom. Every time they stirred in the wind they gave out a stronger almond fragrance.

Abel, as he cleaned his dandelions, breathed it in without noticing. He had been out there all the morning, and had become accustomed to it, as it seems one would to the air of paradise. Moreover, he had seen seventy-eight seasons of blooming peach-trees, and a spring had become like an old and familiar picture on his wall; it had no new meaning for him. And, too, he was harnessed, as it were, with his head down, to dandelions.

Always as he sat there he could hear a heavy creaking step in the forward kitchen. Back and forth it went, and there were also loud rattling and clinking noises of dishes and iron kettles.

Suddenly, as he worked on the dandelions, the step and the noises ceased, and a voice took their place. It was a naturally soft and weak voice that had been strained into hard shrillness. "You mind you clean them dandelions thorough, father."

"I'm takin' all the pains I can with 'em," replied the old man. He examined one which he held in hand at the moment with great solicitude. He could not see the woman, but her eyes were upon him through the crack in the blind. She was at the window nearest the door.

"Well, you mind you do," she repeated. "How near done air they?"

The old man surveyed the pans with grave consideration. "'Bout half, I guess."

"Half! Good land! An' you've been quiddlin' out there all the mornin'."

"It's consider'ble work to dig 'em, mother."

"Work—talk about work! You dun know what work is. If you'd made the pies that I have since I got up from the breakfast-table you might think you'd done somethin'. If them greens ain't done in half an hour I can't get 'em boiled for dinner."

"I guess I can git 'em done in half an hour."

"Guess—there ain't no guess about it! You've got to if I git 'em done for dinner, an' I've got to have somethin' to eat with all them boarders. I want you to git them done, an' then wash up the breakfast dishes. I ain't had a minute. Now don't, for the land's sake, putter so long over that one; it's clean 'nough."

The voice ceased and the step began. Abel labored with diligence at his dandelion greens. After a while another old man came stiffly sauntering across the next-door yard, and took up a stand the other side of the picket-fence. He was small, with sharp features and a high forehead. He had very white hair and a long white beard, and he was smiling to himself. He stood between two of the blooming peach-trees, and looked smilingly at Abel, who toiled over his greens, and did not appear to see him.

"Well, Abel, how air ye?" said the old man finally. His smile deepened, his old blue eyes took on a hard twinkle, like blue beads, and stared straight into Abel's face.

"Well, I'm pooty fair, Ephraim. How air you?" Abel had not started when the other spoke; he merely glanced up from his greens with a friendly air.

"Well, I'm 'bout as usual, Abel." The old man paused for a second. When he spoke again it was more cautiously. He was near Abel, and also very near the kitchen window whence the sound of footsteps and dishes came. "Kitchen colonel this mornin', Abel?" he queried, in a soft and insinuating voice. His venerable white beard seemed to take quirks and curls like a satyr's; he gave a repressed chuckle.

"I dun' know what you call it," replied Abel, with a patient gravity. He took another dandelion out of the pan and examined it minutely.

"Goin' to the meetin' this arternoon?"

"What meetin'?"

"The town meetin: ain't ye heerd of it?"

"No, I ain't."

"It's a special town meetin' 'bout the water-works they're talkin' 'bout puttin' in. There's notices up on all the trees down street. I should ha' thought you'd seen 'em, if you'd had eyes."

"Well, I ain't happened to somehow."

Ephraim cast a glance at the kitchen window, and again cautiously lowered his voice. "Been too busy in the kitchen, ain't ye?"

"Well, I dun know 'bout that."

"I s'pose a kitchen colonel wouldn't git shot if he run for't; but he might git the pots an' kittles throwed at him." Ephraim doubled over the fence with merriment at his own humor.

Abel's face was imperturbable; he kept close at work on the greens.

"Well, I s'pose you'll go to the meetin'," continued Ephraim.

"I dun know."

"I should think you'd want to go, if you was a man, an' have a leetle voice in things. Here they air talkin' 'bout puttin' in them water-works, an' raisin' our taxes four per cent. to pay for't. I've got a good well, an' so've you, an' we don't want no water-works."

"There's some that ain't got wells," observed Abel, shortly.

"Well, that ain't anything to us, is it? We've got 'em.

Anyway, I should think you'd want to go to the meetin', an' see what *was* bein' done, if you was a man."

Abel said nothing. He began to gather up himself and his pans stiffly. The dandelions were all picked over. Ephraim, still smiling, leaned on the fence and watched him.

"What ye goin' to do now, Abel?"

Abel did not seem to hear. When he stood up, one could see how tall he was, although there was a stoop in his gaunt square shoulders. His spare face was pale, and his sharp handsome features had a severe downward cast, although their principal effect was gentle patience. He looked like a Roman senator turned begging friar as he stood there in his overalls holding his dandelion pans.

"Got the dishes washed, Abel?"

"No, I ain't yet," replied Abel, with a mixture of embarrassment and dignity in his tone. He turned on his heel, but Ephraim would not let him go.

"Stop a minute," said he. "Where's Fanny?"

"She's gone to school."

"Hm!" Ephraim, as he sniffed, cocked his head, and rolled his eyes towards the pink top of a peach-tree, as if in a spasm of contempt. "I rayther think *if* Fanny Lee was *my* granddaughter she'd quit school-teachin', an' stay to home an' help about the house-work, an' *I'd* quit bein' kitchen colonel; I rayther think I would."

Ephraim raised his voice incautiously; a woman's head appeared in the window.

"What's that?" she inquired, sharply.

"Oh, nothin'," replied Ephraim. "I was jest talkin' to Abel, Mis' Lee." Ephraim straightened himself from his lounge over the fence, and turned about with a deprecatory swiftness; but the woman's sharp old voice followed him up like a long-lashed whip.

"Well," said she, "if you ain't got anything better to do than to stan' leanin' on the fence talkin' nothin' to my husband all the forenoon, you had better come in here an' help me. I'll give you somethin' to do." Ephraim said nothing; he was in full retreat, and had passed the line of peach-trees. "You'd better go home an' help Mis' Coles carry in the water for her washin'," the woman's voice went on. "I see her carryin' in a pail jest now, an' she was bent over 'most double." Seeing that she could get no response, she stood looking after Ephraim with a comical expression that savored of malice and amusement. She turned around when Abel with the dandelions shuffled into the room. "Now, father, what air you bringin' that pan that you've put the scrapin's of the greens in in here for? Don't you know no better? I should think you'd knowed enough to took 'em down to the hens, many times as I've told ye. They're shut up now, an' they like green things."

"I'll take 'em down now."

"Take 'em down now! It does seem sometimes, father, as if you didn't have no sense at all. If I set you to doin' a piece of work, you're always takin' hold on't wrong end first. Take them greens down to the hens! I should think you'd know better, father."

Mrs. Lee was a small and frail-looking old woman, but she seemed always to have through her a strong quiver as of electric wires. It was as if she had an electric battery at the centre of her nervous system. Abel stood droopingly before her, his face full of mild dejection and bewilderment.

"Ain't I told you, father," she went on, "that them dandelion greens wouldn't get done for dinner if they wa'n't on? an' ain't they got to be washed? You know you ain't washed 'em, an' they ain't ready to put in the kittle, an' here you air talkin' 'bout goin' to the hen-coop! I ruther guess the hens can wait."

"I didn't know jest what you meant, mother."

"You don't act as if you knew what anything meant sometimes. It does seem to me as if you might have a leetle more sconce, father, with all I've got to do."

Abel set the pan of greens in the sink, and pumped water on them with vigor.

"Mind you git 'em clean," charged his wife. She was baking pies, and she moved about with such quickness that her motions seemed full of vibrations, and as if one could hear a hum, as with a bird. If she had about her any of the rustiness and clumsiness of age, she propelled herself with such energy that no hitches nor squeaks were apparent. She stepped heavily for so small a woman; it seemed impossible that her bodily weight could account for such heavy footsteps, and as if her character must add its own gravity to them. Mrs. Lee was but two years younger than her husband; but her light hair had not turned gray—it had only faded—and she did not wear a cap. She had been a very pretty woman, and there was still a suggestion of the prettiness in her face. She had withered complete, as some flowers do on their stalks, keeping all their original shapes, and fading into themselves, not scattering any of their graces abroad.

Everybody called Mrs. Abel Lee a very smart woman, and a very wonderful woman for one of her age. The house in which she lived had been left to her by her father. Abel had mortgaged it heavily, and she had taken boarders and nearly cleared it. Abel Lee had been a very unfortunate and unsuccessful man through his whole life. He had worked hard, and failed in everything that he had undertaken. Now he was an old man of seventy-eight, and his wife was taking boarders to support the family and clear the mortgage, and he was helping her about the housework. It seemed to be all that he could do.

The Lees had had one son, who had apparently inherited his father's ill-fortune. He had a sad life, and died without a dollar, leaving his daughter Fanny to the care of his old parents. Fanny was about eighteen now, and she taught school. Her school-house was a mile away, and she did not come home to dinner. However, Mrs. Lee's boarders all came, punctually at twelve o'clock. The boarders were four women, not very young, who worked in the shoe factory. When they got home, dingy and dull-faced, they always found dinner on the table—plenty of good food. Mrs. Lee was a splendid cook, after the village model. She did the helping with alacrity, and Abel had his portion after the boarders. He had a small allowance of greens to-day; they were the first of the season, and the boarders were hungry for them. The four women could not grasp many of the pleasures of life, and had to make the most of those that hung low enough for them. They took a deal of comfort in eating.

After dinner Abel hurried to clear off the table and wash the dishes. He was usually a long time about it, for he was hopelessly clumsy, although he was so faithful at such work. Abel at the dish-tub with one of his wife's aprons pinned around his waist was a piteous object. He bent to the task with a hopeless and dejected air, and mopped the plates with melancholy fussiness. But to-day he rattled the dishes quite like a woman. "Don't you rattle them plates round so; you'll nick 'em," his wife remarked once, and Abel obediently tempered his movements. Still, the dinner dishes were washed much sooner than usual. After they were set away, Abel took up a stand at the pantry door; he leaned against it, and regarded his wife with a hesitating air. Once in a while he opened his mouth as if to speak, then seemed to change his mind. Finally Mrs. Lee turned sharply on him. "Why don't you git the broom an' sweep up the kitchen, father," said she. "What air you standin' there for?"

Abel did not answer for a moment; he looked across the room at the broom on its nail, then at his wife—"I kinder thought—mebbe—I'd go to—that town meetin' this afternoon."

His wife faced about on him with a spoon in her hand. "What town meetin'?"

"The one they've 'p'inted about the water-works. I thought mebbe I'd better go an' kinder look into it a leetle."

"Look into it—a great difference it 'll make your lookin' into it! I should think you'd got about all the town meetin' you could attend to to home, without goin' traipsin' off there. Here's the churnin' to be done, an' I ain't got no time nor strength for't. I shouldn't think you'd talk 'bout town meetin's, father."

"Well, I dun' know as I'd better go," said Abel, and went across for the broom. However, he swept with more despatch than usual, and when he sat down to the churn it was with a forlorn hope that the butter might come in season for him to go to the town meeting. But the butter did not come until the meeting had been long dispersed, and not until Fanny came home from school. Abel was just lifting out the dasher when she appeared in the kitchen door with her dinner basket on her arm. "Well, grandpa, has the butter come?" said she.

"I guess you've brought it; it's been all the afternoon gittin' here." Abel surveyed her with adoration. Fanny was a pretty young girl. She looked at her grandparents and smiled radiantly, but evidently the smiles were about something that they did not understand.

"What air you lookin' so awful tickled about?" asked Mrs. Lee.

"Oh, nothing. Did you have any pudding left from dinner? I'm most starved."

"There's a saucer under the yellow bowl on the pantry shelf."

Fanny was still smiling when she sat down at the kitchen table with the pudding. "What does ail you?" Mrs. Lee asked again. She was at the other end of the table rolling out biscuits for tea.

"Oh, nothing, grandma. What makes you think there's anything?" Fanny ate her pudding with apparent unconcern, but all the time her eyes danced, and the corners of her mouth curved upward. "I didn't have to walk home to-night," she remarked, finally.

"Didn't have to walk home? Why not?"

"Well, Charley Page came along just about the time school was out, and—he brought me home in his buggy."

"Well, I never!" Mrs. Lee's sharp old face softened; she surveyed her granddaughter with admiring smiles. "That's the second time within a week, ain't it."

Fanny nodded, and bent lower over the pudding. She was blushing pink, and she could not keep the smiles back. Abel, who was starting the fire, stood stock-still, and stared with delighted wonder at her and his wife. "That young Page is one of the smartest fellars in town," he volunteered; "an' his father's wuth a good deal of property."

Abel was so pleased that he paid little attention when, on carrying his basket around to the shed door for more light wood, Ephraim again hailed him from the fence. "Hullo, Abel!" he called; "I didn't see you to the town meetin'."

"No; I wa'n't there."

"Kitchen colonel again?"

Abel picked up wood vigorously. Ephraim surveyed him with a dissatisfied expression. "Who was that I see your Fanny a-ridin' home with?" he asked.

Abel straightened himself, and looked over at Ephraim. "That was the young Page fellar," he said, proudly.

"John Page's son?"

"Yes."

"H'm!"

In a moment Ephraim turned about and walked off. He had a daughter of his own who was about Fanny's age, and she was very plain-looking and unattractive, and was not liked by the young men.

Fanny was much sought for, she was so pretty, and she had such pleasant ways. She dressed nicely too; her grandmother encouraged her to spend her school money for clothes. Her grandparents had always petted her, and exacted very little from her. She did not help much about the house. To-night, after tea, she stood looking irresolutely at her pretty gray dress and her grandparents. "Don't you want me to take off my dress and help about the dishes?" said she.

"Land, no!" answered her grandmother. "Go 'long; it

ain't wuth while to change your dress for this little passel of dishes. Father's goin' to wash 'em while I'm mixin' up the bread."

"Yes, you go right along an' set down in the parlor an' git rested, Fanny," chimed in Abel. "I ain't got a thing to do but the dishes, an' they ain't wuth talkin' about." Abel shuffled cheerfully around, gathering up the dishes from the tea-table.

Fanny went into the parlor as she was bidden; she had about her a sweet docility, and she would have changed her dress and washed the dishes just as readily. Fanny would always perform all the duties that she was told to, but probably not so very many others. She had little original directive power in the matter of duties, although she had a perfect willingness and sweetness in their execution.

She sat down at a parlor window with some fancy-work, and rocked to and fro comfortably. She could look out on the front yard full of green grass, with a blossoming cherry-tree, and a yellow-flowering bush down near the gate. The four women boarders were in the sitting-room, but she did not think of joining them, nor they her. Fanny's grandmother always insinuated her into the parlor when the boarders were in the sitting-room. In her heart she did not consider that these four dingy-handed shop-girls were fit associates for her granddaughter.

Fanny herself had no such feeling in the matter; she would have gone into the sitting-room and fraternized with the boarders, had her grandmother wished her to do so. But they rather repulsed her, and held themselves aloof with an awkward dignity, and Fanny was timid and easily rebuffed. They were quite acute enough to understand that Mrs. Lee did not consider them proper company for her granddaughter, and they felt injured and covertly resentful. They were also righteously indignant because Fanny was so petted by her grandparents, and did not help them more. To-night the four women in the sitting-room whispered together about Fanny; how she was sitting all dressed up in the parlor while her poor old grandparents were working in the kitchen. They thought that she ought to give up her school and stay at home and help. She was not earning much anyway, and it all went on to her back; she need not dress so fine.

While they whispered, Fanny, small and dainty, putting pretty stitches in her fancy-work, sat at the parlor window. When it was too dark for her to sew, she leaned her head against the window-casing and looked out. The yellow bush in the yard still showed out brightly in the dusk; the cherry-tree looked like a mist. Over in the east, beyond everything else, was a soft rise of shadow; that was Eagle Mountain.

It grew darker. After a while her grandmother came into the room, feeling her way. "Don't you want me to light a lamp, grandma?" asked Fanny, in a soft, absent voice.

"No; I don't want none. I'd jest as soon set down in the dark a few minutes; then I'm goin' to bed. Father's gone." The old woman fumbled into a chair at the other window. "Have you seen anything about your hat yet?" she asked Fanny, after they both had sat still a little while.

"Yes; I went into Miss Loring's on my way to school this morning."

"What you goin' to have?"

"That brown straw I've been talking about. I'm going

to have it trimmed with some brown velvet and yellow daisies."

"It 'll be real handsome. When you goin' to have it?"

"Next week—Friday. I've got to have it then, for I haven't a thing to wear if we go up the mountain Saturday."

The old woman's face was invisible in the dusk, but her voice took on a pleased and significant tone, and she laughed softly. "I s'pose that Page fellar will be goin', won't he?"

"I don't know. He was invited." Fanny also laughed with pleased confusion. She had been climbing the mountain with young Page for the last hour in a dream, and she had worn the brown straw hat with the brown velvet and yellow daisies.

"Well, I guess he'll go, fast enough. I see his father down to the store the other day, an' he stopped an' shook hands an' asked how I was, and looked dreadful smilin' an' knowin'. I guess he's heerd how his son's been carryin' you home from school. Well, I guess he's a good, likely young fellar, an' that's wuth more'n his father's money." The old woman spoke the last words of her remark in a lagging and drowsy voice. The two were silent again. Presently there came a long heavy breath from the grandmother's corner.

"Grandma!" called Fanny.

"What?" the old woman responded, faintly.

"Wake up; you're goin' to sleep."

"Well, I dun know but I be. I guess I'd better rouse up an' go to bed. I wouldn't set up much longer if I was you, Fanny."

"I ain't going to." But Fanny sat there and dreamed quite a while after her grandmother had fumbled out of the room.

That was on Thursday. It was the next day but one, Saturday, when old Ephraim Coles came to the fence and hailed Abel as he was paring potatoes at the kitchen door. "Hullo, Abel! how air ye?"

"'Bout as usual," answered Abel.

"Kitchen colonel this mornin'?"

"I dun know what you call it." Abel was cutting the specks from the potatoes with clumsy pains. He sat on the door-step with the pan between his knees. Ephraim stood watching him. He had an important look, and his smile was different from his usual one.

Presently he leaned over the fence. "Abel!" said he, in a confidential whisper.

"What?"

"Come here a minute. Want to tell ye somethin'."

Abel hesitated; he peered uneasily around at the kitchen window. Then he set down the potatoes, arose, and slowly shuffled over to the fence. Ephraim reached over and caught him by the sleeve when he came near enough. "You know Maria an' me own two share in the railroad, don't ye?" he whispered. Abel nodded. "Well," continued Ephraim, "next Saturday there's a stockholder meetin' to Boston, an' Maria she don't care nothin' 'bout goin', 'cause she's goin' to have company, an' Abby she don't want to, an' so if you want to go on Maria's stock you *can*."

Abel stared at him in gentle bewilderment. "Go to Boston?"

"Of course—go to Boston for nothin'; 'twon't cost ye a cent. An' I'll stan' the dinner. We'll go in somewhere an' git somethin' to eat. An' we'll go round an' see the sights. What d'ye say to't?"

Ephraim looked at Abel with the air of an emperor tendering a royal bounty. He drew himself up, put his hands in his pockets, and smiled.

Abel looked pleased and eager. "Thank ye," said he—"thank ye, Ephraim. I'd like to go fust-rate if—there ain't nothin' to hender."

"I'd like to know what there is to hender! I guess you can quit bein' kitchen colonel for one day. The meetin' comes a week from to-day, an' that's Saturday, an' Fanny she'll be home to help Mis' Lee."

"Yes, she will," assented Abel, thoughtfully. "Well, I must go an' finish them pertaters now, an' I'll see what mother says to it, an' let yer know."

Abel pared the potatoes with greater pains than ever; he washed them faithfully, and carried them into the kitchen, and tremblingly broached the subject of the Boston trip to his wife. To his great delight it was favorably received. Mrs. Lee said she did not see any reason why he could not go. She had entirely forgotten about Fanny's mountain party.

All the next week old Abel was in a tremor of delight. He had long conferences with Ephraim over the fence; delightful additions to the regular programme were planned; every day some new scheme was talked over. Abel had not had an outing for many years; he was like a child over this one. Still he did not neglect his household tasks; he worked with anxious zeal, he was so afraid that his wife might see so much to be done that she would veto the plan at the last moment. He was so anxious and nervous over it that he did not say much about it at home, for fear of having some damper cast upon him. Abel had not much shrewdness, but he had learned that a casual acceptance of a situation was much more likely than an eager one to make it lasting when his wife was concerned. Friday night at sunset both of the old men stood out in the yard with uplifted faces and scrutinized the heavens.

"It ain't goin' to be foul weather to-morrow," said Ephraim, judicially; "not if I know anything about signs."

"Ain't you afraid the wind ain't in jest the right quarter?" Abel asked, anxiously.

"H'm! I don't care nothin' about the wind. Everything p'ints square to fair weather, 'cordin' to my reck'nin'."

Ephraim was right. The next day was beautiful. Abel looked out of the window in the morning, and his face was like a boy's. Directly after breakfast he shaved himself at the kitchen glass and blacked his boots. Then he went into his bedroom to put on his Sunday clothes.

He was nearly ready—clean collar and best stock and all—when he heard Fanny's voice and Ephraim's daughter Abby's out in the yard. He did not pay much attention at first; then he stood still and listened with a lengthening face. "No, I can't go any way in the world," Fanny was saying. Her voice was perfectly sweet and uncomplaining, but there was a sad inflection in it. "Grandma forgot all about it, and she says poor grandpa has been counting on going to Boston with your father for a whole week, and it would be real cruel to keep him at home; and it's baking-day, and she's got the sitting-room carpet to put down, and she can't get along alone. Of course I'm kind of sorry about it. I'd been counting on going; but I wouldn't keep grandpa at home for anything, and there isn't anything else for me to do but to stay myself."

"Well, I hope that pretty Rogers girl that's visiting up to Rhoda Emerson's won't cut you out with Charley Page.

I saw him talking to her in the post-office last night," Abby said. Her voice was like her father's.

Abel unwound his stock, and painfully unbuttoned his stiff collar. Presently he appeared in the kitchen, and he had on his old clothes. His wife faced around on him. "For mercy's sakes, father, ain't you changed your clothes yet?"

"I ain't goin', after all, I guess."

"Ain't goin'! why not?"

Fanny was standing at the sink washing dishes, and she stopped and stared.

"Well," said Abel, "I've been thinkin' on't over, an' I've made up my mind I'd better not go, on several 'counts."

"I'd like to know what."

"Well, one thing is, it's kinder cheatin'. I've got to go as Maria Coles, an' I ain't Maria Coles. That's what it says in the stiffikit. I've got to show the conductor 'Maria Coles.' An' it ain't jest square, 'cordin' to my notions. I ain't thought 'twas all the time."

"Well, I think you air dreadful silly, father."

"Well, I don't think 'twould amount to much goin' anyhow, to tell the truth."

"I would go, grandpa," said Fanny.

But Abel stood fast in his position. His wife, and Fanny, who was anxious to acquit herself honorably in the matter, pleaded with him to no purpose. He was proof against even Ephraim's reproaches and sarcasms. "Well, stay to home, an' be a kitchen colonel all your life, if you want to," shouted Ephraim, as he strode out of the yard; "it's all you're fit for, 'cordin' to my way of thinkin'."

Abel went into the house and pushed Fanny away from the sink. "If there's anything else you want to do, Fanny," said he, "you'd better go an' do it. I ain't got another thing to set my hand to now."

Fanny looked at her grandmother.

"If he *ain't* goin', you might jest as well go an' get ready," said Mrs. Lee.

In a few minutes Abel heard Fanny's voice calling over to Abby: "Abby, Abby, wait for me! I'm goin', after all. It won't take me but a minute to get ready." And Fanny's voice sounded sweeter than a bird's to her grandfather at the kitchen sink.

Abel had a hard day of it. Putting down the sitting-room carpet was painful work for his old joints, and then there was churning to be done. When Fanny came home he sat in the old rocking-chair in the kitchen, with his head back, fast asleep. Presently his wife came out and aroused him. "Wake up, father," said she; "I want to tell you somethin'." Abel looked heavily up at her. "I—ruther guess Fanny an' that Page fellar have settled it betwixt 'em," whispered Mrs. Lee.

Abel's head was up in a minute, and he was looking at her, all alert. "You don't say so, mother!" Suddenly the old man put his hand up to his eyes and sobbed.

"Why, how silly you are, father!" said his wife. Then she went over to a window with a brisk step and stood there as if looking out. When she turned around her eyes were red. "I think you'd better go to bed, father, an' not set there dozin' in that chair any longer," said she, sharply; "you're all tuckered out."

The next day, when Abel had to stand a running fire relative to the Boston trip from Ephraim, he gave one counter-shot—the announcement of Fanny's engagement. He listened while Ephraim related the pleasures of his excursion and berated him; then he turned on him with an artfulness born of patience. "S'pose you've heard the news?" said he.

"What news?"

"Well, I s'pose our Fanny an' John Page's son have 'bout concluded to make a match on't."

"H'm!" Ephraim stood looking at him. "When they goin' to git married?"

"Well, I dun know. Mother was saying she thought mebbe some time in the fall."

"H'm! Well, there's slips. Mebbe she won't git him, arter all. It's best not to be too sure 'bout it."

But Ephraim turned on his heel and went home across the yard, and left Abel to his Sunday peace.

Abel had to work harder than usual that summer. It was Fanny's vacation time, and she had been accustomed to assist some about the house-work, so Abel's labors had been lightened a little during hot weather. But this summer Fanny was sewing, getting ready to be married in the fall, and she could not do much else, so her grandfather got no respite in his kitchen work through the long hot days. He grew thinner and older, but he never complained even to himself. He was radiant over Fanny. She was going to make a match that would lift her out of all his own struggles and hardships. Poor old Abel, in the midst of his hard, pitiful little whirlpool, watched Fanny joyously making her way out of it, and no longer thought of himself.

Fanny was married in October. There was quite a large evening wedding, and Mrs. Lee had wedding-cake and pound-cake and tea and coffee passed around for refreshments. Fanny and her bridegroom were standing before the minister, who had already begun the ceremony. Fanny, all in white, bent her head delicately under her veil; her cheeks showed through it like roses. The bridegroom kept his handsome boyish face upon the minister with a brave and resolute air. Abel and his wife stood near with solemn and tearful faces. The four boarders stood together in a corner. The rooms were crowded with people in creaking silks and Sunday coats, and the air was heavy with cake and coffee and flowers.

Suddenly, in the midst of the ceremony, Mrs. Lee nudged Abel. "The milk is burnin', father," she whispered; "go out quick an' lift it off."

Abel looked at her. "Be quick," she whispered again; "the milk for the coffee is burnin'. Don't stan' there lookin', for mercy's sake!"

Abel tiptoed out solemnly, with his best boots creaking.

When he returned, Fanny was married, and the people were crowding around her. He felt a heavy poke in his side, and there was Ephraim. "Had to go out an' be kitchen colonel, didn't ye, Abel?" said he, quite loud.

The bridal couple drove away, and the guests dispersed gradually. Mrs. Lee had to stay in the parlor until the last of them disappeared; but as soon as Fanny and her husband had gone, Abel changed his clothes and went into the kitchen. Things needed to be set to rights a little before morning.

The happy bridal pair rode away through the October night, the wedding guests chattered merrily in the parlor and flocked gayly down the street, and the kitchen colonel fought faithfully in his humble field, where maybe he would some day win a homely glory all his own.

THE REVOLT OF "MOTHER."

"FATHER!"

"What is it?"

"What are them men diggin' over there in the field for?"

There was a sudden dropping and enlarging of the lower part of the old man's face, as if some heavy weight had settled therein; he shut his mouth tight, and went on harnessing the great bay mare. He hustled the collar on to her neck with a jerk.

"Father!"

The old man slapped the saddle upon the mare's back.

"Look here, father, I want to know what them men are diggin' over in the field for, an' I'm goin' to know."

"I wish you'd go into the house, mother, an' 'tend to your own affairs," the old man said then. He ran his words together, and his speech was almost as inarticulate as a growl.

But the woman understood; it was her most native tongue. "I ain't goin' into the house till you tell me what them men are doin' over there in the field," said she.

Then she stood waiting. She was a small woman, short and straight-waisted like a child in her brown cotton gown. Her forehead was mild and benevolent between the smooth curves of gray hair; there were meek downward lines about her nose and mouth; but her eyes, fixed upon the old man, looked as if the meekness had been the result of her own will, never of the will of another.

They were in the barn, standing before the wide open doors. The spring air, full of the smell of growing grass and unseen blossoms, came in their faces. The deep yard in front was littered with farm wagons and piles of wood; on the edges, close to the fence and the house, the grass was a vivid green, and there were some dandelions.

The old man glanced doggedly at his wife as he tightened the last buckles on the harness. She looked as immovable to him as one of the rocks in his pasture-land, bound to the earth with generations of blackberry vines. He slapped the reins over the horse, and started forth from the barn.

"*Father!*" said she.

The old man pulled up. "What is it?"

"I want to know what them men are diggin' over there in that field for."

"They're diggin' a cellar, I s'pose, if you've got to know."

"A cellar for what?"

"A barn."

"A barn? You ain't goin' to build a barn over there where we was goin' to have a house, father?"

The old man said not another word. He hurried the horse into the farm wagon, and clattered out of the yard, jouncing as sturdily on his seat as a boy.

The woman stood a moment looking after him, then she went out of the barn across a corner of the yard to the house. The house, standing at right angles with the great barn and a long reach of sheds and out-buildings, was infinitesimal compared with them. It was scarcely as commodious for people as the little boxes under the barn eaves were for doves.

A pretty girl's face, pink and delicate as a flower, was looking out of one of the house windows. She was watching three men who were digging over in the field which bounded the yard near the road line. She turned quietly when the woman entered.

"What are they digging for, mother?" said she. "Did he tell you?"

"They're diggin' for—a cellar for a new barn."

"Oh, mother, he ain't going to build another barn?"

"That's what he says."

A boy stood before the kitchen glass combing his hair. He combed slowly and painstakingly, arranging his brown hair in a smooth hillock over his forehead. He did not seem to pay any attention to the conversation.

"Sammy, did you know father was going to build a new barn?" asked the girl.

The boy combed assiduously.

"Sammy!"

He turned, and showed a face like his father's under his smooth crest of hair. "Yes, I s'pose I did," he said, reluctantly.

"How long have you known it?" asked his mother.

"'Bout three months, I guess."

"Why didn't you tell of it?"

"Didn't think 'twould do no good."

"I don't see what father wants another barn for," said the girl, in her sweet, slow voice. She turned again to the window, and stared out at the digging men in the field. Her tender, sweet face was full of a gentle distress. Her forehead was as bald and innocent as a baby's, with the light hair strained back from it in a row of curl-papers. She was quite large, but her soft curves did not look as if they covered muscles.

Her mother looked sternly at the boy. "Is he goin' to buy more cows?" said she.

The boy did not reply; he was tying his shoes.

"Sammy, I want you to tell me if he's goin' to buy more cows."

"I s'pose he is."

"How many?"

"Four, I guess."

His mother said nothing more. She went into the pantry, and there was a clatter of dishes. The boy got his cap from a nail behind the door, took an old arithmetic from the shelf, and started for school. He was lightly built, but clumsy. He went out of the yard with a curious spring in the hips, that made his loose home-made jacket tilt up in the rear.

The girl went to the sink, and began to wash the dishes that were piled up there. Her mother came promptly out of the pantry, and shoved her aside. "You wipe 'em," said she; "I'll wash. There's a good many this mornin'."

The mother plunged her hands vigorously into the water, the girl wiped the plates slowly and dreamily. "Mother," said she, "don't you think it's too bad father's going to build that new barn, much as we need a decent house to live in?"

Her mother scrubbed a dish fiercely. "You ain't found out yet we're women-folks, Nanny Penn," said she. "You ain't seen enough of men-folks yet to. One of these days you'll find it out, an' then you'll know that we know only what men-folks think we do, so far as any use of it goes, an' how we'd ought to reckon men-folks in with Providence, an' not complain of what they do any more than we do of the weather."

"I don't care; I don't believe George is anything like that, anyhow," said Nanny. Her delicate face flushed pink, her lips pouted softly, as if she were going to cry.

"You wait an' see. I guess George Eastman ain't no better than other men. You hadn't ought to judge father, though. He can't help it, 'cause he don't look at things jest the way we do. An' we've been pretty comfortable here, after all. The roof don't leak—ain't never but once —that's one thing. Father's kept it shingled right up."

"I do wish we had a parlor."

"I guess it won't hurt George Eastman any to come to see you in a nice clean kitchen. I guess a good many girls don't have as good a place as this. Nobody's ever heard me complain."

"I ain't complained either, mother."

"Well, I don't think you'd better, a good father an' a good home as you've got. S'pose your father made you go out an' work for your livin'? Lots of girls have to that ain't no stronger an' better able to than you be."

Sarah Penn washed the frying-pan with a conclusive air. She scrubbed the outside of it as faithfully as the inside. She was a masterly keeper of her box of a house. Her one living-room never seemed to have in it any of the dust which the friction of life with inanimate matter produces. She swept, and there seemed to be no dirt to go before the broom; she cleaned, and one could see no difference. She was like an artist so perfect that he has apparently no art. To-day she got out a mixing bowl and a board, and rolled some pies, and there was no more flour upon her than upon her daughter who was doing finer work. Nanny was to be married in the fall, and she was sewing on some white cambric and embroidery. She sewed industriously while her mother cooked, her soft milk-white hands and wrists showed whiter than her delicate work.

"We must have the stove moved out in the shed before long," said Mrs. Penn. "Talk about not havin' things, it's been a real blessin' to be able to put a stove up in that shed in hot weather. Father did one good thing when he fixed that stove-pipe out there."

Sarah Penn's face as she rolled her pies had that expression of meek vigor which might have characterized one of the New Testament saints. She was making mince-pies. Her husband, Adoniram Penn, liked them better than any other kind. She baked twice a week. Adoniram often liked a piece of pie between meals. She hurried this morning. It had been later than usual when she began, and she wanted to have a pie baked for dinner. However deep a resentment she might be forced to hold against her husband, she would never fail in sedulous attention to his wants.

Nobility of character manifests itself at loop-holes when it is not provided with large doors. Sarah Penn's showed itself to-day in flaky dishes of pastry. So she made the pies faithfully, while across the table she could see, when she glanced up from her work, the sight that rankled in her patient and steadfast soul—the digging of the cellar of the new barn in the place where Adoniram forty years ago had promised her their new house should stand.

The pies were done for dinner. Adoniram and Sammy were home a few minutes after twelve o'clock. The dinner was eaten with serious haste. There was never much conversation at the table in the Penn family. Adoniram asked a blessing, and they ate promptly, then rose up and went about their work.

Sammy went back to school, taking soft sly lopes out of the yard like a rabbit. He wanted a game of marbles before school, and feared his father would give him some chores to do. Adoniram hastened to the door and called after him, but he was out of sight.

"I don't see what you let him go for, mother," said he. "I wanted him to help me unload that wood."

Adoniram went to work out in the yard unloading wood from the wagon. Sarah put away the dinner dishes, while Nanny took down her curl-papers and changed her dress. She was going down to the store to buy some more embroidery and thread.

When Nanny was gone, Mrs. Penn went to the door. "Father!" she called.

"Well, what is it!"

"I want to see you jest a minute, father."

"I can't leave this wood nohow. I've got to git it unloaded an' go for a load of gravel afore two o'clock. Sammy had ought to helped me. You hadn't ought to let him go to school so early."

"I want to see you jest a minute."

"I tell ye I can't, nohow, mother."

"Father, you come here." Sarah Penn stood in the door like a queen; she held her head as if it bore a crown; there was that patience which makes authority royal in her voice. Adoniram went.

Mrs. Penn led the way into the kitchen, and pointed to a chair. "Sit down, father," said she; "I've got somethin' I want to say to you."

He sat down heavily; his face was quite stolid, but he

looked at her with restive eyes. "Well, what is it, mother?"

"I want to know what you're buildin' that new barn for, father?"

"I ain't got nothin' to say about it."

"It can't be you think you need another barn?"

"I tell ye I ain't got nothin' to say about it, mother; an' I ain't goin' to say nothin'."

"Be you goin' to buy more cows?"

Adoniram did not reply; he shut his mouth tight.

"I know you be, as well as I want to. Now, father, look here"—Sarah Penn had not sat down; she stood before her husband in the humble fashion of a Scripture woman—"I'm goin' to talk real plain to you; I never have sence I married you, but I'm goin' to now. I ain't never complained, an' I ain't goin' to complain now, but I'm goin' to talk plain. You see this room here, father; you look at it well. You see there ain't no carpet on the floor, an' you see the paper is all dirty, an' droppin' off the walls. We ain't had no new paper on it for ten year, an' then I put it on myself, an' it didn't cost but ninepence a roll. You see this room, father; it's all the one I've had to work in an' eat in an' sit in sence we was married. There ain't another woman in the whole town whose husband ain't got half the means you have but what's got better. It's all the room Nanny's got to have her company in; an' there ain't one of her mates but what's got better, an' their fathers not so able as hers is. It's all the room she'll have to be married in. What would you have thought, father, if we had had our weddin' in a room no better than this? I was married in my mother's parlor, with a carpet on the floor, an' stuffed furniture, an' a mahogany card-table. An' this is all the room my daughter will have to be married in. Look here, father!"

Sarah Penn went across the room as though it were a tragic stage. She flung open a door and disclosed a tiny bedroom, only large enough for a bed and bureau, with a path between. "There, father," said she—"there's all the room I've had to sleep in forty year. All my children were born there—the two that died, an' the two that's livin'. I was sick with a fever there."

She stepped to another door and opened it. It led into the small, ill-lighted pantry. "Here," said she, "is all the buttery I've got—every place I've got for my dishes, to set away my victuals in, an' to keep my milk-pans in. Father, I've been takin' care of the milk of six cows in this place, an' now you're goin' to build a new barn, an' keep more cows, an' give me more to do in it."

She threw open another door. A narrow crooked flight of stairs wound upward from it. "There, father," said she, "I want you to look at the stairs that go up to them two unfinished chambers that are all the places our son an' daughter have had to sleep in all their lives. There ain't a prettier girl in town nor a more ladylike one than Nanny, an' that's the place she has to sleep in. It ain't so good as your horse's stall; it ain't so warm an' tight."

Sarah Penn went back and stood before her husband. "Now, father," said she, "I want to know if you think you're doin' right an' accordin' to what you profess. Here, when we was married, forty year ago, you promised me faithful that we should have a new house built in that lot over in the field before the year was out. You said you had money enough, an' you wouldn't ask me to live in no such place as this. It is forty year now, an' you've been makin' more money, an' I've been savin' of it for you ever since, an' you ain't built no house yet. You've built sheds an' cow-houses an' one new barn, an' now you're goin' to build another. Father, I want to know if you think it's right. You're lodgin' your dumb beasts better than you are your own flesh an' blood. I want to know if you think it's right."

"I ain't got nothin' to say."

"You can't say nothin' without ownin' it ain't right, father. An' there's another thing — I ain't complained; I've got along forty year, an' I s'pose I should forty more, if it wa'n't for that—if we don't have another house. Nanny she can't live with us after she's married. She'll have to go somewheres else to live away from us, an' it don't seem as if I could have it so, noways, father. She wa'n't ever strong. She's got considerable color, but there wa'n't never any backbone to her. I've always took the heft of everything off her, an' she ain't fit to keep house an' do everything herself. She'll be all worn out inside of a year. Think of her doin' all the washin' an' ironin' an' bakin' with them soft white hands an' arms, an' sweepin'! I can't have it so, noways, father."

Mrs. Penn's face was burning; her mild eyes gleamed. She had pleaded her little cause like a Webster; she had ranged from severity to pathos; but her opponent employed that obstinate silence which makes eloquence futile with mocking echoes. Adoniram arose clumsily.

"Father, ain't you got nothin' to say?" said Mrs. Penn.

"I've got to go off after that load of gravel. I can't stan' here talkin' all day."

"Father, won't you think it over, an' have a house built there instead of a barn?"

"I ain't got nothin' to say."

Adoniram shuffled out. Mrs. Penn went into her bedroom. When she came out, her eyes were red. She had a roll of unbleached cotton cloth. She spread it out on the kitchen table, and began cutting out some shirts for her husband. The men over in the field had a team to help them this afternoon; she could hear their halloos. She had a scanty pattern for the shirts; she had to plan and piece the sleeves.

Nanny came home with her embroidery, and sat down with her needlework. She had taken down her curl-papers, and there was a soft roll of fair hair like an aureole over her forehead; her face was as delicately fine and clear as porcelain. Suddenly she looked up, and the tender red flamed all over her face and neck. "Mother," said she.

"What say?"

"I've been thinking—I don't see how we're goin' to have any—wedding in this room. I'd be ashamed to have his folks come if we didn't have anybody else."

"Mebbe we can have some new paper before then; I can put it on. I guess you won't have no call to be ashamed of your belongin's."

"We might have the wedding in the new barn," said Nanny, with gentle pettishness. "Why, mother, what makes you look so?"

Mrs. Penn had started, and was staring at her with a curious expression. She turned again to her work, and spread out a pattern carefully on the cloth. "Nothin'," said she.

Presently Adoniram clattered out of the yard in his two-wheeled dump cart, standing as proudly upright as a Roman charioteer. Mrs. Penn opened the door and stood there a minute looking out; the halloos of the men sounded louder.

It seemed to her all through the spring months that she

heard nothing but the halloos and the noises of saws and hammers. The new barn grew fast. It was a fine edifice for this little village. Men came on pleasant Sundays, in their meeting suits and clean shirt bosoms, and stood around it admiringly. Mrs. Penn did not speak of it, and Adoniram did not mention it to her, although sometimes, upon a return from inspecting it, he bore himself with injured dignity.

"It's a strange thing how your mother feels about the new barn," he said, confidentially, to Sammy one day.

Sammy only grunted after an odd fashion for a boy; he had learned it from his father.

The barn was all completed ready for use by the third week in July. Adoniram had planned to move his stock in on Wednesday; on Tuesday he received a letter which changed his plans. He came in with it early in the morning. "Sammy's been to the post-office," said he, "an' I've got a letter from Hiram." Hiram was Mrs. Penn's brother, who lived in Vermont.

"Well," said Mrs. Penn, "what does he say about the folks?"

"I guess they're all right. He says he thinks if I come up country right off there's a chance to buy jest the kind of a horse I want." He stared reflectively out of the window at the new barn.

Mrs. Penn was making pies. She went on clapping the rolling-pin into the crust, although she was very pale, and her heart beat loudly.

"I dun' know but what I'd better go," said Adoniram. "I hate to go off jest now, right in the midst of hayin', but the ten-acre lot's cut, an' I guess Rufus an' the others can git along without me three or four days. I can't get a horse round here to suit me, nohow, an' I've got to have another for all that wood-haulin' in the fall. I told Hiram to watch out, an' if he got wind of a good horse to let me know. I guess I'd better go."

"I'll get out your clean shirt an' collar," said Mrs. Penn calmly.

She laid out Adoniram's Sunday suit and his clean clothes on the bed in the little bedroom. She got his shaving-water and razor ready. At last she buttoned on his collar and fastened his black cravat.

Adoniram never wore his collar and cravat except on extra occasions. He held his head high, with a rasped dignity. When he was all ready, with his coat and hat brushed, and a lunch of pie and cheese in a paper bag, he hesitated on the threshold of the door. He looked at his wife, and his manner was defiantly apologetic. "*If* them cows come to-day, Sammy can drive 'em into the new barn," said he; "an' when they bring the hay up, they can pitch it in there."

"Well," replied Mrs. Penn.

Adoniram set his shaven face ahead and started. When he had cleared the door-step, he turned and looked back with a kind of nervous solemnity. "I shall be back by Saturday if nothin' happens," said he.

"Do be careful, father," returned his wife.

She stood in the door with Nanny at her elbow and watched him out of sight. Her eyes had a strange, doubtful expression in them; her peaceful forehead was contracted. She went in, and about her baking again. Nanny sat sewing. Her wedding-day was drawing nearer, and she was getting pale and thin with her steady sewing. Her mother kept glancing at her.

"Have you got that pain in your side this mornin'?" she asked.

"A little."

Mrs. Penn's face, as she worked, changed, her perplexed forehead smoothed, her eyes were steady, her lips firmly set. She formed a maxim for herself, although incoherently with her unlettered thoughts. "Unsolicited opportunities are the guide-posts of the Lord to the new roads of life," she repeated in effect, and she made up her mind to her course of action.

"S'posin' I *had* wrote to Hiram," she muttered once, when she was in the pantry—"s'posin' I had wrote, an' asked him if he knew of any horse? But I didn't, an' father's goin' wa'n't none of my doin'. It looks like a providence." Her voice rang out quite loud at the last.

"What you talkin' about, mother?" called Nanny.

"Nothin'."

Mrs. Penn hurried her baking; at eleven o'clock it was all done. The load of hay from the west field came slowly down the cart track, and drew up at the new barn. Mrs. Penn ran out. "Stop!" she screamed—"stop!"

The men stopped and looked; Sammy upreared from the top of the load, and stared at his mother.

"Stop!" she cried out again. "Don't you put the hay in that barn; put it in the old one."

"Why, he said to put it in here," returned one of the haymakers, wonderingly. He was a young man, a neighbor's son, whom Adoniram hired by the year to help on the farm.

"Don't you put the hay in the new barn; there's room enough in the old one, ain't there?" said Mrs. Penn.

"Room enough," returned the hired man, in his thick, rustic tones. "Didn't need the new barn, nohow, far as room's concerned. Well, I s'pose he changed his mind." He took hold of the horses' bridles.

Mrs. Penn went back to the house. Soon the kitchen

windows were darkened, and a fragrance like warm honey came into the room.

Nanny laid down her work. "I thought father wanted them to put the hay into the new barn?" she said, wonderingly.

"It's all right," replied her mother.

Sammy slid down from the load of hay, and came in to see if dinner was ready.

"I ain't goin' to get a regular dinner to-day, as long as father's gone," said his mother. "I've let the fire go out. You can have some bread an' milk an' pie. I thought we could get along." She set out some bowls of milk, some bread, and a pie on the kitchen table. "You'd better eat your dinner now," said she. "You might jest as well get through with it. I want you to help me afterward."

Nanny and Sammy stared at each other. There was something strange in their mother's manner. Mrs. Penn did not eat anything herself. She went into the pantry, and they heard her moving dishes while they ate. Presently she came out with a pile of plates. She got the clothes-basket out of the shed, and packed them in it. Nanny and Sammy watched. She brought out cups and saucers, and put them in with the plates.

"What you goin' to do, mother?" inquired Nanny, in a timid voice. A sense of something unusual made her tremble, as if it were a ghost. Sammy rolled his eyes over his pie.

"You'll see what I'm goin' to do," replied Mrs. Penn. "If you're through, Nanny, I want you to go up-stairs an' pack up your things; an' I want you, Sammy, to help me take down the bed in the bedroom."

"Oh, mother, what for?" gasped Nanny.

"You'll see."

During the next few hours a feat was performed by this

simple, pious New England mother which was equal in its way to Wolfe's storming of the Heights of Abraham. It took no more genius and audacity of bravery for Wolfe to cheer his wondering soldiers up those steep precipices, under the sleeping eyes of the enemy, than for Sarah Penn, at the head of her children, to move all their little household goods into the new barn while her husband was away.

Nanny and Sammy followed their mother's instructions without a murmur; indeed, they were overawed. There is a certain uncanny and superhuman quality about all such purely original undertakings as their mother's was to them. Nanny went back and forth with her light loads, and Sammy tugged with sober energy.

At five o'clock in the afternoon the little house in which the Penns had lived for forty years had emptied itself into the new barn.

Every builder builds somewhat for unknown purposes, and is in a measure a prophet. The architect of Adoniram Penn's barn, while he designed it for the comfort of four-footed animals, had planned better than he knew for the comfort of humans. Sarah Penn saw at a glance its possibilities. Those great box-stalls, with quilts hung before them, would make better bedrooms than the one she had occupied for forty years, and there was a tight carriage-room. The harness-room, with its chimney and shelves, would make a kitchen of her dreams. The great middle space would make a parlor, by-and-by, fit for a palace. Up stairs there was as much room as down. With partitions and windows, what a house would there be! Sarah looked at the row of stanchions before the allotted space for cows, and reflected that she would have her front entry there.

At six o'clock the stove was up in the harness-room, the kettle was boiling, and the table set for tea. It looked almost as home-like as the abandoned house across the yard had ever done. The young hired man milked, and Sarah directed him calmly to bring the milk to the new barn. He came gaping, dropping little blots of foam from the brimming pails on the grass. Before the next morning he had spread the story of Adoniram Penn's wife moving into the new barn all over the little village. Men assembled in the store and talked it over, women with shawls over their heads scuttled into each other's houses before their work was done. Any deviation from the ordinary course of life in this quiet town was enough to stop all progress in it. Everybody paused to look at the staid, independent figure on the side track. There was a difference of opinion with regard to her. Some held her to be insane; some, of a lawless and rebellious spirit.

Friday the minister went to see her. It was in the forenoon, and she was at the barn door shelling pease for dinner. She looked up and returned his salutation with dignity, then she went on with her work. She did not invite him in. The saintly expression of her face remained fixed, but there was an angry flush over it.

The minister stood awkwardly before her, and talked. She handled the pease as if they were bullets. At last she looked up, and her eyes showed the spirit that her meek front had covered for a lifetime.

"There ain't no use talkin', Mr. Hersey," said she. "I've thought it all over an' over, an' I believe I'm doin' what's right. I've made it the subject of prayer, an' it's betwixt me an' the Lord an' Adoniram. There ain't no call for nobody else to worry about it."

"Well, of course, if you have brought it to the Lord in prayer, and feel satisfied that you are doing right, Mrs. Penn," said the minister, helplessly. His thin gray-bearded face was pathetic. He was a sickly man; his youthful confidence had cooled; he had to scourge himself up to some of his pastoral duties as relentlessly as a Catholic ascetic, and then he was prostrated by the smart.

"I think it's right jest as much as I think it was right for our forefathers to come over from the old country 'cause they didn't have what belonged to 'em," said Mrs. Penn. She arose. The barn threshold might have been Plymouth Rock from her bearing. "I don't doubt you mean well, Mr. Hersey," said she, "but there are things people hadn't ought to interfere with. I've been a member of the church for over forty year. I've got my own mind an' my own feet, an' I'm goin' to think my own thoughts an' go my own ways, an' nobody but the Lord is goin' to dictate to me unless I've a mind to have him. Won't you come in an' set down? How is Mis' Hersey?"

"She is well, I thank you," replied the minister. He added some more perplexed apologetic remarks; then he retreated.

He could expound the intricacies of every character study in the Scriptures, he was competent to grasp the Pilgrim Fathers and all historical innovators, but Sarah Penn was beyond him. He could deal with primal cases, but parallel ones worsted him. But, after all, although it was aside from his province, he wondered more how Adoniram Penn would deal with his wife than how the Lord would. Everybody shared the wonder. When Adoniram's four new cows arrived, Sarah ordered three to be put in the old barn, the other in the house shed where the cooking-stove had stood. That added to the excitement. It was whispered that all four cows were domiciled in the house.

Towards sunset on Saturday, when Adoniram was expected home, there was a knot of men in the road near the new barn. The hired man had milked, but he still hung around the premises. Sarah Penn had supper all ready. There were brown-bread and baked beans and a custard pie; it was the supper that Adoniram loved on a Saturday night. She had on a clean calico, and she bore herself imperturbably. Nanny and Sammy kept close at her heels. Their eyes were large, and Nanny was full of nervous tremors. Still there was to them more pleasant excitement than anything else. An inborn confidence in their mother over their father asserted itself.

Sammy looked out of the harness-room window. "There he is," he announced, in an awed whisper. He and Nanny peeped around the casing. Mrs. Penn kept on about her work. The children watched Adoniram leave the new horse standing in the drive while he went to the house door. It was fastened. Then he went around to the shed. That door was seldom locked, even when the family was away. The thought how her father would be confronted by the cow flashed upon Nanny. There was a hysterical sob in her throat. Adoniram emerged from the shed and stood looking about in a dazed fashion. His lips moved; he was saying something, but they could not hear what it was. The hired man was peeping around a corner of the old barn, but nobody saw him.

Adoniram took the new horse by the bridle and led him across the yard to the new barn. Nanny and Sammy slunk close to their mother. The barn doors rolled back, and there stood Adoniram, with the long mild face of the great Canadian farm horse looking over his shoulder.

Nanny kept behind her mother, but Sammy stepped suddenly forward, and stood in front of her.

Adoniram stared at the group. "What on airth you all

down here for?" said he. "What's the matter over to the house?"

"We've come here to live, father," said Sammy. His shrill voice quavered out bravely.

"What"—Adoniram sniffed—"what is it smells like cookin?" said he. He stepped forward and looked in the open door of the harness-room. Then he turned to his wife. His old bristling face was pale and frightened. "What on airth does this mean, mother?" he gasped.

"You come in here, father," said Sarah. She led the way into the harness-room and shut the door. "Now, father," said she, "you needn't be scared. I ain't crazy. There ain't nothin' to be upset over. But we've come here to live, an' we're goin' to live here. We've got jest as good a right here as new horses an' cows. The house wa'n't fit for us to live in any longer, an' I made up my mind I wa'n't goin' to stay there. I've done my duty by you forty year, an' I'm goin' to do it now; but I'm goin' to live here. You've got to put in some windows and partitions; an' you'll have to buy some furniture."

"Why, mother!" the old man gasped.

"You'd better take your coat off an' get washed—there's the wash-basin—an' then we'll have supper."

"Why, mother!"

Sammy went past the window, leading the new horse to the old barn. The old man saw him, and shook his head speechlessly. He tried to take off his coat, but his arms seemed to lack the power. His wife helped him. She poured some water into the tin basin, and put in a piece of soap. She got the comb and brush, and smoothed his thin gray hair after he had washed. Then she put the beans, hot bread, and tea on the table. Sammy came in, and the family drew up. Adoniram sat looking dazedly at his plate, and they waited.

"Ain't you goin' to ask a blessin', father?" said Sarah.

And the old man bent his head and mumbled.

All through the meal he stopped eating at intervals, and stared furtively at his wife; but he ate well. The home food tasted good to him, and his old frame was too sturdily healthy to be affected by his mind. But after supper he went out, and sat down on the step of the smaller door at the right of the barn, through which he had meant his Jerseys to pass in stately file, but which Sarah designed for her front house door, and he leaned his head on his hands.

After the supper dishes were cleared away and the milk-pans washed, Sarah went out to him. The twilight was deepening. There was a clear green glow in the sky. Before them stretched the smooth level of field; in the distance was a cluster of hay-stacks like the huts of a village; the air was very cool and calm and sweet. The landscape might have been an ideal one of peace.

Sarah bent over and touched her husband on one of his thin, sinewy shoulders. "Father!"

The old man's shoulders heaved: he was weeping.

"Why, don't do so, father," said Sarah.

"I'll—put up the—partitions, an'—everything you—want, mother."

Sarah put her apron up to her face; she was overcome by her own triumph.

Adoniram was like a fortress whose walls had no active resistance, and went down the instant the right besieging tools were used. "Why, mother," he said, hoarsely, "I hadn't no idee you was so set on't as all this comes to."

THE END.